The Bastards

The Bastards

Bertène Juminer

Translated and with an Introduction by
Keith Q. Warner

CARAF BOOKS

University Press of Virginia

CHARLOTTESVILLE

This is a title in the C A R A F B O O K S series

THE UNIVERSITY PRESS OF VIRGINIA

Les Bâtards Copyright © Présence Africaine, Paris, 1961

This translation and edition Copyright © 1989

by the Rector and Visitors of the University of Virginia

First published 1989

Library of Congress Cataloging-in-Publication Data
Juminer, Bertène.
    [Bâtards. English]
    The bastards / Bertène Juminer : translated and
with an introduction by Keith Q. Warner.
        p.   cm. — (CARAF books)
    Translation of: Les bâtards.
    ISBN 0-8139-1204-0 (pbk.) : $9.95
    I. Title. II. Series.
    PQ3959.2.J8B313   1989
    843—dc19   88-26135
                                                        CIP

TO BRUNO

In vain will you paint the tree
trunk white, the strength of the
bark beneath it still shouts.

Césaire

Contents

Glossary

Adieu Foulards: Literally "Farewell Kerchiefs," a traditional song in the French West Indies, usually sung to bid loved ones adieu.

baccalauréat: Examination certifying the end of secondary school; required for entrance to university.

béké: A creole term designating local whites.

bourrée: Type of dance in the Massif Central region of France.

Cité Universitaire: Student housing complex in French universities.

Code Noir: Edict on status of slaves (1685).

Comédie Française: French national theater company.

France Combattante: French Resistance organization in World War II.

licence: French university degree. The holder in arts is *licencié ès lettres.*

navalais: Familiar term for medical students preparing to serve in the Navy (Santé Navale).

ohé, Zombis bare yo: Yeah, jumbies, catch them.

Glossary

Introduction

There are many who claim that the former colonies of the Guianas—British, Dutch, and French—are culturally linked to South America, and that their allegiance is to the continent of which they are geographically a part. However, as a result of their long historical associations, these former colonies are more closely linked to their Caribbean colonial counterparts in the islands than to the rest of what is popularly termed Latin America. The European powers bickered over the Guianas in the same way they bickered over the various Caribbean islands, and in so doing, drew the former more firmly into the Caribbean basin both politically and culturally. By the 1980s, British Guiana had become the Cooperative Republic of Guyana, and Dutch Guiana had achieved its independence as Suriname. French Guiana, on the other hand, has remained French, technically an overseas extension of mainland France. It is this simple fact of contemporary history and politics, not to mention of contemporary culture, that provides the compelling background to Bertène Juminer's novel, *The Bastards.*

Since European explorers were fond of saying that they "discovered" a region, a waterfall, a river, or a mountain—nearly any natural phenomenon, in fact, conveniently waiting for such a discovery—it is perhaps worth acknowledging that it was the Ojeda-Vespucci expedition of 1499 that discovered the Guianas. Subsequent explorations, notably Pinzon's in 1500, charted the entire region between the Orinoco and the Amazon, and must have provided the initial geographic information used by the countless adventurers eventually attracted to the region by the legend of El Dorado.

Introduction

The seventeenth century saw the arrival of the colonizers. The Dutch were the first to establish settlements in 1616 on the Essequibo River, an area that would become British Guiana in 1814; the British settled in 1634 in the area around the Suriname River, a region that would become Dutch some thirty-five years later; finally, the French began a serious attempt at settlement only in 1663, despite the fact that they were among the earliest to send expeditions—in particular the one by La Ravardière in 1604, which came a mere eight years after the British sent Sir Walter Raleigh in 1596. The 1663 effort saw some 850 white colonists, under the chevalier de la Barre, along with about four hundred black slaves settled in what is now French Guiana. No mention is made of the strength of the native Indian population at the time.

The Guianas suffered the same fate as the rest of the Caribbean islands—namely, the switching of political affiliation and allegiance, depending on what war the colonial powers had won or lost. Cayenne, for example, was sacked by the British in 1667, and was, for the brief period from May to September 1676, occupied by the Dutch. However, the situation settled down to the point where by the middle of the eighteenth century French Guiana counted about nine thousand immigrants, some eight thousand of whom were slaves, and it was estimated that there was an Indian population of between eight and ten thousand scattered throughout their various territories.

From the very beginning, it was clear that this vast territory, covering approximately thirty-five thousand square miles, was disproportionately underpopulated, compared, for instance, with its neighbor Dutch Guiana, and this may have set the tone for the ensuing neglect that has plagued this country. In 1763 there was an attempt to make French Guiana a viable white colony, and some twelve to fifteen thousand immigrants from various parts of Europe went to establish a settlement at Kourou, site of France's current space launching pad. Unfortunately, they were for the most part totally ignorant of how rigorous the conditions were, and in the end, in what came to be called "the disaster of Kourou," thousands of them perished, victims of either disease or sheer hardship. As one commentator has written: "Thirteen thousand persons met atrocious deaths. Mothers were seen throwing their children from atop the Kourou rocks and jumping into the river behind them." [1] One can only imagine the devastating effect such incidents had on the minds of the Europeans in terms of cementing the image of French Guiana as a totally inhospitable part of the world.

French Guiana continued to have mixed fortunes throughout the rest of the eighteenth century. It saw a reasonable amount of progress immediately prior to the French revolution, by which time the slave population had grown to some twelve thousand, in comparison with a white settler population of only two thousand. The abolition of slavery in 1794 made it evident to what extent the colonizers had depended on cheap slave labor. The Europeans simply could not cope with the harsh conditions without the cushion of the slaves. Thus, it was not really surprising when, in 1802, slavery was reinstituted, with myriad inhuman measures used to discourage slaves from running away, or to punish those who managed to do so, and were captured.

Early in the nineteenth century, the continental blockade resulted in French Guiana being cut off from France, allowing the Portuguese to occupy the territory from 1809 until the Treaty of Paris restored it to France in 1817. The other significant events of the nineteenth century were the permanent abolition of slavery in 1848, with the resultant problems created when the freed slaves shunned the manual labor they had just left; the discovery of gold in 1855, and the eventual decimation of a large part of the Indian population as prospectors pushed further and further inland; and the arrival of a new wave of white immigrants—namely, condemned prisoners being sent to the newly established penal colony. The idea of a penal colony in French Guiana had already been broached and tried around the time slavery was first abolished, but this

---

1. Paul Gaffarel, *Les colonies françaises* (Paris: Félix Alcan, 1899), p. 244. My translation.

latest move was to bring a sizable population to an otherwise sparsely populated colony. Furthermore, it was a population that was not in any position to help develop the country, and one that only served to destroy whatever little reputation the country had left. It is estimated that between seventy and eighty thousand convicts were transported to French Guiana before the deportations ended in 1937. Juminer's novel portrays scenes in the lives of many of these ex-convicts—who, upon their release, became part of the Guianese society, for a series of laws made their return to France virtually impossible: "any person sentenced to less than eight years hard labor shall, upon the expiration of his sentence, reside in the colony for a period equal to the duration of his sentence . . . if the sentence is for a period in excess of eight years, he shall be obliged to spend the rest of his life in the colony, and shall not, under any circumstances, be authorized to return to France."[2] The final indignities of the nineteenth century were the annexing of part of Guiana by the Dutch to the west and the attack on Guianese gold miners by Brazilians to the east and south. France's failure to take any retaliatory action prompted one newspaper to comment that "our grandchildren won't believe History."[3] Eventual arbitration in 1899 determined that the country would be reduced to its present thirty-five thousand square miles between the Oyapock and Maroni rivers.

On March 11, 1946, French Guiana, along with Martinique and Guadeloupe, became overseas departments of France. It was a move that seemed to be the solution the colonials desired, since it ensured their full consideration as French citizens, for, according to Brian Weinstein, the Guianese had "fought to remain French. Becoming more French was what the progressives of the time wanted. . . . No one talked of independence."[4] However, as Juminer's novel will make patently clear, they had lost as much as they had gained. Unfortunately,

2. Serge Mam-Lam-Fouck, *La Guyane française: De la colonisation à la départementalisation* (Paris: Désormeaux, 1982), p. 104. My translation.
3. *La Guyane* (Cayenne), 1 February 1896, quoted in Brian Weinstein, *Eboué* (New York: Oxford University Press, 1972), p. 7.
4. Weinstein, *Eboué*, p. 8.

as a result of overdependence on France, these departments have found themselves in a position where they are faced with the dilemma of either continuing in their present state, perhaps with some degree of autonomy, or launching out on the precarious road to independence, similar to the road taken by many of the former British colonies in the Caribbean.

Unlike Martinique and Guadeloupe, French Guiana was thought to possess a harsh, unfriendly climate. Consequently, the attention, however scant, that was paid to the two island colonies/departments, was never paid to French Guiana, and any modern-day visitor to the three French overseas territories in the Caribbean is immediately struck by how much has *not* been done for French Guiana in comparison with the other two territories. Why this is so is difficult to fathom. Is it because the islands with their beaches and sugar plantations conform more to some preconceived European image of the Antillean paradise? Or is it because French Guiana is still perceived as a godforsaken outpost, fit only for the most seasoned of criminals?

From the outset, the relationship of the colonizer (the white minority) with the colonized (the black and Indian majority) was typical of all such relationships under French colonization. Since the blacks were brought in as slaves from the African "wasteland," and the indigenous Indians were never accorded the courtesy of consideration in matters of culture and life-style, it stood to reason, as far as the French were concerned, that the only culture to be inculcated was French culture. Every facet of the administration and every act of the church therefore tended toward the only possible end that would legitimize colonization: assimilation. The French never entertained the thought that they could learn anything from the colonized; on the contrary, it was the colonized who had not only to learn everything from them but had also to become like them in every respect save the color of their skin.

As early as 1938, one of French Guiana's most famous sons, the poet Léon-Gontran Damas, had gone back home on a mission sponsored by the Musée d'Ethnographie de Paris and, upon his return to France, had published his report under the title *Retour de Guyane* (Return from Guiana). It is a scathing attack on French colonization in French Guiana, and makes for fascinating reading alongside many sections of Juminer's *The Bastards*. As one who had suffered through many "convict" jokes when he was a student in France,[5] Damas felt that it was wrong of France to use his country to deposit the dregs of French society, thereby creating a situation in which his countrymen felt permanently insecure owing to the presence of so many ex-convicts. His criticism extended to other areas: "Damas denounced the appalling state of the country where hygiene, public utilities, and the police force were concerned. He revealed the inadequacies of the medical system, the scandal of the leper hospitals, the administrative waste and disorder, the absence of roads and railroads, and the paucity of industries, farms, or mines despite the richness of the soil and subsoil."[6] French Guiana was the picture of negligence, and Damas was not afraid to say so.

Furthermore, Damas attacked the treasured French notion of assimilation: "Ignoring the quality of the people they would assimilate, the French with a certain enthusiasm see their assimilation as a reparation, a declaration that they consider the man facing them to be their equal."[7] Indeed, he was very close to his Senegalese counterpart, Léopold Senghor, who would later maintain that it was actually the African who assimilated,[8] rather than the other way round. Damas wrote: "What they do not clearly understand is that the colonized man whom they hope to assimilate is perhaps an equal but . . . certainly different," an opinion that found what seems to be its

5. Damas claimed that his standard reply when asked about the convicts was that in Guiana they only took them in. The convicts were produced in France.

6. Lilyan Kesteloot, *Black Writers in French* (Philadelphia: Temple University Press, 1974), p. 233.

7. Léon Damas, *Retour de Guyane,* trans. Ellen Conroy Kennedy in Kesteloot, *Black Writers in French,* p. 234.

8. See Léopold Senghor, "Vues sur l'Afrique noire, ou assimiler, non être assimilés," in *Liberté I: Négritude et humanisme* (Paris: Editions du Seuil, 1964), p. 39.

logical conclusion in V. S. Naipaul's comment in *The Middle Passage* that "to accept assimilation is in a way to accept a permanent inferiority."[9] Damas also refused to be tricked into accepting the Europeanization of the Guianese, a stance he had previously adopted in his epoch-making collection of poems, *Pigments,* published in Paris in 1937 much to the annoyance of the French colonial administration, which had seized and burned whatever copies it could find.

As an integral part of this assimilationist policy, the French education system was, quite appropriately, geared to ensuring that the colonies, and eventual departments, would remain permanently under the thumb of those who had set up the system in the first place. In this respect, the French were not unlike the British, who, in their style of colonial imperialism, made absolutely certain that those under their tutelage believed that only things British were of any value. It is this Euro-centric arrogance that precluded the establishment of overseas educational institutions of higher learning, and that, as a result, forced all aspiring scholars to go abroad, usually to the "mother" country, of course. In what can only be seen as a cleverly orchestrated plan of action, indigenous populations were enticed to look toward the metropolis, to go there, and to return to perpetuate the cycle themselves. Guiana was no different, for even in the late 1980s prospective Guianese university students still have to leave the country, though now they can at least enroll at the Université Antilles-Guyane in Martinique.

It is clear that the central administration in Paris did not perceive the overseas departments as anything else but extensions of itself, which would be attended to in due course. Indeed, the very concept of "overseas" departments held in it the seeds of discontent, since one is "overseas" only in relation to a particular locus, the way the terms Middle and Far East are only understandable in relation to a Euro-centered world. Consequently, since there was no great urgency pushing this

9. Damas, in *Black Writers in French,* p. 234; V. S. Naipaul, *The Middle Passage* (Harmondsworth: Penguin Books, 1969), p. 181.

Introduction

administration to develop what it saw as peripheral to its own existence, no serious attempt was made to develop this outpost beyond a modicum of convenience and progress. Furthermore, the idea that anything associated with Guiana was difficult was evident in the government's attitude toward serious infrastructure development. One reads the following statements in documents prepared by the French Press and Information Service in New York: "The Guianese forest, the Department's most important resource, has not yet been exploited. . . . Natural conditions for exploitation are not very favorable: species are widely scattered; building tracks in the forest is very expensive (roughly one mile of main forest road is needed to exploit forty-five hundred acres); it is difficult to bring the rough timber to market (floating the logs is impossible because of their density)." The same documents contain similar statements concerning agriculture and stockbreeding. Finally, under the heading "Problems in the Development of Tourism," one reads: "It is unlikely that Guiana will ever attract mass tourism the way the West Indies do. However, because of its unusual possibilities for outdoor pursuits and special-interest tourism, Guiana is the perfect answer for the growing numbers of tourists from the developed countries who are tired of ordinary vacations and eager for a new form of escape." [10] That, in short, is the overall tone of the administration's attitude: Guiana is full of problems, but a few possibilities do exist, most notably in tourism.

Meanwhile, what about the many blacks (Creoles and so-called primitives) and Indians comprising the majority of the population, some forty thousand out of a total population of approximately sixty thousand? The white administrators and their families came and went. They always had France or another administrative appointment in another outpost to fall back on. The ex-convicts were forced to stay and eke out a living however they could. This meant that the blacks and Indians were able to see both the high and the low of white so-

10. Promotion packet on French Guiana distributed by the Ambassade de France, Service de Presse et d'Information, New York, n.d.

ciety, although they aspired to neither station. Guiana presented very little promise, since there were few industries and no large-scale organized farming, mining, or timber production. The Indians—huddled together in their remote villages, the object of a few curious anthropologists—and the blacks struggled to obtain whatever jobs they could, mainly in the lower ranks of the civil service.

The net result of this state of affairs is that, according to the same information service, the working population today is sparse, for: "while the demographic situation in French Guiana is relatively healthy, it is nonetheless true that the problem of populating the country still remains unsolved. Guiana lacks manpower just as it lacks consumers. Only large-scale immigration . . . can remove this primary obstacle to development."[11] The French government's policy on immigration is not wholeheartedly supported, however, and is puzzling at best, since it actively encourages young black Guianese to go to France, with the hope, it is felt, that they will disappear into the mass of other Frenchmen, and not bother to return to their native land.

With the development of the Space Center at Kourou, a new wave of immigration was begun, with many of the newcomers arriving from Brazil and smaller numbers from Haiti. Unfortunately, as Roland Delannon of the Guianese Movement for Decolonization points out in his attack on the entire procedure, the Brazilians were ruthlessly exploited, and enabled both foreign and Guianese businesses to make excessive profits because of the illegally low wages paid and the long hours workers were forced to put in. In addition, because of the obvious competition that the Brazilians represented for the native Guianese vying for the same jobs, open hostility and resentment quickly developed toward these outsiders.[12] However, while the situation upon their arrival was virtually the same as the one that the Haitian immigrants encountered, it must be

11. Ibid.
12. Roland Delannon, *Spéciale racisme* (Cayenne: MOGUYDE [Mouvement Guyanais de Décolonisation], n.d.), n.p.

noted that other immigrants, notably those from certain European countries, have not suffered this fate, leading Delannon to conclude that the entire undertaking is based on a racist premise pure and simple.

This, then, is the Guiana into which Bertène Juminer was born, and about which he has chosen to write in *The Bastards*. The period he treats is the one immediately following the Second World War, but for all intents and purposes, it could just as well be a period much closer to the present, so little have things changed over the years.

We were fortunate to be able to obtain, via written correspondence and telephone calls, the following interview with Bertène Juminer. It provides the essential elements of his biography necessary for a keener appreciation of his work. As a supplement, it is worth knowing that he is a medical doctor, with specializations in parasitology, bacteriology, and immunology, among others; that he has taught at universities in France, Iran, and Senegal, and was, from 1981 to 1987, Recteur (president) of the Académie Antilles-Guyane in Martinique; that from 1987 he was once more attached to the Faculty of Medicine of the Université d'Amiens; that he holds the distinction of belonging to the Legion of Honor; that he has published three other novels: *Au seuil d'un nouveau cri* (On the threshold of a new cry) (1963), *La revanche de Bozambo* (Bozambo's revenge) (1968), and *Les héritiers de la presqu'île* (Inheritors of the peninsula) (1979), for which he was awarded the Prix littéraire des Caraïbes in 1981.

Interview with Bertène Juminer

K W: *Can you tell me what prompted you to write* The Bastards? *Perhaps you can begin by saying a little about your background.*

B J: *I was born in Cayenne on August 6, 1927. My mother was from Guadeloupe, and my father was Guianese.*

Introduction

At the tender age of one, I was sent to live with my maternal grandmother, with the result that my view of the world is colored by her. I spent my childhood in a matriarchal atmosphere, one filled with affection, but also with authority.

My grandmother, despite her obvious mulatto features, was acutely aware of her Africanness. Although a staunch Catholic, she also carried in her the cultural heritage and memory of an Africa she had only known through tales orally handed down from mother to daughter. Through this syncretism, which I only learned to appreciate in retrospect once I had become a man, she achieved a fair balance. The result was that, despite our rather modest circumstances, my childhood saw a happy blend of the real (the presence of Europe), and the imaginary (black mythology). No doubt I was already a "bastard" without knowing it, incapable of realizing it because of the happy life I was leading.

At age twelve, I left for Pointe-à-Pitre, where I was to spend seven years at the Lycée Carnot, following which I spent an even longer period as a student in the south of France. This disruption, contrary to what might be expected, did not cause any bitterness or frustration in me. I wanted to succeed, and had convinced myself very early that, in the absence of money, my only hope of success lay in academic excellence.

While studying in Montpellier (1946 to 1956), I once again found myself at the crossroads between Europe and Africa: Europe, constantly renewed, reassuring, showing postwar humility, seeking to please rather than to rule, whose lordly attitudes the exiled student unconsciously adopted; Africa, even more tangible than before, now only an arm's length away through the smiling, brotherly students who shared my condition. The real and the imaginary of yore blended into one. Blacks had come to Europe. As "overseas students" we were aware of living at the dawn of a new

*day. This was the triumphant time of the cultural re-
naissance of the black world, strongly supported by
existentialists. Negritude dared to raise its head, to
pursue its goals for decolonization, and above all this
juvenile fervor there was Marxism. We quoted, pell-
mell, Césaire, Damas, Senghor, or Sartre. There was
a veritable telescoping of lively forces from all points
of the compass, exerting mutual influences and condemned to tolerate one another. The backdrop for* The
Bastards *was set.*

K W: *And did you set about writing the novel right away?*

B J: *It was only much later that I wrote this work. The idea
came to me following a two-year professional stint in
Guiana (1956 to 1958), a period that had struck me
for two reasons. First of all, it was evident that the
French-trained Guianese elite knew nothing about the
problems of Guiana and were, in fact, an aggregate of
foreigners forced to adapt themselves to their own
country and scandalized by certain shortcomings or ini-
tiatives of their countrymen. Second, the European mi-
crocosm handling the administration of Guiana was
totally different from that fraternal Europe known and
loved by my colleagues ten years before. I could not
understand how these two continents harmoniously installed in my subjectivity could cause me such turmoil
when I had to deal with them objectively. But how
could you recognize the African mother you seemed to
deny, the European father who denied you? In order
to diagnose, then analyze, this dilemma, I had to
move away, to see from the outside these two parental
worlds, like an entomologist hunched over his magni-
fying glass. By chance, I went to Tunisia, in the midst
of a third transitional civilization. The Algerian war
was in full swing, and Tunisia itself was beginning,
dangerously but obstinately, the decolonization process. And there I was, a French worker who was also
black, once more torn between two contrary alle-*

Introduction

giances: to a Europe gagged and devoid of power and to the colonized desperate for dignity. That's when I thought I must do something, and I started writing this work. The Bastards, *which was only a pretext for my settling the score with a reality I had lived, hence the heavy autobiographical and realist content, conceived as an element of authentification.*

K W: *To what extent is* The Bastards *an autobiographical novel? Is Berjémi Turenne really Bertène Juminer?*

B J: *My novel,* The Bastards, *is indeed largely autobiographical, to the extent that the events described are real: student life in Montpellier, then working in Saint-Laurent, etc., even if they were not actually all lived by the author. Besides, which of the characters is really the author?*

We're not dealing with one character, but three; and it's through this trinity that I wanted to circumscribe its [the character's] true nature, comprised as it is of revolutionary idealism (Turenne Berjémi, whose deliberately transparent anagram was instantly appealing), of lucid pragmatism consciously assumed even to the point of failure (Robert Chambord), and of revolt against family conformity (Alain Cambier), with all that such an attitude implies with respect to vain trembling and gratuitous provocation.

The aim of this symbiosis was to show, from the outset, the principal types of men called to come together, to confront one another in one and the same camp in the struggle for emancipation: those who sooner or later will opt for violence (Turenne); those who, by their sterling example, prefer to work patiently in the socioprofessional arena, in order to instill a certain moral and civic sense in their countrymen (Chambord); and finally, those who wear their bourgeois legacy like a curse and will be ready to try anything, including terrorism, to prove that they are not enemies of the people (Cambier).

Introduction

I say all of this to say that The Bastards *was written*
with a twin ambition in mind: descriptive and pedago-
gical. With the passing of time, it seems that that ambi-
tion was not realized, either because it was not prop-
erly articulated (due to the clumsiness associated with
one's first novel), or because the reader was not in a
position to grasp its significance (the usual discrepancy
between the visionary and his contemporaries).

K W: *I am sure that your readers will readily notice the great*
influence of Sartre and existentialism in The Bastards.
Would you care to comment on this?

B J: *The influence (it would be better to speak of "aware-*
ness") of Sartre and existentialism is not accidental. It
shows the adherence of the postwar colonized youth to
new ideas, exactly as had happened with regard to sur-
realism after 1914–18. It also shows the interest mani-
fested by this youth in Sartre's activities (his "Black
Orpheus" preface to Senghor's 1948 anthology, etc.)
in favor of peoples of the Third World. It was not by
chance that Sartre would later write a preface for
Fanon.

K W: *What effect would you say your works have had on*
the Guianese?

B J: *Only very few Guianese read, and it is not certain*
whether this minority of readers is interested in works
written by their compatriots. We have in that situa-
tion a real dilemma. The Guianese writer, in principle,
writes for his people, but it is the whites who read him,
and to whom he owes his renown (a situation that is
true for the entire Third World). The Guianese public
only recognizes its writers posthumously, and even so!
Let me give you an example of what I mean. René
Maran was born in November 1887. His centennial in
1987 saw no official ceremony in Guiana. A few years
ago, one of the municipalities in Guiana wanted to
honor the memory of this same René Maran by nam-

Introduction

*ing a street after him. When the plaque was unveiled,
the inscription read: René Marrant Street. That says it
all!*[13]

*However you look at it, you notice that the Guia-
nese chooses the easy way out—in other words, the
least effort, both in his professional training as well as
his creations (where they exist) or his projects (when
he has any). In this respect, it is significant that Guiana's literary production contains very few novels,
though it has many small volumes of "poetry." This is
terribly sad, when you know that there's so much to
say. The Guianese wants everything, and wants it right
away, even if it means losing it all the next day. The
essential is to show off, to pass for superior to others.
Our lives are total imposture. One wonders if this
mentality is not a survival from the days of the gold
rush which, several decades ago, made and lost fortunes in the twinkling of an eye. One came to Cayenne
to spend one's gold on women and gambling; quickly
wiped out, one returned to the forest. Meanwhile, one
had demonstrated that one was somebody. In those
days, this propensity to show off was less shocking
than it is today, since there were the dregs of Europe,
the convicts, who served as scapegoats for everyone,
including the most pitiful Guianese. Nowadays, these
convicts have disappeared. Furthermore, the new
whites in Guiana very often own property, and the few
poor whites who go around begging in the streets of
Cayenne aren't self-conscious about it. But the mentality has remained. As a result, there are attacks on
immigrants. Haitians in particular, or on fellow countrymen. Such a context naturally fosters a climate of
hollow vanity, of wiliness, thus of mediocrity. The race
for political office is fraught with tragic bitterness, for
the holding of elected office, however modest or fleet-*

13. The pun is lost in translation, but the mistake is tantamount to naming the street "René the Joker."

*ing, confers overnight more notoriety than any univer-
sity degree. This is what Edouard Glissant calls "successful colonization." Under those conditions, literary
works have no chance of being noticed, still less of
being influential in any way.*

K W: *What was the reaction of the authorities with regard to
your portrayal of colonization in Guiana?*

B J: *When the book came out, and for many years afterwards, I was not in Guiana (I was in Tunisia, Iran,
Senegal, etc.). Thus, I could not say what the local administration's reaction was concerning my portrayal of
the colonized Guianese. However, in 1962, one year
after the book was published, the central government
of the time opposed my going to Martinique, where I
had been appointed to work at the Pasteur Institute in
Fort-de-France.*

K W: *As you are aware, many writers in your situation are
seen as* engagés, *even though they might not consider
themselves as such. Do you consider yourself a committed writer?*

B J: *All writers who stand up for their people are* engagés.
*In this respect, I'm a committed writer, just like James
Baldwin or Chester Himes, whose works, in their own
way, are authentic testimonies on blacks in the U.S.A.,
and on the conditions in which they live.*

K W: *Are you for or against departmentalization? What future do you envisage for the overseas departments?*

B J: *It is obvious—and all my books show this—that I
am not in favor of departmentalization, which is a
neo-colonial absurdity, and whose logic subsumes the
total disappearance of the Guianese soul. The depart-
mentalists, white or black, are aware of this, and have
embarked with absolute villainy on the road to this
ethnocide. The assimilationist phantasmagoria is so
overpowering that it goes to the extent of choosing any*

Introduction

*solution rather than giving up the overseas territories.
Thus we have in Guiana a sort of transfer of tutelage
from France on behalf of Europe through the Kourou
Space Center.*

*Where will all that lead? Will the future confirm
what I wrote in* The Bastards: *"Assimilation will replace malaria"? That boils down to saying that Guiana
will achieve independence only when the whites are in
the majority, as is the case in Australia, in the U.S.A.,
etc., to mention only the English-speaking countries.*

*As far as I'm concerned, I see the future of the over-
seas departments—at least, that's what I would like—
as being very diversified, within the framework of their
accession to the status of managing their own affairs.
With regard to Guiana, I would like it, one day, to
become part of a confederation (similar to the Swiss
Confederation) with the other Guianas. The pooling of
their natural and human resources, within the framework of cultural autonomy, could in the long run be
a model state for the South American continent.*

K W: *And what of present-day Guiana? In view of the long
history of neglect on the part of the French government, how do you see things developing?*

B J: *Present-day Guiana is a challenge to good sense. One
thing is certain: right now, the inhabitants of Guianese
extraction (Creoles, Amerindians, refugee blacks) are
economically and numerically in the minority, even if
some of them have a few political posts. They can lose
these posts overnight, without the slightest difficulty;
it's just a matter of "others" deciding that it must be
so. It will all start with the town of Kourou.*

*But, paradoxically, Guiana's way out remains its
ethnic diversity. I mean that a well-understood pluri-
ethnicity can be a source of sane competition, of solidarity, in short, of economic, social, and cultural progress. Should such an opportunity be lost, the country
will face the worst; in other words, the risk of "Cale-*

Introduction

donization," since immigration from Europe is on the increase. Given that these immigrants receive vast amounts of land, there will soon develop a group of Guianoches, patterned after the present-day Caldoches in New Caledonia.[14] *We are currently seeing what such a system can do.*

K W: *Let's change the subject a bit as we conclude. Who would you say are some of your favorite authors?*

B J: *It's difficult for me to say who my favorite authors are. I like many, for I'm an avid reader of all works dealing directly or indirectly with the Third World (and I include the black minority of the United States in this group), and, in particular, with black people, be they in Africa or elsewhere in the diaspora. However, in the final analysis, authors are less important than their works, so, to name just a few:* Nations nègres et culture *(Black nations and culture) (Cheikh Anta Diop),* Cahier d'un retour au pays natal *(Notebook of a return to the native land) (Aimé Césaire),* Amers *(Seamarks) (Saint-John Perse),* Les Damnés de la terre *(The wretched of the earth) (Frantz Fanon),* Chaka *(Thomas Mofolo),* La Nausée *(Nausea) (Jean-Paul Sartre),* Voyage au bout de la nuit *(Journey to the end of the night) (Louis-Ferdinand Céline). . . .*

K W: *And finally, do you have any one of your books that you prefer?*

B J: *Books are somewhat like children: you always prefer the youngest. In other words, my particular preference is for the work I'm now finishing, which is called "La fraction de seconde" (The split second). Actually, even*

14. Juminer is predicting for Guiana a political-ethnic conflict of the sort that has divided New Caledonia for several years at this writing. Descendants of European settlers—Caldoches—oppose independence from France, whereas ethnic Melanesian inhabitants of New Caledonia support independence. "Guianoches" is a neologism to designate the new European settlers being attracted to Guiana.

Introduction

> *though it's not readily apparent, my works are part of*
> *a cycle of positions vis-à-vis colonialism, and each one*
> *deals with one aspect of this positioning: awareness in*
> The Bastards, *surgical treatment in* Au seuil d'un
> nouveau cri *(On the threshold of a new cry), psycho-*
> *therapy in* La revanche de Bozambo, *postoperative re-*
> *covery in* Les héritiers de la presqu'île, *and synthesis*
> *and distancing in "La fraction de seconde."*

In what has become an almost classic introduction among black writers to the experience of writing a novel, Bertène Juminer turned to autobiography for the main subject of *The Bastards*. True enough, as is usually the case, one cannot rightfully say that the novel is a carbon copy of this author's curriculum vitae, but it is obvious that many elements of his life form the basis of what comprises the novel. In this instance, Juminer has admitted, we are witnessing not only snatches of his own personal experiences, but also those of other close friends, lending to them a tone of authenticity "even if they were not actually all lived by the author."

Invariably, such novelists see themselves as using their own situation, which they obviously know best, to make a statement; to complain, for instance, about what was done to them, to their race or their culture, and by whom; to reflect nostalgically on what they have lost; to stir their people into action; to lament what their leaders are doing to the people; etc. In other words, they once more fit the classic mold. They see themselves as committed; they speak *for,* if not always *to* their people. But do they at the same time use the opportunity simply to write, to show their mettle as artists? Do they write because, as William Gardner Smith says, "a writer is a man of sensitivity; otherwise he would not be a writer"?[15]

There are those who maintain that black writers must per-

15. William Gardner Smith, "The Negro Writer: Pitfalls and Compensations," in C. W. E. Bigsby, ed., *The Black American Writer* (Baltimore: Penquin Books, 1969), p. 72.

force be committed, and Caribbean writers are no exception. "West Indian writers, whether novelists, poets or playwrights, are almost never adherents of the doctrine of art for art's sake," writes Beverley Ormerod.[16] The time has not yet come, it seems, when these writers can afford the luxury of mere storytelling on colorless universal themes. There is as yet no acceptable solution to the artist's dilemma in this regard save perhaps the wish that the black writers would do both at the same time, though even then critics will carefully scrutinize and dissect the works to see to what extent one aspect has won out over the other. Again, according to William Gardner Smith: "Too often . . . we witness the dull procession of crime after crime against the Negro, without relief in humor or otherwise. These monotonous repetitions of offenses . . . only serve to bore the reader in time; and in so doing, they defeat the very purpose of the writer, for they become ineffective. One might even say that the chronicles of offenses constitute truth; however, they do not constitute art. And art is the concern of any novelist."[17] Equally often, too, at those times when writers do attempt to concentrate on pure artistic expression, readers and critics insist that some message be forthcoming, some cause be espoused, some position advocated. It is a burden few writers can escape, and it is therefore interesting to look at Juminer and *The Bastards* in the light of the foregoing comments.

Essentially, *The Bastards* deals with the lives of a few French Guianese students completing their studies in France following the Second World war, and with what happens when a couple of them return home to help build their country. Aimé Césaire states in his preface to this 1961 novel that to his knowledge, it is the first novel "to analyze the situation of the colored student and to consider the problem of his integration into colonial society."[18] Thus, one finds two distinct sections

16. Beverley Ormerod, *An Introduction to the French Caribbean Novel* (London: Heinemann, 1985), p. 3.

17. Smith, "The Negro Writer," p. 73.

18. Aimé Césaire, Preface to Bertène Juminer, *Les Bâtards* (Paris: Présence Africaine, 1961), p. 7. My translation.

of uneven length, the first dealing with what one could term the black student in the white world and the second with the plight of a black country with white administrators.

The students are shown in fairly typical situations in the university town of Montpellier, and the various episodes ring true even to anyone who has not had those particular experiences. There is the usual round of parties and dances, student committee meetings, examinations, and the resultant anxiety or joy, flirtations and budding love affairs, etc. Chief among the Guianese are Chambord, studying medicine, the "dean" of the group so to speak, and Cambier, who is studying dentistry. It is these two who eventually return to Guiana to work and whose adventures comprise the major portion of the novel. Apart, perhaps, from Turenne, whose ambition is also to return and build his country, the other students do not really stand out, and they are obviously composites of characters of the author's acquaintance.

Each of these secondary or supporting characters is shown to have some trait that tends to stick in the reader's mind rather more than the character himself (for all these Guianese students are young men): Sugert, the law student, is ashamed to admit he is from Guiana, preferring instead to claim South American origin; Ségaye is plagued by "the myth of the second," and is so elated after his eventual conquest of a white woman that he celebrates the event by scrawling his victory cry all over the wall of his room; Décamport, a prospective pharmacist, tries his hand at some currently modish poetry; Aresquier is involved in pseudoscientific experiments; and Borgier is comically drawn as a budding flamenco dancer, complete with castanets. All in all, then, Juminer presents a typical, and utterly believable, motley band of students, held together by the bond of origin and color—for even the mulatto (Cambier) loses his so-called privileged status in Europe, where the color line is more tautly drawn.

For all the similarities uniting Cambier and Chambord, "their identical preoccupations are different. Cambier is obsessed with the psychological problem of coming to terms with himself as the bastard product of West Indian colonial society. Chambord's gaze is turned outward as he focuses his attention on the establishment of a place for himself and his native Guyana [*sic*] and the liberation of his own people from the yoke of colonialism."[19] One major difference, as it turns out, is that Cambier is a mulatto, an in-between individual who suffers from being of neither one race nor the other, although white Europe readily shows him which side he is on. In this respect mulatto and bastard are not too far removed one from the other, with all the unsavory implications of illegitimacy and miscegenation.

An existentialist, Cambier is understandably swept up in the postwar fascination with Jean-Paul Sartre, the committed writer par excellence, and with the external trappings of the existentialist movement: "Cambier had insisted on going to Paris, and had gone to Saint-Germain-des-Prés. He had expected to chance upon geniuses with brilliant minds holding forth before avid, attentive disciples on the terraces of famous cafés." Black students in France during that period openly admitted their love for existentialism, which they frequently coupled with Marxism. Both doctrines appeared to make good sense to blacks and other oppressed groups faced with the absurdity of what the mainstream white world was offering.

The Bastards contains many references to *La Nausée*, "a book that had made a great impression on him [Cambier], that he was rereading for the umpteenth time, one whose ideas he devoured with a passion." Juminer obviously patterns Cambier's search for meaning to his existence on Roquentin's, and there is even an echo of the latter's obsession with the tune "Some of These Days" as Cambier and Turenne listen to "Body and Soul." Furthermore, the passages outlining Cambier's internal struggle with his "reality" and with his "darkness" seem to come straight from *Being and Nothingness*. One is so unaccustomed to this type of philosophical musing in novels written by blacks that Cambier's struggles with himself seem

19. Randolph Hezekiah, "Bertène Juminer and the Colonial Problem," *Black Images* 3, no. 1 (Spring 1974): 30.

Introduction

to reflect Juminer's own struggles with the genre. It is as if he decided that he must sharpen the intensity of the novel, giving it an air of artistic seriousness. Unfortunately, the relevant passages seem to stick out like the proverbial sore thumb.

On a more positive note, however, it is not unlikely that Juminer used the Sartrean model of Roquentin as indicative of a similar effort necessary on the part of Antillean and Guianese students in particular, and of other Antilleans in general, who needed to experience this same type of sudden awareness of their condition. However, such an undertaking does not seem plausible on a collective basis, at least not at this stage, since an awareness like Roquentin's operates on a very personal level. "To live," Cambier exclaims, "is to run counter to Darkness; to move along side by side." Paradoxically, then, the individual is almost forced to concede that the true Sartrean model will not work for his own circumstance, since the struggle of the French West Indies to gain some measure of self-respect and dignity must necessarily be a joint effort first, an individual effort second. We are led to conclude, like Gary Warner, that "the quest for ideological purity, for absolute revolution, is presented as both myopic and contrary to human experience."[20] Clearly, Cambier's conclusion that "we don't need other people to exist" can only be seen as the result of "his impassioned espousal of certain ideas," and as counterproductive in the case of these black students in their attempt to find some meaning in their lives.

It is Chambord, on the other hand, who best illustrates how the individual, as part of the oppressed group, can overcome the obsession with personal salvation and concentrate on the overall welfare of his fellow countrymen. Significantly, whereas both Cambier and Turenne have white girlfriends, Chambord "steered clear of any emotional involvement." It is as if he wants to keep himself pure in body and mind, ever ready for the monumental task ahead of him, ever mindful of the risk of contamination. In fact, he is the essence of discretion, as

20. Gary Warner, "Bertène Juminer: The Ethics of Revolt," *Black Images* 3, no. 3 (Autumn 1974): 14.

Introduction

Turenne comes to find out: "And to think that he, who had been friends with Chambord all these years, who had eaten with him day and night, was completely in the dark about his activities! From this, he deduced that discretion had to be the most important quality in a militant." Chambord is consistently shown as rational and levelheaded, "colonized, written out of History, dreaming he could build triumphant tomorrows without hatred or rancor," and so it is not surprising to see Juminer have him deliver, during his farewell dinner with his countrymen, the key lines in the novel, the ones that explain the concept of the bastards:

> We are bastards born of a Gallic male and an African girl abandoned by him on the banks of the Amazon. By laying full claim to our European blood, we discover our position as beings culturally born of a mother we did not know; and our choice of culture itself makes us aware of another blemish: we are, historically, anonymous or outlaws. In short, our loss of identity is two-faced: cultural and historical. But Africa, matriarchal and powerful, survives in us, in spite of the vicissitudes and humiliations suffered. Guiana, our mother, the unwed mother, awaits us to grant us legitimacy and salvation!

He is so sincere, so idealistic, so enthusiastic, that we want to follow him and his adventures as he returns to his homeland: "They need me back home. I have to go back. To stay here would be cowardly. I'd feel I had abandoned my country, that I'd fled." It is the dilemma of anyone who has ever left his homeland to study and/or work in a distant country, even though, as is the case here, one is dealing with the so-called mother country. The sense of betrayal is acute.

For the most part, these black students are seen only by themselves, for there is relatively little interaction with the white people among whom they live. We never see, for example, a white university professor, not even the ubiquitous radical, a character who would have been a natural addition to such a setting as theirs. What we do see of the white world

Introduction

comes directly in the form of the girlfriends and their parents or guardians and of the occasional male classmate, like Farnabe, and indirectly through the reactions of passersby to the Guianese students as they accompany their girlfriends.

Juminer is unapologetic about having his black students flirt with, and eventually bed, white women students, though one suspects that, if pressed to explain his reason for this, he would probably resort to the standard explanation given by colonial students in similar situations—namely, that there were no black women around. This is the same explanation that English-speaking African and Caribbean students gave when asked why they always gravitated toward white women when they went to study in the United Kingdom, and when they, inevitably, returned home with white wives. The black Antillean or Guianese student in Europe also complained that where there were any black women, they were often inaccessible, rather plain, and inexperienced; in short, they were sexually unattractive: "A young woman from the Antilles joined them. Like all the others who came to the Club, she wore no makeup, spoke little, and was easily shocked." The picture of these women could not be more unflattering, and we are even told categorically that they are not beautiful, since the "beautiful girls are married off while still young and don't have time to go to university."

Still imbued with the moral values inculcated in the Caribbean—values that did not permit the easy flirtation indulged in by the European woman—the Caribbean women in France soon found themselves avoided by their own countrymen, who could not bring themselves to think of them as objects of sexual attraction: "We'd be real scamps to try to seduce them. Our role is rather to protect them." In other words, here are black men finding it difficult to see black women as potential mates; instead, the latter are seen as needing protection, the way one looks after a sister or a good friend of the family, where a sexual liaison is out of the question.

Of course, there was always another reason why these students virtually abandoned their Caribbean sisters, one that Frantz Fanon had examined in his penetrating study, *Black*

Introduction

Skin, White Masks, a soul-searching analysis of the black psyche. Who else but the white woman, Fanon conjectured, could make the black man be recognized as white? By loving the black man, she was proving that he was worthy of white love; he was being loved as a white man. He thus became white. Ségaye clearly alludes to the anecdote related by Fanon concerning the black man who, on achieving orgasm during intercourse with a white woman, is alleged to have shouted: "Long Live Schoelcher" (the French abolitionist)![21] As he hesitates over what to scrawl on his wall, he is sure that he did not want to write the name of this Frenchman. He "no longer had anything in common with a newly freed slave swooning in the arms of a white mistress. [He] had passed that stage." Now, whereas the impression is given that great strides have been made in the personal relationship between the black man and the white woman, one is led to wonder, in view of the frankly derogatory treatment of the black woman in the novel, whether in fact Fanon is not being proven right.

On the whole, the white women in the novel are sympathetically treated. They show political awareness (Brigitte is Marxist, for example) and the ability to hold important jobs in the administration (the case with Gisèle). The girlfriends are understandably naive about what life in Guiana really entails, and are possibly attracted and intrigued by the sheer exoticism of their friends' distant homelands. They are also aware of, and suffer from, the constant staring of the French as they show up in public with their black escorts and stand up for their Guianese friends even if it means disagreeing with their own relatives. In fact, Juminer actually manages to see the humor in such situations, and his portrayal of the scandalized aunt as she comes face to face with the black visitor is obviously done more for comic effect and relief than to show maliciousness on the part of the whites.

While the white women play a symbolic role in their relationships with all the black students, it is in Cambier that

21. Frantz Fanon, *Peau noire, masques blancs* (Paris: Editions du Seuil, 1952), p. 71.

Introduction

we see illustrated the full extent of the psychological struggle involved in the black from the Caribbean being allowed to face the world as an individual, not as a black individual. "Cambier's relationship with Charlotte," writes Randolph Hezekiah, "can be interpreted as a perpetual struggle to eliminate all traces of self-doubt and to assert himself as an individual in his own right." [22] First of all, when he and Charlotte are in public, he is painfully conscious of the severe physical constriction of inhabiting a black skin in a white country: "To Cambier, the few hundred yards between the house and the tramcar stop seemed unbearably long. Strolling about at that hour of the day, under the gaze of the passersby, with Charlotte on his arm, filled him with a stifling sensation. Burying his head in his shoulders was pointless, since all those who walked by, as if unsure of what they had seen, turned around to look at them." Second, when they are alone, and when Charlotte finally offers herself to him, Cambier is unable to consummate their union. His impotence, only imagined as it turns out, must then be seen for what it is: a psychological paralysis brought on by the inability to convince himself that he is having this woman because he deserves to as a man, and not because he is just another black man desperately desiring white flesh. Nor is he about to have her because she as a white woman wants to experience the reputed virile sexuality of the black stud, thus satisfying the curiosity created in her by years of the stereotyping to which blacks were subjected.

It is precisely such stereotyping and prejudgment that we see in most of the other members of the white world with whom these black students come into contact. The conversations of the parents and relatives of the girlfriends reek with platitudes and paternalistic banalities as every attempt is made not to betray any latent racism, not to abandon the assimilationist "civilizing mission."

To be fair to the younger whites, however, several of them are opposed to what the French were doing to countries like Guiana, and "felt that it was only through direct action and

22. Hezekiah, "Bertène Juminer," p. 31.

Introduction

violence that the bastion of colonialism could be breached,"
seemingly going along with Fanon in his assessment that "decolonization is always a violent phenomenon."[23] Indeed, it is
ironic that these zealous comrades at times appear more militant than many of the very ones undergoing the suffering: "it
was paradoxical to see how moderate the colonials were in
the face of the vehemence of those who were not affected by
the same system." It is also ironic that it is perhaps these very
types who, with laudable missionary zeal, would go out to
work in the colonies, becoming part and parcel of the white
administration in a black country, and perpetuating the very
colonial attitude they originally set out to eradicate.

The many white characters we could have seen in France,
and did not, turn up on Guianese soil, and allow Juminer in
the second section of the novel to excel in his portrayal of
what it means to live in virtual colonial conditions under an
administration that views cultural and political domination as
an inalienable right. The scene shifts to Guiana as Chambord
returns to take up his job, to start the task he had set himself
since his days in Montpellier: lifelong devotion to his country.
Unfortunately, he receives an unexpected baptism of fire, as he
immediately finds himself embroiled in an outrageous example of administrative cronyism. Thereafter, Chambord is
able to see how the entire spectrum of officialdom operates,
and this in turn forces him to concede that, in many ways, he
is now a foreigner in the country of his birth. "Are we mere
tenants on our own soil?" he is forced to ask himself.

We are able to see some of the internal workings of the
French colonial administration (colonial, because the new departmental status apparently brought no appreciable difference in the day-to-day running of the civil service and other
organizations). Juminer literally starts at the top, with the prefect himself. Bertrand, who seemed to have used various postings in the colonial network to move up the administrative

23. Frantz Fanon, *Les damnés de la terre* (Paris: François Maspero,
1968), p. 5. My translation.

ladder, has ended up in Guiana, but really (and typically, one might add) has no love for or commitment to the country and its people. His decisions show a bureaucracy interested only in ensuring that its various divisions run more or less smoothly, but from a metropolitan, not strictly a Guianese, point of view. He is so technically and professionally oriented that he cannot see, for example, that the cutbacks occasioned by his austerity program hurt the very people he claims he is helping by instituting them.

One cannot escape the impression, confirmed outright in a few cases, that the majority of these white administrators have come to Guiana only because of the relatively favorable working conditions, despite the reputed harshness of the country. Their salaries are considerably higher than any offered comparable Guianese workers and are supplemented with paid vacations in France, special hardship allowances, and housing far better than the paltry quarters provided Guianese recruits. In short, the overall luxury of living conditions, which these metropolitan workers recognize they would hardly ever be able to afford in France, shows the extent to which the white administration thought only of itself, and would even resort to downright dishonesty to maintain the status quo. How else could one explain the episode with Quintaine and the alleged mix-up in Chambord's appointment? It is evident that any inconvenience to the Guianese doctor never entered anyone's mind.

What is so devastating about the dominance of the white metropolitan administrators is that most of them manage to convince themselves that they are working for the eventual good of the country. They believe they have nothing but the noblest of ideas and plans as far as the Guianese are concerned, and they therefore rally to one another's assistance, ostracizing anyone who appears not to be thinking or acting along the same line, for "the white minority was duty-bound to band together," and even though "they hated one another, . . . did it according to protocol." This explains why someone like Police Commissioner Gélazothes, "Bertrand's eyes in Saint-Laurent" and an obvious caricature of a character popular in anticolonial literature (shades of Gosier d'Oiseau in Ferdinand Oyono's *Une vie de boy,* to be sure), appears to succeed, while Subprefect Vincent, portrayed as sympathetic toward the Guianese, is returned to France. Juminer has the last laugh, though, when he has the commissioner unexpectedly recalled to France a mere few days after his ecstasy over Vincent's departure.

The humor we saw in some of Juminer's portrayals of the Guianese students in France is again apparent in some of the portrayals of the whites in Guiana. Poncet, the departmental director of health, is comically ill-treated by Bertrand, and Quintaine's irrational fear of the bat that enters his room and his peering under his bed to make sure nothing is lurking there are instances of comic relief in the unfolding drama of Chambord and his struggle to achieve his goal in his homeland. Also presented with a touch of levity are the many ex-convicts with whom the Guianese characters come into contact. Having paid their debt to society, and unable to return to France, they are seen at a variety of odd jobs, ever willing to regale anyone who will listen with their exploits in times past.

By far the most interesting aspect of this section of the novel, however, is Juminer's presentation of the effect of years of French rule on Guiana. One senses that Juminer could not resist taking several shots at the French government, and in many passages, what he writes sounds very close to what Damas had written several years before: "He [Chambord] scathingly attacked the mediocrity of the administration which, by refusing Guianese the right to self-government, seemed to undo the work of the great abolitionist [Schoelcher]. He had refuted, one by one, the accusations of stupidity leveled against the colonized world, brilliantly rehabilitated his race, and castigated the politicocultural alienation to which it had fallen victim." In other words, Chambord, and by extension Juminer, tried to celebrate his negritude, though he did not do so by mouthing empty slogans and clichés.

There was every need for Chambord to make his position abundantly clear, for despite the fervor he held within him, and his deep commitment to work for the improvement of the lot of his countrymen, the overriding Frenchness that he exuded upon his return made him appear one of "them:" "At the airport and on the street, people had seen a black man in a tie and a woolen suit. They had looked at him with insistent curiosity, and had discovered a foreigner. He had done nothing to reassure others, to show that he knew he was a willing accomplice. . . . He had acquired this type of behavior, and despite his profound desire to leave Europe and plunge himself all the more back into his country, he couldn't help imitating the white man." In addition, he did not even speak the local creole properly, so that "from the very start he had everything against him: language, dress, behavior." It is Chambord's gradual journey toward having things go *for* him that constitutes the thrust of this section.

At times, his journey seems a lonely one indeed, for he does not garner much support from his countrymen, who are mesmerized into believing that nothing can be done or that where a little was being done, it was not beneficial. The plight of the Indians is brought up as an example of how what appeared to be beneficial turned out to be quite the opposite:

> The young Indian was taken away from his milieu; he was baptized, raised, and sent to school up to adolescence. The educator was proud of the job he had done. Chambord however saw no reason for rejoicing. Once back in his tribe, the Indian lost all constructive contact with the world that had tried to mold him: no more going to church, no more reading books, no more speaking French. All he had learned gradually dwindled away, and his memory became as empty as an hourglass. He was forced to readapt. Far from being a motivating force, he became a dead weight for his people.

The situation was hardly different for the so-called black primitives, who "as former slaves, came from the same source as he [Chambord], and, as primitives, remained solidly united with the Indians. Struggling for true freedom meant uplifting them both."

Chambord's friend Cambier, having left his girlfriend in

France, joins the small group of Guianese professionals working alongside the Frenchmen on Guianese soil. It is an opportunity for the reader to discover the source of Cambier's deep-
seated problem that plagued him as a student, to learn that he
did not have syphilis as he had thought, and to be taken
through his complicated family history. The reader now fully
understands the neurosis that undermined Cambier's self-
assertion and that produced his impotence, and also sees
Cambier literally return to his senses through his contact with
Guianese soil, and through his acceptance of his Africanness:
"He had found the path he was to take; it was beautiful and
led in one direction. And this time, he would not let his chance
slip by. By rehabilitating his grandmother, he was rehabilitating himself, and Africa, and Guiana, and all their children." For Cambier, too, the journey had been a long one. His
bourgeois mulatto family had cringed before any association
with Africa and its descendants, the real reason his sister's relationship with Marcel had not found approval. Now with
one sister still in suspended animation mentally, waiting for
her black Prince Charming, and the other virtually cured
of her physical infirmity but refusing to leave the people among
whom she had achieved the cure, Cambier is still ready to pursue the struggle for the liberation of his people on a level that
is far less personal. It is only after that psychological purging
that he reaches the stage Chambord had attained long ago.

In the end, the novelist plays with his readers somewhat, for
we witness the painful process Chambord has to go through
following the administration's decision to have him return to
France. We suffer his self-doubt with him, along with his sense
of failure to motivate his people to stand up and reject their
French masters:

> Chambord saw only deception, betrayal, tears of blood.
> But he still held out hope; that was all he had done over
> the past two years. . . . What was he waiting for to under-
> stand that nobody wanted to decipher his messages? Soon
> men from his own country would rise up and spit in his
> face, and chase him as if he had the plague. And he would

shout to them: "I'm one of you! I want to save you!" But no one would want to be saved in this manner, and the very ones he would have wanted to elevate to the rank of free men would stone and chase him away.

It is heartbreaking, for Chambord cannot but conclude that "he was now an out-and-out bastard, since his own mother, Guiana, was disowning him." He reluctantly decides to return to France. In fact, Gary Warner's article says as much: "At the end of *Les Bâtards,* faced with the prospect of being victimized by the administration, and unsuccessful in his attempts to overcome the general submissiveness of his compatriots and to mobilize popular support, *Chambord decides to leave Guiana.*"[24] There is no mention, as there is in Randolph Hezekiah's article, of the last-minute change of heart: "In the plane, he had made his decision: he would return, *would accept* anything to remain with his people." Juminer, having mulled over all the possibilities open to his characters, eventually concludes that "to reconquer what is ours does not necessarily imply hatred of the white man." The atmosphere of reconciliation seems to come straight from Léopold Senghor, perhaps because his writings also have similar conciliatory tones; perhaps because he too wrestled with the problem of cultural *métissage* or mixing, thus with the same problem of bastardization.

We can be sure that what Juminer has chronicled, to return to the William Gardner Smith passage quoted earlier, constitutes truth. What we need to establish is whether it constitutes art. Léon Damas also chronicled truth in *Retour de Guyane,* yet we do not have the same expectation when we read that text as we do when we read Juminer's novel. The novelist, though using the same facts as the essayist, must do much more with his material, must create characters who are believable, must interest the reader in the situation created in a way that leaves one the richer for having read the book. I believe that Juminer has done this.

24. Warner, "Bertène Juminer," p. 5. My emphasis.

Introduction

In his preface to the French edition of *Les Bâtards*, Aimé Césaire points to what he sees as its shortcoming: it lacks horizon, or rather its horizon is far too restricted to individual destinies and does not extract precisely the lesson of the individual's failure in order to prepare us to move to the level of a collective problem: namely that of a people who must struggle for true freedom. And Randolph Hezekiah seems to agree: "The novel lacks vision," for "Juminer has offered no real solution to the problem."[25] I do not entirely share these views, for they seem to want the novelist, as artist, to come up with "lessons" or to "solve problems." It is somewhat surprising to see how much is expected of artists. After all, whatever "solution" they propose can only be one of many, and is not guaranteed to work in every case. I daresay Césaire as playwright could be told exactly the same thing. What have his plays solved? In other words, one can always examine a work looking for horizon, for solutions, for vision, etc., but not finding what one is looking for—and we know how the search can vary from individual to individual—can conclude that the work is not up to par.

One can, for example, bemoan the absence of any treatment of religion or of its effects on the Guianese. Surely, the church actively colluded with the administration to keep blacks in their place, a situation that was both devastatingly and humorously treated by Oyono in *Une vie de boy*. One can also regret the fact that we are not shown any other young black Guianese women beside Cambier's sick sisters. But here again, one would be imposing a mold into which the novelist must fit rather than giving him credit for what he actually does.

Juminer, whether deliberately or not, eloquently conveys the alienation suffered by the colonized individual facing a dominant white culture. He has not always avoided the pitfall of the black writer referred to by William Gardner Smith: "He is driven often to write a tract, rather than a work of art. So

25. Césaire, Preface to *Les Bâtards*, p. 9; Hezekiah, "Bertène Juminer," p. 33.

conscious is he of the pervading evil of race prejudice that he feels duty-bound to assault it at every turn, injecting opinion into alleged narration and inserting his philosophy into the mouths of his characters."[26] The consciousness is definitely there, but the lapses into tract writing and propaganda are few. Chambord does preach a little in his attempt to convince his countrymen of the desperate nature of their situation, but he proceeds more often by personal example and commitment. While not seeking to excuse this openly didactic aspect of the novel, we should note from Juminer's admission in his interview that he saw himself as settling a score, and that this is precisely what such a tone sets out to do.

One of the strengths of the novel is the way in which Juminer shows the tragic implications of the French policy of assimilation, which actively sought to produce, as Chambord comes to realize and admit, "white minds in black bodies." In fact, the characters' recurring confrontation of the "myth of the second" (where the "first" is obviously white) symbolically shows the extent to which this second-class status is ingrained in the black psyche. Finally, the entire concept of bastards (and we cannot rule out the possibility that there was a hint of Sartre's *salauds* lurking in Juminer's mind) is dealt with in a manner that evokes the reader's understanding of, and sympathy for, the Guianese dilemma of having been placed in a situation of illegality and immorality with respect to both their race and their culture.

The style in which the novel is written is not particularly Caribbean, the way, say, the region's novels in English have a definite Caribbeanness about them. The language is standard French to perfection, almost to superperfection one might say, and typifies that of the well-educated French West Indian, which the novelist is. His admitted uneasiness with creole has him avoid any genuine attempt to incorporate it into the speech of his characters, even when they are in Guiana and are in situations where such a language would surely have

26. Smith, "The Negro Writer," p. 72.

been the one used. From a translator's point of view, this made it easier to render in English the many conversations of the Guianese without too much loss of the vernacular.

It would be futile to try to pretend that *The Bastards* is a major novel—in the same league, say, as the great Russian, French, or English novels of the nineteenth century. The breadth (perhaps what Césaire referred to as horizon) is just not there; nor are there the finely drawn characters we end up referring to as if they actually existed in real life: in short, it does not have the universality and timelessness characteristic of the great novel. But while not a great novel, it is nonetheless a good novel in its own right. It takes hold of the reader and richly rewards him or her with a sensitive portrayal of a significant moment in French colonial history and of the continuing battle of one of the world's minorities to gain respect and dignity from one of the ruling majorities. In this respect, *The Bastards* is a very contemporary novel.

Keith Q. Warner
George Mason University

The Foyer

They are peaceful, a bit surly,
they are thinking of Tomorrow; in
simpler terms, of a new today.

Sartre

CHAPTER ONE

Cambier was waiting at the station.

The streetcars labored their way up the sloping avenue, jolted to a stop to discharge their occupants, and set off once more in a screech of metal.

Cambier had leaned back against the wall to avoid the rush and was smoking impatiently. He regretted having gone to that anatomy class which his friends in dental school shared with the students in medicine. Every Saturday, there would be great excitement among those present, and the amphitheater, bursting at the seams, and appearing about to crumble as if its inside were eaten away, took on an air of festivity.

Before the class, there had been an all-out paper-ball fight. The scene had unfurled according to the established rite: the student who had the ball, and who was wearing the traditional beret, was rushed by some of the impatient; he tried to bluster, but suddenly his beret was seen flying through the air; caught and thrown again from one place to the other, it went spinning throughout the amphitheater.

From the start, Cambier, hidden by a blond student in glasses, who had taken evasive action at the very last minute, had received the ball full in his face. The person who had thrown it had put into the shot all of his strength as a rugby player for the Catalan XIII team. Turenne, a medical student and Cambier's countryman, took care of the return shot. Almost immediately there were shouts of "Apology! Apology!" Custom had it that the clumsy one had to apologize if the ball touched a young lady. The victim would allow herself to be kissed.

That day, everyone got ready to enjoy the spectacle: a black man, a white woman, a kiss in public.

The Bastards

There had been no hesitation on Turenne's part. He had undone his scarf and had thrown it to his neighbor. "My apology!" his mocking lips uttered like a challenge. He lunged forward. His tall body hovered several times above a sea of tangled arms, heads, and backs, before tumbling down the steps. It emerged in an attempt to continue its course. In vain . . . The professor appeared amidst thundering applause. The class began.

A streetcar let off its passengers; Charlotte was not among them. Would she show up?

Cambier had not ceased thinking of this rendezvous with that excitement he always felt at the prospect of meeting his girl friend. Yet whenever she appeared in the flesh, looking the way he dreamt her to be, he would be at a loss for something to say to her, and the time would go by in emptiness and pockets of silence. She would soon appear, and he would again look at her, unable to express what was going on inside him. He loved her. He knew she loved him. All of that was possible in this town, for a time. Here the young woman maintained her equilibrium. Would it be the same when he asked her to follow him? He could not abandon his folks, but what of her, would she accept going into exile? The day would come when he would have to throw his hat in the ring, and join those who, down there, were engaged in a struggle against certain men of the same origin as she. What then? Wouldn't he have to start all over again?

He gave a start. Someone had just touched him on the shoulder: Sugert. He did not care much for this fellow, ever since the day he had tried to conceal his true origin under the term "South American." Sugert was no doubt ashamed to admit he was from the country with the convict prison, as if he feared people would think he was related to those accursed men sent there to pay for their crimes.

"What the hell are you doing here? You're after someone?"

He felt Sugert's stiff thumb against his hand. In the midst of a brawl, this thumb had penetrated into the mouth of the adversary, who had clenched his teeth, severing a tendon.

"I'm waiting for a streetcar."

The Foyer

"Come, come! Admit it, you're on the prowl!"

Sugert thought about women a great deal. He was working on his doctorate in law, and practiced his glibness on the young female *licence* candidates, who were only too happy that a more advanced student had noticed them. Even as early as when he and Cambier were at the lycée in Cayenne, he would get into frequent fights over "matters of the heart." These quarrels were generally settled on the Place des Palmistes. A pack of brats never failed to turn up to egg on the fighters until a policeman intervened, pulling ears and delivering blows indiscriminately.

"I think it's coming."

Cambier pointed his head in the direction of a bright carcass wobbling along in the station's turning area. Sugert continued on his way and disappeared behind the theater.

The streetcar came to a stop after swaying on its rails. Charlotte alighted and ran to meet Cambier without worrying about who was looking at her. She kissed him furtively, and he pretended he was whispering something in her ear. In public, he made every effort to have their relationship appear like a game.

The tearoom resembled a confectioner's store. In the discreet fluorescent lighting, made-up faces lost their distinctiveness and blended together in an iridescent ashen hue. Built-in speakers dispensed light, easy music; muslin drapes fell in waves of fine folds, impalpable shadows of passersby brushing against them in robotlike movements. The setting was ripe for dreams, for whispered confessions.

Cambier, alone at a table, tried to collect his thoughts. When he married Charlotte, she would have to leave all this. In Guiana, neither this refinement nor this comfortable abandon was to be found. One had to face nature, which had scarcely been penetrated and which was still renewing itself, still invading. On one side, the calm, steaming sea, thick with alluvium, came lapping against the sand, its mud dirtying the twisted roots of the mangroves. On the other, the forest, rich in fauna spreading to the edge of night, displayed its sun-drenched greenness; rivers cut sinuous openings in it, lazily carrying toward the unknown their humus-laden waters. In that jungle lived a sparse population, constantly obliged to defend itself, ignorant of the rest of the world and unknown to it.

Yes, this void was all he could offer his wife!

When the plane carrying them flew over that yellowish sea and the interminable frizziness of the forest, Charlotte would be panic-stricken. She would have seen, a few hours before, the chain of adorable islands in the blue sea; she would have seen the enchantment of it all, then she would come face to face with an overpowering world.

After the night landing, she would fall asleep, exhausted, oblivious to the disenchantment. The shrieks of the parrots would rouse her from sleep at dawn. She would open her eyes, surprised but as yet unafraid. It's at night, when the red monkeys begin to howl, when vampire bats and giant insects take to the air and brush against you as they fly, that fear sets in.

And what would Charlotte do when he put her in an air-conditioned bungalow, a small domestic prison within the vast natural prison? She would soon find her confinement unbearable. Of course, there was the beach, but the color of the ocean did not make sea-bathing a very attractive proposition. As for suntanning, the breeze could intensify, or there could be a sudden warm, stinging downpour, without so much as a thunderclap, a flash of lightning, or a cloud. Bewildered, Charlotte would want to flee. She would scarcely be on her feet when it would all be over, and all that remained would be the sand smoking in the sun. Drives in the car would give rise to the same disappointments. You left the town; you drove straight ahead; intoxicated, you began to hope again. But the asphalt soon gave way to a mud road, marked with potholes and sometimes cut off by uprooted trees.

Charlotte was coming back.

Before sitting down, she arranged her skirt and slid between the table and the chair against the wall. For a short moment, the cloth, stretched at the hips, lightly touched Cambier on his fingers, as he had let his half-open hand wander, filled with Charlotte as with an offering. She was in no way offended by this.

The Foyer

"So, you found the record?"

"No. Unfortunately."

"What's the name of the tune you were looking for?"

"It's by Gershwin . . . I've forgotten the title."

The music changed. He recognized the tune, and realized it was the one Charlotte had chosen. He leaned towards her.

" 'The Man I Love'!"

She smiled.

Once more he let his thoughts take him to his country. After hours in his dental office, he would return to the bungalow, and his wife would be calm again. They would band together against nature and would not let themselves be conquered by it. They would go off to await the awakening forest; would take their baths at night in that warm sea whose hideousness they would no longer discern; they would join the bridge club, and take up tennis. . . .

"You're not asking me what I've decided, as far as the Club is concerned?"

"What?"

"I've been observing you for some time now. You seem far away."

"No, no. What is it, then?"

"It's yes."

"You want to work with us. You're sure?"

"Certain."

"You've thought seriously about what you're in for?"

"I wanted to. At first, I came up against something obvious. So, I stopped thinking."

"And what was so obvious?"

"How shall I put it? I feel certain . . . in fact, certain that you and I must go all the way, otherwise . . ."

"Otherwise?"

"Nothing."

"What do you mean nothing? You said: 'we must go all the way, otherwise . . .' I'm waiting for the rest."

"There's nothing to say. I came face to face with something obvious, something certain."

"Which was?"

"Stop torturing me, Alain! Why make me say things one can only feel . . . that you too certainly feel? Any explanation would be a letdown."

Cambier recalled the train of events that had led Charlotte and him to the Club.

Turenne had been the first to appear, attracted by Brigitte, whom he would not have won over without that concession. He had become aware of doctrine, and on contact with it had reinforced his convictions as well as Brigitte's feelings. Cambier had followed him there, at first out of friendship, then he had absorbed the manna. Charlotte had come along in turn.

Charlotte had covered a lot of ground. Initially engaged to an American officer, she had come close to leaving for the U.S.A., and once there God alone knows how she would have judged those of Cambier's race. At present, she was considering marriage to a man of color, whose ideals she had no hesitation in choosing. She was getting into it fully aware of the pitfalls. He thought it necessary to place her once more on her guard.

"I'll tell you this, though: you're going to be my wife one day. Within me, beside the husband, there'll be the colonial, the man without any recognized historical support, without any personal future, but with a thirst for self-fulfillment. You've never experienced this thirst because no frustration has ever befallen you."

"You're not a colonial. France adopted you."

"Adopted! That word that turns us into foster children, with all the implied hazards: an unknown past, an uncertain future . . . In class, they forced idiotic things down our throats."

"Idiotic?"

"Yes. For instance, that my ancestors were insignificant people, and that it was better for me to claim I was Gallic . . . as if my people had always been part of history without having taken part in it."

"Well, if that's the way you see things!"

"I can't accept this ease, this abandon. That's what we're

fighting against in the anticolonial Club. We want each of us to know who he is, where he came from, without false shame or false pride. Coexistence will be meaningful only after this has been sorted out."

Cambier's last words made her jump. She drew herself up, an unusual glow in her eyes.

"Do you love me, Alain?"

"Careful, people are watching us!"

At a nearby table a couple was leaning over photographs which the young man was examining ostentatiously, an arm around his female companion's shoulders, his lips lightly stroking her neck. Those two were too engrossed to pay attention to what was going on around them. Further away, a dyed blonde was enjoying a cup of sweetened coffee. She was waiting for someone, turning her head in all directions and blinking nonstop. Her demeanor was irritating. The old civil servant sitting to her right was not looking at anybody; he was merrily downing a Chartreuse, allowing his cigarette to burn itself out in the ashtray.

Charlotte repeated her question. Seeing her friend's discomfort, she continued after looking around her: "I couldn't care less! I love you. The rest means nothing to me."

At these words, he all but gave in to a feeling of bliss. If only there hadn't been this "rest," those eyes trained on them!

With Charlotte, he was himself only in a setting of intimacy, though this intimacy was not to exceed certain limits. In public, he felt a sort of inhibition.

"Yes, Lotte. I love you, you know that."

An absurd shame gripped him. The acrid atmosphere and surrounding mustiness suddenly weighed heavily on him. He found them unacceptable. He had to leave, to flee from that room, those people, those witnesses. He paid for the drinks.

At the Place de la Comédie—*L'Oeuf*—the icy mistral took their breath away. Against his shoulder Cambier imagined the luster of the long hair through which he loved to run his fingers. In the privacy of the dark, he was happy to feel

Charlotte's body pressed close to his; but as they passed in front of the Café Riche, which sheltered behind its stained glasswork a clientele avidly seeking warmth, he instinctively moved away.

The theater clock struck seven. There remained more than half an hour before Charlotte had to leave. He wanted to make the most of this last moment alone with her to tell her of his love, to make her understand that he too was certain that they should go all the way. But it was she who spoke: "Alain, my aunts would like to get to know you. They're beginning to be a little worried."

"Why? We're not doing anything wrong!"

"True! But I broke my engagement . . . Obviously, you didn't ask me to."

"It was better like that. That way, everything is clearer."

"Some friends of the family have already seen us together. My aunts are embarrassed. You must understand their position, Alain. They're from another world."

She had tried to extract from the spectrum a basic color. He still found a hint of iridescence. "They're from another world!" Weren't they above all from another race? What a shame for these old ladies if a black man was taking advantage of their niece! That, he thought in his egotism, was why they were embarrassed. But he calmed himself immediately, thinking that they would probably have felt just as uneasy had he been white. Their niece had broken her engagement some nine months ago; she was being seen with a man, at dances, in tearooms, on the street; wasn't she going to compromise herself?

"Don't you want to come to the house?"

"Sunday, I'll come to see your aunts."

They moved along under the plane trees on the Esplanade. The stalls of the autumn fair had for the most part closed. All that remained were a few huts here and there, or the faces of merry soldiers having their photographs taken from behind boards picturing women's bodies in swim suits.

They left the main walkway. To their right, the small lake where, by day, haughty swans glided gracefully, shimmered brightly. Through a lattice of bare branches, the new moon

The Foyer

showed its pale crescent. Under the halo of a street lamp, Charlotte looked at the time on her watch, then turned to Cambier with a pout in anticipation of her excuse. He guided her to a dark corner.

* * *

He looked at the streetcar as it drove away, and a terrible feeling of loneliness came over him as the grinding noise, over which he had not been able to hear Charlotte's last words, faded into the night.

He walked slowly back to the Foyer. He was returning to that motley hive where he would have to listen to Décamport and his "unrealistic" pronouncements, to put up with Sugert and his sententious, albeit original, judgments, to hear his friends gossip about their absent friends to their heart's content.

Since Turenne was not in his usual spot, Ségaye said: "Monsieur Berjémi Turenne, as he does every Saturday, has abandoned us to have dinner with his woman!" He spoke with a deliberate eloquence to emphasize all the more his countryman's indiscretion. Sugert, who couldn't stand anyone making fun of Turenne, came up with an appropriate rejoinder. Ségaye tried in vain to disarm him: "I'm surprised, old boy, that, like me, being one of the *spared* ones, in other words those who have carefree liaisons, you allow yourself to come to the defense of a defector, of a *mutant!*"

Silence ensued, and Décamport took advantage of it to hold forth with one of his ideas on the fantastic in modern poetry; his words met with indifference all round.

Cambier recalled how he had met Charlotte, how he had been forced to declare himself . . .

A dance was being held at the Foyer that night. He had put on his special navy blue suit, and he sat smoking a cigarette under a mural depicting Africa.

"You have a date?" Turenne had enquired.

"Yes."

"Student?"

"No. She lives with her parents."

"Middle class?" the other insinuated with a smile.

"Probably. I met her at the science students' dance. You don't remember?"

Turenne had thought a bit. He could not but have noticed Charlotte with whom he, Cambier, had danced continuously, a heroic deed that did not go unnoticed by friends constantly searching for something to gossip about. His bow tie, the thin line of his moustache traced under his nostrils like a circumflex, and his furrowed brow made him look ever so conservative. Clearly, it was all an act on his part.

"You really don't remember?"

"Wait a minute . . . tall, dark, somewhat slim?"

"Correct."

"Oh, yes! Nice body! . . . Any prejudice?"

Actually, he had asked himself the same question. How could he admit it? Turenne would have criticized him.

Around midnight, he had taken the girl to the end of the garden. She had shown no surprise when he had said, in a business-like tone, after dancing with her: "Come, Charlotte! I'd like to talk to you."

She had followed him; and had sat beside him in the dark. Faced with such submissiveness, he had lost all self-assurance. An idea flashed into his mind: with what authority was he going to question her? He couldn't very well ask her to raise her right hand and swear to tell the whole truth, nothing but the truth, then ask her if she was prejudiced. "Blasted Turenne and his ridiculous insinuations!"

As if on purpose, her eyes never left him, and that bothered him.

"Charlotte, I love you."

He had uttered those trite words, and he was unspeakably ashamed for doing so. He tried to compose himself, but when his eyes met Charlotte's, he realized that this platitude had hurt and disappointed her. He blurted out the first explanation that came into his head:

"Listen, I'm very serious. I . . ."

He dared to look at her once more, and detected an unfathomable glow in her eyes; the lights from the hall were reflected in them and sparkled like diamonds. He could not continue.

"You're crazy!" she whispered.

In Cambier's head, rusty wheels began to turn: prejudice was there, as deep-rooted as ever. For having dared to break into a well-regulated life-style, he couldn't be anything else but crazy. Once the reins were slackened, out came the outrageous pretensions! Unexpectedly blurting out a word in this harmless vocabulary that was to mark his dealings with Europe! Couldn't he see that Charlotte was a sort of ready-made symbol, like that God, those saints in the churches, which he had to respect, but which looked nothing like him. God had created man in his image. What a joke! How could he recognize himself in Him? Not even a slight family resemblance! One had only to look at Balthazar in the nativity scene!

"We'll have to be just friends. I should have understood."

She shuddered and held his hand tightly. A leaf from a shrub whirled down in a ray of light. The pressure surrounding his relationship with Charlotte became more intense.

He had a feeling that something was going to happen—the life-style was about to shatter, to blow its barriers to smithereens, its splinters lodging in flesh that had experienced life. He waited for the blast and the exquisite pain that would follow.

He closed his eyes as an embrace caught him by surprise. Burning lips were pressed against his, and a wave of intoxication welled up in him, sweeping him away. He felt himself plunging, foundering amidst seaweed whose touch delighted him; he felt a warm wetness on his face. Charlotte was crying. Dumbfounded, he shook himself.

"What's the matter?"

"You won't get mad at me, Alain?"

"Quite the opposite! Tell me what's bothering you! Tell me I'm mad! Enlighten me!"

"You're silly to think me silly."

"What do you mean?"

She disregarded that question. From her blouse, she had taken a handkerchief, and was drying her eyes. Then, hesitatingly, she continued: "The other night, I lied to you. It's not one of my friends who's engaged to that American, it's me. I was getting my papers ready to join him."

"Then that means you've stopped?"

She would have liked to be made of glass, to be able to reveal herself to him in one piece, with her violent feelings, her life filled with principles she had always believed in, ones she hoped to adapt to their life together: in short, principles she was ready to abandon if need be.

She had longed for the confession, and when it did come it had been brutal, avenging all her doubts. She had wanted it so much that the sound of it now deafened her, made her complain, the same way that, in the aftermath of an explosion, one is unable to listen properly for having been subjected to excessive noise.

She picked her words from among the torrent that stuck in her throat and surged within her.

"You've got to understand me, Alain. I live with two old aunts, who raised me after my parents died. I had the feeling I would never love a man. So, that one, or some other man . . ."

She stopped short, as if afraid to make a confession full of consequences.

"Alain, you've got to believe me. It's you I love."

The flame had been kindled; it flickered within Cambier's heart. No doubt that's what happiness was: a rush of crazy heartbeats and a flame triumphantly making your blood boil.

"What are you going to do? Your aunts surely must think highly of this man? They'll know that . . ."

"As far as I'm concerned, he's no longer my fiancé."

Then, without the slightest touch of remorse, she had uttered these words: "He would be worse off if I were forced to marry him."

* * *

"Hello there, Mr. Existentialist!" Décamport said as he saw Cambier arrive.

"Leave him alone!" Ségaye advised.

"It's nevertheless reassuring to see a tooth puller show an interest in things of the spirit!" the other continued, seemingly not paying any heed to Ségaye.

The Foyer

During the last vacation, Cambier had insisted on going to Paris, and had gone to Saint-Germain-des-Prés. He had expected to chance upon geniuses with brilliant minds holding forth before avid, attentive disciples on the terraces of the famous cafés. Instead, he had found a bunch of sloppy youngsters who treated their bodies with disdain, who relegated love to nothing more than insipid gymnastics, and who sprinkled their conversations with annoying clichés. On his return, he had come to the conclusion that it was better to imagine some things than to live them. He had shared his impressions with Décamport, who had had a good laugh at such naiveté, and who, since that time, never missed an opportunity to harp on it.

"Chambord's not with you?"

"He's spending the weekend with Farnabe!" Cambier replied.

Chambord was in the final stages of studying medicine; in fact, he had finished studying some time ago, and was an intern at a sanitorium, having pushed back the date of his thesis defense. From his very first year, he had become friendly with Farnabe, a European classmate. Gradually, he even began to feel himself part of the family of his friend, who often invited him home.

"Say, you believe this Farnabe business?"

Ségaye, sensing he was on to something, had just placed the ball in Cambier's court.

"What exactly do you mean?"

"My mind tells me that, on occasion, this Farnabe person is really a fine lady in whose ear Chambord is whispering sweet nothings." As he spoke, his eyes had not left Décamport, *licencié ès lettres*, who fancied himself a poet. He wanted to show that, pharmacist though he was, he was still able, when the occasion arose, to come up with a literary turn of phrase. The pitiful look in his friend's eyes convinced him of the mediocrity of this aspiration.

At that moment, Sugert came in and sat down with a thoughtful sigh.

"The doooor!" someone bellowed.

It was Borgier.

He sat at the end of a table exposed to the drafts, and to the waitress's balancing act. Little by little he had accommodated himself to the misfortune, and was waiting for the right moment to "make a change," as he said. But the right moment never came. He fussed and fumed without naming any names. When he saw the waitress round the bend as she left the kitchen, he drew himself up in anticipation, his eyes taking everything in. If perchance she spilled soup or sauce on him, he grumbled listlessly: "Agaaain!" In the end, he admitted, in his fake southern accent: "Aw, she's not bad, after all!" Gossip had it that his all-too-easy acceptance of things was not unrelated to certain payments in kind, an insinuation whose libelous nature everyone admitted, and which really exasperated him at times. But the more he let it annoy him, the more the gossip spread.

Sugert had recognized the voice. Ungraciously, he closed the door, and, turning to Borgier with his arms raised, did a pirouette as he chuckled: "Olé!" He had not found any better way to avenge his having been taken to task, but it was a gesture full of treacherous allusions.

Indeed, Borgier, after a trip to Barcelona, had returned enchanted with folklore. The pair of castanets he had brought back were always with him, and just about anywhere was good enough for one of his ridiculous Spanish dance demonstrations, the irony of his pretended admirers escaping him as he performed. Already at several Student Union dances he had simply left his partner smack in the middle of a paso doble, taken out his castanets, and done his little number, complete with contorted face and clicking heels. His partner, after a few seconds' hesitation, had no other choice than to leave the floor and go far away from the antics of this joker around whom students were standing in a circle.

"What a chap, this Borgier!" Décamport said. "Perhaps one day he'll end up at the Comédie Française."

"What?"

"I went to a classical play Thursday afternoon. Listen to this: I recognized Borgier in a bit part. He was dressed as a Roman soldier."

"Really!"

"Say, Borgier!" Sugert shouted. "Seems you've traded your castanets for the phalanx?"

There was no reply, and since no one had caught what he was referring to, the matter ended right there.

Sugert was literally showing off. He would have loved to have Borgier take him on so he could cut him down to size. He tried to fall back on Cambier.

"Caught anything?"

"What about you?"

"Oh!" Décamport said. "There's a strong smell of Russian leather since Sugert came in."

Sugert, clearly not coming across too well, did not pursue the matter. What could he say? One could vent one's foul mood on Ségaye the youngster. But Décamport was a trusty old fellow. He was entitled to say anything.

They ate in silence.

It was only during the dessert that Ségaye said something: "Let's get a move on, you guys! I'm going out tonight." "Monsieur is going to spend a boring evening alone in the cinema?" Sugert insinuated.

"Alone, not quite! I have a date."

"You're interested in women nowadays?"

Ségaye assumed a boastful air. "More than you think! You wouldn't by any chance be thinking that they are there only for you?"

Sugert looked at him from head to foot. Ordinarily, whenever he did not like what someone had said, he would retort: "Quiet, Freshman!" But that night he concealed his irritation, for he wanted to find out the finer details of the affair. He would have yet another story to spread at the Foyer.

"Where did you find this old hag?"

"Beaux-Arts, my good man! If you could spend some time with her, you wouldn't find her such a hag as all that."

The others could not get over what they were seeing: Ségaye wasn't doing too badly for himself; his replies contained a touch of mystery, and he had even managed to arouse their curiosity. He was so convinced of this that he tried to exploit the situation, but, as was his custom, he soon became boring.

The Bastards

"Besides, you know that the girls at the Beaux-Arts are really something to see. It's public knowledge."

This publicity spiel was even more annoying to Sugert, who was anxious to get the whole thing over with.

"She's your mistress?"

Ségaye raised his large arms and assumed a noncommittal expression. He played the perfect gentleman, carefully watched his every move. Intoxicated by his role as a star, he did not show enough caution in dealing with Sugert, who had a trick or two up his sleeve to trap people into revealing themselves.

"You've inherited quite a burden, if I may say so."

"Burden? No, indeed! I'll have you know that I'm the second man to have the old hag, as you call her."

The others sniggered noisily. All the diners turned around, surprised at the brusqueness and racket made by the laughter. Ségaye, taken aback, looked at the fools around him and wondered what was so laughable in what he had just admitted. His naiveté would become the Foyer's best joke that year.

"The myth of the second!" Décamport shouted. "That's delving into the fantastic for you, messieurs. Ségaye, you're a poet, and don't know it."

"Virgin, looks like!" Cambier whispered scornfully.

And Sugert chimed in, with a false look of desolation: "To think that Max Müller attributes the origin of myths to a speech disorder!"

* * *

Brigitte had cleared space on the desk and was setting the table while Turenne was over an electric hot plate trying his best to cook steaks that spattered little drops of boiling oil. He felt a sharp burning on the back of his hand, and reacted with an obscenity.

"What's the matter?"

He turned his head. He looked really stupid with that towel around his waist, his long legs spread like a wrestler, one hand to his mouth, his pink tongue licking the burn.

"Nothing! It spattered up . . . When I think that the guys at the Foyer . . ."

"What about the guys at the Foyer?"

He was about to say: "When I think that they think we're eating at a restaurant!" He had stopped short, wanting to avoid another one of the sudden angry outbursts he had come to expect from her.

With her, things always started the same way: a question would bring an answer deemed offensive; one word would lead to another, deliberately uncalled for, and Brigitte would become angry. She would pout, threaten, leaving him no choice but to admit he was wrong. What else could he do, alone in his room, once she had walked out, slamming the door?

"I think they must be having a good laugh over my place setting!" he said.

"They're so childish. That's just like them." She was right. At the Foyer, generally speaking, stories had a tendency to grow, to multiply. Since it was always the same ones that were repeated, they were embellished to everyone's liking. For instance, they had recently spent their holiday as a group in a rural district in Lozère; Ségaye had been hooted down by some *bourrée* dancers he had wanted to join. Now the entire Foyer was talking about a mob of wild peasants who had chased him into the night with clubs. Sugert added that he had seen the "flash of a clog propelled by a sturdy foot in the direction of a pair of fleeing buttocks."

Turenne went back to his cooking and was not at all unhappy he had managed to avoid the gathering storm. Had Brigitte allowed herself to be taken in? She was aware of how much he feared losing her, of how willing he was to accept anything from her. In the beginning, she had been very stubborn, but had quickly disarmed him: "Don't for one minute think that your color has anything to do with it. I'm simply studying you, that's all." She agreed to be taken to the cinema, to dances, and that convinced him that if he persevered a little he would end up winning. Gradually, she had appeared to take a liking to him. She had asked him about his country, his tastes, his ideas, his projects. He in turn became quite talkative; this country, so beautiful, so misunderstood, was waiting to be saved by men like him; he, Turenne, would return to put the education he got in France to the best use; he was sure that in less than ten years, with the help of other countrymen, he would change everything down there. She interrupted him: "What language do they speak?" He answered, as if it was all so obvious: "French, of course!" "I mean, your national language?" she specified. He then admitted: "We have no national language, no national culture." She did not hide her disappointment, and in the end he asked her, "What did you expect?" She had replied: "And you're happy like that?" She had taken him to the Club.

"Have you read *Darkness at Noon?* What crap, eh, don't you think?"

She had asked the question and answered it right away, a typical answer for a young Marxist woman, disgusted that the communist world could be criticized.

At the Club, she was one of the hard-liners who felt that it was only through direct action and violence that the bastion of colonialism could be breached. Most of the European comrades shared this view, and it was paradoxical to see how moderate the colonials were in the face of the vehemence of those who were not affected by that system.

"I've read the whole thing. Didn't seem too bad to me."

"You! And what would it take, then?"

He thought of Chambord. He too must have found this book rather honest, but must not have been foolhardy enough to reveal his impressions so easily.

On his first visit to the Club, he was in for a big surprise: Chambord was on the committee, and was presiding over the meeting. All the members, even Brigitte, used the familiar *tu* when addressing him. And to think that he, who had been friends with Chambord all these years, who had eaten with him day and night, was completely in the dark about his activities! From this, he deduced that discretion had to be the most important quality in a militant. He also realized that, with

The Foyer

him, Brigitte had only pretended not to know anything; taking advantage of his feelings, she had totally bamboozled him.

"Some wine?"

"Sure."

She drank it down in one gulp, felt her head spin, and remembered that she had never been much of a drinker. Before the meal, the punch had shaken her up a bit, but she had completely regained her composure as soon as she began to eat. Her own voice thundered in her ears; she seemed to be floating in from far away, her body trembling ever so slightly.

"I'm so happy."

He looked at her in surprise. She was not in the habit of making such confessions; she was constantly in control, except when she berated him sharply for his excessive aggressiveness. Instinctively, he reached for the bottle of beaujolais and drew it toward him.

"What exactly do you mean by that?"

"I meant that tonight seems exceptional, a sort of 'privileged moment.'"

"Listen," he said wearily, "keep your Sartre quotations for your friends in the Faculty of Arts. Here, we have a man and a woman who love each other, who are searching for each other if you prefer."

"I'm drifting. It's the wine that has me a bit tipsy."

From that moment, he was certain she would give in to him, and it worried him somewhat. He did not want to make love to a drunken woman; such an exploit held little attraction for him, and above all not with Brigitte, whom he would expect to make up her own mind, as opposed to having it made up for her.

"You're not drunk by any chance?"

"I feel a little light-headed, but I know what I'm doing."

Reassured, he was ready to try his luck once more. The previous Saturday, he had almost succeeded. He had turned off the bedside light. Brigitte had raised herself up, full of hostility.

"Put the light back on, please." He had done as she asked, then had replied: "You call yourself a Marxist; in fact you're acting like a petty bourgeoise. You're just bursting with principles." She had looked at her watch. "It's time to go."

Now, he could tell she was within his grasp. Was she a virgin? Time did not permit any further questioning. A burst of laughter resounded in his head, and he pictured the red shock of hair of Bernieder, a Saarlander student who worked alongside him in the hospital. That very morning, Bernieder had set everyone talking. The professor had just completed a difficult operation: "Gentlemen, this old girl made us work for our money; her hymen was as hard as a suit of armor!" The entire room found what he said funny, all except Bernieder, who had taken out his French-German dictionary, and had begun to leaf through it feverishly. Turenne had whispered to him: "Armor!" The latter had turned a few pages. "*Panzer!*" he had finally blurted out, noisily laughing in his corner long after everyone else had changed the subject.

"Would you like us to go to the cinema?" Turenne proposed.

"I don't feel like the cinema tonight."

"We'll go downtown for a bit."

He would go out with her. He would put his large arms around her shoulder, and she would walk along very close beside him, smothered by his protective body. She was small, blonde—too blonde, too small, in fact, for this dark giant she thought she had tamed, but who had been so adroit at conquering her. He had worked quietly, accepting her whims, even to the point of anticipating them in order to better conform to them. Indeed, each time he gave in to her, it created a new bond between them, and the net drew tighter around them. She hid her weakness beneath a touchiness that surprised even her, after the fact. She ill-treated him, threatened him, yet he gave in; he grumbled a bit, searching for words that stung, but all in all he was like her: ripples on the surface, but calm and serene underneath.

"Where shall we go?" she asked.

"Wherever you wish. To the Student Union. . . ."

"Oh, no. Not tonight."

The Foyer

"Why not tonight?"

"Because there's the 'Apache Ball'. I really don't want any problems."

At the Montpellier Student Union, the "Apache Ball" took place once a month in an atmosphere of rowdiness. Everyone tried his utmost to come up with an unexpected face, and the burnt cork worked overtime: some drew whiskers, moustaches, or necklaces; others wore caps or bowler hats dug up from the family attic, sweaters with horizontal stripes, crumpled trousers, odd-size shoes; straight, long clay pipes were to be seen along with shorter ones of similar material, or others of briar, the entire collection equally filled, equally foul-smelling, equally glowing. Some students played pimps, eyes askance, half-closed, a cigarette butt hanging from their bottom lip. Others dressed as characters in some bohemian novel. Sundarive, the son of one of the professors, had even come up with a famous gag. He had pinched an enamel plaque from a public W.C., and had hung it from his buttocks. It read: "The public is asked, upon leaving, to ensure that this place is as clean as it found it on entering."

In such an atmosphere, tempers flared easily, and there were occasional altercations. One night, Turenne had been in a fight over Brigitte; that squabble had almost degenerated into a free-for-all, but it had all ended amicably, especially since the overseas students had stood resolutely by him, with the exception, however, of that cowardly Borgier, who, when it was over, was found crouching behind a column near the exit. "I wanted to create a diversion," was his excuse.

The light projected from the bedside lamp onto the wallpaper outlined an orange spot with a halo that quivered ever so slightly before blending into the darkness. Brigitte had grasped Turenne around his neck with both hands and was looking straight into his eyes; for his part, he ran his fingers through her hair, its blond locks strewn across the pillow.

They said nothing. Their lips sought each other's. They were still for a while, then their burning cheeks slid against each

The Bastards

other. The black hand moved slowly up the bolster; it groped around, caught hold of the switch, and the lamp went out. Brigitte made not the slightest protest.

* * *

The bus, all windows rolled up, made its way along a winding road at the foothills of the Causses. The muffled whine of the engine seemed to rise from the bottom of the valley where the rocky garigue surrounded a few acres of cultivated land.

Heads swayed as the bus bounced along, and the driver, who had taken off his cap, bumped up and down in his seat, his hands tightly gripping the steering wheel. The women had almost ceased gossiping, while the men were smoking.

Chambord had read and reread his newspaper. He had even gone through the classified advertisements and noticed that his landlady had lost no time: his room, which he would be leaving in three weeks time, was already being offered to prospective tenants.

He would have loved to give that room to a fellow countryman, to Cambier, for instance, of whom he had a very high opinion. After six years, the room was in a way part of him, and he would have liked to see a friend of his occupy it after him. From afar, he could then imagine all the goings-on, the surprises, even the disappointments: every morning, you would turn on the washbasin faucet and the usual whistling would greet you; you would just miss falling off as you sat astride the wobbly bidet, and you had to go through all sorts of gymnastics to regain your balance. At night, upon your return, you would trip over the raised edge of the carpet; you would discover the small heap of dust hidden there by the cleaning woman; the radio would crackle every time a mechanic on the ground floor, who worked at impossible hours, turned on an electrical appliance.

That room encapsulated an entire era: it was there he had prepared his first exams, stayed up to study for the competitions, made love to his mistresses, and elaborated all his projects.

The University, the Foyer, the Club, this fine town of Montpellier marked his life and belonged to him, though he shared them with others. How could he brutally strike all that from his existence? Everything came back to him, from the very beginning . . .

The war had just started. He was a first-year medical student along with Farnabe, and together they had been mobilized and confined to barracks. Just as their military training was coming to an end and they were getting ready to see some action, armistice was declared.

They had gone back to the university, where they had studied side by side, sharing the same anguish, the same joy, inextricably bound one to the other yet so radically different in origin, in race, in worldview. Farnabe, despite what had happened, had no problems: son of a doctor and a budding doctor himself, middle-class blood in his veins, sure of the future and of himself. Chambord, on the other hand, colonized, written out of History, dreaming he could build triumphant tomorrows without hatred or rancor. And these were the two beings who were moving along hand in hand.

The days lingered on over the town in the grip of the occupier. In each family there was someone absent, lost beyond the border, in concentration camps, or in the factories. Chambord, too, for all of his freedom, was absent, even dead as far as his people were concerned. Now that all communication with his family was virtually impossible, he had not ceased wondering whether his father and mother were still alive. The last time he had written, he was still in those barracks, waiting to be directed to an operational zone.

In this town he endured, like everyone else, the shame and restrictions of the vanquished, and could not bring himself to admit that the France he had always seen as a symbol of strength and love was now reduced to submission. It was then that he made contact with one of the Resistance networks.

He was a frequent visitor at Farnabe's. He would make the trip on his bicycle, and always felt completely at home, staying as long as he pleased. No one knew what role he played; no one asked any questions, so he did not have to lie.

But there had not been only dark days. The Navalais from

The Bastards

Bordeaux had, in the meantime, descended on the University of Montpellier, engulfing the town in a tidal wave. In the amphitheater, their mascot dog accompanied them, and quietly watched their eccentricities. Once they even clashed with a somewhat prudish female student. "Strip her naked!" a voice had shouted. There was a rush. The student disappeared under an avalanche of uniforms. In all the shouting and shoving, a man's hand held aloft a pair of pink run-free panties: "O.K., guys! Got it!" There was a moment of stunned silence; but it did not take long to figure out that the trophy, far from being ripped off the victim, had come straight from a store in town.

Then there was the Liberation, with the arrival of the first contingents of young compatriots attracted by the climate and the fame of the university; and above all Cambier and Turenne, who had left the army to further their studies. Here were two young men full of ideas, who had confidence in him, and who were getting ready to help him later on in the great enterprise of decolonization. Sugert, Décamport, and Ségaye cared little for politics, and saw no attraction to it even in the future; the first two were interested mainly in women, and their adventures were aided and abetted by the utter scarcity of good men in those days just after the war. As for Ségaye, he thought of his university days as an inconvenience to be endured while waiting to take over the family dispensary.

Some of the earlier students, stuck here on account of the war, had finally been able to leave. He had been there to see them leave, some joyfully, some regretfully. Some thought of their families thousands of miles away, and paid little attention to the problems that awaited them. Others gave them a great deal of thought and were quite distressed at the idea of returning home, whereas in France everything had seemed so easy: human relationships, possibilities for improvements, etc.

The bus stopped at a village square. The sudden burst of passengers' voices woke Farnabe, who had slept all through the trip.

"Oh, Robert! Where are we?" he asked as he stretched.

The Foyer

"Gignac."

The bus drove off as they lit their cigarettes.

They had finished dinner and had repaired to the living room.

The older Farnabe, overworked by a large, demanding practice, made a point of freeing himself at mealtime whenever Chambord was staying with him.

Mme Farnabe, a pleasant, eager woman, treated "Robert" like her own son and called him "my dear." For his part, he found her so natural, so perfect in her motherly role, that he would sometimes ask himself if she had ever been different: a simple woman without any useless airs either in her dress or in her speech, a woman who seemed not to age. "You have good news from home, my dear?" He talked about his latest letters, then they went on to life on campus, the upcoming vacation, which would be so pleasant if the exams . . .

Mme Farnabe's mother lived with them. She was a sprightly, tireless grandmother, who had immediately told him: "Robert, call me Mémé, like the children."

The children in question were Farnabe and his younger brother, Pierre, who showered Chambord with unswerving childish affection. Five years younger than his brother, Pierre was still in short pants the first time Chambord had come. No one appeared to have changed except him, who had just started studying medicine as well.

Over dinner, Chambord had announced that he would be defending his thesis in three weeks time, but he still had to say what his projects were. Already, upon hearing his plans, his boss had expressed surprise. Yet, one could not remain a student all one's life. The boss would have preferred to keep him, to push him to the limits of his career.

"I'm thinking of leaving a week after my thesis defense."

"No!" Farnabe said in surprise.

"I've been offered a job in a hospital at home. I've accepted."

This first lie had filled him with uneasiness. He had not

The Bastards

been offered anything. It was he who had seen the announcement of a competitive examination to recruit a doctor for a
hospital; he had sat it on his own and passed. That was the
truth, pure and simple.

He had told his boss the same story, giving the impression
that he was facing a fine future full of optimism. In reality, he
knew that his upcoming posting would only sidetrack him,
and that, once on the job, he would have to give up any idea of
professional promotion.

"The hospital is in Cayenne?"

"No. In one of the communes . . . Saint-Laurent," he added,
embarrassed.

"The convict prison's down there. I hear the climate is
lousy."

"It's the climate I was born in."

"But you'll be cut off from everything, in that godforsaken
place."

"I'll be like the rest of the people living there."

He was fully aware that he was deliberately anticipating
certain constraints. In this country, he was not isolated from
anything, except of course his native land, his countrymen; he
felt free but useless. Could he resolve to let his people continue their dull existence while he enjoyed the benefits of the
mother country? Back home, at least, his contribution would
count for something.

From this point on, he had made his choice, to use the expression he often repeated at the Club: "Freedom revolves
around choice, even if we choose not to be free."

"Why do you want to leave . . . so quickly?"

The older Farnabe only added "so quickly" to soften the
sharpness of the question. Above all, he wanted to know why
Chambord, after so many years among them, was so eager to
return to that country where everyone had probably forgotten him.

Whatever he thought, Chambord had for his part lost contact with his folks. He had acquired a life-style, new habits
and needs. Could he ever re-adapt to his milieu or succeed in

transplanting a convenient portion of this new world which had molded him?

"They need me back home. I have to go back. To stay here would be cowardly. I'd feel I had abandoned my country, that I'd fled."

He thought: "Still, I've never had *arouara* soup." In his country, around Easter time, the *arouara* palms were laden with bunches of shiny, plump, apricot-red fruits; once these fruits were picked, a delicious soup could be made from them. It is said that anyone partaking of it is bound to return to Guiana. Over there, a few Europeans became superstitious and drank the soup, wishing that it would bring them good luck.

"You're sounding like a future politician."

"It's not a question of politics, only a moral debt to the country incurred by my fellow students and countrymen. You can't imagine the void we experience. France maintains itself, perpetuates itself thanks to certain values I call historical; it offers them to us, and that only aggravates our feeling of destitution. Before appropriating French values, we deem it our duty to take a look at what we have."

"And you think you're the one to do it, with what in mind?"

"Today France has accepted us as we are physically. There are also other fundamental parts of our being—cultural and social. It's not normal to reject them out of hand. The better we come to know each other, the more our association with France will make sense. Men like me who have spent a long time among the metropolitans, who have come close to what is most valuable about France, cannot give up this sudden awareness. Renouncing it would be tantamount to betrayal."

"Betrayal for whom?"

"The men here, and those over there."

He would have liked to tell them not to judge his people by him. Being an intern, almost a doctor, what he represented was only the end, the result of what Europe had done to a being it had clutched in its grasp since his childhood, a being drawn to it, a being full of material acquisitions, and driven to the edge of self-denial.

The Bastards

It had all transpired as if he had never possessed anything personal, anything natural. The Marxists at the Club used to talk about cultural alienation. They would observe one fact and not go beyond it, whereas for him, what was essential lay much farther off. He and all his people, who had penetrated to the very heart of this adopted culture, recognized in themselves an intense thirst to know their own, to find themselves. What was most troubling was the feeling of being off balance, of being a bastard, easy prey to alienation.

The history of his country consisted only of European attempts at colonization, with all their difficulties and their failures, biased accounts of which notoriously discredited this land of his birth. For many—and Farnabe had just proven the point—Guiana meant only prison, a harsh climate, dangerous forests, and an almost hellish atmosphere of terror. The existence of his compatriots, those who remained over there, seemed to blend into legend. The country was nothing more than vast uninhabited bushland, a special type of desert. But it was because of this discrediting that he loved his country and that he intended to devote his entire life to it.

"Culturally speaking, we are less than hybrids, since, in our present form, we contribute nothing to what Europe gives us. We are condemned to lose our memory. Yet, there is no doubt that we do have our own values, so necessary to our equilibrium."

"One almost gets the impression that you regret the things you have acquired from us."

"Quite the opposite. Only, I'm not European and don't want to be just a well-trained monkey. My purpose is to find myself so I can be more assertive."

"I don't follow."

"If I were to abandon myself completely to European values, I'd look like a deserter, or worse, like a dowry-chaser. In the long run, I'd go down in your esteem."

"Robert's idea of things does hold up," said the older Farnabe, who till then had left the two young people to their arguments.

"We'll miss you, son."

The Foyer

"Me too. But I must go. Even if when I get there I come face to face with racism, I'll remember that in your home . . ."

He did not finish what he was saying. He felt a sob well up in his throat, and he turned away to avoid becoming emotional.

* * *

Ségaye had just entered the room. It was 2 A.M. by his watch. He badly wanted to take a shower before going to bed. Fortunately, as was the case every Saturday night, there was hot water at the Cité Universitaire. He felt dirty after those minutes of lovemaking, too short for his liking, such as he had just experienced with Christiane, the Beaux-Arts student.

He turned on the washbasin faucet. A blast of steam obscured the water flowing into the basin. The sound of the water on the porcelain reminded him of something: as soon as he had had his climax, Christiane had jumped up from the bed and run to the bathroom, from where he could hear the noise she made washing herself.

What a girl, this Christiane! She had not made any fuss. During her short absence, he had thought, as he snuggled up in the bed, his ebony head protruding from the sheets: "It would be funny if she had a little mulatto." He hadn't dared to wash up when it was his turn; he felt ashamed in front of her, and furthermore, he wasn't satisfied as yet. When she returned and lay beside him, he was quick to enter her again, making her gasp and gnash her teeth. He held himself back; a wave shuddered throughout his body; he remained still and did not flinch as the awesome sensation took hold of him.

She had shaken him roughly to wake him. "You have to leave. It won't look good for you to be seen walking out of here tomorrow morning." He had put on his clothes, and made his way to the Cité. He was happy. Second or not, he had made love to a woman. "The myth of the second! What a jackass, that Décamport!"

As he passed in front of the *préfecture*, his eyes automatically glanced toward the gate. It was there one Christmas night his compatriots had found him dead drunk, or almost, unable to walk back to his bed under his own power. He even recalled telling them, once he made it to the hallway: "Let me go. I'm going to do the crawl up those stairs." He had taken one half-hearted stroke before collapsing on the tiled floor.

He turned off the faucet, and began to undo his tie. Finally, he had *his* mistress. "France is a lovely country," he said, smiling at his reflection in the mirror.

An idea suddenly struck him. He ran to his desk, and grabbed a large red pencil he used to underline the titles of his classes. He turned toward the wall, one hand up-raised. He needed some document, some lapidary formula to mark this event.

He started to write "Vi," but his hand faltered. "If I write *Victory* the guys will catch on right away, and they mustn't."

He must write something that would be meaningful only to himself, something that his friends would wrack their brains to figure out.

He read "Vi." Nothing was to be erased. "Did the Greeks or Romans cross things out on their monuments?"

A word came to him: "Viva." Yes, but Viva who, Viva what? He gave it some more thought. "Above all, not 'Viva Schoelcher!'" He, Ségaye, no longer had anything in common with a newly freed slave swooning in the arms of a white mistress. No, sir! Ségaye had passed that stage.

So he wrote: "Viva Guiana."

CHAPTER TWO

As he pushed open the main door, Cambier set off a bell somewhere in the villa. The muffled ringing surprised him, like a
stabbing pain deep in his belly. On seeing him, an Alsatian dog
leaped from its kennel and reared up, restrained by its chain.

On the other side of the street, faces peered through windows. Glancing over his shoulder, Cambier caught sight of
their white outline parting the drapes. "As soon as I stop observing them, they'll start their scrutinizing again."

It was beastly cold. In the middle of a garden path, Charlotte
was approaching. Despite the paleness in her face, she was
bubbling with happiness.

"How nice to see you."

She had hardly moved her lips. Hand outstretched, he
reached her; she took him by the arm, then stood on tiptoe to
kiss him.

"They'll get the message," she continued, casting an insolent look toward the house opposite.

"Those women can look if they want, can't they?"

"I hate them."

She had spurned the American to go right to the end with
him, Cambier; she would take him along with her, against his
will if need be; she would hate others, would stand up to them
with her heart laid bare. Had she fully understood the quin-
tessence revealed the night before? A disconcerting halo was
beginning to form around her attachment. He wanted to be
seen neither as a deserter nor as a hater; had she understood
that he wasn't really asking her to be either?

"Don't let it bother you, darling."

"I want to show them."

"To show them what?"

"Our relationship."

"What for? Since we don't need other people to . . ."

"To what?"

"To . . . know for certain."

At the entrance, she quickly introduced him. He paid close attention to the faces of the Levasset spinsters, searching for a hint of surprise; he found only unmitigated joy on two faces colored pink by the makeup they used in their belated attempt at stylishness.

"We're glad to have you."

"Charlotte has told us so much about you, about how nice you are. . . ."

They helped him off with his coat and directed him to the warm, cozy living room. He settled down on a couch covered with a Beauvais tapestry, and Charlotte sat beside him.

The walls were hung with very dark paintings: a Lohengrin scene depicting the messenger from the Holy Grail saving Elsa de Brabant; another showed the Damnation of Faust. In a crystal vase was a lovely bouquet of carnations he had thought of sending.

He had remembered their names, but would not have been able to determine whether Beatrice was the one serving coffee or the other sitting across from him, legs together, hands in her lap. Dressed in black, like widows, their necks emerging from small white starched collars, they looked a picture of serene old age. They showed no wrinkles, apart from the lines at the corners of their heavy eyelids, stretched by twists of graying hair.

"I, too, was anxious to meet you."

"You certainly have changed Charlotte. We've never seen her so happy, so anxious to go out."

"Oh, Aunt Beatrice, please!"

"There's nothing wrong in saying that, is there?"

Ever since the previous evening, he had constantly thought about them with some apprehension. Eager aunts, women without any airs about them, women quite willing to welcome him to their house—that's what he was seeing. He had imagined that with them he would be free from the sentimental blackmail of those women who had watched him grow up, so that the slightest languidness on their part crushed him under an unbearable feeling of depletion. He was expecting to experience a shared friendship.

On the contrary, he was suddenly seized by a feeling of anguish he knew only too well. He detected its furtive, tenacious nature, like the time he was living with his mother and sisters after his father had succumbed to a heart attack. The only man henceforth among them, a stranger to their preoccupations, he could not withstand this imbalance. Their frailness, their tenderness evoked in him a feeling of inhuman constraint. Overcome with powerlessness, he avoided them. One day, he had joined *France Combattante,* and he had left.

"One sugar or two?"

The pair of tongs hung suspended over his cup.

"Only one, thank you."

Once away from them, he was filled with remorse. What would they do?

His elder sister, Caroline, was neurasthenic and spent her life consumed by the fire of a thwarted love; Hortense, the younger one, was wasting away at high school. Their mother would never manage to improve the latter nor to have the former respect the stubborn opposition steadfastly upheld by their father until his death. But what could he undertake or say against them? He had constantly come face to face with an African survival: the matriarchy.

Even the elder Cambier had suffered on account of it. His tyranny vis-à-vis his daughters took on an air of liberation. With his brother, they had grown up under the maternal fluid; their father, a European, might perhaps have seen his own way triumph if he hadn't died so early. With him gone, a dormant Africa, unbeknownst to his widow, had molded his children.

And now this same bewitching ambiance came back to haunt the grandson: Charlotte, her aunts—no man around, not even to provide opposition for him. Could it not be his fear of feminine confrontation that had kept him from seeking this visit for such a long time? He had always been the center of a system, continuously turning on his own axis. With just one leap he would be hopelessly flung into the same orbit as these women. Could he calculate how much thrust he needed? The weight of his atavism and his problems kept him bogged down. Even if he managed to overcome their inertia, he would carry them around, without any possibility of escape.

"Did Charlotte tell you I plan to return to my country as soon as I finish studying?"

"Yes. It must be a beautiful country, eh? Sun, sea . . ."

"Indeed."

"I'd love to know it," said Charlotte. "No more coats, no more woolens, eternal summer. How lucky!"

She had no idea that it was precisely this monotony that drove you to despair: never ever feeling cold; seeing week after week, month after month go by, all the same; feeling warm rain all over you, like the perspiration that made your clothes stick to your skin; opening your wardrobe and finding, every morning, your clothes covered with mildew formed by the night's dampness. She, like all European women, would come to long for snow; a feeling of frustration would begin to take hold of her.

"Nothing like the United States, obviously!"

Aunt Julie had said this without any hint of embarrassment; she was comparing two countries and, despite herself the comparison had centered on two men. Cambier thought: "Will they consent to give me their niece?"

"I guess you know what my intentions are concerning Charlotte. . . ."

"Well, er, I mean . . ."

"I'd like to marry her. Otherwise, I wouldn't have dared come to your home."

"Of course. We have no objection, if that's what Charlotte wants."

"Oh, yes."

Charlotte couldn't wait to lean over, as if about to kiss him. She had stopped halfway, somewhat self-conscious, her hand clutching the young man's sleeve.

The Foyer

One of the aunts offered cigarettes; the other, pretending she had gotten over her discomfort, said:

"There's no hurry. Your studies . . ."

"Many of my friends are married; that's not stopping them from continuing their studies."

Charlotte came to his rescue with an objection filled with allusions, that in its quasi-insolence was addressed directly to the two old ladies.

"At least, our engagement should be announced . . . so people won't have anything to say against us."

He remembered something she had said the day before: "Some friends of the family have already seen us together." Hadn't those friends gone a bit too far? Some more people to hate! This tendency to vengeful anger seemed to him quite a heavy, useless burden. "Where will it all end, in practice, if she tries to get even, and if I, for fear of making things worse, become neutralized in a network of precautions?"

After his visit, he would take a streetcar to a meeting at the Club. There he would pillory colonialism and polish his arms in preparation for his attack on it. Would Charlotte be able to differentiate between those he was rejecting and the others?

"Charlotte's probably right. We do go out together; your friends could be shocked."

"That's right."

Aunt Beatrice, who spoke as head of the family, had made this concession. He tried to exploit this semisuccess.

"Last night, for example, we were at La Cigale."

"A very nice tearoom," aunt Julie admitted.

"You're familiar with it?"

He hadn't been able to hold back his startled reaction; he just could not picture the old spinster in a setting so evocative of the free and easy life.

"Yes. Long ago, it was called . . . er . . ."

"Le Lido," Charlotte prompted.

"That's it: Le Lido. It's quite different now. We used to go there often with Charlotte's parents . . . before the accident."

The other aunt, momentarily oblivious to what they were saying, suddenly spoke.

The Bastards

"However I look at it, I see only one possibility for your engagement. You have to wait till we come back from Megève."

"You're going away?"

"In ten days time. We go there every year, to please Charlotte. We don't stay very long. My sister and I are getting more and more susceptible to the cold. Happens at our age, right?"

"Yes, of course."

That involuntary ungentlemanly remark added to Cambier's uneasiness. What could he add to keep the conversation from dying?

"A while ago, you mentioned an accident," he said, turning to Aunt Julie.

It was Charlotte who replied: "My parents were on their way to Megève, as it turns out. Their car . . ."

"Oh, I'm sorry."

Charlotte's eyes began to grow dim. He had upset her, and that troubled him all of a sudden. He barely heard her lament: "I'd be so happy if they could see us now!"

"I wouldn't like to impose. I'd like your permission to be on my way."

He stood up amidst their protests.

They were still congratulating him as they stood in the vestibule. The aunts repeated how delighted they were to have met him, and insisted that he come see them again before they left for the mountains. Charlotte saw him out.

"If Turenne were to see me surrounded by these women, he would accuse me of deviationism, with his contempt for the bourgeoisie." Ever since Brigitte had taken it upon herself to initiate him, Turenne was blinded by doctrine. He had never been made to see that middle-class values can coexist with a certain spiritual uplift and do not necessarily imply racism. He preferred to believe that a man owed it to himself to be, ideologically, pure enough to give up love for doctrine. Yet History, the source of life's experience, was against him. In his own country, there had been the *Code Noir*. This manifesto of segregation was to guarantee the purity of two races, the white masters' as well as the slaves'. Exemplary punishment had been instituted for any infraction. What was there left of this Code after two centuries of contact between races, when a revolution came along to abolish it? A fine piece of parchment. Men and women had, in the meantime, made it into the best seasoning for their forbidden love affairs.

To Cambier, the few hundred yards between the house and the streetcar stop seemed unbearably long. Strolling about at that hour of the day, under the gaze of the passersby, with Charlotte on his arm, filled him with a stifling sensation. Burying his head in his shoulders was pointless, since all those who walked by, as if unsure of what they had seen, turned around to look at them.

"Eight!" she said.

"Eight what?"

"That's the eighth person to turn around."

They finally arrived at the stop. He would now be able to make his world smaller and to escape this intolerable feeling of astonishment. He slowed down, but Charlotte leaned against him and kept him moving.

"Let's go."

"They're expecting me at the Club, you see."

"When?"

"Right now."

"Your friends are always late. You've often said so yourself. We can just as well walk. I'll go with you. That'll be my first contact."

Such stubbornness had convinced him.

He had to introduce Charlotte into that den where very harsh words would no doubt be uttered about people who on the outside were similar to her. Was it paradoxical or foolhardy, his wanting to juggle studying, dabbling in politics, and having a love affair? The university was, to a very large degree, and without meaning to do so, inculcating its culture in him. Charlotte had already given him almost everything, whereas she had only promised herself to the American, passively. With him, on the contrary, she wanted to become involved: in love, in a great demystification enterprise, in help-

The Bastards

ing to cleanse a land of common minds which sprang up in abundance, like weeds. Would she know how to discern the true meaning of her action and stick to it without the feeling of betrayal?

They walked through the narrow streets of the old town with its rugged landscape. There were fewer people about, and, by the same token, fewer curious stares. The ramparts formed a sort of barrier between two worlds: on the outside, furtive curiosity; on the inside, almost provocation.

A pensioner with a thick moustache, his hand clasped behind his back, passed close to them and looked at them out of the corner of his eye. They turned around. The man had stopped, one foot in the gutter as if petrified.

"The old dog," Charlotte whispered.

"Leave him alone. He's from another era."

"So are my aunts. They've never had any doubt about you. What right have these people examining us like that?"

The man had set off again with a shrug of his shoulders, his aggressive cane blocking his silhouette. "He must have lived in the trenches not far from men like my father, my uncle. His regiment, like theirs, marched under the Arc de Triomphe. Hasn't he ever felt that all contact could not end there?"

It had become suddenly dark. They arrived in front of the Club, whose lights pierced the semidarkness. On the geometric screen of the windows, seizing the beams of light, shadows danced in confusion.

* * *

Aresquier had invited his friends to a housewarming party and had used the opportunity to show them that he did in fact have a magnetic fluid.

He was in his third lodging in six months, for after a few weeks there would be a lot of activity around him: paintings falling off the walls, furniture broken, objects moved from one place to another. Many times, he had awoken with a start, in the middle of the night, to see his Mesmer, a thick volume, floating above the desk. Faced with so many levitations, his only alternative was to move.

The Foyer

He looked like someone out of his mind, with his wasted face, thick eyebrows over hawklike eyes, and hair that came down to his neck. He never went anywhere without a stick, which, if one were to believe him, had often struck him in his sleep. He maintained that this licentiousness was the result of the lingering presence of fluid.

His guests had listened to him, wishing that something would happen.

Sugert's date for the evening, Suzy, who looked perpetually sleepy, had surprised everyone by her tenacity, up to the moment when Aresquier's will made of her a mere executant writing a series of disconnected words in Spanish.

Sugert didn't really appreciate this. Above all, his main concern was to have a quick end to the evening so he could take Suzy back to his bachelor quarters.

Turenne, accompanied by his Brigitte, had brought along a blood-pressure gauge and a stethoscope in the hope of confusing Aresquier, but it was he who had lost face. Under the fluid of the magnetizer, Ségaye's blood pressure and pulse had risen to alarming proportions, and Christiane had gone into catalepsy.

As for Cambier and Charlotte, they had escaped with a mere fright.

Aresquier passed around petits fours, while addressing those present: "You can help yourself. They're not contaminated by my fluid."

For his finale, he did what he called "little things." He made his fluid work on Suzy from a distance; he asked Charlotte to go with Brigitte to another room. They closed the door behind them. He made a few passes, and Charlotte came and flattened herself against the folding door. They could hear Brigitte pleading: "Come on, Charlotte. Don't allow him to do this to you. Get away from that door!"

"I don't want to."

Then Turenne goaded Aresquier: "Try to throw me down."

They stood face to face in the middle of the room like two enemies. Aresquier, hands outstretched, ready to pounce, tried to draw his friend forward, but the latter resisted. A circle was formed around them. Turenne swayed but did not lose his footing; then, all of a sudden, as if he had succeeded in sizing up his rival, he stopped swaying. His belly puffed up under his shirt every time the other pulled him. This made him look fat and ridiculous.

"You're not responding. You're getting me tired."

Then it was Cambier's turn. He took his place in the middle of the group. Aresquier, who was taking a drink, had his back to him.

There was a long wait, filled with uncertainty. Aresquier was taking forever to finish his beer. Fleeting, elusive ideas flashed through Cambier's head. The other friends were looking at him standing there like a scarecrow.

"He'll make it. Aresquier is worn out."

"No, he won't. He's very sentimental."

Yes, he'll make it; no he won't. If only he could think of something, so he would not have to chase after his ideas shooting by like meteors. He won't make it. Stars. There was the ring of crystal from a glass. He'll make it. Aresquier had drunk it all.

Rattling exploded in Cambier's skull; in the depths of his galaxy, a ball of fire appeared. He thought he recognized the red head of Roquentin-la-Nausée who shouted, in a peremptory tone: "One must not introduce strangeness where there is nothing." He'll make it.

Aresquier undertook to put his client to the test, but he had resisted. All his excitement was to no avail and absolutely wasteful. His grin, his contortions, his pulling; nothing worked. Cambier looked at his belly. "Turenne!" Aresquier burst out laughing and gave up.

Ségaye was highly amused by all that was going on. He laughed so much, he was beside himself with joy, unaware of what awaited him.

Sugert, his patience stretched to the limit, was the first to leave with Suzy. Ségaye was quick to follow, accompanied by his girl friend.

Then Aresquier told those remaining: "In ten minutes, Ségaye will be coming back. He has no idea that I've ordered him to. We'll turn off the lights, lock the door, and wait for him in the garden."

Ségaye returned and tried unsuccessfully to open the door. They thought he was going to call out to Aresquier. But no. His giant form scaled the gate, and Aresquier had to step in to restore him to his normal state.

When he came to, he looked as if he had had a nightmare. Where was Christiane? What was he doing here again? Luck was really not with him: yet another story to make him the laughingstock of the Foyer.

Leaving Aresquier to his occult forces, Ségaye, Turenne and Brigitte, Charlotte and Cambier set off in the direction of the Esplanade. Not a word passed their lips until they were a tidy distance away from the magnetizer.

"You can't recover once you've given in."

"Looks like autosuggestion to me."

"You feel a sort of warmth within you. It's irresistible."

"He should be doing medicine, not law."

"The worst part is that your friend could be dangerous."

"Dangerous? How?"

"Abduction, and fraudulent use of a third party to commit a crime!" Charlotte informed them, betraying a strange sort of captivation.

Spectators at the Pathé cinema were puffing away at cigarettes. Behind the open windows they could be seen clustered in little groups in the opaque atmosphere of the smoking room. From time to time, women made their way through them, the play of light on a jewel causing it to sparkle for an instant. It was intermission.

Aresquier's guests made their way slowly over the paths of the Esplanade, unable to avoid a disturbing presence. The magnetic fluid persisted among them like a wad of cotton whose fluff had enveloped them in unreality. Blotted out by the sound of the bell at the Pathé, it continued to haunt Cambier, painfully exquisite, like the annoying insistence of a dentist's drill working on a molar.

Behind them, the sound of the bell faded slowly. Turenne suggested they go to his place for the evening. Like his friends, he needed a break; they had to place some new adventure between Aresquier and their approaching loneliness.

Ségaye preferred to go looking for Christiane.

In the stairway, Brigitte was not embarrassed when Turenne put his arm around her waist, to walk up in step with her. Cambier and Charlotte came behind them, and it was she who, out of jealousy, took his hand and placed it on her hip.

Turenne sat down and took Brigitte on his lap. His hands stroked her neck, her shoulders, her breasts, and she trembled with lascivious pleasure. He wished he could get drunk, his escape from an evil spell, and gorged himself with tangible reality as his means of staving off that hunger that Aresquier's world had aroused in him.

Cambier leaned against the desk with his hands in his pockets, pretending to be unaware of what was happening right before his very eyes. The same hunger gripped him, but an unspeakable torpor thwarted his urge to act. From her chair, Charlotte motioned to him; he and Turenne were in the same position, not daring to satisfy the need that tormented them. An avalanche of brown curls showering down on his eyelids, he could not see the other couple. Turenne's hushed whisperings to Brigitte were all he could hear.

"Say, darling, prepare us something. Hey, you two, would a punch be O.K.?"

Charlotte stretched, pulled her hair back over her neck, and pinched Cambier on his chin. His ever-hungry lips parted to let out a sigh of satisfaction.

Brigitte played the mistress of the house. She crouched in front of the improvised bar, and her provocative curves bulged in her skirt.

"What a character, that Aresquier!" she said.

"You don't think we've talked enough about fluid for one night?"

Turenne's reply, showing aggressive fatigue, cut short her reminiscing.

"Chambord's defending his thesis in two weeks," he continued.

"Do you know what he plans to do?"

The Foyer

"He's going back home. I hope he'll do a good job down there."

"I know he'll leave one day; but I don't think it'll be right away."

"Still, he's planning to leave in three weeks at the outside . . . at least that's what he hinted to me."

Cambier viewed the announcement of this departure as a threat.

"It'll be a great loss for the Club," he said.

"But an investment that could pay big dividends."

Attentive and obstinate, Charlotte tried to make sense of what they were saying. She knew one thing for sure: they had all traveled the same path. First the rigor of physical attraction, then the flow ending in total identity, something she called *certainty*.

In the street marked with the pale cones of the lamps, Charlotte snuggled close to Cambier.

"What are they going to do?" she asked.

"Who?"

"Turenne and Brigitte."

"What do you mean, Turenne and Brigitte? He's taking her home."

She showed just a touch of complicity; a fleeting glow appeared in her eyes, making her strangely beautiful with naive sensuality.

"And after!" she said.

"What about after?"

"He'll take her home, *after*."

He refrained from pursuing the matter. A young man, a young woman tied to each other by gut-wrenching certainty—that was the couple Turenne and Brigitte. Left to themselves, in the dead of night, in a room, they would soon feel its weight; it would engulf them and drive them to yield to it. Charlotte had made a prediction, so to speak: Turenne would take his friend home only *after* the fluid had stirred in them.

The Bastards

They continued toward the avenue. A short man, staggering, feeling his way along the wall, allowed them to pass him without bothering to look at them. "O.K., O.K. Long live America!" he stuttered in a thick voice.

Cambier was in a hurry to take Charlotte home, to take her from the double charm that did not seem to frighten her.

"Take me to your place!" she begged.

"Why?"

"Take me to your place!"

"Do you know what time it is?"

"I couldn't care less. I want to see what your room is like. You've never had me over. Turenne invites Brigitte over all the time."

He turned into his street. Since he had known Charlotte, he sought ecstasy in contemplation, and his sexuality had become an affair of the mind. He felt fulfilled, withdrawn in a tower and dreaming about her. He began to practice self-denial, persuaded that in this way he would be all the more worthy of her. But wasn't she expecting more from him than abstraction?

When he arrived at the main entrance, he had an idea.

"I can't find my key. I'll have to call the concierge. She'll see you."

"So what? Ring the bell."

He searched in his pocket and produced the key. The squeaking it made as it worked the lock stabbed him like a pain; the steel seemed to be digging into his flesh.

As was the case every weekend, the central heating was on. In the veiled brightness of the wall lamps, the room appeared desperately suggestive.

"Your place is lovely. You've got two rooms."

"An alcove and a study separated by a curtain, that's really only one room."

She disappeared behind the curtain. He did not want to pay any attention to her, yet to his surprise he found himself listening. She sat on the bed, tested its softness. As she lit the bedside lamp, she knocked over a book, which she picked up immediately. "Must be *La Nausée,*" he thought; a book that had made a great impression on him, that he was rereading for the umpteenth time, one whose ideas he devoured with a passion. There was some rustling against the curtain, and Charlotte reappeared, a picture of expectation.

"Come."

"It's senseless, Charlotte."

"I want you to . . . you and me to be like them."

"Like who?"

"Turenne and Brigitte."

"What do you know? Come now, don't be . . ."

She sank down, curled up against him, and drew him to her. He did not feel that twinge announcing imminent orgasm; instead, he was seized by a ridiculous panic. Lying on Charlotte, he shook her violently.

"It's that fluid, that punch that made you drunk."

"I hardly had anything to drink. I love you, Alain."

Panicstricken, he went back into the study and regretted it almost immediately. What was this charm that excited him once he was far from a woman, yet paralyzed him when she came close? Was Charlotte's authoritarian love a match for that other love that had forced him from the family house?

"Forgive me, Lotte," he said as he moved to kiss her.

"Why do I scare you? Because I'm a virgin?"

"We must rid ourselves of evil spirits."

"Are you sure you love me, Alain?"

"Yes. Otherwise . . ."

"Otherwise what?"

"Otherwise I'd have used this opportunity to . . ."

"But, Turenne and Brigitte?"

"I repeat. You're getting ahead of yourself. And furthermore, everyone is free to do what he likes."

They left hand in hand. Throughout the entire walk back, he wanted her, as if to prove to himself that his inhibition was not an illness, that it came from a crystallization that prevented him physically from carrying through with it. All he had to do was turn around. Charlotte, quite docile, would have followed him. But as always, things that bothered him did not influence his actions, and his intention did not get past the impulse stage. Even if Charlotte had called upon him to act, he would still have refused.

They moved instinctively along the dark boulevard. Their halting step did nothing to stop the flow of their thoughts. Each in his own peculiar way, they confronted the same torment: she, assessing their love and its sterile incantations; he, imputing his reticence to a malaise that verged on impotence.

* * *

Ségaye lit a match and searched for the switch. He did not see it right away, though he was looking straight at it. The glow, growing redder before his face, had filled his head with a wave of light that penetrated through the sockets of his eyes and shot backwards in a painful whirl. His grimace intensified when he felt a burning on his fingers as the flame finished consuming the match. A sudden dizziness made him sway, and he stumbled against a step as he tried to spread his legs in an attempt to regain his balance.

He was lost in that black hole where the slightest noise took on a particular resonance. The echo of footsteps as a night walker strolled along the lane reverberated against the walls and up the stairwell, where it hit Ségaye, making him grimace. "Hope she's in."

A second match scraped against the box, and burst into flame. The shadow cast by the black hand ran along the wall like a huge spider and blended into the live hand that pressed against the switch. The light went on, as did the automatic timer, making a funny-sounding noise that accompanied Ségaye as he climbed the steps.

He was worried that he was probably climbing up those few flights in vain. After all the stairs, he had to take one of those labyrinthine corridors, the kind where you would suddenly run into a wall, and where the corridor would turn either left or right after forcing you up or down a few steps.

The Saturday before, he had found it absolutely exciting to slip, at night, into the room of a consenting young woman, who walked in front of him, most often not in a straight line, her finger on her lips to urge him to be careful. Spurred on by a great feeling of adventure, he had savored the joke he was playing on those fools at the Foyer. "Did they ever have a minute like this, those jackasses?"

He had reached the second floor when the light went out. Now was not the time to make a mistake. All those damned floors looked alike in these old buildings. It would look like he was up to no good if he were to knock on the door of a complete stranger.

Why had Christiane left him? He remembered leaving Aresquier's place with her and quickly breaking away from Sugert at the first intersection they came to. He had wanted to show this so-called Don Juan that he wasn't the only one interested in women. Then there was a void until the moment Aresquier had given him a fatherly tap on the shoulder. "So, Ségaye, we came back to see old Aresquier?" And those clowns Turenne and Cambier had started their stupid snickering.

He recognized the door and knocked. "Hope she's in." There was no answer. He knocked more loudly and waited. Still no answer. "I'm sure she didn't go to the cinema. When I passed in front of the Pathé with Cambier, Turenne, and their old ladies, it was intermission." He called out: "Christiane!"

In a neighboring room, there was some commotion, and a mattress could be heard squeaking. A sleeper had been rudely awakened, and was grumbling as he tossed in bed.

"Should I call her again?" Having come this far, he might as well continue.

"Christiane!"

"Yes. What is it?"

"It's me."

"What?"

"François."

"François who?"

"Ségaye."

"What d'you want?"

After having him specify which François it was—as if she knew several—she was now using the formal *vous* to address

The Bastards

him, as if he were a stranger! Then, to top it all, the light had just gone out again. Christiane repeated:

"What d'you want?"

"I looked all over for you," he whispered through the door, which was still not open.

"That's a good one. You looked for me? You forget what you said to me earlier?"

Had he said anything to her? He couldn't remember. Yet, his exact words to her had been quite straightforward: "Sorry, but tonight I can't take you home." He had then walked off and left her standing in the middle of the street.

He spoke more loudly.

"What did I say?"

"Shut uuup!" shouted the tenant they had awakened.

Ségaye became afraid. He would die of shame if people were to come out of their rooms to put him in his place. He was so easy to spot: a black man. He took off at breakneck speed and was soon lost in the darkness of the stairs.

* * *

Turenne slid beside Brigitte. "Basically, I'm the one becoming middle-class. I'm settling for a little sex once a week!" Was that the truth? Did his juvenile eroticism not demand much more? Tonight, when he took her home, he would have this pressing desire to have her once more. Already he could feel the longing taking root inside him, even as they shared one last embrace at her front door. This desire grew more intense as he got further from Brigitte, going back to savor a certain fragrance that lingered in the sheets. He took a long time to fall asleep.

"You think they're sleeping together?"

"Who?"

"It's true, Charlotte is so middle-class."

She would have liked to know if Charlotte had given herself to Cambier, if their union was in response to the one she had with Turenne. She sought a sort of consolation in solidarity. Her own case would seem less odd if she could be convinced that their two friends shared the same intimacy. Such a flagrant insult to middle-class values, of which this act would have made Charlotte guilty, would have filled her with a satisfaction guaranteed to ease her conscience.

"A woman can be part of a milieu without sharing its principles," Turenne asserted.

She saw some insinuation in this remark, and felt the same uneasiness that had bothered her before: an indefinable shame mixed with a feeling of guilt. Was she betraying Marxism? Was it betrayal to have a certain modesty? Wasn't she rather showing her conformity? She had on many occasions felt the urgent need to carry through with the physical consummation, to throw herself into that adventure to the brink of which their every embrace was leading them. On each occasion, she had checked herself, and that brutal, voluntary interruption, like an abortion, left her in deep shock. It was stronger than she. Restraint was needed. It was quite clear that she still harbored middle-class values. A critical look at herself had just proven it to her. And to think that she had thought herself totally liberated!

But how could she get Turenne to say what he believed? Whatever their milieu or their race, didn't young men immediately see any young woman as easy prey? Perhaps he would betray his true feelings if she enquired about Cambier.

"What about Alain?"

"What about him?"

"What type of person is he?"

"My best friend."

"All the more reason you should know what type of person he is."

"That's vague."

"I mean, with women, with Charlotte?"

"Oh, you know, he and I, we never discuss our affairs, unless we have to."

"Have to?" she asked, frightened at the thought that one day all that had transpired between herself and him would be exposed.

"Yes. Have to, because of certain circumstances."

He recalled one of those circumstances. It had happened

when he and Cambier were still at the Cité Universitaire. During the month of August, the concierge of Colonial Hall would go off to Belgium, and his replacement, who had his hands full anyway, would do only a symbolic job of watching the place. Most of the overseas students, who spent the summer in residence, took advantage of this.

One night, Turenne had hoisted a woman through the window of his room. Their carrying on had greatly inconvenienced Cambier, alone in the adjoining room. The shaking of the bed, the whispering and muffled laughter, the sighs, were all the more unbearable since he was in the habit of leaving his door wide open whenever it was hot. By dawn, he had managed to doze off. The young woman had then asked Turenne: "Where's the toilet?" and he, dead tired, had mumbled in a distant voice: "Down the corridor, first door on the right," and had added "after the stairs," but she was already out the door.

As it turned out, the first door on the right was Cambier's. The young woman entered and bumped into the bed. You can imagine how surprised this lone occupant was to open his eyes and find in the semidarkness an alabasterlike creature stark naked in front of him. "What's the matter?" She had jumped, and slapped her hand over her pubic area. "Darn! Excuse me, I made a wrong turn." He burst out laughing—a hearty, black laugh from deep down inside him, as if to make up for his recent loneliness, and Turenne had come running.

"What type of circumstances?" Brigitte insisted.

He lied: "For instance, a year ago, Alain had brought a woman to his room at the Cité. I was his neighbor and heard all their frolicking. He had to apologize the following morning."

She imagined a third party listening and could not help exclaiming: "How horrible!"

He pulled her beneath him, and she squeezed him tightly in the vice formed by her legs digging into his black spine.

* * *

The news had taken them all by surprise, though they were half expecting it. Macombo, an African friend of theirs, and an arts student, had just died after a protracted illness that kept him in hospital for months. A black drape hung over the door to the Foyer, and the condolence book filled with signatures.

Chambord went into the salon, where he saw Gervais absorbed in a book and sitting off in a corner of the room.

"You're all right?"

"Sure. Bad luck is certainly following us. Last year, Brienne. Now, Macombo. It's sad to die a student."

Gervais had a tendency to launch into ridiculous commentary whenever there was bad news. One got the impression that he thrived on it. Sinister in outlook, and always on the alert for his friends' bad intentions, he had ended up earning the nickname Malaise.

"We knew he couldn't be saved," Chambord said.

"It wasn't like that with Brienne."

Chambord could sense it coming. Gervais was about to regale him with a complete rundown on Brienne's death. Hadn't he witnessed the entire thing? That untimely death had swooped down on the victim, and on them, with alarming suddenness.

They had spent a month vacationing in Lozère. Minor events, and everyone's setbacks were to be transformed into indescribable adventures once they returned to the Foyer. The suitcases had been repacked; they had piled into the bus and were on their merry way back home, relaxed, recharged for the new school year. Brienne and some others had wanted to ride back on their bicycles. He had ended up in a ravine in the Cévennes hills with a shattered skull.

"The burial's tomorrow."

They would see a catafalque in the middle of the salon, surrounded by the sad faces of the students in their dark clothes. There would be speeches, choked sobs, and periods of painful silence in the large room where multicolored frescoes created a paradoxical, unbearable decor. Then the hearse would leave, speeding toward the suburbs. There would be a dash to catch a streetcar to the Saint-Lazare cemetery. The absolution was given right there in the chapel.

"Hello, youngster!"

The Bastards

Cambier took his hand away from Chambord's. He did not allow himself to join in with the ritualistic "Hello, old prostate," his term of address for his older friend. His eyes met those of Gervais; as conspirators, they did not need words to understand each other. A danger hovered over the Foyer, over them. Fate had struck twice. Would it stop there?

Sitting around the same table, no one dared to speak or touch the cards strewn on its green covering. They were afraid. Afraid of what? They had no idea. Their worry went no further—a numbness they recognized, but were unable to avoid.

Chambord turned around, letting his eyes wander over the room, to the ping-pong tables, the radio that for six months would be turned on only for newscasts or cultural programs, and the piano condemned to silence. He was almost engrossed in thinking that he would soon be leaving all of that. The Foyer was entering a new period of austerity. The break would be less painful.

A young woman from the Antilles joined them. Like all the others who came to the Club, she wore no makeup, spoke little, and was easily shocked. She had come forward with an unaccustomed spontaneity. This death created a bond among them. Everyone gathered together in a corner of the huge salon, which seemed even more immense because it was empty and silent, and looked like victims waiting for help.

"How old was he?" Gervais enquired.

He had just remembered the dynamism shown by Macombo when the new committee was elected for the Foyer's Student Association. He found it difficult to think of him in the past, completely in the past. Macombo had shown some originality in his candidacy, running an American-style campaign, distributing smiles, cigars, and handshakes. He had even stuck a humorous manifesto on the walls of the vestibule: "Overseas Students! Vote for Macombo! You will not be disappointed, for he has made no promises!"

"Twenty-four or twenty-five."

"Was his family notified?"

"No, they hadn't been told how serious it was."

"Why?"

"They thought they could send him back home but the illness claimed him faster than they imagined."

Cambier was listening to them, a burning question on his lips, one that only Chambord could answer. But Gervais with his horrified look, and the female student with the sapodilla-colored face were upsetting his plans. Just his luck! He desperately wanted to know: "Am I impotent?"

The others continued speaking of the deceased. Cambier, on the other hand, centered on himself and, without realizing it, stared at the female student, making her embarrassed. She bowed her head with a sigh, causing him to realize that he was in fact staring at her. He rubbed his chin to regain his composure. Another question flashed through his mind. "Why don't they flirt?" All the women from his country remained apparently indifferent in the warm, seething milieu of the Foyer. They passed through it without getting bogged down, escaping one day like will-o'-the-wisps, remaining just the same, impenetrable, impossible to fathom. They were not beautiful. "Besides, in our country, beautiful girls are married off while still young and don't have time to go to university." They were worth our interest, all the same, although they were generally rebellious. "We'd be real scamps to try to seduce them. Our role is rather to protect them." He let go of his chin as a last thought came to him. "Then, too, it's possible they do their flirting in secret!"

He put his hand in his pocket, looking for his pack of cigarettes. His fingers found a few coins, his change from the cinema. He was unaware of the mourning at the Foyer when he had bought the four tickets for Brigitte, Charlotte, Turenne, and himself. Now, it was too late to change his plans.

He passed cigarettes around to everybody.

* * *

They took their seats in the empty row, and the usher walked away, tottering on heels that were too high. The cinema was flooded with many-colored lights to which the arabesque patterns of the fluorescent tubes lent an air of exoticism.

Turenne and Brigitte sat with the other two between them.

Cambier felt protected, no longer afraid of the environment. He was brave enough to look around.

Up behind him, a French friend greeted him with a small wave of his hand, which he replaced gently on the female shoulder whence it had risen. He returned the greeting, and the lips of the young man's companion began to twitch.

Brigitte addressed Turenne ironically: "Must be quite a change for you to find yourself on the extreme right!"

"Maybe. But I see you're in your true place!"

Seated between them, the two others moved their heads from side to side in order to catch what they were saying. Cambier was searching their eyes and their words for some sign that would replace an impossible confession. Had they been able to rid themselves of the evil spirits the day before or to achieve the chaotic duet denied Charlotte?

A couple came to their row, and they had to stand up to allow them through. The houselights were dimmed. On the screen, a few beams of light flashed, then the credits appeared, accompanied by background singing.

"Another documentary on Africa," Turenne whispered.

"Looks like it."

"They're going to show us Negroes running about half-naked."

"Don't fly off the handle yet. Wait for the first few scenes."

"You're always so damned naive. It can only be lousy, as usual."

"Look. It's in color."

A black dance, pulsating with realism, flashed onto the screen. Cone-shaped, almost erect breasts bobbed up and down convulsively; copper-colored buttocks swiveled and throbbed; mouths rich in ivory opened wide to shout in lascivious joy or to twist as if entranced.

Highly annoyed, Turenne fumed: "They've not understood one damned thing! They'll always be caught by surprise."

Charlotte clutched Cambier. That hand of sympathy she wished to extend felt like a foreign body. Turenne was right: always the same nonsense. One got the impression that was all the black people could do and that his presence at the university was the result of a wave of a magic wand. The Levasset spinsters never went to the cinema. "Thank God for that! They'd never accept a savage, newly introduced to clothes, who could possibly offer their niece to cannibals as a snack."

From that moment on, Cambier remained frightened. He discovered suddenly that he was moved by the aggressive sensuality of African women. Did his frigidity with Charlotte stem from a breakdown of his senses, then?

The *thing* was right there, turbulent and hidden. She enjoyed smothering it and refused to show any outbursts. Why had he failed with Charlotte? He hated conformity, rejected it by denying all its defects. If he had kept some trace of it, he would have conceded: "We don't yet have the right." Instead, he had shouted: "We must rid ourselves of evil spirits." This last exhortation could not apply to him; he had no need of exorcism to rid himself of a spirit that tormented only Charlotte. Whenever she looked at him, in her veiled innocence, he wanted her. Whenever she gave in, he no longer felt any desire. There were stories of millionaires brought to ruin by the ecstasy of possession. Was he impotent in his excess? Some saw in the function a creative virtue. Was it written somewhere that a purely functional perspective could be destructive?

They split up in the street. "Turenne seems at ease. He's going home with Brigitte. And what about me?" He desperately wanted to take Charlotte to his room. But the intention ended right there.

"Take me back quickly. I want to be ready to pack my suitcases."

"That's true. You're leaving tomorrow."

"I'll write often, darling."

He was alone in his room, thinking about the *thing*—that frightening doubt—that kept gnawing away at him. And he was incapable of telling whether or not it was a question of impotence.

This *thing* existed within him. He felt certain that he could neither prevent it from existing nor even identify it. He knew only one thing, namely, that he *did not know*. His certainty

The Bastards

ended there, in blinding negation. But when he broke the circuit to fly off toward Charlotte, at least in his thoughts, he believed he possessed another certainty: that he would see it through to the end. This latter certainty he thought of as brand-new, whereas it was close to the previous one, for love cannot be reduced to thinking as a couple.

Thus, his certainty turned round in circles within his fear, and his fear turned within him.

Meetings were out at the Foyer because of the mourning. Chambord, who had just defended his thesis, had held his celebration party in his room.

Cambier had brought his guitar, and they had sung songs from Guiana, recreating in the very heart of the old town a piece of their homeland. "*Ohé, Zombis baré yo!*" The guitar played with frenzy. Vestiges of Africa filled bodies jigging up and down in front of one another, carried away by the rhythm. Décamport and Ségaye, arms in the air and bellies almost touching, were swaying in front of each other. "*Ohé, Zombis baré yo!*" Cambier played with such passion that his fingers seemed to be on fire. The rhythm changed all of a sudden. "Wasn't that the cause of all his pain in the cinema the other evening?" Africa was still there, immortal and powerful; why be ashamed of it?

They had been drinking; heads began to feel light, and the women couldn't stop giggling.

Meanwhile, Charlotte was enjoying herself in the mountains, and Brigitte, who was ill, had indicated that she could not make it.

Something unusual was happening.

Cambier surveyed the calmly sensual faces of Chambord, Turenne, Sugert, Borgier and Ségaye eagerly awaiting the right moment. Farnabe, the only white man in the group crowded into the room, also knew where he was headed, despite the bright redness in his face.

Suddenly the lights went out.

They were shrouded in a silence thick with mystery, secret deals, and tacit agreements. There was the pounding of foot-

The Bastards

steps, like lost people looking for one another in a crowd. Sporadic whispering interrupted the creaking of a divan.

In the darkness engulfing them, Cambier felt the isolation of a diver stranded in the deep. His ears hummed as a result of the alcohol.

"My partner is abandoning me," a woman's voice said.

Partner. Actually, there were as many men as women. Chambord became angry. By the very tone of his voice, it was obvious that he was tearing himself away from a very pleasant task.

"Hey, Cambier, what the hell are you doing?"

Cambier did not reply.

"He's drunk. Probably fell asleep. Look after him, Gisèle."

He heard close to him the wheezing of air expelled from a cushion. The brightness filtering in from the street was crossed by a silhouette that brushed against them.

"Alain!"

"What?"

"Here. Drink this!"

The rum burned into him with fierce mellowness. He returned the empty glass. Before slipping it under the chair, a hand lingered on his in a caress.

The shadow bent over; its warm, panting, alcoholic breath ran over the face of the young man whom a weight then crushed as it came to a rest against him.

The image of Charlotte yanked him from his predicament. He saw himself once more on the platform of the station, saying good-bye to the Levasset spinsters, their heads nodding in a doorway like faded withered stalks on some plant. They had pleaded: "When you're married, you'll come along with us, won't you? Charlotte's room looks on to Mont-Joly. A breathtaking view!"

He would sleep in the same bed with her, at the foot of a glacier. She would invite him to make love to her, only to find herself in the middle of two glaciers: the other and himself!

The shadow was still holding him close, and continued its flirting. He wanted to know. He had to know.

The Foyer

"Let's not stay here," he said.

"Where are you taking me?"

"My place."

He disappeared in the night, dragging after him a woman and a guitar. The cold sting of the wind helped him recover.

He tried to play the strings of the instrument hanging from his neck, but to do so he had to let go of Gisèle, and, furthermore, his fingers were fairly stiff.

"You want to play something?" he asked Gisèle, handing her the guitar.

She put her arms around his neck and kissed him so violently he stumbled.

"No, darling, I prefer to listen to you."

His fingers clumsily tried to find a chord. He knew that inspiration would fail him. Thus, as he walked, he began to think about Gisèle.

Before running into her again at Chambord's, he had only met her once. She was sitting in the Foyer casually thumbing through a file on her lap and studiously puffing scented cigarettes while attempting to look inspired. Sugert and Chambord were reluctant to approach her, although they lacked a fourth for a game of bridge. He had taken a chance, and she had accepted him as her partner. "A real premonition!"

She had doubled all and sundry, and he had gone down several times. Sugert, in his perpetual pose—tie untied, hat balancing on the back of his head, cigarette hanging from his half-open lips, leg over the armrest—was highly amused by so many blunders. Chambord totaled up the score. "What manna, my friends! Even at a cent a point, you're going to have to fork out quite a sum."

She took no notice of them, and was more interested in posing like a star with her cigarettes no one could find on the market. "Unlucky at cards . . ." she said.

He had spent a long time caressing delicious curves with his brown hands. He had thrown himself on her. In that way, he

The Bastards

was assured that he was not impotent, but began to discover that appeasement was not around the corner.

His fear had just been swept away in a blast of fireworks, but another one had taken its place. Fireworks? It looked more like the vivid blue of a Bengal fire, except that it was as sinister as an auto-da-fé.

He could hear crackling in his head, which seemed about to explode. The more the fire crackled, the more it worked its way into him. He became the heretic, the apostate under fire from the Inquisition. Each color of the flame revealed something to him: the red parodied his weakness; the yellow, his cowardice; the green, his hypocrisy. Within this spectrum, he saw only red, yellow, and green. No easing touch. Nothing but red, yellow, and green!

It was fire, too, that had destroyed a village where, as a child, he had spent his holidays. Animals had been caught in the stable, in the pigsty. Yes, in the pigsty. Burnt, shriveled pigs passed before him on an assembly line. He identified the most charred, the most shrunken of all: a boar whose bloated face— black, hairless, almost human—grunted in a voice from beyond the grave: "It's me, Alain Cambier. Look at me!"

He had become a boar, a pig roasted in its own muck, in its own filth. The mutation had sprung forth like a flood in the night. He felt his skin stretch, his inside lose its importance, fading into nothingness. He was making his exit from the human throng. Henceforth, he would have to go about on all fours, naked, the way he now was, as naked as Gisèle.

Suppose the celestial fire were to galvanize him in this ungainly posture! It was then that self-disgust gripped him, penetrating everywhere, into his flesh, into his blood. Each beat of his pulse against his temple murmured in his ear the awful toll: "Son of a bitch! Son of a bitch!" It was impossible to escape it, to stop it, to crush it. It stuck to him like a shadow.

And Gisèle was there, in his bed, snuggled up against him, and smelling like a flower in full bloom. She had accepted him with a strange smile, conscious of success, and had only stopped talking long enough to moan as she abandoned herself to the drunken pleasure. Then she had reacted, had intensified her prattling. She confessed as her voice choked slightly: "Alain, you're the second."

The risk he had taken obliged him to listen to the tales of a hussy who handled eroticism like a lute: the myth of the second! He saw again Ségaye's pitiful face, heard his friends laughing their heads off. He, too, had come to that. It was heartbreaking. He stood up, shouting with vexation, his hand in the air:

"Get the hell out of here, before I . . ."

He saw the fear in Gisèle's eyes, and it made him forget his own. The young woman drew herself up against the bolster and pulled the sheet over her.

"Don't look at me like that, Alain. It's awful. I feel like I'm staring my tomb in the face."

"Enough of this nonsense. Get the hell out!"

He felt strong. His strength in front of her, of her dilatory candor, was tantamount to repentance and prepared him for grace. He wanted to see in her a fear that would swell up and burst hideously into pieces. He began to hate her. He was going to inject his hatred into her in small doses, and would feast on a vain desire for love she had been incapable of concealing. He would degrade her, would make her beg, like a beggar stretching out his hand when pangs of hunger attack him. What a splendid kick it is that sends his modest bowl flying while the man flounders in despair!

She would never overcome that hatred that sought to overwhelm him with its bitterness, to avenge him for having been afraid. To hate as one loves, blindly; the opposite of love at first sight! Hate oneself, so as to hate her more; so one could punish oneself for not hating earlier.

"Look at my hands," he said.

"Yes. I'm looking."

"My friends say I'm a virtuoso."

"I know. I think so too."

"These same hands can reach all the way up to your throat and squeeze . . . squeeze, you understand? So, get the hell out!"

She left.

There was none of the charm left, only a new uneasiness.

The Bastards

He was not mature enough to hate, for hatred is not a spur-of-the-moment thing; his earnest desire to hurt Gisèle had yielded to his own suffering.

His body heaved with a hiccup, the way it would with a sob. No tear came to his eyes. Did he need tears to realize that he was still distressed?

He had wanted to prove himself physically, but beyond the fact of his performance, his disgust seeped through like forgiveness.

The young man in medieval times became a knight after a prayer vigil before the altar; he, on the other hand, had found himself after an hour's pantomime in a bachelor apartment.

* * *

"A fantastic evening, huh?"

He looked at Turenne without replying. A man about town? A man of experience? His friend was out of his mind. What was the use of tarnishing his pleasure? He was happy with his night of orgy, and his satisfaction gave his eyes a dreamlike appearance. "He devoured his erotic fare beside females of his species, with others like himself, including me."

Since the abominable conspiracy, Cambier had been trying to make sense of the dramatic turn of events. The unwholesome flood lurking beneath his host's words brought them back to him. He would have wanted to say he was right so that he wouldn't have to come up with his own version. But that would have been too costly.

A sensual lower lip adorned Turenne's face. His fingers rested on the desk as though dead—fingers that, a couple of days previously, had plundered relative modesty, had effortlessly conquered a bit of abandoned flesh, while Brigitte was fighting a bout of tonsillitis. They took off, glided, landed on a book.

"You've read Décamport's collection?"

"Yes, I was part of the subscription."

"It has a funny title: *Accords macabres,* but I like parts of it."

"Certain lines are rich in assonance, I find."

"Except that, at times, they're somewhat aggressive. A sort of overflow of eroticism. Furthermore, the poem dedicated to you illustrates what I'm saying. Listen to this."

Turenne began to read "Arpeggio":

You wished to sit in my lap
so you could vibrate,
guitar of mine!
Allegory spewed forth its burning
exhalation:
for pause a frozen Priapic sigh.
Around your neck my left hand
sought a chimerical
chord.
I dreamt of fleeing the ergastulum,
far from the burning lava.
My right hand, at your navel,
plucked strings high and low.
Up rose your lament, sinister
and beautiful . . .
I opened my eyes;
You were grimacing, strangled!

Silence followed, then Turenne declared: "That's what Décamport calls 'Unrealism.'"

His hand smoothed the binding, and in so doing caressed all the unclad women in *Accords macabres*.

A taste of metal filled Cambier's mouth, a taste of blood, almost one of disgust. He felt a bit woozy, as if he had been hit on the chin. How he wanted to crush his fist against Turenne's face, to make him see clearly into himself, to make him judge himself, pity himself. But Turenne, with a glint in his eye, pursued an idea: "You're a lucky one. A woman from Paris!"

"Paris?"

"She works in the ministry."

"Which one?" asked Cambier, who seemed to be doing nothing but asking questions.

"Come on, don't act surprised. She accepted Chambord's invitation on one condition."

"Oh, is that so?"

"That you be there."

"What?"

"She insisted that you be invited as well. Chambord found it quite funny. You can't really blame him!"

Those words confirmed what Cambier had suspected: there had indeed been a conspiracy; Gisèle had insisted. He felt guilty for having treated her so terribly. "Suppose she was in love with me?" At any rate, he would find out. She was about to return to the capital; if she wrote . . . Charlotte, too, had promised to write. Charlotte, his fiancée of tomorrow, his wife for always. How, then, did Gisèle get into all this? No, he needed to forget instead, and to take no chances so that Charlotte . . ."

"They spat in my face. I thanked them," Turenne shouted.

"What?"

"They spat in my face, I said."

"Who?"

"The Knights of the Round Feather."

"Are you sick or something?"

Turenne's head was unsteady. He rubbed his forehead, concentrated, looked around, and seemed for a while not to know what was happening. On April first, before playing a joke on anyone, you had to put your hand behind your back. In a way, this was what he was doing.

Outside, it was drizzling. A light breeze, filtering through a broken pane, made the curtain ripple. In the street, a Gypsy hawked rabbit skins, and his guttural cry rose like a cry of distress; it was life.

"What's the matter with you? For an hour now I've been relating a sort of nightmare. It came over me after the wild party at Chambord's place," Turenne continued.

"I didn't follow what you were saying. Must have been thinking about something else."

Seized by a sudden feeling of ridiculous loneliness, Turenne continued wearily: "This is how it started: a dinner for young modern poets . . ."

"Like Décamport!"

"Perhaps. I had read a few poems before falling asleep! . . . Huge appetites: The Knights of the Round Feather. I was part of the whole thing."

For a fleeting moment, something clicked in Cambier. In a few seconds, each poem in *Accords macabres* came to life; white, hairy cyclops, muscular and covered with sweat, were chasing black, vociferous females deep in a wood, while two weeping nymphs, Charlotte and Brigitte, begged them to stop. The flow of words from Turenne ended the hallucination.

"Lots to eat and drink. I arrived late; they were already eating. I came in, swinging a denture on my index finger. I recited *my* lines. The Knights spat in my face, and that made me happy. I thanked them . . . Suddenly, I felt uncomfortable. I wanted this dream to stop. It's awful to know you're dreaming, and not be able to stop dreaming."

"I know what you mean. What happened next?"

"There was a duel. Yes, that's the word for it: a duel, between my projection and me. I was boiling with anger at the other. . . . I struggled. Against what, against whom? Wasn't it against myself? I wanted to kill that character exasperating me with his ambiguity. My double had two faces: humility and conceit. His pretentious gestures with this denture, his expressions of thanks: it all reeked of paradox, of hypocrisy. It continued, despite me. Spit was all over it. And *I* was the one who felt a sharp burning similar to the one you feel when a razor . . . A bad dream, wouldn't you say?"

"Are you sure you spoke the truth over at Chambord's?"

A huge fly began to buzz around the room; it could be heard every now and again butting into an obstacle. After a while, it would start again, as if it had been stunned each time it flew into something. Turenne, completely unaffected by this, was looking at Cambier.

"Spoke the truth?"

"But, for heaven's sake, you're sleeping with Brigitte! You're in love with her!"

"So what? You're doing the same thing with Charlotte."

"Answer!"

"You're complicating everything."

The Bastards

"Listen, Turenne, you can fool some women. You can't fool yourself."

"What about this nightmare, then, an attempt at correction?"

"On my way back from that party, I had my bad dream with my eyes wide open. Say what you want, we're in the same boat."

This admission embarrassed Turenne, who seemed to withdraw into an imaginary shelter. Fear gripped him as well, but he put on a jaunty air; it was his way of escaping. "I won't get anything from him. He's too immature," Cambier thought. He was right. It was futile pursuing Turenne; he would slip through his fingers as always. Even if he found himself cornered, he would not surrender. It was only Brigitte who could manage to unravel the complicated mess of his revolutionary ideas, to sidestep the delaying tactics he used to camouflage his reasoning. Cambier tried to trap him: "If only one of us had spoken the truth, he would not have endured either nightmare or duel."

"Then it's repression?"

Cambier had thought that he was moving along a straight path, but there was his friend trying to give him the slip. Everything had seemed clear to him, so much so that he felt a halo around his head; he had become clarity. And the result was: "Then it's repression?"

The word had, of necessity, betrayed him; it was left to him to find the error and correct it. He decided to withdraw into himself, all the way to the very depths, and the adventure continued to seem admirable to him. His clarity wavered. "Am I going mad?" He noticed a faint glow, like when you close one eye: a flash. The shadow swept over him; he had no time to recognize himself in all this. Thousands of huge flies began buzzing around somewhere: the sound of thunder. The storm was upon him.

He was aware that going any further was out of the question, overcome as he was by the dizzying depths. "Nausea was probably not far off!" He was struggling close to a frontier beyond which the storm was raging, the frontier to a forbidden world: his Night. This Night was revealing itself to him, and he was unable to penetrate it.

There was a tightening in his throat, and he almost fainted. "Am I going mad?" There could be no more delay! He went into reverse! He had to regain the light, that blinding light whose brilliance made everything escape him.

He was so near his goal. He had at least picked up his own scent for a fraction of a second. Even if he had been strong enough to explore that Night, he would only have been able to feel it; any attempt at explanation would have changed its nature. Essentially his, it was not compatible with the language used by everybody. He alone could discern it; he alone could try to understand it, without any hope of objectifying it. Had he been an artist, he would have captured it in a work of art: a song, a marble sculpture, a painting, even a poem. He would have had to end up with something unfathomable and infinitely variable. Could he claim to have rendered it? Would he have surrendered his privilege to it, this gift of existence?

A few moments ago, he had felt it possible to represent his Night, his *Reality*, by bitterly colored sounds, with a rugged fragrance, like his blood that made a tart ruby sound, and had a bumpy smell like corduroy. A few moments ago, his *Reality* was on the verge of emerging right there where everything became explainable; a bubble of *Reality* was about to burst. He got ready to receive it, like grace, at his own risk and peril. Don't marshy depths proclaim their truth in noxious fumes? A few moments ago, everything had seemed to fall into place logically; now that he had wanted to identify his blood, he no longer enjoyed the privilege. It was no longer his blood, but that of just about anybody, of any person who came to mind. His bubble floated away, balanced between two waves. . . .

"It's not repression, but an expression of your Reality."

"What?"

"Fishes in the deep live in darkness; each one makes its own light to recognize itself by. Reality is a bit like that: a great Night that lives on in the individual, that he alone can experience, that he feels when he is certain of his existence."

"Certain of his existence?"

The Bastards

"Existence is no simple feat. A constant inner commotion, a constant searching, down to the very impression that one's own self is about to stop . . . so many privileges forgotten by the *Living*. To live is to run counter to the Night; to move along side by side."

Turenne, disappointed, looked at him inquisitively. What was happening? He had been expecting to spend a long time chatting about the goings-on of their evening together, recalling together how ridiculous Borgier had been, how Farnabe's cooking had tasted, how the women had gotten drunk. Hadn't Suzy taken off her clothes? Chambord had said: "Who's the youngest of these ladies?" After all the questions, it was agreed that she was. "Good. We're going to put you through the customary questioning."

She had climbed onto the table, and he had begun asking her questions. "Full name and status?"

"Suzanne Castella! . . . Er, what do you mean by status?"

"Virgin or nonvirgin!" Farnabe had shouted, all excited.

She did not back down. Taking up the challenge of their little game, she contrived to have the joke on Sugert instead. "Virgin!" she confessed, delighted at this lie.

Turenne had retorted: "Excuse her. Her memory's failing her!" and Chambord chimed in with: "We want to check it out."

"Impotent, Sugert!" Farnabe had shouted a second time, much to the chagrin of Suzy's lover.

She had begun to take off her clothes while Cambier still smarted from that accusation of impotence, which was in no way meant for him. Sugert had had to intervene, energetically at that, to prevent Suzy from stripping off the last bit of clothing not already flung about the room.

That was what Turenne wanted to talk about; instead he had to deal with rambling digressions. How on earth could a young man like Cambier, apparently levelheaded up to this point, suddenly allow himself to be sucked into that sort of intellectualizing about existence? "Hope he's not going off, like his sister!"

Cambier continued with even more gusto: "We don't need

anyone else to exist. Life favors a blending of the individual. Our brains cannot think in unison. Otherwise, they would have to work in the open, in permanent telepathy."

Turenne reached for a bottle. The fiery liquid shook in its glass prison, then settled after a final upheaval. He had to go all the way to the draining board to fetch the glasses.

"What about a punch?"

At this invitation, Cambier's thoughts were once more in full flight. A punch could make one drunk, could free the individual and make him surrender without any constraint. He could act as herald for the truth; the principles by which Charlotte had been brought up had not resisted it. The other night, it had made him a toy in Gisèle's hands, up to the moment she had gone too far. One New Year's eve, Décamport, drunk or up to one of his hoaxes, had harangued his reflection in the window of a large store: "Negro, looking at me in the dark night; Negro, who are myself in that glass, you dazzle me." Two policemen had passed by, and Décamport had to go with them to the station. Did he have the time to know his *moment?*

Turenne wrapped his fingers around the bottle. Rum poured into the glasses. A few drops formed a chaplet on the table, and their aroma tickled Cambier's nostrils. As a child, he had had a playmate called José, whose parents ran a café next to where he lived, so that he often went over to see him. He would cross the room with its strong aromas and go up to the counter. José's older brother would be standing near the cash register. "He had already completed his military service; I was his protégé, since he used to flirt with my sister. He would shout: 'Hey, José!' then, turning to me: 'Everything O.K. at home?' A yellowed notice, swollen by the dampness, was posted on the wall. It announced: Law on the suppression of public drunkenness and regulations on the serving of drinks. . . ."

"Cheers!"

Turenne emptied his glass in one gulp and shoved it far from him. His action was methodical, traditional, *routine*, as Cambier was in the habit of saying.

The Bastards

"Don't be bashful. Put it back."

"With liquor, I never have a second."

Cambier would have liked to see him lose his vigilance, become himself one more, and do his prospecting safe from constraints, like Décamport. But Turenne had no pretention of virtue; he was an Epicurean and quick to react to anything that bothered him. Only political heroism seemed to arouse his interest, even if, to achieve it, he had to rid his action of all subjectivity and to have it mirrored in the absolute. He wanted to be a pure militant.

"Pity! Your mask would probably have fallen."

"Sorry about your theory, old man," Turenne conceded.

"It's reassuring to understand some things that escape others, even if what they understand escapes us. We have the glimmer of exception left."

"You said it; a sort of consolation, right?"

This irony annoyed Cambier. He stood up all of a sudden, and Turenne's laughter stuck in his throat, then disappeared altogether. His annoyance increased when he realized how difficult it was for him to make himself understood. Yet, before speaking, he had thought everything was so clear.

"I've bored you enough. I'm leaving now."

However, he added: "What I have against life is that it prevents us from being constantly faithful to ourselves."

His friend did not budge, but was sure that the conflict would unfurl in him as well. Outside, thunder rolled; within Turenne, the same chaos must have existed, only to a greater degree.

He went outside. It was raining harder. Between Turenne and himself, complicity grew thicker, abstract but full of certainty on the scale of Reality.

* * *

Cambier walked up the narrow street, head down, sometimes on the sidewalk, sometimes on the pavement. A steady step behind him was his signal to move out of the way. "What if I had told Turenne how my Reality manifested itself?"

It was, in a way, because of Turenne, his dream, and his mu-

sic that he had felt Reality encroaching. They were listening to
jazz records, the wonderful music of "Body and Soul," the
soul of a race impeded by _Routine_. The drama stemmed from
the music itself, which captured a nostalgia, interpreted a suffering that would allow no repentance or disavowal. The race
played the game ardently, for the future—messenger of salvation—was there, forever vigilant, confronting the present.
The musician with the metal serpent dramatized his melody,
changed it to a lament, to a funeral oration: that of a decadent
intellectual police in the midst of which black people, desperately needing to become, swarmed like termites. The end was
near. Did Turenne understand this message? He did not even
suspect the myriad of sound waves bombarding his antennas.
He explained how he had come to see Staffer again.

"Do you remember that American Negro, the one who was
always in a fight, in the port in Fort-de-France?"

"Yes."

"We ended up together in North Africa a year later."

"How did that happen?"

"I was with a convoy of troops on their way to Italy."

The first contact with Staffer had been dramatic. It took
place in Fort-de-France, where Turenne was doing his military
service. One night he saw two men in a clinch on the ground
inside the port compound: a black astride a white man, whom
he was pummeling with blows. For him, race was secondary.
He was amused above all to see two adults sizing each other up
like a bunch of kids fresh out of school; two sailors from the
same warship, who had used the visit to go from bar to bar, but
who were now paying certain dues to the Antillean rum.

Suddenly, events took a dramatic turn. The black man, taking his adversary's head in his hands, proceeded to crack his
skull on the cement. The victim howled as he thrashed about.

Turenne intervened. He grabbed the black by his neck, and
forced him to release his grip. The white fellow rolled over on
his side and passed out.

The tragedy changed form and place. It was now played out
in awful silence between two blacks, out of breath and standing face to face, toe to toe. Meanwhile, the white man re-

The Bastards

gained consciousness; he shook himself and paused to look at the two blacks. He crawled further away on all fours, then stood up, and scampered off in the dark, convinced that his enemy had received reinforcement.

The other fellow cursed Turenne: "*You can't understand, you goddam French nigger!*" He was appalled to see a man of his own race butting in against him; it filled him with hatred and despair. Clearly, it was hard to understand. . . .

"What's his name again?"

"Jim Staffer."

"Doesn't ring a bell."

"Nice guy, actually. These records are from him."

Turenne drew a brief picture of Staffer's life. In Cambier's eyes, this entire picture was nothing more than one of "over-whelming routine." After early years of beatings, periods of silence, and mysticism, Staffer had ended up at a university, from which he graduated with a degree. What next? He was driven by the urgent need to feed and clothe himself, to make something of his life. He held various jobs: elevator operator, delivery man, and, finally, pimp among the riffraff of a large city. He just barely managed to stay out of prison. The war saved him. He became a sailor, and found himself every morning, with mop and bucket in hand, swabbing the deck of a ship.

At this juncture, an invisible grasp seized Cambier by the throat and shook him: Turenne, himself, blacks like Staffer, no more! Their studies completed, they would never stand for such a letdown.

He felt cornered: there was no escape from Routine! Question. Answer. Quick! Otherwise, he was ruined. Yes or no, would he accept Reality, that prize of truth, that freedom to do whatever one pleased? Actually, he had no choice, not really. The answer was yes.

Turenne played the other side of the record. A woman was singing. Her voice, uncertain at first, came and licked Cambier like a flame; a burning voice. "*I got a man crazy for me.*" Yes! Crazy indeed, all those who believed things would remain static. Reality scouted around. Cambier could feel it hovering above his thoughts, like a hawk eyeing its prey. It offered an alternative that was only a trap: either be just plain crazy, and end up sterile and stupid, or be crazy with Reality, and justify the gift of life. Cambier's madness, brutal in nature, was upon him in a flash: extricate himself from the Routine, like the masterpiece of formless clay. Reality molded him, used his servile abandon to inculcate in him his share of madness, of certainty.

Cambier passed through the main entrance and disappeared into the concierge's apartment, where he heard about the incident. One of the tenants on his floor had just killed herself. The concierge gave her account of what had happened, punctuating her words with an excessive show of sympathy. She handed him his mail as she dried her eyes. He went outside on the patio.

"Did this woman who just killed herself have her share of certainty?" Gas, slow death, intoxication. While the rest of life was unraveling, had she at least the faintest trace of conviction: that she would reconquer herself, that she would escape without calling upon that man who wanted to punish her? For one second, did her entire drama flash before her eyes? Did she relive that night the gestapo came to get the lover she had reported? "This woman has told us everything!" No point resisting. In a flash, pity made the maquisard insensitive to kicks and blows. He had come to town in search of a night of love, but met hatred, death perhaps. What fate awaited his mistress? "Poor dear, did they threaten you, torture you?" A flurry of blows forced him to shut up; he stumbled as the man with the swastika laughed heartily. He was completely surprised and overwhelmed by what he heard. "No! I told them everything because I can't stand you." She thought that she had rid herself of him forever. Mistake! He had been able to pluck himself from that hell. The previous month, he had written to say he would return to punish her. He was on his way? Wasn't he already here, observing her, making his victim's panic all the more acute, just waiting for the right moment to pounce? Perhaps he would never reveal himself. Only, he had known captivity, known what it was to be condemned;

The Bastards

he was aware that the anguish and the long wait to die were more deadly than the executioner himself. . . .

"Your papers!"

Cambier took out his wallet; a postcard fell out, the one he had just received from Charlotte. "Beautiful weather, but anxious to get back. Best Wishes." Rather brief. "Best Wishes," when deep down inside her certainty was saying something else.

"Good. You may proceed to your room."

In the corridor, there was a strong odor of gas, combined with a catafalquelike smell of death.

He put his key in the lock as he took one last glance over his shoulder. The stockier inspector was saying something in the ear of his colleague, who nodded in approval.

"Monsieur!"

He already had one foot in the door. What did they want with him? A woman was dead. So what? She was entitled to die, wasn't she? They, too, would one day be like her, despite their chests full of decorations.

"Yes?"

"It's about this woman. Please remain at our disposition, for the inquest."

"Now I'm mixed up in a matter involving death." But he was alive, by God! Alive? No, not this condition. He didn't deserve feeling so low, despite Gisèle and her mythology. He existed. He felt himself exist. Because of him, even the dead woman began to exist; but, in her case, where was her certainty? Did she feel herself exist? How important was it for her to exist in him, if she did not have her own certainty?

She needed him to exist; he wanted no part of such an existence, for it was too close to that of a colonial and his relationship with a dominant power. An existence that is merely given could not mean Reality, even if it was opposed to Life. Actually, did it really oppose it? Participation was necessary, with its horrors and its joys.

The dead woman kept her certainty within herself, just as he kept within himself his share of Charlotte and of Africa. Yes, the dead woman kept within herself that zone that was off-limits to all who were not herself, even if they experienced their own certainty of existence, of making her, the dead woman, exist.

"They want me at their disposition for the inquest!" He would have to tax his memory. Memory of what? Must he remember anything about this woman? Why hadn't he waited before coming home, at the risk of upsetting Turenne or of being upset by him?

He knew her as a neighbor, that was all; a free woman, responsible for her actions. Free to commit suicide after being so bizarre recently. She scrutinized the stairs before entering her room; there would be a quick turn of the latch, and an even quicker closing and locking of the door. The two police officers would not get over how she had escaped them and managed to remain faithful to herself. Would they ever understand that, these two who made a name for themselves dealing with thought burglars, with vampires?

The dead woman would soon be taken away. All that would be left of her would be concentrated in one little document, legalized by wax seals. She had thought she could come to terms with her remorse, but it had grown excessively, catalyzed by the fear of punishment, by the fear of Life.

And what of the man? Would he keep this taste for ashes which, sooner or later, would fill him with nausea? He had dealt death, applying with interest the law of retaliation.

Already, a disgusting palatability was filtering through to Cambier like a rolling sensation, while all he had done was broach that certainty that bound him to Charlotte. Love's invitation had found only death in him; in order to pour some life into it, he had needed a parody of love, and this led to another parody, that of grace.

The postcard lay on the table, covered with fingerprints; were they Charlotte's? Or those of the salesclerk, some unattractive woman who allowed the winter visitors to make her feel wanted? "Anxious to get back." What if she found him changed?

He turned the card over; it showed a skating rink, the same one they had seen in a documentary. Charlotte had said: "I go skating there every year!" . . . "Is that so?" . . . "You don't seem to believe me. I'll send you a card in which you can see my silhouette."

She had not misled him; he recognized her, with a small cross written in by hand above her. The photographer had caught her with one leg in the air, her body leaning forward. He wondered how many men, their heads full of lust, like the stocky inspector he had just met, had experienced moments of ecstasy on seeing her in this pose; how many had extrapolated; how many had begun to daydream. Mental rape, it was! "Oh no! I don't want her to go skating anymore!"

* * *

There was a knock on the door, but Turenne knew at once it was not Brigitte. He would have been happy to see her; he needed her. He opened the door, and recognized Ségaye, who entered, looking dejected.

"I must talk to you."

After the directness of that opening, Ségaye began to beat about the bush; he noticed on the desk the copy of Décamport's poems, flipped through it, then said: "What do you think about these?"

"Some good, some bad."

"I really like 'Let my canopies burn!'"

"Wait a minute. That's what you want to talk to me about?"

Ségaye was embarrassed. What he wanted to talk about was rather delicate, though its delicate nature was only in the end result: a favor Turenne could do; what led to it couldn't be any clearer, so clear in fact that the atmosphere was fraught with details. He had made up with Christiane. She had been so good about the whole thing!

Two weeks before, when she had refused to let him in her room, she wasn't yet afraid: she was only three days late. One whole week had gone by, and still not seeing anything happen, she had begun to get worried; not overly so, all the same, since she was often a few days off. She had not tried too hard to talk to her friend, whom she often saw strolling in the square with his countrymen. Besides, he appeared to ignore her.

The Foyer

Then he had come to invite her over to Chambord's. She had gone with him, had allowed him to caress her. "François, I think I . . ." "You think what?" "I think I'm going to have your child!"

"Then what happened?" Turenne asked.

"A terrible story."

He felt desperately ridiculous, naive, and unlucky. Ridiculous because he was there with Turenne who had greatly appreciated, after the fact, the quip about the *myth of the second*. Naive because he had swallowed so easily Christiane's frank admissions, and had allowed himself to be so readily carried away, to the point of writing "Viva Guiana" on the wall of his room, and in red at that. "I must remember to erase that nonsense." Unlucky, because the whole scenario had been played out at his expense.

How would his father take it? After all, he did have to inform him of the situation he found himself in viv-à-vis the young lady. He would marry her, unless Turenne . . .

"What type of story?"

"She's pregnant!" he said, thinking aloud.

"Who?"

"Christiane."

"Well, my friend. I guess we can say you were right on target this time, weren't you!"

"This kind of thing only happens to me."

Turenne consoled him: "Of course not! Most of the guys decided to get married when the woman was already expecting. And well on the way too! You'll just be like the others."

"I thought you could help me."

"Help you?"

"You're studying medicine . . ."

"You must be mad!" Turenne exclaimed. "You come here from down in the bush, you screw the women, and now you want to force stuff up inside them for them to have an abortion! . . . You are out of your mind?"

He was exaggerating; his friend had not seduced women, but had taken advantage of a stroke of luck, the first one, which turned out badly. Faced with Ségaye's continuing si-

The Bastards

lence, he added: "And on top of that, you're trying to involve me! This could ruin my career if anything went wrong. . . . A fine pharmacy career you'll have, later on, if you start off with ideas like that!"

"What can I do then?" he asked sheepishly.

"Go and find her, and tell her you're going to marry her, stupid."

"I'm only twenty-two."

"So what? You didn't think you were twenty-two when you jumped in bed with her?"

They were both the same age. When he was with her, he seemed to attain a sort of fullness that made him feel as if nothing mattered. Was that love? If he were presently living anywhere else but in this town, everything would be so simple. But he had to contend with his friends from the Foyer, their perverse humor, their teasing which, more often than not, was quite sarcastic. His beating about the bush stemmed from the acute embarrassment he experienced when it came to showing his feelings. His countrymen all pretended to be big and tough; so then, why couldn't he?

Among those young people at the Foyer who tried to appear blasé, he could not think of any who were like him; either they showed morbid discretion, like Cambier and Turenne, or, like Chambord, they steered clear of any emotional involvement; as for Sugert and Décamport, they did not think of women as anything above utility objects. Too bad, he would shoulder his responsibility.

"I'll go and see her parents," he promised.

"They live here?"

"No, in Sète."

"You'll see, they'll treat you like a prizefighter."

"Promise me you won't say anything to the guys at the Foyer," Ségaye pleaded as he left.

* * *

"By Easter, he'll be married!" Turenne thought as he sat at his desk. No more evenings of fun and frolic at the Foyer! Little by little, the group was disappearing, and each member was moving toward new responsibilities: Chambord would be going back to his home country to play a role he had prepared for; Ségaye was staying on as an apprentice. They were all resigned to growing old, to turning their backs on their carefree, gilded youth; after all, was it really a bother being forced to take an examination at the university every year; could they really compare their economic situation as overseas scholarship students to the difficulties faced by the French students from poorer families?

And Turenne? Why was he afraid of escaping the years of adolescence? How else could he designate, if not as adolescence, that in-between position he occupied. Of course, he had seen action in the war, had taken part—on a tank—in an important confrontation between millions of men; but that epic event had been for him nothing more than the escapade of an adolescent anxious to live his life.

He became conscious of his own case. It was easy for him to play moralist with his friends, to harass them into acting like men. But when it came to himself, despite this baptism of fire, what had he done so far? He had behaved like a child, a spoiled child to boot, a middle-class weakling who had chosen hypocrisy by making love to a former mistress in a bed still warm from Brigitte's body. He needed Brigitte, whose absence left him in disarray; and he hadn't even been able to take this absence gracefully. Cambier had warned him: "You can fool some women, you cannot fool yourself!"

He was ashamed; he needed Brigitte. He wanted to see her, to touch her, to talk to her.

He went out.

What would he tell her? Nothing, rather than tell her a lie! He would ask how she was, and not mention the night at Chambord's except to say that it had been very nice. Above all, he would tell her that it was becoming urgent for them to marry before an accident happened, making their marriage seem hastily arranged. He would go to see her every day until she got better, till she could once again come to his room, to his bed, to his arms.

He arrived in front of the building, and went into the stairwell. He saw some mailboxes and on one of them read the name of Brigitte's parents. "Third floor," the little sign instructed. The parents? The father who complained every Saturday when his daughter came back home. He imagined him tall, fat, bald, authoritative, with a thick moustache—an ogre, in other words!

He climbed the stairs. On the second floor, he hesitated. "I'll go and see her parents," Ségaye had promised. Could he, Turenne, be any less courageous than this youngster who dared to talk about a visit after what he had done? He had not impregnated the daughter of the lady of the house, not yet anyway! He resumed climbing, and knocked.

As the noise of slippers came closer, he could feel his heart beating wildly, and the door opened to reveal a small bespectacled man, an unfolded newspaper in his hand.

"Excuse me, monsieur! Does Mademoiselle Brigitte live here?"

"Yes. I'm her father."

This nice family man, tiny, fragile . . . nowhere near as terrifying as he had imagined him to be.

"I've come to find out how she's doing."

"And who are you?"

"A friend. Berjémi Turenne."

"Oh!" the father said with a smile, "I should have known! You're the famous Turenne. She talks about you a lot . . . only, she hadn't *specified*. Come in, monsieur."

As he slipped through the half-opened door, Turenne thought: "She hasn't specified that I'm black." The father placed his hand on his shoulder, and guided him almost cordially into the corridor.

"I had a very good friend *like you;* we went through almost the entire war together—not this last one, the first. He was killed a few weeks before the armistice. He was from Guadeloupe."

They passed the entrance to the living room. Turenne had time enough to observe that the furniture seemed expensive.

"Brigitte, your friend Turenne's here to see you," the father said, turning immediately on his heels.

The Foyer

The mother was in the room; she rose from the armchair where she was knitting, and Turenne turned on the charm. He bowed as if about to bestow a formal kiss on her hand.

"My respects, madame."

"Good day, monsieur."

"Turenne, I'm happy to see you. It was so nice of you to come."

He went towards Brigitte, who did not seem to be doing too badly; he wanted to extend his hand to her.

"You can kiss me in front of Mom, you know."

"I'll get us some coffee," the mother said as she disappeared without waiting to see whether the young man accepted her proposition or not.

"How are things?" he asked as he slipped from Brigitte's embrace.

"A bad attack of tonsillitis. The fever has subsided. I'm improving."

There she was, sprawled out in a chair in the corner of the room; her blond, somewhat disheveled hair swayed with every move of her head. He finally had her before him, just as beautiful and desirable as ever. He preferred her like this, without makeup, without anything artificial . . . natural. Never had he been able to see what she was like as she got out of bed, since he had never spent an entire night alone with her. How happy he would be if he could gaze upon her as she awoke, later on!

And here he was, in her house, unexpectedly. Chance had spared him long days of waiting, the anxiety that precedes visits arranged by mutual consent. His decision had been made suddenly; he had dared, and had found the father reading, the mother knitting, the daughter in her room. He had penetrated a world where each person, including himself, was concerned only with private matters: the father who had almost embraced him; the mother smiling, discreet, young-looking, as small and blonde as her daughter. "They'll treat you like a prizefighter."

"He already mentioned his Guadeloupean?"

"Yes. Quite nice, your father."

The Bastards

"You'll see, when he knows you better, he'll tell you about their adventures. And, believe me, there are adventures aplenty."

"Why didn't you tell your parents who I was?"

"Who you were?"

"Yes: a man of color."

"I didn't see what good that would do."

"It would have made things easier."

"Easier for whom? If you had to tell your folks about me, would you say that I'm white?"

"It's not the same; you're French."

He found this conversation suddenly painful; it made apparent the vast difference between Brigitte and himself: a difference of race and origin. He gave up.

"Your mother looks so young."

"We're best friends. I tell her everything."

"Everything?"

"Yes, everything. So, she knows about you and me."

"Knows what?"

"Knows everything."

"And your father?"

"With him, it's different."

He wanted to escape. The mother would soon return with her coffee pot, and she knew everything. She knew he had . . . Oh, no! It was unbearable. He would never be able to look her in the face!

"You're not ashamed to tell her?"

"I'm not a petite bourgeoise. I tell the truth, for I want to shoulder my responsibilities."

"Brigitte, we must get married."

"Why are you mentioning that now? Because my mother knows?"

"No. That's what I came to talk to you about."

"It came over you all of a sudden?"

"I knew that an accident could happen. I don't want any part of a forced marriage, of anything hastily arranged."

"Come sit beside me," she said.

The mother returned as they were kissing; she coughed to

alert them of her presence. Brigitte casually let go of Turenne, whose eyelids were both swollen—it was his way of blushing.

* * *

That Saturday night's meal was a strange one indeed; for once, all six of them were around the table. Chambord, the dean, who was about to leave them; Décamport, who, for a swan song, had just published his volume of unrealist poems; Sugert, about to defend his law thesis, and still swooning as a result of a recent female contact; Cambier, sad as usual, more contemplative than ever; Ségaye, who was inwardly rehearsing arguments for his impending conversation with Christiane; finally, Turenne who had just told Brigitte's mother of his intentions. "She confides in her; might as well tell her everything right away!" And now he was observing his five compatriots. How many would be left in three months? Weren't Chambord, Ségaye, and he himself going to disappear shortly from the number of guests? Sugert was the only one in good spirits.

"There's no getting away from it, your party was tops," he told Chambord.

"You think so?"

"Was it ever! It wouldn't have been so fabulous if we'd been able to get together here."

"There's a few more memories for you!" Décamport added. He tried to lessen the chagrin he thought he saw in Chambord, and to paint a rosy picture of things, although he knew that parting always meant an unpleasant break.

Even in his poems, there was this sort of imminent uprooting; his verses anticipated, on each page, a sudden plundering of man—wasn't it Décamport himself?—in his habits, his likes, his loves. The strangled guitar-woman, the blazing canopies, it all showed the conflict between self-abandonment—the dream—and atrocious reality, burning, brutal, irreversible.

Of them all, he was undoubtedly the most hurt, for it was he, along with Cambier, who endeavored to plunge the deepest into himself. There was this difference, though: he remained completely lucid with himself, and made no claim to conquer the forces about him.

"Yes," Chambord said. "I looked like a patriarch surrounded by his sons. That made me understand it was time to leave."

"Life is only now beginning. You're going to move to the action phase, place yourself at the service of our country," Turenne declared.

"Oh, no! No politics!" Sugert intervened. "Here, we're still students, despite our ages. For instance, take Borgier; he's Chambord's age, but that doesn't prevent him from staying in shape. Castanets and prehistoric old hags, that's what I call living."

At Chambord's party, Borgier had been asked to do a number with his castanets, under the amused eye of a mature woman whom he had brought with him, and whom everyone examined with a look of pity.

"This party taught me at least one thing: the guys have two types of women, their regulars and the birds of passage, some of whom even come from the capital."

Cambier did not take the bait. Décamport had not had an opportunity to tease him since Charlotte no longer frequented the Foyer; the Gisèle affair was a gold mine he did not fail to exploit. He insisted: "Turenne had to scrape the bottom of the barrel to come up with a pre-war mistress; Cambier intercepted a stork; Borgier shook the coconut tree to pick a grandmother. It's funny!"

Cambier was dying to get up, to run away, to go back to his room. He was fed up with Sugert, Décamport, and their silly gossiping. Was this the type of conversation they should be having on the eve of departure of one of the older guys?

Dessert was about to be served; it would be easy for him to find some flimsy excuse to leave. But could he separate himself so soon from Chambord and Turenne? He heard Sugert object: "I beg your pardon! I was with my regular girl. I'm a proletarian, you know. I don't have spare chicks for after-thesis parties!"

"Me too, I brought my regular!" Décamport pursued. "So did Ségaye who, I presume, isn't crafty enough to collect an entire set. Say, Ségaye, was that the mythomaniac?"

The Foyer

"Don't insist, please. I'm not really in form tonight," Ségaye said, looking genuinely tired.

Chambord was not taken in by the forced lightheartedness of the two older ones; they had gone so far out of their way, the care they took to be convincing missed its mark. But wasn't he, too, trying to put the others on the wrong track? He presented his usual face, and any evaluation of his distress by another was well within reality.

"We are bastards born of a Gallic male and an African girl abandoned by him on the banks of the Amazon. By laying full claim to our European blood, we discover our position as beings culturally born of a mother we did not know; and our choice of culture itself makes us aware of another blemish: we are, historically, anonymous or outlaws. In short, our loss of identity is two-faced: cultural and historical. But Africa, matriarchal and powerful, survives in us, in spite of the vicissitudes and humiliations suffered. Guiana, our mother, the unwed mother, awaits us to grant us legitimacy and salvation!"

That was the message Chambord had prepared for them in his mind. Meanwhile they were fidgeting around the table, cheating themselves, insensitive to any plea that was not soothing, or did not advocate oblivion. Which of them would have understood him? Turenne, perhaps, although his sidestepping Sugert's apolitical stance was rather disappointing.

He wanted to leave a message, and on examining his conscience, he discovered that, reluctantly, he was writing a will without even possessing the resignation of men looking calmly behind them. It was already on his part a sign of weakness, of advanced degeneracy, to compare his return to Guiana to death.

"I must leave. The country needs me!" There was to be no more thinking. No more remembering. One had to become insensitive to the metropolitan fluid. Refuse to give up, no discussion, no scrutiny. Rehabilitate oneself by choosing Guiana, passionately, blindly.

He felt suddenly lucid, ridiculously lucid. He saw himself attending his own funeral, walking at the head of the procession, his mouth wide open, chanting the Requiem, while at the side of the road people he knew were laughing their heads off to see a man leading a part of himself to the tomb. "I'm burying Europe!" He hardly suspected that something like an afterbirth had torn itself from him, and he floated in an acrid atmosphere reminiscent of an operating room, feeling a strange sensation of painful relief.

CHAPTER FOUR

Christiane's parents had received Ségaye like a prince. She had reacted with a start when he declared his intention: "I want to meet your family. I'm marrying you. The sooner the better!"

He was afraid she might think of this gesture as a sacrifice and, yielding to her innate amour propre, turn down his proposition. He had hastened to add: "Sooner or later, we'd have to come to that, for as far as I'm concerned, it's serious between you and me."

She seemed to hesitate, and this made him more worried. "As far as I'm concerned, too, it's serious between you and me," she ended up replying. There was scarcely any further conversation between them. The following morning, he had left his friend's room in broad daylight, but did not meet anybody, since it was Sunday, and all the tenants in the building were late getting out of bed.

"This is it," he said to himself as he put his glass down. Christiane's father, who had retired from the Navy, treated him with warmth, admiration, and spontaneity. He liked Ségaye's robustness and his genuine moderation. His ambitions, all modest, amounted to nothing more than being grandfather in a fairly well-to-do family. Yet, he was nowhere near guessing what state his daughter was in. He had worked his fingers to the bone so she could teach in the arts, but she had upset his plans, and he had to settle for sending her off to the Beaux-Arts. Now, here she was bringing home a pharmacist!

"Do you like soccer, François?"

François, already! None of this hemming and hawing here. He was being called by his first name and asked what sort of things he liked. He smiled before answering. One of his favorite themes came to him: "France is a charming country."

The Bastards

"Yes, a lot. I used to play long ago."

"That's great! There's a team from Paris playing this after-noon. The stadium at Métairies will be filled to overflowing."

"Come now, you're not thinking of dragging him off to the stadium, are you?" the mother said.

She was a dark woman with brown hair, quite plump, of similar build to Christiane, and much younger looking than her husband. She wanted to keep her daughter's intended near to her, to question him, to study him. The father continued to tempt Ségaye: "We have a colored player on the team; he's fantastic. They've nicknamed him 'the black wizard.'"

The entire conversation was in the lilting accent of the Midi. Ségaye just loved it.

Christiane was going to be his, to bear him a child, to forge for him new attachments that would free him from the stranglehold of the Foyer, where he had encountered nothing but derision, and from which he could not escape, there being nowhere else to go. He felt happy, oddly so. Even that winter Sunday's exceptionally fine weather was unusual; it looked like a day in spring. Christiane's parents' villa sat high above the corniche. On his way up he had spent a long time admiring the purity of the sky, and the beautiful blue of the sea, whose calm waves leisurely lapped against the sand.

He finally had an affectionate father, a compassionate mother, a fiancée in love with him. Gone forever those painful weekend evenings, that loneliness in the midst of a crowd that refused to understand. Every Saturday, he would take the bus with his fiancée, and spend two days with the family, his family.

"So, François, are we taking in this match or not?" At that moment, a bell rang in the narrow vestibule, and the mother got up: "Who is it? We're not expecting anyone."

There were several exclamations, followed by the sound of kisses on cheeks.

The father winced expressively, and Christiane was heard to mutter: "That's all we need! She always arrives at the right time."

It was Aunt Agda, one of the father's sisters, a typical village shrew: cantankerous, talkative, and scandalmongering. Whenever she showed up—always unexpectedly—she was always griping about a long-standing inheritance matter that had not been resolved to her entire satisfaction.

She came in, small, wrinkled, her face almost hidden under a veil, an umbrella and a suitcase in her hand. She kissed her brother and her niece, without apparently noticing the guest. He was introduced to her: "Christiane's fiancé."

She smiled stupidly: "Monsieur! . . ."

The father added, by way of clarification: "He's a student."

She sat down, using her legs and hips to push the chair noisily back on the tiled floor. She placed her suitcase and her umbrella between her legs, bit her lips, and looked around, her eyes falling on Ségaye.

Christiane could tell she was about to launch into her well-known refrain: "oh, poor dear, you know that . . ." The aunt peppered everything she said with the word *poor*. It was a sort of all-purpose expression that covered everything from surprise to joy or contempt.

"Why don't you put your things away?"

The mother had said this almost reluctantly. She knew only too well what this unexpected visit meant. The suitcase by itself said a lot; its presence indicated that the aunt had come to Sète on business, and was going to plant herself in this house, and proceed to drive them all out of their mind with her whining and complaining.

The suitcase and umbrella changed hands, and while her sister-in-law had her back turned, the aunt said to her: "What about some garlic soup?"

Ségaye gave a slight start. Christiane and her father were seething with disappointment; yet the aunt was only now warming up. She turned to her brother: "Oh, poor dear, you know the notary . . ."

But she checked herself as she noticed Ségaye. She asked her niece: "He understands French?"

"Why, of course."

"Oh, good. I'll continue when this gentleman has left."

Christiane preferred not to take this impoliteness too seriously. She said, in a tone of affected irony: "Excuse my aunt. She's not accustomed to city people."

But Ségaye was not put out by what his future aunt-in-law had said; it was really too absurd, too ridiculous to be offensive. And hadn't he heard worse at the Foyer?

The father was beside himself with anger. Not only would he miss his soccer match, but wouldn't his sister possibly scare off the suitor?

And the aunt, who had for the time being ceased her tattling, examined those around her, seemingly surprised by that sudden reserve. She had her garlic soup, which she drank down quickly. She gave an occasional furtive glance, then buried her head in her plate. In the end, she forgot that Ségaye was there.

"Oh, poor dear, you know that . . ."

Christiane gave a little kick under the table, but the aunt exclaimed: "Hey, you're scraping me, poor dear. You'll ruin my stockings!"

Finally, exasperated, the father accompanied the young man to another room: "Christiane, bring us coffee in the living room."

* * *

Things were not going well for Cambier. Ever since that time he had left Charlotte, he was constantly worried, and it became worse at the slightest show of emotion.

He had always come across as listless at heart, and his close friends saw this as the result of his impassioned espousal of certain ideas. He was forever analyzing himself, but this breaking down of the self that he indulged in only served to turn him into a mixed-up individual. The more he searched within himself, studied himself, scrutinized himself, the more inaccessible he became.

After each of his attempts, there was new destruction, new ruin. He deepened his Night as he came to its edge, and what he believed to be self-exploration was, in fact, simply an unending series of impulses, of failures that were slowly edging him toward a loss of control, a quiet delirium willingly entertained.

He was afflicted with a hopeless incapacity for synthesis. He envisaged every new fact, every emotion, as self-contained, devoid of any context: Macombo's death, Charlotte's disappointment, Chambord's departure, his experience with Gisèle, his neighbor's suicide. And this patchwork of voluntarily disconnected events, though linked to one another by his own self, was strangely akin to his very concept of existence. "We don't need other people to exist."

It was raining.

Cambier raised himself in his bed, sat up, and let his feet hang above the carpet. Raindrops had splashed against the windowpanes, and trucks full of vegetables drove by under the windows.

From that room, he had witnessed the birth of a tear-filled dawn, while in the adjoining apartment, its doors under seal, the musty smell of death still filled the air. He would have to return to the clinic, and his uncertainty caused him great anguish. "Waiting, always waiting. Life is nothing else: a perpetual waiting until you have nothing else to wait for."

The previous Thursday, a new worry had crept into his life. It had begun in a very mundane manner, when Turenne had taken him to one of the health centers.

"Claudia, please show my friend, Monsieur Cambier, in as soon as the boss is finished with his patient. My friend's a medical student."

The nurse complied. It was impossible for Cambier to guess the exact age of this withered face with the painted smile. In the tropics, women age rapidly. Was it because they were more precocious, and gave up their love of finery at a very early age? Back home, faced with someone as experienced as Claudia, he might have said: "She's fifty." But here, criteria were different. Claudia must have passed that stage years ago. She assumed a businesslike air as she considered the Monsieur-to-be-shown-in, who was no medical student, but was trying a trick to gain easier access to the examination room.

The Bastards

"I'm going back to the office. Come and see me when you're through. It's nothing to worry about, believe me."

Turenne disappeared in the hall; his white jacket was too short, emphasizing his huge size. Claudia "sounded" Cambier with her eyes.

"Do you have an examination?"

"No."

"First time?"

"Yes."

"Something wrong?"

"You could say that."

Realizing that she could get nothing from him, she motioned him to enter the dressing room.

A bulb on the wall, under a globe of frosted glass, gave off a faint red glow when the closing of the door shut out the daylight. Cambier started to undress, but stopped halfway when he remembered that for what he was about to show the doctor there was no need to take off so much.

He sat down. "In a few minutes, I'll be out of this dungeon like a bull from a pen, and be ready for battle." Already he was dramatizing. Each passing minute brought a sad thought, sadder than the preceding one but not as sad as the one to come.

"It's nothing to worry about! Turenne thinks I'm stupid. Yet Hortense . . ." His sister Hortense's body was covered with spots. They said it was because she spent too much time playing with lizards. She would catch them with a blade of grass, tie them to tiny wagons, and make them race one another. Sometimes, she would arrange fights between the *big greens* and the *little reds*. Their differing sizes made the assaults spectacular. She did not realize that the green ones were the males, and the red ones the females; in her naiveté, she could not distinguish a genuine duel from mating, an act from which the female could not extricate herself. One morning, her mother had caught her by surprise: "Don't play with those nasty creatures. You see how they change color. They have poison in their skin, and if this poison touches you, you'll get a rash."

The Foyer

"But I like to play with them."

"It's not something to play with. A pretty sight you'll be, with spots all over your body. . . ."

"I'm lonely. Alain is never home, and Caroline is always on the balcony."

"Get your doll."

"I'm fourteen; I'm too big for that."

"You're unbearable. You've got an answer for everything, just like that Negro woman, your grandmother. A plaster for every sore . . . I'm sorry you're so much like her."

"I don't want to play with any doll."

"Go and play with your little friend next door."

"She plays with lizards too."

"Leave me alone. You're bothering me!"

She ran off; like a boy she scaled the boundary wall, and her mother shouted: "For heaven's sake, leave those creatures alone!"

The door opened. He went into the examining room where half a dozen students were standing around the supervisor. Several of the faces he recognized smiled discreetly as they saw him. One night after a dance, he had found the big red-faced fellow at the end sleeping off the effects of wine on the stairs of the Cité Universitaire. The student on his right was the makeshift doctor who had once wanted to render assistance to an athlete who had fainted. He had scraped the sole of his foot with a pin, and this surprising operation had set the whole stadium laughing. A bucket of cold water on the patient's head had restored the situation.

"Please sit down. What seems to be the matter?"

"I've got a spot on my leg."

"How long have you had it?"

"About two weeks."

He took his shoes off and exposed his bare leg to the doctor, who took a pin, and proceeded to prick the skin before him. "I see, that pin pricking is a real obsession with this guy!" The scribe on duty noted: "Nummular macule on the right internal supra-maleollar region. Light central hypaesthesia." This hermetic jargon, reserved for the small group of

The Bastards

initiated of whom he was not part, made Cambier lose interest in the examination. He was frustrated by all the poking, and, without his realizing it, this set him thinking about Hortense. He pictured her with her friend Ginette, both of them sticking aloe prickles in their arms. Ginette took it very well—not a grimace, not a word. Hortense's eyes were filled with tears, but pride made her press on her prickle. "It's not as hard as you make it," Ginette said. "Your prickle is not sharp. Try mine a bit." The tip changed arms. Hortense tried. Her face grimaced with pain, but she continued. The important thing was not to appear any less brave. . . .

The voice of the doctor speaking to his assistant once again caught Cambier's attention.

"Brévaux, since there's a question of race here, take a specimen of his blood. He'll be back in a week. We'll see whether we have to do a biopsy."

That's how it had started. For a week now, Cambier had been in pure hell.

He finished washing up, put on his clothes, and left.

* * *

"I'm here for the results."

"Your name is Cambier, isn't it?"

"Yes."

A rustling of paper made him turn around. The intern was looking for his file. The sheet of paper went from hand to hand all the way to the supervisor.

"Tell me, are your parents healthy?"

"Yes. At least my mother. My father's dead."

"What did he die from?"

"I don't know. I wasn't home."

"Do you have brothers and sisters?"

"Two sisters."

"Healthy as well?"

"I believe so."

"Your mother never had a miscarriage?"

"No, er . . . never!"

The Foyer

He had told two lies. The supervisor sensed there was some hedging in his answer.

"Think carefully. It's important."

He retorted that he had always been at boarding school, and that as a result he could have missed some of the details of his family life.

"Never mind. Ever had a button on your penis?"

He quickly looked around the room; among the interns, there was one woman. Had he been white, he would have blushed in confusion. He protested curtly.

"O.K., don't get annoyed," the doctor said.

"What's wrong? Exactly what do I have?"

"Can't say for sure as yet. You'd better not keep anything from us. You could be in for some serious problems later on."

His fear resurfaced. A sentence he had read somewhere burned in letters of fire before his eyes: "We are united by syphilis." His blood test had just officially admitted him to a brotherhood. Routine made him victim of an abominable segregation. With a start he realized that he desperately wanted the redemption that was to rid him of that curse in as short a time as possible.

"I believe there were two abortions, and that my father was a heart case."

He said nothing about his sisters. "Too much proof!" As the female intern laboriously took down what he was saying, he asked again: "What's wrong?"

"Listen. As of now, it's only a series of presumptions. It could be a serious disease, as well as a simple anomaly that's nothing to worry about. In order to be more certain, we'll have Brévaux take some more blood. Come and see me in a week."

Cambier bit his lips as his blood filled the syringe. He saw once more the agony of his father as he suffered his heart attack; the spots on Hortense's body; Caroline in the throes of her delirium, which she suffered regularly at dawn. He saw his mother commiserating with each one, suffering for the others. He did not think of himself, not yet at any rate. He was only a result, the quotient of a simple division, with a remainder that proclaimed its presence. He had to acknowledge this existence to the specialist who, spurred on by the rigor of the medical evidence at his disposal, already considered him a number among so many others.

Only when he was outside did he think of Charlotte. Centuries of Routine would get the better of her and her certainty. Henceforth, he officially entered the realm of rebuff through the front door. It was better to disappear before Charlotte told him it was all over. However, everything would have been so beautiful with a little less Routine. Instead, things were the way they were before: unrelenting reality—Life, according to those who were all tied up.

At the first intersection, he turned around to look at the peaceful old structure from which the attack had come. The Living Being had just been swept aside. No more misunderstanding. Reality again took hold, making him the exception. The dazzling revelation vanished; he felt close to his Night, a whisper away from understanding it, from understanding himself.

Ahead of him a road stretched toward the suburb. It was the same road that led to the mental hospital, to the sanitorium. It wound its way between two rows of bare plane trees, and appeared to him like a symbol. It was *his* road, at the end of which stood cells where ex-Living Beings were confined permanently to suffer and to see one another suffer. Some suffered because they were afraid; others were afraid to suffer. Wasn't it along a similar route—only a maritime one this time—that men of ebony had experienced centuries of exile, herded together in the bellies of ships, and transplanted from one continent to the other? Wasn't it under the same depressing conditions that Reality's intangible factors had confronted everyone's Night, in that infinitely variable song of Reality?

Did mad people know that they had severed connection with life, and that living persons isolated them in an area of fantasy where man's attributes were called impulses, fixed ideas, and sudden dejection?

The Foyer

Those from the sanitorium knew, or thought they did. It was the stimulus for their nostalgia, for their despair. Wouldn't ignorance have been a better proposition for them?

It was here that he encountered once more what was indeed real, through that very Routine with which man has been struggling ever since he became a slave to reality. He again saw the participants in the duel just as they had appeared to him, after Turenne's nightmare: the Real against Reality; Existence against Life; the exceptional man—the Individual—against the Living, the prisoner of Routine!

"Reality, the spark comes from you." What were the powers that be waiting for to treat these insane minds with respect, to eradicate the complexes affecting those at the sanitorium, to make the sons of slaves like him forget the past? What were they waiting for to punish the poets, those socially acceptable mad people, whom the Living had been ashamed to confine and whom they were forced to praise so they themselves could give the illusion of wisdom?

"We are united by syphilis!" He suddenly remembered: Desnos! It was Desnos who had shouted that. Desnos, the man who managed to have a split personality, to place himself in suspended animation, to seek the Night so he could bring back exceptional trophies—something Aresquier, despite his fluid, could not do without help from someone else. The poet revolted as a result of great oppression. His message exploded desperately in the vastness of an impeded, mechanized Thought. It was a message dripping with the distress of existence. The poet transmitted; a few select persons succeeded in picking up his waves; interference brought resonance. What did people like in a poet, if not his aversion to Routine? Didn't Desnos hone his astounding wordplay when he was freed from the constraints of Reality?

What was real existed somewhere. "It escapes me, but it *must* exist, since I expose everything that is not part of it." He could feel it quite close, almost in his thoughts; he proved it through the absurd, and, in his own way, tended to show it through his unreality.

He returned to his room.

Frost covered the window panes, making them look like large tear-filled eyes. "I must leave! No looking back, so there'll be no time to think, to regret! Drug myself with flight!"

For a week, he had been ignorant of the result, and buzzed around a problem that did not exist, like a moth around a lamp whose attractive brightness masks a deadly caress. Routine was there, too, more cruel than ever; and he was getting ready to experience it without flinching.

That day, he discovered how attached he was to this room. Earlier, he found only faults in it, even blaming it for the laziness that kept him from looking for a better one. Wasn't he like those grave-side eulogizers, who sing a man's praises once he is dead? Besides, this room even looked like a tomb; Alain Cambier had just died. Someone else was born in his own coffin. Was there any difference?

A blade was about to fall on the slice of life Charlotte had shared with him. Would its fall not mark the beginning of an existence that was more oppressive, more inescapable, more exceptional?

* * *

As he waited his turn in the line, Cambier found himself between two men who appeared to be seeing each other again after a long separation. He was preparing his own from Charlotte. His studies, his friendships, his love affairs in that town, it was all about to crumble.

The train that, in a few hours, would take him to Paris, would also drive a shaft between his drama and those of which he refused to be a part.

He would try to survive, to blank from his existence the wretched world where he had gone astray. He had not seen Turenne again. He did not want to see him. Nor did he wish to see Charlotte again either.

The two men in front of and behind him continued chatting. The taller man had a scar on his temple; the other kept moving constantly. Standing sometimes on one foot, sometimes on the other, every time he swayed his elbow dug into your stomach; it was enough to make you sick.

The Foyer

"You pay your rent regularly?"

"Sure."

"What he wants to do is unfair. It's against the law to raise the rent."

They had to stop, for the man in front of Cambier was almost at the ticket window.

A little girl began to whimper at the other end of the line, filling the information booth with her cries and causing a stir among the small wave of persons stretching toward the man with the schedule.

"Shut up!"

At the same time, a hand delivered a sharp smack; it moved away, then grasped the child and dragged her off. A woman could be seen disappearing in the station with her daughter in tow.

"Let's see, Paris . . . there's a train at seven. . . ."

Cambier did not listen for the number of minutes past the hour. He remained standing, as if in a daze, in front of the clerk, who had closed his book. For him, it was the start of everything, and already the end of a dream, a tomorrow heavy with reality.

"Next!"

This request, in its heavy southern accent, made him step out of the line. He moved aside, keeping his eyes on the man: a middle-aged Living Being who, his day at an end, would go home, put on his slippers, and go through the local section in a newspaper before dinner; a Living Being imprisoned by Routine, nothing more.

It was almost dark as he left the station. It was about the time the mistral began to blow harder. He clinched his fists in his pockets, and the shiver running down his back stopped. A row of taxis waited along the sidewalk. Drivers in lumber-jackets smoked patiently, their berets pulled down to their eyes.

The policeman at the traffic circle yielded his raised platform to his replacement. He shook his hand hastily and strode quickly across the avenue, stopping at the stall of an oyster vendor about to close up shop for the day.

Cambier went around the theater. At the bottom of rue des

Etuves, the last bus was leaving in a cloud of smoke and shouts of good-bye.

At that moment, he only had time to duck into an opening on his left. Behind the bus, a woman, her head down, was coming toward him on the sidewalk, but she had not seen him.

From his hiding place, he kept an eye on the passersby; the crowd moved along in jerky movements. He saw Brigitte go by, struggling against the wind. She had the usual look on her slightly pale face. "If she had seen me, she'd have asked me a lot of questions: 'How was the after-thesis party? I had to stay in with that damned tonsillitis. . . . How are things with you? Good news from Charlotte? Not too painful being alone?'"

So many questions, which would rub salt in his wounds. Just thinking about it seemed to make him itch on the inside; his body ached, but he could not tell exactly where.

In his haste, he had sought refuge at the entrance to a public W.C. A client, an easygoing sort, entered and placed a coin in the hand of a woman sitting near a pedestal table. She stopped knitting and was looking intensely at Cambier, one eye half-closed, her lips distorted by repeated twitches due to a tic. Her fingers rattled the coins in the pocket of her apron.

He read on a sign: "Urinals Free. W.C. Five Francs." He went to the urinal. After a somewhat convincing show, he again passed in front of the woman with the twisted face.

"Try your luck, monsieur. Only winning tickets!"

He continued on his way without saying a word.

He had finished packing.

He was leaving Montpellier with these images in his mind. Their banality had seemed exceptional. Every day, he had been close to those same people, those same buildings, and it was only that very evening that he noticed them, he thought. He was leaving, and every part of that town remained in him like a splinter. He wanted to carry with him all that had been part of his existence, but he was carrying away only what Routine had decreed.

He took up the guitar from the bed. He recalled Décamport's poem. "I opened my eyes; you were grimacing, strangled!" He suddenly hated that guitar. "Why carry this with me?" He grabbed its neck and smashed it against the wall.

In a few days, he had come close to everything, known everything, lost everything. The following day, life would find him in Paris in the fog, a fog similar to the one he felt creeping within him. He refused to imagine what Charlotte would do when she got back from the mountains. He refused to imagine anything, so he wouldn't weaken, wouldn't change his mind, wouldn't have to reveal himself, and thus be exposed to an agonizing breakup.

The Adopted Family

They are princes of exile and want
nothing to do with my song.

Saint-John Perse

"So, how was your first night?" Poncet enquired.

Before replying, Chambord took the time to look carefully at the person speaking to him. The night before at the airport he had not been able to look him over at leisure, since the plane had arrived shortly before midnight, which is very late in this country. Everyone was anxious to get to bed.

A young smiling European had come toward him, his hand outstretched, and had said: "Doctor Poncet, Departmental Director of Health." A car had whisked them away and had left Chambord in front of the quarters where most of the contract doctors stayed when passing through Cayenne.

Completely worn out, he had fallen into a deep sleep, despite the crashing waves, the squeaking insects, and the croaking frogs.

Voices from the gang of men working on a neighboring site had awakened him early.

Now, in this office, he was face to face with a man approximately his own age, rather short and plump, with a sad countenance and blue eyes: his director.

"I haven't yet seen much of the place," he said, sidestepping the question.

"I'm happy you're here. We need doctors."

Chambord glanced at the official map on the wall. The coastal region was dotted with red circles showing where the health facilities were located, and these had lines linking them to the principal town.

"You're referring to the interior, aren't you?"

"Not particularly. There are so few people living there, it wouldn't be profitable to post a doctor in each sector. I'm especially upset by the lack of genuine commitment to this country on the part of the medical profession."

Chambord wanted to say how committed he was, but refrained, because he had made himself a promise to mind his p's and q's since he had met, somewhere between Vigo and the Azores, a European doctor called Quintaine, who was also on his way to Guiana.

"I met Quintaine on the ship. He'll be here in two days; he's stopping over in Trinidad."

"Another one who wanted to see Caracas," Poncet said ironically.

"He told me he was assigned to the hospital I'm going to. That means two of us passed the exam?"

A shadow came over Poncet's countenance; Chambord's words were proving highly embarrassing for him.

As if on purpose, everything had gone topsy-turvey. They had wanted Chambord to arrive after Quintaine, but it was Chambord who was the first to arrive.

In principle, he had been recruited for a hospital; but Quintaine had high-level contacts. He was almost fifty years old; since his mentor moved in certain ministerial circles, he had been spared the rigors of open boat trips and treacherous jeep outings over pot-holed roads.

"Actually, we need only one doctor for Saint-Laurent," Poncet said. "You were successful in the exam, but Quintaine was on top, and you second."

"What do you mean second?"

There it was, this *myth of the second* again! Indeed, Ségaye wasn't the only one to believe in it! Livid with anger, Chambord was about to say something else, but Poncet continued, as if to convince him: "Quintaine, having placed first, could choose where he wanted to work."

"He told me himself he'd never heard of this exam."

Poncet turned livid with disbelief. "Quintaine, that joker!" What else could one say, after such a blunder? It was futile pursuing a line of defense that Quintaine's indiscriminate chattering had nipped in the bud. He was being credited with topping the applicants, yet by his own admission he was completely unaware of the very existence of an exam. Should the matter be dropped? This type of action, already hardly noticed in a country where the white minority was duty-bound to band together, could have disastrous consequences for Poncet's career.

Shortly before Chambord was to arrive, a member of the government had said to Poncet: "One of my young countrymen has informed me that he has been recruited to work in Saint-Laurent. He's a young man you should keep in mind; I just wanted to draw him to your attention." Now, a disgruntled member of government could ruin the future of a civil servant.

To further complicate matters, there were the differences between Poncet and Bertrand, the prefect.

For a long time, both these men had been the best of friends, but Bertrand, in his desire to implement an extensive austerity program, had decided to cut back on all spending, and the health services had not been spared. This made Poncet unhappy, since his idea, on the contrary, had been to set up throughout the territory a network of highly equipped health centers. Bertrand, in whose judgment this reaction was unwarranted, had issued threats that were not exactly veiled: "You're young, Poncet. You've moved up very fast. Don't forget that the higher you go, the harder you fall."

Poncet counted on returning to his good graces by going along with the deception surrounding Quintaine. He would agree to assign him to the postion in question.

Meanwhile, relations had deteriorated following an affair that, for the time being, seemed to be going on and on. A doctor posted to a rural area, angered by Poncet's way of doing things, had ill-treated and slapped him in his office; as ill luck would have it, a door had remained open, and some of the employees had witnessed the entire episode. Poncet had demanded forthwith the dismissal of his hot-tempered subordinate. Bertrand, who favored radical measures, instantly issued an order claiming "Breach of contract for professional misconduct." But the victim, along with a representative from the medical fraternity, had lodged a protest: one could not call professional misconduct an attack on a superior's person. It was horrible.

If the argument was valid, the fact still remained that this doctor was quite a character. A second order from the prefect rescinded the first, and stipulated, moreover, that the aggressor was being let go because his position had been abolished. This meant that the department had to pay the dismissed doctor six months' salary, plus remuneration in lieu of leave, and his return passage to France. The great financial austerity program was about to suffer a major setback, all because of Poncet, who let one lousy little slap from a former colleague turned subordinate upset the running of the administrative machinery.

Bertrand had vented his anger at Poncet. From that incident on, he systematically refused to see that "former sanitary inspector catapulted to a position he was incompetent to fill." Bertrand had himself only been a subprefect prior to his Cayenne appointment, but that he willingly put out of his mind.

That was how far things had gone. Poncet saw no honorable way out. And Chambord, still seated across from him, was waiting for explanations.

"I feel terrible about the whole thing," Poncet said. "I'm really on your side. I know you'll see yourself as a victim of injustice, but Quintaine *must* go to Saint-Laurent. It's all part of a chain of events I have to follow."

"And where do I fit in all that?"

"Yes. I know, I know. You must understand."

"I'm only asking one thing of you: honor your signature. You sent me the official results of an exam I had passed. I'm here to take up my job. That's all."

Chambord looked ready to fight for his rights. The affair could have serious repercussions if word got around in France. Then, what would become of Poncet? Cayenne was his first posting as director. Imagine having everybody unanimously against you: the prefect, the doctors, your supervisor, your subordinates! What a feat! What a handicap for the future! No, it was too unfair; he had to let everyone shoulder his responsibility.

"I'll call the prefect and ask him to see you. You'll tell him your grievances."

Bertrand was in a bad mood. He had just had a rather unpleasant meeting. Faced with a respectful, but firm councillor, he had had to concede that he was as weak and fickle as Poncet. Within one week he had issued two conflicting orders on the same issue. The whole of Cayenne was already talking about it, and soon it would be all of Guiana's turn to be amused. "Yet another one the heat has driven clean out of his mind!"

To get rid of a dispensary was to expose the councillor from the penalized district to the wrath of the voters, to mortgage his political future. A councillor just could not allow his constituents to suffer as a result of a dispute between two civil servants soon to return to France, leaving the elected official at the mercy of popular rage. Bertrand had made a few concessions, and since his visitor's departure, his anger against Poncet only grew deeper.

The telephone rang. Bertrand took the receiver, and heard his secretary's voice: "Sir, it's the director of health. Should I say you're busy?"

For a few days now, Poncet had been receiving that answer whenever he wanted to speak to his superior.

Bertrand, a smile lighting up his face, said in a tone of sarcasm: "Put him through."

As soon as Poncet began speaking, he smiled broadly, and made himself comfortable by crossing his outstretched legs on his desk.

"Hello, Mr. Prefect, I have here with me Dr. Chambord, who came in last night. Would it be possible for you to see him before he starts work?"

"And where do you plan to send him?"

Poncet became worried. All his plans crumbled at this brutal, unexpected question. If Chambord had not been sitting a mere arm's length away, listening carefully to every word, he would have made a suggestion which would surely have met with Bertrand's approval. He found a compromise position.

"I was thinking that in the meantime he could get that position made vacant by your last order."

"Do you take me for an ass, Poncet?"

"Of course not, sir," said Poncet, spontaneously coming to attention where he stood near his desk.

"A councillor just this minute left here. The population has signed a petition demanding that we keep the doctor who allegedly roughed you up."

"That's a political move, sir."

"It's you who have been making the moves. You made me look foolish! Yes, you Poncet, and your childish pranks!"

"What do you mean, sir?"

"Shut up! My last order is sheer nonsense: it abolishes a position. Now, how can you ever appoint a doctor to an abolished, therefore nonexistent, position?"

"I hadn't seen the matter in that light, sir."

"Well, no use starting now. I'm issuing a third order keeping your aggressor in his job. If you don't like it, I couldn't give a shit!" Bertrand shouted as he slammed down the phone.

Poncet, paler than ever, also hung up, then turned to Chambord: "The prefect completely misunderstood what I was saying. Unfortunately, we were cut off. I'll try to call him again tomorrow."

Chambord was flabbergasted. He was right in the middle of a ticklish situation. His case was of no importance in a conflict that was taking place in high places. He was already a man alone. He had only to wait.

"Would you like to have lunch at my house today?" Poncet proposed.

Chambord accepted. He had understood that Poncet, too, was an unhappy man.

* * *

Poncet's villa, situated a few miles from Cayenne, was perched on the side of a rocky cliff overlooking the sea. From the road you entered flush with the floor where the bedrooms were located. A steep stairway took you down to the living room off a hall. A few feet further on, and you were actually on the beach, washed by a dirt-colored sea whose spray would sprinkle you through the shutters.

Poncet's children were having fun teasing a little capuchin monkey that, after constantly moving up and down a pole, was virtually strangling itself with its chain. A talkative parrot on a perch was preening its newest feathers.

The Adopted Family

Mme Poncet, who hailed from Paris and was all smiles, had quickly taken to Chambord. He noted how close he was to those Europeans, how sensitive he was to their manners. Since returning to Cayenne, he had reacted like them, always shocked by the behavior of some of his countrymen, whose reserve he detested. But wasn't he in a way responsible for this reserve?

At the airport and on the street, people had seen a black man in a tie and a woolen suit. They had looked at him with insistent curiosity, and had discovered a foreigner. He had done nothing to reassure others, to show that he knew he was a willing accomplice. On each occasion, he had gone his merry way, unperturbed, like in France when you avoid speaking to someone to whom you've not been introduced. Didn't many white people come into contact with one another, pass one another on the sidewalks of Montpellier without acknowledging each other's presence? He had acquired this type of behavior, and despite his profound desire to leave Europe and plunge himself into his country all the more, he couldn't help imitating the white man.

In France, people knew their place. Over here, on the contrary, you had to take the initiative, talk to them about anything. But you had to be careful not to talk down to them or to be too familiar with them. Speaking French all the time was already seen as bordering on being snobbish; always speaking Creole smacked of contempt for some compatriots, who could get the impression that their knowledge of French was being questioned.

Chambord hardly ever spoke the local Creole; in fact, he spoke it rather badly, since he had been raised in Guadeloupe, and nothing is funnier to Guianese than to hear Guadeloupean Creole, which they find heavy and comical.

A childish shame made him hide behind the white man's language. From the very start he had everything against him: language, dress, behavior. Soon, the people he saw would be added to that list. His first visit was to a European, whose invitation to lunch he had even accepted. He had been seen sitting next to this man as they drove through the streets of Cayenne. It embarrassed him somewhat, not because he was seen with a white man, obviously, but because of the priority he afforded him, because of this typically European courtesy he had shown with regard to a white man who, without doubt, was keeping something from him.

Snatches of sentences reached his ears: "Injustice . . . Quintaine *must* go . . . forced to obey." There had been some hesitation on Poncet's part during the phone call to the prefect. They were definitely keeping something from him!

"I mentioned you to several Guianese. They all claimed they didn't know who you were, except one government official who thought he had met you in France," Poncet said.

How could they know who he was? Shortly after he was born in Cayenne, his parents had emigrated. When he was about ten, he had returned for a short while. Every day, his playmates had made fun of him. He had completely forgotten everything, except that painful image of faces laughing at the odd way he spoke.

"I've hardly lived here any time."

He thought it useless to do any more explaining. A feeling of mistrust was now creeping between Poncet and himself. He had absorbed it like hemlock, convinced that it would poison only whatever whiteness was left in him. He had thought of late that he had rid himself forever of Europe, but it remained in him, as deep-rooted as before, not allowing itself to be given the slip. Years of cohabitation, of shared experiences, had made of it a companion that was regular, complacent, or intrusive depending on the mood, but always dominant. "If I were to abandon myself completely to Europe, I would look like a dowry-chaser," he had said to Farnabe. The bet was already lost if one was adamant about taking things in a block: Europe versus Africa. "There's no one-to-one fight between two continents; only colonizers and colonized squaring off against each other." Europe was far away, ignorant, or indifferent; Africa seemed even farther away, even more ignorant, even more indifferent. If they still existed here, they were each as diluted, as unnatural as the other.

The Poncets and others, even when at war, were one family,

which turned its back on liberal Europe, though claiming to belong to it, elevating it to the status of a myth, benefiting from it in spite of itself. As for Chambord, he uttered a stifled cry toward Africa in its suffering, in its burglarized state, but an Africa no less unreal.

The colonial vocation had had the same effect on Poncet and his counterparts as did slavery on Chambord and his. For some, exile had brought prestige; for others, it had meant only one problem after another. But in either situation, and with centuries between them, one was dealing with men made different from their basic nature. In Guiana, the Europeans, like the Africans, had ceased existing as such, to make way for the privileged and the frustrated, indeed for the *bastards* who had ceased belonging to a race to become mere men struggling for opposite ideals.

"Whisky?" Mme Poncet asked.

"A little."

"Perrier or water?"

"Perrier, thank you," Chambord said, raising his glass.

He wondered whether in France Poncet could afford to drink whisky as an aperitif, to live in a villa by the sea, or to let his children tease a monkey and a parrot.

"Lovely home you have here," he said.

"Really nice."

"Official housing, of course?"

"Yes. It comes furnished, with a car, chauffeur, and other perks. Actually, all directors are in the same situation," Poncet added, as if to tone down the unusual nature of his privileges.

"You like it here in Guiana?"

What a question! It was obvious that whoever held Poncet's job would find the country extremely attractive.

"In the beginning, I didn't want to remain, but little by little I discovered how much this country needed people to love and serve it. So, I came to love it. I've even thought of staying on, but the administrative atmosphere is not what it used to be, especially since the latest round of budget decisions. My section is the target of all the restrictions."

"And what about the people?"

"The people?"

"You mention the administrative atmosphere, the restricted budgets. But what about the Guianese people in all this? What's their reaction?"

"I'm afraid I don't understand."

"I'd like to know whether the administration is aware of the existence of popular masses. When you say you want to love and serve Guiana, are you thinking of its people, or . . ."

"Or what?"

Chambord had just realized that he was, after all, speaking to his boss, and that the tone of his voice was definitely disrespectful. Did the fact that they ate at the same table, that they were both alert to problems in the same country, that they discussed them, give him any right to put aside the subordination of guest to host?

He had not dared complete his question, which would have sounded quite insolent: "or of your future?" He concluded: "Or are you so busy that you float above the masses?"

"If there's one office that remains in contact with the masses, it's ours. I've inspected all the health sectors, seen all the facilities, met with all the doctors in charge. . . ."

"Did you visit people's homes? Did you see what conditions are like?"

"That's the responsibility of the Departmental Office of Population."

"Oh!"

Poncet thought it wise to elaborate a bit.

"There are serious problems involved in making a visit to the rural sector. First, it's hard to get there: special plane, motorboat, jeep, etc. The distances to be covered are considerable. Once in a particular sector, I can't stay very long because I'm needed in Cayenne. Added to that, the population in the rural areas is either very timid or very aggressive. I make do with the reports filed by the doctors."

"Agressive, you say?" Chambord said, surprised.

"For example, I recently had a bone to pick with one of your colleagues. In fact, you'll soon be hearing about it in detail. This doctor's really hotheaded."

"Guianese?"

"No, a Frenchman. He's well liked by the people in his sector. A few days after the incident, when I went to inspect the health district, my car was surrounded, and I was insulted and threatened. I only got away thanks to my chauffeur."

Poncet could not understand how the people could like this doctor. In his mind, all problems could be solved by issuing official memos to these ignorant masses. There were attempts to make them happier, in spite of themselves; but instead of showing their gratitude, they reserved their support for a fanatic, and their hostility for a man who spent sleepless nights putting together plans for reorganizing the health services.

"The people probably love this doctor because they feel he is close to them," Chambord said. "A departmental director only turns up to inspect, whereas a doctor is a permanent element in a sector."

A permanent element. Poncet found this term quite unpleasant. And to think that he had already arranged to put an end to this permanence! It had taken a councillor coming to scare Bertrand for the entire question to be reopened. Never again would he, Poncet, agree to set foot in this health district, to undertake the slightest reorganization. He would choke off the fanatic. When all was said and done, he was the one in charge, and he would show him! He wanted to make them happy, those unknowing people, led astray by a demagogue of a doctor who used to take it upon himself every night to go crocodile hunting with them on the river. Did the department pay doctors to take boat rides, and in official boats to boot? Was Bertrand aware of this abuse, he who made such a fuss about saving money?

Poncet began to think of various ways of exposing this wastage, in order to force Bertrand to take more powerful measures. His plan was simple: alert the prefect, act as if the fanatic doctor's sector did not exist; then people would see what became of the so-called permanence.

Thus, without realizing it, he was conceding that Chambord was right. By wanting to penalize a doctor, wasn't it the population he was penalizing? He proposed suspending all supplies and reducing expenses or stock to the minimum. Who else but the Guianese would suffer the consequences of this victimization?

During the course of the meal, Chambord filled them in on the details of his life, but made no concession: he wanted to take up his position. Poncet could see that all would not be plain sailing. Success for Chambord would mean defeat for the secret forces behind Quintaine. No compromise was possible. There would inevitably be an expiatory victim, and more and more Poncet saw himself as the one.

Chambord was totally unmoved by all the threats and all the fighting. This was a dispute between tenants on the first floor, between colonizers. He was on the ground floor. Should he knock on the ceiling, or go up and restore order? Had they condescended to come down to his level? He would block his ears.

"I'd really like to see this country prosper," Poncet said excitedly. "The former prefect tried his best, but was transferred. His successor's only program is to undo all that was done. The administration lacks a sense of continuity, of cohesion."

"Do you think it's possible to build a Guiana without the Guianese?"

"What do you mean?"

"You seem to see everything from an administration point of view. With the help of a few senior civil servants on short-term assignments, it takes a global view of the country, ignorant, or at least pretending to be ignorant, of the fact that there is a Guianese elite trained in French graduate schools, one that is growing impatient."

"It is not ignorant of the fact."

"At any rate, it's hiding it quite well."

"You're obviously referring to your own case; that's a simple accident which, in my view, must be corrected quickly."

There was no doubt that the administration knew of a Guianese elite that went to graduate schools. Since Chambord's departure, his friends back in Montpellier had become aware of this. They had all received a letter from Bertrand reminding them that they were expected to reimburse, and immediately upon completion of their studies at that, whatever grant they had received.

"How many doctors are there on contract or in the civil service in Guiana?" Chambord asked.

"About twenty."

"And how many are Guianese?"

"Two: Faustin and yourself."

"Do you know that, in France or elsewhere, there are enough Guianese doctors to fill all the positions in the country?"

"Why don't they return home, then?"

"No doubt because of accidents!" Chambord replied ironically.

* * *

Chambord had been in Cayenne for two days. As he still had not been posted, he divided his time between his residence, situated behind the hospital, a stone's throw away from the ocean, and the office of his supervisor, who received an unending stream of complaints. "In this country, the white man sees another white man as a wolf. As for the white doctor, he's like ten wolves with another white doctor. I'm the victim these gentlemen dreamed of; even when they attack me, they go unpunished."

Chambord would have preferred not to be present at these confidential meetings, but he had been told that by going to the office of the director of health he would be more likely to run into his colleagues. Poncet took the regularity of these visits for friendship. He confided in him over and over. "Among your colleagues there's a traitor and a coward: the traitor is a white who's in collusion with the prefect against me; the coward, I'm sad to say, is your countryman Faustin, who never had the courage to defend me, when he knows how devoted I am to this country."

Chambord had met Faustin and a few other colleagues, either those on contract—Europeans all of them, including the *traitor*—or those in private practice, all of whom were Guia-nese. Nobody had had anything good to say about Poncet.

As he was still unable to see Bertrand, Poncet went to see Arnaud, the secretary general. The latter, very young, married to a woman doctor, was reputed to hold all doctors in utter contempt. Poncet had warned Chambord: "This man hates all of us. He's taking it out on us because his wife rules him."

"We don't have a posting for you as yet," Arnaud said.

"I'll wait," Chambord replied.

"Unless you take over the Cayenne Exterior Sector. The person in charge is on sick leave. What do you think, Mr. Director?" he asked.

"You have my approval, Mr. Secretary General," Poncet conceded.

Despite his disappointment, Chambord was inwardly amused to see two men his age playing at being important, both separated only by a double pedestal desk, and just a thirty-six hour flight from their home country. The whites in Guiana were a surprising lot. They hated one another, but did it according to protocol. Sitting across from each other, Mr. Secretary General and Mr. Director retracted their claws. They would attack each other only when there was some distance between them. The awful struggle would end only with the elimination of one of them; in other words, when one was recalled to France with a file full of incriminating information.

"You approve, you say? This is obviously the proposal you wanted to make to the prefect?"

Arnaud, with a Machiavellian smile, enjoyed embarrassing Poncet. He was a master at doing this. Weren't all those un-popular decrees, though originating from him, always signed by the prefect?

The proposal to Bertrand? He was very familiar with it, having heard about it as soon as it was formulated. He had to make Poncet own up and show himself for what he really was: a small-time laborer. The struggle continued.

"No," Poncet said evasively.

"Oh, I thought it was. You had another suggestion?"

"I approve your idea, sir," Poncet said in despair, deeply pained by these questions.

But Arnaud was not about to believe all he was hearing. He insisted: "But in order to approve so quickly, you must at least have given the matter some thought already."

"No, Mr. Secretary General."

"Good."

"There's no doubt, Mr. Secretary General, that Dr. Hortez's accident has thrown things into great confusion. I think Dr. Chambord could hold the position until the substantive holder returns."

"What accident?" Chambord enquired.

"She broke her leg."

"It's a woman, then?"

"Yes. Furthermore, this job is too rough for a woman."

"Let's get back to the point," Arnaud interrupted. "Dr. Hortez won't be able to return to work for another four months, and . . ."

"But I'm here to go to Saint-Laurent."

"As of now, that position is to be taken up by Dr. Quintaine, who's coming in tonight," Arnaud said firmly.

Chambord was definitely going to object to the unfair appointment of Quintaine. He had solid arguments: an official letter, Quintaine's own admissions. Now it was Poncet's turn to begin to be amused. There was one snag, however: the letter bore his signature.

Chambord began to read the famous letter he had promptly taken from his pocket. Arnaud listened without turning a hair. Silence followed the reading.

"I was recruited for the hospital in Saint-Laurent, it seems."

"There's no hospital in Saint-Laurent."

"No hospital?"

"Please don't interrupt!" Arnaud pleaded. "This so-called exam you took is worthless. . . ."

But Chambord interrupted him again.

"What do you mean, worthless? There was an official announcement in the medical bulletin. I applied, and was asked to supply copies of my degrees. The jury deliberated, and informed me that I had passed. . . ."

"They had no right to organize this exam. The hospital in question has no legal status. In other words, it doesn't exist. The exam is therefore null and void."

"So?"

"So, the administration can appoint any doctor it pleases."

"And I'm out. I'm being penalized for allowing myself to be taken in."

"It's not that at all, doctor. We're glad you're here, you, a son of the soil. . . ."

"Doesn't look so to me."

"Dr. Quintaine, in view of his age, cannot be sent to a rural sector that demands sportsmanlike fitness. I'm hoping you'll fill the bill."

"If Quintaine was accepted as fit to work overseas, then he can be sent anywhere. The medical checkup one takes prior to leaving France . . ."

"Medical checkup! You know only too well how it's administered."

"Very well," Chambord said. "I know what I have to do."

Arnaud gave a start. He sprang to his feet to see his visitors out.

The telephone was ringing for the third time. Rousing himself from his siesta, Chambord ran, barefoot, to the receiver.

"Hello, Doctor Chambord?"

"Yes."

"This is Arnaud."

"I beg your pardon?"

"The secretary general. Am I disturbing you?"

"Not at all."

"Would you like to have lunch at my house on Monday?"

Chambord hesitated. Monday was three days away. He seemed to recall that there was something important planned for that day. But what? In his head, still groggy with sleep, his ideas were moving in slow motion. He searched in vain; he could conjure up only bits and pieces of a dream he was having: a sticky fight between Poncet, Arnaud, Bertrand, and Quintaine, all completely naked, sweating and puffing, shouting, bent over after each low blow.

"Monday at twelve," Arnaud specified.

Chambord saw once more Poncet's blue eyes, about to be filled with tears; his standing to attention as he spoke with Bertrand on the phone; Arnaud's haughtiness; the embarrassment of Quintaine caught unexpectedly between the devil and the deep blue sea, and forced to admit his ignorance.

He had no right being among them. Deceived and ridiculed, he had no desire to be part of their scheming.

"Monday?" he said.

"Yes, Monday."

The constant repetition of this word refreshed his memory: it was on Monday that he started work in the exterior sector.

"I begin working that day. I've got to go up the river, and won't be back till late in the afternoon."

"Very well, very well," Arnaud said as he hung up in anger.

For him, this excuse, coming after so much hesitation, was tantamount to an insult, for there was hardly anyone in the upper echelons unaware that he had already been invited to Poncet's place.

"Hello, hello!"

Chambord, anxious to propose another day, shouted in vain into the receiver.

"One enemy already!" he sighed.

* * *

An early afternoon shower had turned the narrow street leading to the place des Palmistes into a mass of mud. Carefully pulling up the legs of his pants with his fingers, Chambord picked his way, skipping between puddles.

He felt like strolling through the town; the popular district appealed to him above all.

From a distance, he saw the closed shutters of the Ministry of Health, whose offices were only open mornings. Two tennis courts had been laid down in the center of the square. Taking advantage of the reappearance of the blazing sun, players were warming up with a few exchanges, and little kids darted into the damp, smoking grass to retrieve lost balls.

A primary school let out its pupils amidst a din that reminded one of a fowl run. Chambord was quickly surrounded by hordes of brats; on the lawn there was a noisy mixture of shouts in Creole, somersaults, laughter, and tears.

On the terrace of the Café des Palmistes, a few drinkers were talking around tables.

A little farther on, on the side of a building, an inordinately large sign indicated the location of a dentist's office. Everything seemed to point to the fact that it was not yet very effective, because the dentist, lacking patients, was standing in the doorway smoking and staring dreamily at the street. From time to time, he would acknowledge a greeting from a passerby, or exchange a few quick words with another who did not bother to stop.

At every intersection, there was a general store run by a Chinese shopkeeper. Most of the oriental immigrants had businesses. Clever retailers, they rose early and stayed up late; they sold a little of everything and were quite a force on the market. Attached to their customs, they formed a veritable enclave among the population.

Cayenne was a living paradox defiantly challenging History: South American location, European vocation, African essence. All races could be found there, except the true natives of the continent, who had been almost totally forgotten. On occasion, for some folk festival organized to please a few important visitors, a dozen or so Roucouyennes or Oyampis would be brought from the interior. They would arrive, with their feathers and false ferocity, to yell and send a shudder down the spine of an august assembly. Happy at having their fear come at so little cost, people would pat themselves on the back; the natives would be given some worthless token and sent on their way.

There remained, therefore, whites, orientals, and blacks: the doers, the spectators, and the other puppets. Indeed, since the orientals were impermeable or indifferent, the entire colonial interplay was one between a handful of white admin-

The Adopted Family

istrators and a mass of dehumanized blacks of more or less mixed blood, who were artificially assimilated to Europe. The former, like true molders of destiny, set to work achieving the impossible without bothering to think about the upheavals created in the lives of the latter, the very ones whose destiny they were molding.

Chambord went down a hill toward the Crique, that foul-smelling river that rose or fell with the tide and served as the dividing line between the poorer people and the rest of Cayenne. Many streets came to it, but not all of them crossed it, there being no bridge.

The Crique was bustling with activity. Back in port, fishing boats attracted housewives on the bank. A fisherman, squatting before a chopping block, was hacking an enormous fish into slices. Splinters, bones, and scraps were flying everywhere.

Through the legs of the women about to make their purchases, and near their motionless bare feet, could be seen a rusty scale, whose arm fell noisily whenever a slice of fish was thrown into a tray.

A man's voice gave a figure. A woman leaned over; her skirt eased up on her legs, hugging her ample buttocks. A crumpled, dirty bank note rolled on the ground. A hand snapped it up, unfolded it, put it away. One by one, coins fell at the same spot. Another hand picked them up. Then the woman waddled away from the group, arm folded, hand shoulder high, carrying a chunk of white flesh on the palm of her hand as in a cup. Behind her, the hacking continued.

The paved section of the road went only as far as the Crique. Beyond that, the roads were of mud, easily flooded and slippery. Despite the embankments that had been provided, they looked like crossing points on a river forming a sticky grid on this waterlogged suburb. Down from these roads were shacks that could be reached only via culverts of rotten wood; they had been pieced together from empty soapboxes and oil drums that still bore the name of the manufacturer and the origin of the merchandise. "Department of France, indeed!" Chambord sighed, suddenly relieved that he had turned down Arnaud's invitation to lunch.

He had been careful to wear a short-sleeved shirt and open

sandals, and carried a raincoat on his arm. He would have been asking for trouble had he worn a suit in such a neighborhood. He could feel countless eyes peering at him from deep inside the dark shacks.

He heard a baby crying. The voice of a woman, no doubt the infant's mother, was singing a Creole lullaby. How many mothers had to resort to lullabies as a replacement for milk! Do the white man's laundry, be his maid, stand respectfully behind his chair, look at his dog, its stomach full, asleep beside a half-full bowl. And it was not true only for the white man. The middle class and the local nouveaux riches held on even more fiercely to their condition and haughtily imprisoned you in yours. You would go off at the crack of dawn to use your hands to make the master's easy life even easier; you would return home at night dog-tired to a little hungry being conceived beyond the Crique. . . .

In one of the side streets, he recognized Faustin's car. The day before, he had talked with his compatriot, though in the presence of Poncet. Today, he would have liked to put Faustin to the test by talking about all the things they found so distressing.

The car was in front of a dispensary.

A few persons were waiting at the entrance. A social worker was filling out information sheets, screening the patients, taking only those who patently could not afford to pay.

"Good day, mademoiselle. I'd like to see Dr. Faustin, please."

"And who should I say wants to see him?"

"Dr. Chambord."

She got up, and he used the opportunity to glance at one of the sheets she was still to complete. Under the heading "Income" he read: "Makes four thousand francs a month doing laundry; says she has no other source of income to raise her four children from unknown father." The social worker had written "unknown fathers." What was sad was that she was not wrong.

Faustin came in, wearing a white jacket, visibly happy his countryman had come to see him.

The Adopted Family

"Hi, man! What good breeze blows you here?"

"I went for a walk, and I saw your car."

He was already being taken to a room where a patient was standing with his pants off, his shirt covering the upper portion of his legs.

"Today, we're seeing VD cases," Faustin explained.

"Do you have many cases?"

"Fewer and fewer, thanks to antibiotics; but malnutrition is hampering us a bit. Medication is more effective on people who are properly fed."

Faustin scribbled a prescription and dismissed the patient, who went over to a treatment room.

"I've had a look at the neighborhood. It was very painful for me."

Not so very long ago, he had compared Guiana to an unwed mother. That woman without money, saddled with a bunch of bastards, relating her woes to a social worker, came along at just the right time to make his comparison all the more telling.

"You end up getting accustomed to it," Faustin admitted.

"We really can't afford to. This blight is unacceptable. I just saw on a sheet next door that a mother and her four children were living off four thousand francs a month."

The bitterness of that reply surprised him, but he could not help baring his soul, expressing the pain he had felt.

Faustin did not seem unduly alarmed. When he arrived six years earlier, many things had shocked him as well. He was part of the local middle class and had, in order to be with his folks, given up his practice in a small town in the Midi. But it wasn't long before he thought he should never have done what he did.

"Often, patients exaggerate," he said.

"What do you think this woman really makes?"

"Ten to twelve thousand francs!" Faustin suggested with a shrug of his shoulders.

"With five mouths to feed! That's scandalous."

"My friend, everything here is scandalous. The example comes from the top. We're in bad shape in the health sector.

The Bastards

You have a dentist extracting as many as forty teeth from one patient; you have a doctor, hooked up with a pharmacist, giving out bogus prescriptions; all that so they can collect non-existent fees from the administration."

"So?" Chambord asked.

"So, Bertrand is beginning to flex his muscles, and the small fry are caught along with the big shots."

* * *

A sign had just gone on, telling passengers not to smoke and to fasten their seat belts. The plane would be landing shortly.

Quintaine looked through the window. In the blackness of the night he saw only a navigation light at the tip of the wing.

He had made quite a few discoveries since leaving Le Havre: cold, foggy England; the Bay of Biscay, its green waters specked with oil slicks; Spain with all its contrasts; the verdant, calm Antilles. Caracas was not what he had imagined. There was hardly any of the feeling of remoteness from his own surroundings that he was seeking in leaving Europe. And so, shortly after this stop, while they were flying over the continent, he had discovered marshy shores, a dense forest, and wide, winding rivers—a whole new world. It was too much to take in all at once.

If Caracas bore too profound a mark of the civilized world, the succeeding stops gradually introduced him to the realm of adventure. Quintaine did not wish to go so far. Already in Port of Spain, modern and colorful, the coexistence of white and black worlds seemed to follow a certain conventionalism: segregation, forgotten in the long run, kept the haves and the have-nots (whites and blacks, in other words) restricted within respective limits. To Quintaine's eyes, this situation was fraught with all sorts of dangers that could explode at any moment. At his age, living dangerously was out of the question.

A lull in his life had brought on a belated colonial vocation: he would serve overseas while awaiting his inheritance from a father who, now in his eighties, had been a rice farmer and was quite well-off. He had contacted a few influential friends, asking them to see what they could do to speed things up, since he was caught between a demanding mistress and his family obligations.

He was offered a position in Guiana, a country about which he had had only the worst of information. He would have turned down the offer had he not, in the meanwhile, met Poncet, who was on vacation in France, and who had set his mind at ease. A harsh climate? Unjustified denigration. A difficult life? Lies. The high salaries gave Europeans many possibilities. Secondary schools? Cayenne had plenty of them.

That was all true. What was not quite true, though, was giving the impression that there were many outstanding men among the whites, that the Guianese people lived in a state of total happiness in a land of plenty.

Quintaine began to have his doubts some time after leaving France. He had sought further information from the man in the cabin next to his, a Guianese lawyer, who had retired to Martinique. That was how he learned that the body and soul of the country were wasting away in abject misery. Local intellectuals, intent on putting things right, met with hostility from the administration, and therefore had only one alternative: submit and be part of the suffocation of their people, or resign and abandon them. Many were opting to leave. Some returned to France; others went to work in the Antilles or black Africa. The result was the following paradox: a country rich in educated men and natural resources lacked people in management and was wallowing in mediocrity. It was inevitable that one day or the other the popular masses would wake up and rise up, making things even more difficult. At least, if those in control made up for their errors with a few concrete achievements, then there would be a sort of absolution. But on the contrary, they were incapable of any undertaking, because of a lack of imagination, or of any success, because of a lack of competence.

The lawyer had ended this dismal tale with a disturbing flash of wit: "After being, through the prison, the dumping ground for the nation of France, Guiana, through assimilation, has become the dumping ground for the administration."

There was a sudden shaking of the plane. Quintaine felt his

heart leap. He hated air pockets; they always made him feel some disaster was about to occur. Behind him, someone grumbled a complaint. It was Retter, a veterinarian he had met during the trip and who was also taking up a job in Guiana.

Retter had spent many years in North Africa; he had behaved so well there that, at the first hint of popular revolt, he had deemed it useful to disappear.

On the ship, as he introduced himself to Quintaine, he said in a military tone of voice: "Retter! a symmetrical name: R-e-t-t-e-r!" One night, while they were together in the smoking room with the disillusioned lawyer, Retter had confided: "I've broken the card." Quintaine and Chambord had looked up with indifference, and the lawyer had to explain that this legal jargon meant that Retter was divorced.

The lights of the airport were in sight. The stewardess gave final instructions.

Standing in the hall, Poncet waited for his two new staff members. He had insisted that Chambord accompany him. He could only find one available room in the town's one decent hotel, and it was being given to Retter, who had his children with him. Quintaine would share accommodations with Chambord. It was better to take it all in from the scene of the action than to stay up alone waiting for a colleague.

The veterinarian and his brood took the jeep with the chauffeur, while Poncet, driving his own car, left with the doctors.

From his seat in the back, Chambord merely followed the conversation of the two others, whose profiles he could see in the glow of the headlights.

Poncet spoke mainly about things in general. Quintaine, on the other hand, wanted to talk shop; for him, since Chambord was part of the white colony, there was no need to be embarrassed. Despite all his efforts, he was unable to make Poncet open up. Because of the difference in ages between his director and himself, he thought it all right to show some self-assurance in his manner of speaking. The other alarm bells he heard, as well as Poncet's suddenly fearful attitude, encouraged him to persevere. He was not conscious of the *circumstance* he was now experiencing: two white men carrying on a conversation in front of a black man. Could they talk freely? It was some challenge for Poncet, who at one and the same time had to share the official enthusiasm over Quintaine while avoiding offending Chambord. It was exactly like Faustin and Chambord who, the day before, had clearly not gone into the details of their personal problems when they were with him.

"So," Quintaine said, "it seems that Chambord and I have been assigned to work in the same place?"

"Who told you that?"

Dumbfounded, Quintaine turned to Chambord: "You did say you were going to Saint-Laurent?"

"Yes."

"You even mentioned an exam, didn't you?"

"Yes," Chambord repeated.

"So, Poncet, why act so surprised?"

He addressed the other by his name, directly, to show from the start that there was to be no formality between them.

"It's getting late. We'll talk about it tomorrow, in my office."

"As you wish. I'll ask Chambord to drive me over."

"Apparently, you don't want to leave Chambord alone," Poncet said ironically, not wishing in any way to talk with both these men at once.

"Say, this fellow Poncet, I find him strange," Quintaine said, emerging from the bathroom, a towel tied around his potbellied body.

Chambord, sitting in a deck chair, sipped a glass of fruit juice.

"Ah, yes?"

"Really strange! Yet, in Paris, he was rather informal."

"There must have been new developments."

"Well, we'll see."

The Bastards

Quintaine walked toward the middle of the room, and his feet left damp prints on the carpet. With one hand, he filled his glass, while with the other he continued to hold the towel in place.

"Quite nice down here: furnished house, a refrigerator full of stuff, a bathroom, fluorescent lights. It's perfect!"

"It's all right, I guess," Chambord agreed somewhat glumly.

He could not erase from his mind the shacks he had seen beyond the Crique nor the sickening feeling within him.

"Is that the sea we're hearing?"

Without waiting for a reply, Quintaine, his buttocks swaying from side to side, went over to a shutter and opened it just a little. Moonlight bathed the ocean in a silvery whiteness.

"It's beautiful."

"I'm going to bed. Good night," Chambord said. He had already stood up, and was on his way to his bedroom.

Quintaine remained looking at the sea for a long time. A fresh breeze blew in gusts, and he felt the rush against his skin. He calculated that with his settling-in allowance, and his high salary, he would definitely save enough money to have a good start in France. If his practice had been in bad shape, it was because he had been stupid enough to set it up in a spa town where, under normal conditions, a doctor worked only four months every year. He would remain here just long enough to be able to start up again in a sound position.

He had never worked in a hospital, but it was not too late to start, especially in this country where people were clearly not hard to get along with. Besides, he would have with him Chambord, who, if the need arose, could always intervene. He spoke the same language as these poor people and was a man of color. He was an ideal partner.

A bat flew into the room and knocked against a partition. This abruptly ended Quintaine's happy thoughts. He had forgotten how dangerous this damned country could be. How careless of him leaving the window open so long!

Armed with a tall broom he found in the corridor, he attempted to chase the creature, to catch it with a blow and kill it. He shook the broom as he twisted his body to avoid being touched by the bat as it flew dangerously around.

"What's the matter?"

Chambord, alerted by the commotion, and still in his pajamas, arrived as the animal flew out through the shutters.

"Nothing," Quintaine said, naked and breathless.

"I heard you scream."

"Me? Scream?"

"That's what I heard."

"I screamed? How?"

"Never mind," said a tired Chambord, returning to his bedroom.

Quintaine picked up the towel he had dropped in the pursuit. He went to his room, untied the mosquito net, and looked carefully under his bed. There had been all those stories about colonialists finding a rattlesnake curled up in a corner of their room. He turned off the light, and darted under his mosquito net.

The room did not become dark right away. He looked up at the ceiling and noticed that the fluorescent lamp gave off a diffused glow. "That's reassuring," he thought as he turned and faced the wall.

* * *

Quintaine, snug in a leather armchair, was listening to Bertrand, who had a way with words, and who moved from one subject to the other with bewildering speed.

He was now in Cayenne less than twenty-four hours, and already he was sitting with the country's highest official. He had received a call as soon as he was up; it was the prefect, through his secretary, informing him that he would see him at ten. Quintaine did not even have the time to see Poncet.

"What time is it?" Bertrand asked.

"About eleven thirty."

"I don't have anything planned before twelve. We can talk some more. So, you were saying that your father was one of the first colonizers to try to grow rice in the Oran region?"

The Bastards

Quintaine had the annoying habit of always putting his father in everything he was saying. At his age, such a tendency was clearly ridiculous.

"Yes. Things did not work out as planned; he had to move to Camargue, and was very successful there."

"Do you know I'm from Algeria?"

"No."

"From the Oran area to be precise."

They discovered mutual friends. Quintaine's father had been a close friend of one of Bertrand's relatives. He felt almost part of the family. A maid appeared with drinks and cookies. They continued talking over aperitifs.

"My advice to you is to leave for Saint-Laurent by Monday."

"Why so soon? It's already Saturday, and I've got some shopping to do."

"I know why I'm saying this. If necessary, you'll return on official business in a few days. But it's important that you start work as soon as possible. Besides, your voucher is being prepared right now for the flight on Monday."

Chambord had hinted that he would not take the matter lying down. If the position in question had someone assigned to it, then he would not have a leg to stand on for the time being. Everyone would sympathize with his misfortune, but tell him that the department could not undertake any additional expense to recall Quintaine, and send him, Chambord, to Saint-Laurent.

"There aren't any buses, then?" Quintaine inquired.

"No roads to speak about. Over here, the plane's the only decent means of transport."

Another plane, more air pockets, more flying over an impenetrable forest, those bumpy landings . . . Quintaine was not exactly thrilled at the prospect.

"It's safe traveling like that?"

"What do you mean?"

"You have to fly over jungle. Is it a long flight?"

"One hour. Maximum one hour and a quarter to cover the seventy-five miles between here and Saint-Laurent. There are never any accidents."

The Adopted Family

It would have been more correct to say that accidents were rare. Bertrand's predecessor had narrowly escaped death some sixty miles from Cayenne. The plane carrying him and the deputy at the time crashed in a river, and the deputy was killed. There was even talk of political assassination. Another plane was rotting away at the bottom of the Maroni, near Maripassoula.

That accidents were not more frequent was really more a matter of luck. Because of weak radio transmitters, a plane could still fly more than fifteen minutes without ground contact, which would be reestablished only a few minutes before the plane landed.

As for landing the plane, this called for great skill on the part of the pilot and great resignation on the part of the passengers. At times, the runway, carved out of virgin forest, was too short, and the plane had to come in very low, skimming the tops of trees, and stopping a hair's breadth from their trunks. At others, as was the case in Saint-Laurent, mounted police officers chased away water buffaloes, sometimes with rifle shots, in order to clear the runway.

"What's Saint-Laurent like?"

"Very nice small town," Bertrand replied. "One problem though: too many ex-convicts hanging around. As you know, they make up most of the whites; their past and their present wretchedness definitely hurt us. It would be better to send those people back to France."

He was ready to reject the ex-convicts solely because these men—who, by the way, had paid their debt to society—hurt the whites' reputation. What was even more irksome to him was how well they got along with the population, which, in the end, saw them only as men just like any others, poor fellows, nice sorts, who have grown attached to the country and are simply trying to make a new life for themselves.

"Are they dangerous?"

"They're not crazy! They know that the slightest recurrence means the guillotine," Betrand said, pretending to slit his throat.

"So much the better, then."

Reassured by the fact that his life was not in danger, at least as far as that was concerned, Quintaine did not detect what was worrying Bertrand.

How could one demand respect from these blacks if so many whites were less respectable? Bertrand saw in this promiscuity between Saint-Laurentians and the ex-convicts only proof of the formers' Machiavellianism; they pretended to like the transplanted men, but in reality they were using them to extract vengeance from Europe. Such a conception showed a total misunderstanding of the Guianese way of thinking, for since the native was at heart gentle, tolerant, and hospitable, he was not capable of being as calculating as Bertrand thought him to be.

Consequently, most of the people under his command were psychologically unknown to Bertrand. His predecessor, although somewhat of a demagogue it seemed, had tried to become very close to the people, going as far as agreeing to be the godfather of a score of kids born on the other side of the Crique. He, on the other hand, did his best to avoid these people, which did not prevent him from making harsh judgments about them, however. Whenever he went to Saint-Laurent, it was almost invariably incognito, and on many occasions, he had left his official quarters and spent the night in a room at the police barracks.

"What's the hospital like?" Quintaine asked.

"Very big . . . too big even! Some top-level staff should be moved. Persons appointed by my predecessor are objecting to the way I do things."

That much was clear. It mattered little whether these people were doing their work efficiently or not, once the patients received adequate care. It was the way each one performed that guaranteed his administration's worth, and in Bertrand's eyes toeing the line was the sole source of favors.

Seeing that Quintaine looked dejected, he continued reassuringly: "I ask for only one thing: help in restoring order to the overabused finances of this department."

At first glance, this ambition did look legitimate; the desire to clean up the financial situation was basically sound, particularly when attempts were under way to eradicate abuses.

But reality was quite different. The increase in abuses had never brought any benefit to the masses. By asking those in charge of a hospital to reduce their orders for medical supplies, by arbitrarily restricting the list of products for the poor, they were punishing the innocent masses. Restrictions were placed on the hiring of medical assistants, throwing heads of families out of work; dispensaries were closed down, or normal operations were made impossible, which amounted to the same thing. Exceptional measures were taken to reduce the amount of money given as family allowances.

From the people's point of view, if there were abuses, they could only be on the part of those in power.

"As soon as you arrive in Saint-Laurent, get in touch with Gélazothes, the commissioner of police. He'll clue you in on everything."

"O.K."

Quintaine agreed, not without some reservation. In all circumstances, the medical profession was instinctively suspicious of the police, who, with their constant digging around, constituted a permanent threat to professional secrecy.

Gélazothes was Bertrand's eyes in Saint-Laurent. Every plane brought back to Cayenne thick police reports, with everything noted, tagged, filed, interpreted. An operation turned out unsuccessful? There was a report indicating that the accident could have been avoided had it not been for the surgeon's excessive sexual dalliances, or his playing bridge late into the night. A boat sank on the Maroni on its way to the interior? There was another report implying that the whole thing had been staged to camouflage the theft of vast sums of money, part of which was probably destined for a certain civil servant from the subprefect's office. One of the European women was pregnant? A detailed list of her lovers, black or white, was drawn up, with the promise to see what the infant was like at birth. . . .

Among the whites, there were two distinct areas that

aroused the curiosity of Gélazothes, who fancied himself a specialist in General Information: private wrongdoing and an abuse of trust. As for the Guianese, they became interesting only above a certain salary range, when they were in the civil service, or above a certain income, when they were not. They were called racist, or separatist, or communist, sometimes all three at once.

A list of Gélazothes's deplorable literary works would have supplied material for entire volumes.

"What about Vincent, the subprefect?" Quintaine asked. "I hear he was chairman of the hospital board."

"Oh, him!"

"What do you mean?"

"Not to be trusted! He's part of the old team!"

His aversion for Vincent stemmed from considerations that were somewhat hazy. Vincent, the young subprefect, was in charge of nine-tenths of the country—an artificial administrative unit certainly, but a zone rich in mining resources, called the Inini District. This sort of state within the State had more or less the status of an overseas territory in the department. Moreover, there were scarcely any inhabitants, apart from a few managers and workers in the office of mine research and some natives.

Already it was hard to imagine a subprefect with a territory that was bigger than the department. Where things became really unacceptable was when relations between this district and the central administration were carried on directly, without passing through the prefecture. According to an angry Bertrand, Vincent had become the "petty king of the Inini."

There being no decent facilities anywhere else, the Inini subprefecture had to be located in Saint-Laurent; but Saint-Laurent was part of the Cayenne district, therefore part of the department. There was no way that could continue. This petty king had to be made to feel that they were doing him a favor by allowing him in a town that was not part of his fief, and that he did not enjoy extraterritoriality while there.

Like any other citizen, and no doubt more than others, Vincent suffered from Gélazothes's indiscretions. Even old escapades, going back to the time he was still a bachelor, were exhumed, accompanied by scandalous memos, and forwarded to Cayenne.

"I don't want to take up any more of your time, sir."

"Not at all, dear friend."

"I'd like to see Dr. Poncet today, especially if I have to leave Monday morning."

"See him while you can, for it's not likely he'll be here very long."

Quintaine, in pensive mood, strolled casually under the mango trees lining the square in front of the prefecture.

Over here, everything seemed so easygoing that it became embarrassing—a telephone call in the morning, and a well-trained orderly showed you into the office of the prefect, a silent maid brought you whisky as you chatted with her master, who was also master of the country. And to think that after so many years in France, he, Quintaine, had never been near, or even seen, the prefect of his department.

He already had some idea of what Saint-Laurent was like. Lines of demarcation clearly separated groups. At no time had they talked about the indigenous people; they must have no real existence. Only whites appeared to exist, summarily classified in three categories: at the top, those trusted by Bertrand, and headed by Commissioner Gélazothes; in the middle, those from the old team, men to be cut down to size, and led by Vincent, the subprefect; and at the bottom, the ex-convicts, the shame of Europe, elements that Bertrand had promised himself to eradicate. In short, everything was set for a white purification, done by whites to the detriment of other whites.

Quintaine felt caught, and, in spite of himself, he recognized himself among Gélazothes's acolytes. He would oppose Vincent, the main person running that hospital where he pictured himself introduced like a worm into a fruit.

Poncet received him warmly. He had phoned during the

morning, and Chambord had said that Quintaine had gone to see the prefect. He had not pressed the point, sensing the humiliation felt by the Guianese, who, for two days, had been cooling his heels while waiting for Bertrand to be kind enough to see him.

"I see things are moving quickly for you," Poncent said as he sat down.

"I should've seen you first, but the prefect called to ask me to drop by his office."

"That's better than I thought. Bravo!"

"He urged me to go to Saint-Laurent by Monday. My voucher's being prepared."

"In that case, I have nothing further to add."

Stung by Poncet's every reply, Quintaine felt unbearably uncomfortable. From the very start of his interview with Bertrand, Poncet had been on the carpet, criticized, ridiculed. He, Quintaine, was only now arriving in this country, and was unfortunately caught in the cross fire. The weather, the isolation, and the difficulty in adapting were nothing compared with that other climate, the psychological one, in which he would have to exist for the next two years. In Cayenne, it was open warfare; in Saint-Laurent, it was armed peace.

"What about Chambord? When do you think he'll leave?"

"The prefect didn't tell you?"

"We didn't talk about him."

"Do as you're told, and don't worry about Chambord."

Little by little, because of their respective rebuffs and disappointments, Chambord and Poncet had grown closer to each other. It had all happened without their realizing it; they had discovered their dependence on each other, despite the difference in their situations.

Chambord, with Faustin in tow, was in charge of the external sector, working at times in the suburbs, at others in remote areas accessible only by boat.

Travel on the rivers was terrible. There was a sudden change as you went from drenching showers drumming on the surrounding forest into bright sunlight slowly baking your body. You had to shout to be heard above the drone of the motor.

Dense vegetation varying in color from ultramarine to dark green, depending on the light, reached the water's edge, where it died in a maze of twisted lianas.

At dawn, noisy parrots appeared, flipping above the water from one undergrowth to the next. A giant anaconda, in a state of torpor, or simply unable to move after a meal, was wrapped around a large branch, almost becoming one with it, and did not move as the boat went by.

They crossed other small craft driven along by the rhythmic strokes of their paddlers. People hailed and greeted one another, then were out of sight at a bend in the river.

They reached a makeshift landing stage, and took a slippery path up to a dwelling-cum-dispensary filled with patients, most of whom had come from very far; one lived a half day away by boat; another had given up going to tend his land. Far in advance, they had noted when next the doctor would be coming.

Faustin had done this all by himself since Mme Hortez's accident, and he still continued his visits now that Chambord was around. He grumbled a lot, complaining he was overworked, but would have been very sorry if he were not allowed to visit these isolated dispensaries.

They returned to Cayenne at nightfall.

Chambord loved this life. The more the days went by, the more pointless all the intrigue seemed to become. He was making himself useful to his people; everything else faded in importance.

It was now some two weeks since Quintaine had left, and there was no word from him. No doubt a third order would soon come from Bertrand stipulating that Poncet's attacker would go unpunished. All those men who opposed one another would soon disappear, going off to wherever else their new postings took them. But Chambord and his people would remain. They would build this country. That was what counted.

One morning, as he was helping Faustin in the Crique dispensary, Chambord was asked to see Poncet about an urgent matter concerning him; it couldn't be discussed on the phone. He had to come over.

The door was barely open when Poncet shouted: "Quintaine has resigned!"

"You're joking?"

"Here, this is his letter of resignation sent by the prefecture. You may read it."

"No point," Chambord said, unmoved by all the commotion.

He had seen so many obstacles along his path that now that they were falling by themselves, he no longer felt like continuing.

"I'm happy," Poncet continued. "Quintaine received a hefty settling-in allowance; he's entitled to a first-class ticket back to France at department expense. We'll see what becomes of the famous abuse-eradicaion program!"

"He'll have to pay it all back."

"That's not in his contract. I'd give anything to see Bertrand's face right now."

An Unwed Mother called Guiana

Long have I wandered and I return to
the deserted hideousness of your wounds.

Césaire

CHAPTER ONE

"*Adieu Foulards.*"

The nostalgic, wrenching ballad touched those hearing it in their very souls. There could be no wavering now, despite the blaring of the ship's horn, a sound that made one's blood run cold, and brought a lump to one's throat. The record was worn. The overamplified scratching of the needle distorted the clarinet player's chorus.

Beside Cambier, those who, like him, were leaving, waved their hats and handkerchiefs. He recognized not a single face among that gesticulating mass growing gradually smaller on the quay. He remained fixed to the rails, anonymous, useless.

The ship left the harbor channel; the first perceptible rolling indicated that it was setting out to the high sea. Night was upon them, and the coast of France blended little by little into the fog. "It's over. . . ."

Cambier had spent two years in Paris, two years during which he had not dared attempt anything, or at least anything of significance. But life had relentlessly made an attempt on "his" exception; it threw him in the midst of crowds where no one seemed to recognize him. *Living Beings* adopted him without question. He was one of them, they felt, and that was sufficient. He did not, for all that, abandon his eccentricity. In the middle of the pack, where he nurtured that crazy aspiration of his, life did not give up trying either. Race, disease, certainty, all that should have isolated him and separated him from what he had in common with others, was under constant siege.

The first breach occurred when he saw Gisèle again.

His military background had made it easy for him to settle back down to university life. Although his move had taken place during the school year, he had been allowed to register, and to take his exam.

Transferring his scholarship money, however, took much longer.

For three months, he had cooled his heels in Paris, existing thanks to help from his mother, who could not understand this sudden decision to leave the southern sun. In her last letter, she had told him that she had to be admitted to a hospital. He saw difficulties she had not had the courage to mention. He wanted to deliver her from himself.

He should have accepted this new twist of fate that only reinforced a privilege he was enjoying; material straits, coupled with the segregation he had chosen, should, normally, have made him supremely happy. Instead, he had wavered; he wanted to *live*.

He returned to the ministry. In spite of the genuine courtesy shown by the employee who received him, there was still a touch of pessimism in his voice: "We've taken the necessary steps. Everything now depends on your former university. As soon as your file arrives we'll let you know."

"But it's been three months. . . ."

"I know; but that's a short time, really, for something like this."

As he listened, Cambier felt a sharp itch in his lower abdomen. He tried not to scratch, since the man to whom he was speaking was staring fixedly at him with sea-green eyes that showed little life behind thick glasses; this gave him a vague contrite look that was emphasized by his runny eyes. Though aware of the civil servant's indifference, Cambier nonetheless admired the administration's shrewdness in placing a weepy-eyed man in a job that dealt with so many hardship cases.

Each time the word *scholarship* was mentioned, the frustrating itching seemed to spread. And this word, a veritable switch that turned it on, was being mentioned over and over. He would soon be over the edge.

The door made no noise as it opened. A green file appeared in the space; it was held by a woman's hand glowing with nail polish. The civil servant looked toward the entrance.

"Yet another scholarship matter, probably!"

Cambier could not help taking a violent scratch. Gisèle entered.

"Just in the nick of time, mademoiselle! Perhaps you can help this gentleman."

He made the necessary introductions. Gisèle pretended not to know Cambier. Her soft, warm hand slid into that of the young man, who felt he was squeezing the neck of another Gisèle, naked, in his bed. He had wanted to kill that one; if she had defied him, he would surely have done it. Now this one was giving herself to him, with her fingers, oblivious of the risks previously incurred.

"What can I do for you?" she asked.

"I've been in Paris three months now. My scholarship still has not been transferred."

"Three months?"

Unlike the employee, who had no clue what had happened, he immediately caught the reproach in her question. He couldn't very well go to see her and say: "I almost strangled you. Let's not talk about it! I've just come to Paris, and dashed over to say hello!" He found no way out of his embarrassment without arousing the suspicion of the weeper, who, without realizing it, presented him with an excuse: "Please tell mademoiselle what the problem is in her office. If this matter is not solved by month's end, then you'll have to come and see me, won't you?"

He followed her.

In the corridor, she gleefully wiggled her hips as she walked, as if to excite him. It worked. Before opening her door, she turned around to see how she had done. He came close to her, quite close in fact, almost touching her. With all the skill of an experienced woman, she avoided him, and went into her office.

"Why did you come to Paris?"

"To continue my studies."

"Come on, be serious! The university you were at has not closed down, as far as I know."

It was Gisèle's turn to make her strength felt. The one who had humiliated her was now seeking her help, in order not to starve to death. She could not have hoped for a more opportune moment. He had spurned her desire; finally, she was going to have her revenge. She needled him: "You mean you actually abandoned your friends, your province?"

"I'm an individual. I don't need friends."

"I see that; cowardly animals travel in herds, the lion walks alone! Yet, it . . ."

"If you're settling an old score, you'd better let me know."

"You're conceited."

"Why do you say that?"

"You knew quite well I could help you with your problem, and you didn't condescend to come and see me . . . for three months."

Things were about to take a turn for the worse. He was trapped. His mother, from her hospital bed, could do nothing for him. He had brutally sacrificed his past, his friends. His fate was in Gisèle's hands. She could have done with him whatever she wanted, and he would have no recourse. It was futile disparaging Routine; he needed to live. He had to effect a reconciliation, to try to win Gisèle over.

"If I told you why I came to Paris, you wouldn't believe me."

She ignored what he had said. She spoke of herself, in order to bring Cambier back to the grudges she harbored against him.

"I've got my own way of doing things. When I'm brutalized, I get close to the person. I was sure I'd meet you. I wanted to."

"For vengeance?"

"To try to understand."

He was quick to accept the helping hand she offered him. He relented in the hope of softening the way Gisèle felt, without losing sight of the risk involved in such a maneuver. Did she not just admit her admiration for tough men? Intuition told him she had lied. They were both lying. She had mentioned masculine brutality because he had been brutal. It was a way of confiding in him. If she liked rough treatment, she wouldn't have been so afraid when he attacked her, to the point where her fear had neutralized that other fear, the one that would have stopped her from leaving his room, alone, at two o'clock in the morning, and making her way through dark, narrow streets.

"There's nothing to understand. It's clear."

"Come now!"

"I, too, wanted to see you again. But then, once I got here, I dillydallied."

"You were ashamed."

"Perhaps."

Thenceforth, they became friends. She agreed that, basically, he was a "nice follow," and that he became "obnoxious, because he was obviously spoiled rotten by women." She asked about Chambord, Turenne, and Sugert. He invented an entire novel: his friends wrote regularly; Chambord had left, and had set up a thriving practice. She swallowed all his lies.

She telephoned the Foyer. While waiting for the call to go through, she proposed: "How about us having lunch together?"

"Your treat! You think I'm that broke?"

"What are you getting at?"

"Then you'll tell me I'm too spoiled by . . ."

The sound of the telephone interrupted him. Gisèle discussed the case with the ventriloquistlike voice coming from the receiver. The director of the Foyer promised he would forward Cambier's file within forty-eight hours.

"See," she said as she hung up, "all you have to do is want things to be simple."

They had lunch at a Chinese restaurant in the Latin Quarter.

For several months, she invited him to her place, and he had her over to his; they were just friends. The scholarship adjustment he had received meanwhile allowed him to occupy some of the nights of his former one-night stand. Then suddenly, she told him this unexpected bit of news: "I'm getting married."

"You're joking!"

"No. I'm getting married to a colleague from the office."

"When?"

"Next month."

"Why didn't you tell me anything before?"

The Bastards

"I made so little impression on you. When you're out with me, it's like you're still alone. You go, you come, you take me for . . . I don't know what! You're distant, preoccupied. You, who had been so sublime down there!"

"Down there?"

"When I met you at the Foyer, then at your friend's place that time he invited us over, then even in your room. . . ."

"In spite of what almost happened?"

"In spite of that! Now, you seem spent, as if something was gnawing away at your insides. You're constantly on your guard. So, what's the use of continuing?"

"Spite?"

"Not even that. I'm getting old; I have to settle down. You understand what I'm trying to say?"

"You're annoyed with me, aren't you?"

"I repeat: no. There's nothing between you and me, not even sex. There's only this big void, and that never united people."

"You told me we were going out just as friends . . . so?"

"So what? It's not possible for you to have changed so drastically. There's something worrying you. You should tell me everything."

"I thought you were getting married. Why should I tell you anything whatsoever?"

"Alain, you'll be unhappy the rest of your life, and it'll be your fault."

"Coming back to this marriage, it's serious?"

"Yes. I can't continue like this. I'm long past twenty-five, and still unmarried."

"What's all this? You're the same age I am!"

"Same age, yes, but that makes you almost a young man, and me a grown woman."

"You've been through all the formalities; you have all your papers?"

"Everything's ready . . . You must be surprised that I'm still seeing you. Actually, what are we doing wrong?"

"What if I invite you to have sex, as you say?"

"I'm still single, therefore free."

An Unwed Mother Called Guiana

He became her lover once more, out of jealousy. The thought that someone else was going to have her made him want her passionately. It was only later on that he remembered that he was sick, contagious. But hadn't he already been her lover before he was told? He felt a sort of pity for her; she wanted to delve inside him, to track down the cause of his loneliness. She gave herself to him, deliberately, for to her he crystallized something that, while not being strictly love, was not sheer eroticism either. They had to remain friends, almost partners. But does a partner allow herself the sort of confidential disclosures she had made to him that night?

"I'd so love to have had your child!"

"Ah, he'd be handsome. A real degenerate!"

"What do you mean?"

There was something irresistibly moving about her. She arrived, in all her innocence, in the midst of a circumstance, and, without her realizing it, began to mold it, to make it *privileged*. Beneath her ordinary exterior, she held a fluid that meshed with Cambier and forced him to emit his own truth. When they were both face to face, he could feel this truth about to burst out of him, and he had only one alternative: confess or break the confrontation.

Already, in Montepellier, she had barged into his life, making it pathetic. The duo was broken up in the nick of time. He had then managed to pull himself together, and he had thought he detected a ray of hope within himself. There was no physical evidence of his wound, for, just as the stroke of a sword in water leaves no trace, his lips had immediately closed again, while an inner whirl spent itself out, the only hint of what was taking place being concentric waves that gently parted on the surface.

But this physical evidence had since manifested itself. It spun its spidery web in Cambier, foreshadowing banishment and death. He had created the circumstance in collusion with Gisèle, who, herself, ran the risk of suffering from it, like a foetus that poisons a woman and ends up killing her and itself at the same time.

The Bastards

Cambier experienced sudden stabbing pains in his chest, and he started sobbing. He heard himself cry and was unable to stop. It was horrible and unfair.

Gisèle cradled him in her arms like a child. It was painful for her to witness the downfall of someone she had considered, only a short time ago, so sublime, so strong, so sure of himself. He was pitiful; he, a warrior, a strong man, was relegated to the ranks of the persecuted and the vanquished. How right they had been at the health center to put up posters that proclaimed: "Syphilis: a flaw in human steel!" The germ was nothing. The flaw was nagging at him, in his head, pursuing him in the form of a complex.

"Alain, tell me what's eating you."

"What's eating me? I have syphilis! Everyone in my family has it. We've always had it, from father to son."

"What are you telling me? That's madness!"

"Syphilis, I tell you. Madness will come later."

"Whoever put such an idea in your head?"

"It's not just an idea. It has shown up in my blood. That's why I left, why I didn't want to start anything with you again."

"How long have you known?"

She asked her questions calmly. He had expected her to jump up, insult him, threaten him; but nothing of the sort took place.

"Come on, take it easy!" she said. "Let's try to make sense of all this."

"A few days before that evening at Chambord's, I had gone to the health center. There was a spot on my leg."

"Do you still have it?"

"It disappeared."

"What did they tell you at the health center?'

"They took some blood. It was syphilis. I only knew for sure after you left."

He wanted her to understand that he had not intended to do her any harm; if he cared little whether he came across as a brute, he rejected, on the other hand, any Machiavellian intent. She said simply: "You could have given it to me. How come my test is negative?"

"What? You did a test of your . . ."

"Of course! It's compulsory before you get married. Wait a minute, I think I have the form in my purse. I'll show you."

She sprang from the bed, and scurried, completely naked, to the couch where she had thrown her things. Her shapely posterior jumped around in the semidarkness, and disappeared through a doorway. She returned, immodest and sensual, equally indifferent to his gaze as to her own nudity.

"Here, look!"

He snatched the form from her hands.

When he began to read, a nauseating lump, like a figurine in a water-filled vase, stuck in his throat. This figurine whirled around, appeared larger, brushed against the walls, lingered awhile, and waltzed off, becoming smaller as it did so. This mad dance continued with the soft hum of a sleeping top. The movement reached Cambier from inside; a gust swept him away. He had become figurine; he had become top. He himself spun, and everything spun around him: pieces of furniture, various Gisèles, printed forms. The furniture passed by, dull and uninteresting. On a floating desk, huge molars of pink plaster, left over from the session at which the model was made, grinned grotesquely, imitating in the semidarkness someone whose face was disfigured and who was forced to present himself sideways.

He closed his eyes to chase away this hallucination. It was a bit as if he had pulled the curtains and plunged his inner self into darkness. He felt supremely light, almost absent. "I'm going mad!" Phosphorescences appeared in that darkness that had engulfed him. Two locks of brown hair parted to reveal a made-up face, shrouded in an unreal ashen color: "You love me, Alain?" He did not see the head that replied; he did not need to see it. He was behind it, behind the voice, inside this voice: "Careful, people are watching!" The warning was immediately ignored, reduced to nothing: "I couldn't care less! I love you. Nothing else matters. . . ." A burst of genuine black laughter quickly brought toward him an impassive face. The snickering belonged to this face, but it remained rigid and petrified: "I'm not getting it out of you: a consolation, you know!"

The laughter had given way to these words, familiar in tone to the ones that made Turenne so devastating at times. But another voice covered everything with its purulence: "A great Night: the certainty of existence!"

As he touched Gisèle's hand, Cambier shook himself.

"You read it?"

"Yes."

"You see for yourself; everything's normal. They even asked me if I wanted to sign up as a blood donor."

He had retained the name of the hospital. The very next day, he went there and asked for a blood test, saying that he needed one as he was about to get married.

During the week he awaited the results, he tried to recall the events that had led to his flight. The specialist had shown no conviction. Hadn't he simply tried to zero in on a case by the process of elimination? Why had he, Cambier, allowed himself to be alarmed? Suppose, all of a sudden, he were to learn that he was in excellent health, like the time when he was deemed fit for military service? The military authorities had sounded, analyzed, and x-rayed him and had found him physically perfect. Why hadn't he told the specialist this? In that way, he would have shed some light on his case and put him on the right track. Consumed with remorse, and devastated by a feeling of impurity he had not been able to back away from his personal drama and reduce it to real proportions.

The result was negative.

As it turned out, then, Cambier had worried himself to death for nothing. "Gisèle was right. I'll make myself unhappy all my life."

He had to write to Charlotte. She would forgive him his escapade. "She and her aunts must think that I was scared off by all that marriage talk, that their formal promises forced me to show my true self." And suppose Charlotte never replied? No, how could she not answer! But what would he say to her when he wrote? For instance, that for family reasons . . . Family? What about his father? His sisters? What disease did they have? Hadn't the specialist made some allusion to his ancestry and his relatives? His father's heart had given out; his sisters still carried an unknown evil within them. Didn't he himself have a germ, the germ, within him in spite of this result? He could not return to Charlotte without being certain, certain that he was pure.

* * *

For two years Chambord had followed the routine of his work at the hospital and had led an uneventful life on the banks of the Maroni.

Contrary to what had happened in Quintaine's case, there had been no one to meet him on his arrival. After a fruitless twenty-minute wait, he had had to get a ride in the van of one of the airline employees. Along the way, they had met Vincent: "Excuse me, doctor. I did hear the plane, but I couldn't leave right away."

This was not the first time Chambord had seen him, for soon after Quintaine resigned, they had met in Cayenne and had even had dinner together. Vincent had two hobbies: the hospital and ethnology. He wanted to reorganize the hospital and lived in the hope of proving one day that the Indians had immigrated from the Far East. During the entire meal, the conversation had been about those subjects.

Chambord climbed into Vincent's car, and was taken to the "Stone Shack," a sort of transit house reserved for visiting dignitaries. He rather liked the accommodation there: shower, W.C., a devoted, submissive Boni maid who, without fail, answered Vincent with: "Yes, Mr. Subprefect" at such unbelievable speed that the words made a strange whistling sound between her teeth.

But Chambord had to leave, and move to another temporary shelter while awaiting the completion of a dwelling promised by the hospital. That, of course, had none of the amenities. Furthermore, there were many rats, huge, grey, hairy creatures, with white tails, that scampered all night around his mosquito net. "That's nothing. They're opposums!" one of his countrymen had told him by way of consolation.

At the hospital, he had come face to face with a blatant conspiracy. Were all the supervisory positions not held by whites?

The Bastards

What on earth was he doing here among these people? In spite of his status as resident, he lived about a mile from the hospital. This meant that he was forced to walk this distance four times a day, sometimes in the broiling sun, sometimes in the rain. Once, a heavy shower caught him midway; by the time he reached his house, his pants had shrunk a good few inches.

In the absence of private doctors, he had been asked to organize a series of house calls, but there was no vehicle available. There was the ambulance, but, according to Vincent, "it must be used only for the seriously ill patients."

Chambord had grown suddenly stiff: "Under those conditions, there'll be no house calls. Those who need to see me will bring their sick here, or will come and get me by taxi." How naive of Chambord! The members of the board, despite their surprise, could not help smiling. Just as there was no running water, no hotel, there weren't, there had never ever been any taxis in Saint-Laurent. Surely, this "nice little doctor," as the vice-president referred to him, thought he was still at the foot of the Tour des Pins.

By happy coincidence, Vincent wanted to change his car. The one he was going to get rid of could be used by the doctor. The deal had been struck on the spot: the subprefecture of Inini had been lucky enough to sell one of its scrapped cars; and the purchaser was the hospital, which also belonged to the subprefecture of Inini.

A few days after that memorable meeting, Chambord had stormed angrily into the office of the treasurer, who was being replaced by a nun while he was on leave.

"Sister, this cannot continue."

"What?"

"My house is abominable. No water: the tank is clogged with leaves and other debris. There's no W.C. . . . ."

"You have a chamber pot."

"Yes, since you mention it. It's awful."

"What do you mean awful?"

"Build me a septic tank."

Thereupon, the saintly woman gave one of those delicious replies that brought Chambord back to his place: "But, doctor, you're being rather difficult; all your countrymen are in the same boat."

Well, yes. For all the doctor that he was, he was still one of a carefully catalogued whole. People referred to the stone and bronze ages; he and his kind clearly had not yet reached the age of the septic tank.

Thus, in a few days, he had been able to obtain an idea of where he stood in that hospital. Vincent was undoubtedly the nicest of the whites. On one of his trips to France he had secured significant funding and had given Chambord the go-ahead to erect, according to his specifications, a building for those patients with tuberculosis. But, as soon as it came time to grant it official status, a certain reticence had become apparent, for by doing so the administration was at the same time removing it from the exclusive authority of the subprefect.

Chambord saw Vincent frequently, and this annoyed Gélazothes, who would have liked to have one of his spies among the hospital management. All the same, Chambord did not go along with all of Vincent's ideas. They had disagreed violently over a question of medical fees. Another time, Vincent, upon his return from a mission to the interior, had spoken of the border *between France and Brazil,* and Chambord had taken exception to that insult to Guiana. "Furthermore," Vincent had replied, "I sincerely believe that the Maroni separates France and Holland!"

That, then, was the country Chambord had *chosen,* a vast alluvial plain—marshy, empty, forgotten. A border river, the Maroni, oceanlike, blue at dawn, yellow at midday, green then black at dusk, dotted with lush green islands; a river separating two European nations: on one side, Holland; on the other, France. Twice a day, the liquid giant shook itself from its torpor, rose up at the onslaught of the rising tide, and the current changed direction. All around, a raging forest at the edge of the village, ready to swallow it up, was already attacking it at ground level with its encroaching undergrowth. Between these two forces of nature, there were those people, the society he wanted to serve: a forgotten world that seemed not to exist. There were two forces present: a river, a forest. Two forces that were themselves part of two nations: France and Holland. Beyond that, nothing.

Nothing! That was really what his country was. A land he thought was his, but where nothing belonged to him. "Are we mere tenants on our own soil?"

No one denied his claim to be Guianese; not at all. In fact, from a folkloric point of view, it was even recommended; he could be of immense help to colonialism's perpetrators. "You who stand in judgment on us, take a look at what we made of this boy: a doctor!" One almost got the impression they had taken the necessary examinations for him.

Yes, no one denied him his claim; only it had no real value. He had a choice: either admit that as a Guianese one was out of it and suffer the resultant integration that, in theory, made one assimilated, but, in practice, turned one into a lifelong debtor; or reject self-denial, self-neglect, and expose oneself to the perverse accusations of flunkeys like Gélazothes. Wasn't he in exactly that situation now? Wouldn't his every attempt at restoring his self-image come up against those same facile arguments: communism, racism, secession?

The more he thought about it, the more he saw the impasse disappearing. It was now as thin as a thread: on one side, self-neglect and a few crumbs in return; on the other, the refusal to self-destruct and the attendant hatred and persecution. They had made him a tightrope walker, and the rope on which he was advancing was gradually becoming frayed. Could he reach the end before it broke?

"I'm too alone. Others do not understand me." Would he ever be understood?

He was sitting on a bench, with the river flowing before him, and once again, he asked himself this same question. Would he ever be understood? In order to get to where he sat, he had crossed the place de la République, where a statue had been erected to commemorate the centennial of the 1789 revolution. Wouldn't it have been better to honor the 1848 revolution, which had brought about the abolishment of black slavery? Every year, this square was the scene of a celebration on the occasion of Schoelcher's birthday. The last speech had been delivered by Chambord who, taking advantage of the opportunity, had said all that was on his mind, what all his people ought to have on theirs.

He had scathingly attacked the mediocrity of the administration, which, by refusing Guianese the right to self-government, seemed to undo the work of the great abolitionist. He had refuted, one by one, the accusations of stupidity leveled against the colonized world, brilliantly rehabilitated his race, and castigated the politico-cultural alienation to which it had fallen victim.

Criticism was rife all around: the whites had grumbled, the blacks had expressed alarm; on both sides, people were afraid.

He had thought that he could open his people's eyes. He had taken his case to them, but his words had had little effect. Some had considered him with astonishment, had feared being compromised. "Oh, but you're getting into *politics!*" No attempt was made to understand; this word was uttered for its shock value, and no one waited around for the fallout. Did they not realize that the fact that they paid their taxes, that they did their military service, gave them the right to get involved in politics? Were they so bastardized that they gave their blood, opened their purses, and kept quiet? That an old man like Ségaye's father would refuse to lift a finger was understandable; but that some young people, surrounded by mediocrity, incapable of showing their full potential because of a lack of opportunity, should manifest such resignation was unacceptable. He had said to one of them: "You're expecting manna from heaven . . . a new Schoelcher!" The other, his eyebrows raised, his arms folded across his chest like a Buddhist monk, had smiled sadly: "At first, you want to reform everything; but after a while, you end up taking things easy." Wasn't that the same thing Faustin had told him in that dispensary at the Crique?

There he was, sitting on a bench, a stone's throw away from Vincent's private residence—the very Vincent who was beginning to understand him, and who had become his friend. How could one fight administrative incompetence if its perpetrator was a friend?

The Bastards

Shadows cast by the coconut trees danced on the waters of the river. In the distance, on the landing stage, the beam from an electric light swept over darkened spaces underneath the girders: the guard from the prison was doing some fishing. There was one who had no more problems, there being no more prisoners! He remained here as surety for a liquidation. He had been waiting for years, and in the end, he too had been forgotten. He did not complain; he showed visitors passing through around the *Transportation Camp*. Every night, he went fishing. He went to France on leave every other year, in order to rest from the *harsh conditions in the colony*.

Had Chambord tried something? He had wanted to jolt his compatriots awake. He had spoken to them in words that were new, direct, adapted to action such as was carried out in France. Was it not, for him, a contradiction, his wanting to exhort his people to free themselves, whereas he himself remained prisoner to an ideology, to borrowed tactics?

He had tried to act, so he could make it very clear he was not afraid. With the help of a few liberal Europeans, he had founded a cultural, apolitical club. The undertaking had been swiftly sabotaged by the usual means; intimidation and police reports. Gélazothes had broken all records. Those members with nothing to lose, since they were neither civil servants nor on contract, continued to frequent the club. Those who were more courageous paid their dues but did not attend any meetings. As for the others, they had suddenly become insolvent or invisible. Only Fedène and Méverit, though civil servants, were brave enough to remain faithful friends who kept coming. Gélazothes had gotten the better of them though, accusing Fedène in particular of having smuggled in a shipment of automatic weapons. It was possible to deny this sort of stupidity with some degree of success; but how could one refute the outlandish accusations of racism, communism, and secession? Hadn't Gélazothes, between two rounds at the bistro, followed by those other "rounds" with which he satisfied his unhappy wife, declared to some stupefied Guianese: "Your Chambord is a known entity, you know. The authorities keep a file on him in France; he's already been involved in some underhanded political matters!"?

An Unwed Mother Called Guiana

Nothing could be done against the lie, the mystification, the threat. A Guianese could not think of realizing his full potential. In his immaturity, he could only be wrong on the very meaning of his aspirations. Every one of his impulses was an error to be cured of; every one of his leaders an evil spirit to be avoided.

* * *

The liner had just left Vigo and its tattered brats illegally selling cigarettes and pestering you for the odd handout.

The ship's band was about to end a concert. The smoking room was full of passengers. It was then that the incident took place. Cambier came face to face once more with racism.

D'Ablancourt, a white cane farmer born in the Antilles, was the object of everyone's attention. Opposite him, a Marxist lawyer and an anticonformist agricultural engineer—both black—sat in their chairs looking important. They enjoyed seeing someone of distinction make a fool of himself. If d'Ablancourt had come into some money, he could not have behaved any better. He was shouting: "I was one of the first to build a dispensary for the little Negroes. Without me, you'd all be degenerate . . . and now you dare . . ."

The lawyer cut him off: "In spite of your money, it is you who are degenerate! Your inbreeding is slowly gobbling up your race."

Some passengers drew closer. A few Venezuelans, unable to decipher the subtleties of the French language, had what was happening explained to them by a volunteer interpreter. One of them was carried away by the encounter, and greeted each remark with a vigorous nod that made a huge cigar between his teeth move up and down.

In the end, d'Ablancourt left the room.

The engineer continued, for the benefit of his friends: "They're hopeless, these *békés!* On the one hand, they don't mix with the Europeans; on the other, they hate black people, the very ones making them rich. They remain mired in their negativity. What idiots!"

Cambier joined the group. The doctor, another black, who till then had not said anything, proposed a game of bridge. An obsequious cabin boy, white, set up a table for them, and brought a pack of cards. He disappeared after collecting his tip, a broad smile on his face.

"It's like that one," the lawyer said. "I know him well; this is my sixteenth trip. He's all polite today because we're still in Europe. You'll see how he changes as we get nearer the Antilles."

At the time of the slave trade, a slave had only to set foot on French soil, and he was a free man. Without men even realizing it, history repeated itself in a curious irony that favored the opposite: as Antilleans returned to their native lands, they encountered prejudice once again.

As for Cambier, who proudly considered himself black when he was in France, wasn't he in fact a mulatto, midway between d'Ablancourt and those who were at loggerheads with him? Hadn't he acquired, with usage, certain rights over his fellow blacks, certain debts toward the white man? He had never given any thought to this stratification, but a chance incident forced him henceforth to be on his guard.

There were only two days left before the boat arrived. The ceremonial gala was in full swing in the winter ballroom, despite the rolling of the ship that sent the passengers stumbling in space and lulled them with immateriality.

The tuxedos and evening dresses were all brilliantly bedecked with jewels, insignia, epaulettes, and Legion of Honor decorations. There were people of all sorts: whites, blacks, so-called whites, pseudoblacks.

The band was as lively as a seven-headed monster, each head bellowing in turn, or several of them doing so in unison.

In the midst of this riot of perfume, colors, and sounds, there was a drum roll, and the judges took their places for the fancy-dress contest.

What was d'Ablancourt doing among the judges? Uncomfortable in a short jacket that was definitely too tight, he held his graying crop of hair bent over in the direction of an English woman on his left. A red rose in his buttonhole was

crushed against the shoulder of the young woman, bewildered
by the atrocious French spoken by this gentleman beside her.
He was hardly bothered by this, and continued prattling in a
language he did not at all master.

The contest was about to begin.

A woman disguised as a cauliflower skipped by; she was
pursued by a man dressed as a chef, a shopping basket hanging from one hand, the other brandishing a knife. Applause.
The master of ceremonies was shouting himself hoarse, and
the judges made notes. D'Ablancourt's face became redder
and redder; he almost looked like a real white man, now that
the blood was going to his face, and put some color in his
complexion that, heretofore, looked like musty papyrus.

There was another drum roll and a clash of cymbals.

The stage was now set for exoticism: animated flowers,
tutus with roses, pineapple-woman with prickly hips and
palm leaves for hair; maharajah sparkling with precious
stones, huge ruby-colored turban, false moustache, false frills,
real paunch. More applause. The scenario was becoming
irritating.

Cambier went out onto the deck. As he approached, two
shadows broke from their embrace. Feeling that he was about
to be seasick, he went back to his cabin.

In the translucent dawn, mountain ridges stood out like a dor-
sal fin on the Caribbean island. The rising sun dotted the
bluish hills with eerie shadows.

Between the passengers leaning against the rails and their
friends standing on the quay, welcome greetings were being
exchanged. There were shouts from afar and anxious questions as the gangway was being readied at the side of the ship.

Cambier was ready. "Tonight, a plane will set me down
among my people as they grapple with their problems, my
problems. My mother and father are dead; my sisters are
wasting away in hospital."

He was about to enter a circuit where facts would have
their priority; the whirlwind that awaited him would not

come under control unless he, Cambier, managed to free himself. He was going to have to give up the privilege he thought he earned by being the exception. "There's no exceptional being; only problems have the appearance of exception, and it is this appearance that is blown out of proportion according to one's overall concept of them."

His dilatory thoughts had brought on a feeling of solitude, but reality had never deserted him, since he remained a complex individual, persecuted by his own visions. It had even placed the fate of his sisters once again in his hands. The clock marking the time for action was about to strike, and the ringing that vibrated in him tolled like a knell.

* * *

Fedène, comptroller of customs in Saint-Laurent, scratched his head lazily. He was bored stiff.

Since the founding of the club with Chambord and a few others, he had become choice game for Gélazothes, who cast around for something to pin on him since he had more or less exhausted all local scandals, past, present, and future; the overzealous policeman in General Information did his job so well that he would overreport the story.

All the same, that morning, it happened that Fedène's safe refused to open. If this bit of news were to get to the policeman's ear, what a tale he would invent.

Fedène stooped down and began to try some of the eleven thousand possible combinations. He became angry, cursed, and fumed; he couldn't have forgotten, Jesus Christ! There was surely a mechanical failure. But what good did it do him to know that? Only one thing mattered: he had to open this safe.

"You look real busy. You're changing your combination?" said a voice behind him.

It was Saivol, the agent for one of the shipping companies. He dealt frequently with customs as part of his job. His office was nearby, and he often passed in front of Fedène's door.

"I've got a blasted problem."

"What's wrong?"

An Unwed Mother Called Guiana

"This fucking safe is playing the ass. Can't get the damned thing open at all. I sent a telegram to Cayenne, and they said: 'Try to solve this one on your own, but above all, no blow-torches.'"

"If Gégé-the-terror knew about this, he'd already have an inquiry under way," Saivol laughed.

He too tried his hand at feeling the locks and turning the knobs, but it was all in vain. He finally suggested: "You've got to bring in a burglar; there are some famous ones among the inmates. They'll do it for you in the twinkling of an eye."

Warrant officer Fontès from the gendarmerie came and sat down heavily in front of Chambord.

During a mission in the hinterland, he had fallen over a tree trunk that was lying across a path. He should easily have been able to step over it, but, as it turned out, there was always a snake lurking underfoot at such times. He had tried at first to climb over the obstacle before rushing off. His boot had skid-ded on the moss.

He thought he had simply wrenched his back, but to his surprise there was now talk of doing an x-ray of the spine.

Chambord liked Fontès a lot, and the feeling was mutual. Had it not been for the presumed seriousness of the accident, he would again have teased his patient, whom he insisted on addressing as "Mr. Brigade Commander." All he would have had to say was: "And what's become of that famous buffalo?" and Fontès would have burst out laughing as he replied: "It stinks!"

This water buffalo had the annoying habit of preventing the planes from landing properly. On every occasion, it had to be chased away, and on every occasion it would return. Finally, to avoid any further complications, it was decided to kill it. It had been able to flee with seventeen rifle shots in its body. Riddled with wounds, it continued to cast its stench over the surrounding farms. And as soon as any attempt was made to corner it, it disappeared in the woods.

"You'll have to go to Cayenne," Chambord said.

The Bastards

Just then, the phone rang. It was Fedène on the line: "Say, old man, I have quite a problem on my hands. I need an ex-convict who's an expert safecracker."

"What's all this?"

"My safe is stuck."

"Well, that sure beats the buffalo story! O.K., I'll see what I can do."

He gave Fontè a brief account of Fedène's misfortune. With a smile that was one of mere politeness, Fontès took the visit register that listed the doctor's recommendations and limped off, one hand holding his hip.

"An expert safecracker!" Chambord sighed. There must be at least one hundred or more former convicts among the elderly at the hospice. Was there any expert in anything whatsoever? Now, they all boasted about legendary abominable crimes so as to make themselves respected.

There was Fernandez, but he was more of a conjurer; he knew remarkable card tricks, and with his lips alone, could make a lighted cigarette disappear and reappear intact from his mouth.

Since he wrote nothing but Spanish, he had dictated his memoirs to a colleague, a recurrent mental case confined to the psychiatric ward. He had filled an entire exercise book, which he had given to Chambord. In it, he told of having committed his first burglary at a bank on Calle Florida, Buenos Aires, in 1913; of having spent eighteen months in a Tierra del Fuego prison for this crime. Perhaps he still had his touch, but was he speaking the truth? The occasional scribe, though mad himself, had thought fit to add an appendix to the tale: "Do not believe Fernandez, he is totally mad."

Chambord summoned his orderly: "Alexis, get me Fernandez!"

After examining the safe, Fernandez sounded it very carefully, eagerly watched by Fedène.

"Even a novice could do this. The safe will be open in a flash, you have my word on it."

"Good, good!"

"Besides, it's an old model, similar to the ones I knew long ago."

"What luck!" Fedène added.

"But I want ten big ones for the job!"

Fedène jumped. Ten thousand francs! He couldn't very well be expected to come up with such a sum just like that, for an old rusty safe belonging to the administration.

"I've got to seek approval from Cayenne," he said.

To be on the safe side, he told Chambord what his patient was demanding.

"Let me talk to the son of a bitch."

Fedène handed the receiver to Fernandez: "Dr. Chambord wants to talk to you."

A violent rush was all that was heard from the receiver, and Fernandez could not get a word in edgewise. When the flood of insults had died down, he promised: "O.K., doctor. I'll give it a try."

A tiepin was inserted in a crack, as he pressed his ear against the steel, and turned the knob slowly. His face contorted, he waited for a click. From time to time, he chewed on his sticky tobacco to help him relax. This went on for some time.

"Nothing doing!" he admitted. "It's completely fouled up. Well, well . . . that's the first time!"

He left, cursing his bad luck.

Fedène's worry intensified. He again called Chambord, who had to be fetched from one of the wards.

"Hello, Chambord. Your man's a joker. You have to send me another."

"I'll see."

Chambord was not surprised at the failure. Fernandez also claimed he was a chef by profession. He had boasted so much that Vincent, a bachelor at the time, had hired him. And every night poor Vincent had had to eat a bowl of unappetizing left-over porridge for dinner, as a result of the poor quality of Fernandez's work.

While waiting, Fedène began to fiddle with the locks once more, and the safe opened. The second expert arrived shortly thereafter, but was immediately sent away: "Pity!" he said. "If you had called me first, everything would have been over a long time ago. Fernandez is a braggart, absolutely no good, just a lot of hot air! Me, I . . ."

"That O.K., that's O.K." Fedène interrupted.

* * *

They drove along in the dark of night with the forest and its noises on both sides of them. Huge moths flitted in the beams of the headlights before smashing against the windshield with a light thud. Small animals darted hither and thither on the asphalt and headed for the ditch when the car came too close to them.

The taxi, after passing through the Crique with its foul smell, headed for the heart of Cayenne. The harshly lit, perfectly straight streets were no longer a deathtrap. As midnight approached, patrons had left the cafés, and the last strollers had deserted the sidewalks.

A short distance from the prefecture, the grass in the vast square bristling with century-old palm trees was damp and intermittently showed patches of light from the nearby lamps.

The car stopped in front of a hotel.

"Get some rest. Tomorrow we'll talk about all that again."

Cambier looked at the taxi with his uncle driving off. At the airport, this uncle had seemed tense, had looked older than his years; he had embraced his nephew somewhat coldly. His wife was not with him.

"Auntie is not with you?"

"She sends her apologies. She feels rather low these days. Since it's so late . . ."

"I understand."

Cambier was forced to dash off in search of a taxi. When he had managed to find one in all the hustle and bustle, he had to carry his two suitcases himself. His uncle climbed in, settled down as best he could, and only spoke when he had to answer a question.

"And how are Caroline and Hortense?"

"All right, I guess."

"You must see them often. How are they doing? What's wrong with them?"

"They're improving."

"Come on, let's have some details. Did you tell them I was coming?"

Fearing that his letters would go astray if he wrote directly to the hospital, he used to write to his sisters in care of his uncle. They never wrote. He had insisted that they be told personally of his arrival.

The reply he received this time caught him by surprise.

"I wrote to them."

"They're not here?"

"They've been moved to Saint-Laurent."

"Oh! That's news to me."

"Actually, they were transferred several months ago; your aunt and I preferred to wait till you got here to tell you. We didn't want to scare you."

"He's the perfect type for this sort of underhandedness," Cambier thought. In fact, it was really the aunt who was like that—an Afro-Asian mulatto who appeared so gentle, but who was very firm and all the more effective since she operated on the sly.

There would be some more questions for this reticent uncle, who evaded attacks. His sudden nod to the chauffeur cut short Cambier's spurt of questions.

Cambier was thus going to spend his first night quite close to his sisters without having received any clarifications; there would be a sleepless night, filled with conjectures, between the enigma and himself.

The following morning, he hurried over to his uncle's; he found his aunt alone and by no means in low spirits. He thus remained very distant in the face of her welcome.

She glided over to him, enveloped in a kimono that hid her feet and made it look as if she was airborne. She showered him with kisses. The suffocation he felt produced erratic quivering in his throat, and a network of bluish, swollen veins could be seen throbbing.

"My son! At last you're here!"

"Uncle is out?"

"He went to the post office."

"Will he be long?"

"Just long enough to check our post office box . . . Tell me, how was your trip?"

"I'd like some news about Caroline and Hortense."

"Your uncle didn't tell you anything?"

"It was difficult, in the taxi."

"Caroline is in the hospital in Saint-Laurent, and Hortense is at the center for the treatment of Hansen's disease, not too far from Saint-Laurent."

"Hansen's disease? She's with lepers?"

"But she's almost cured now. She went there to recuperate."

"And why wasn't Caroline kept here?"

The uncle arrived at this juncture. He had been caught in a shower on the way. He shook himself on the doorstep, and put below the verandah an old umbrella he kept constantly with him.

"Not too tired?" he said as he embraced Cambier, almost stealthily.

"I've come for news of my sisters."

"Your aunt didn't tell you?"

Their manner of placing the ball in each other's court was beginning to be annoying. Earlier on, he had to keep quiet because there was a third party present; now, these two were refraining from talking, so as not to repeat themselves. They had been afraid to tell him anything sooner because they did not want to scare him; now that he was on the scene, they still had this absurd fear. He guessed what they were thinking. The more they beat about the bush, the more he despised them. In their minds, his return had been possible only because they had kept quiet. They were conscious of the fact that they had trapped him, for, in his place, they would not have returned on their own to face such calamities.

"Listen!" he said. "I must know. Legally, the fate of Caroline and of Hortense depends on me."

"You're right."

"So, what is Caroline doing up there?"

"It's the psychiatrist who decided to transfer her."

"She's so bad that he's giving up?"

"You shouldn't exaggerate."

"How does one get to Saint-Laurent?"

"You want to go there?"

"How can I arrange it?"

"Well, there are three flights a week. One should be leaving in two days, I believe."

"Why 'should'?"

"You must always expect a last-minute change: mechanical trouble, special flight on another airline."

"And how can I make a booking?"

"The agency is right next to your hotel."

Cambier got up. He paid scant attention to his uncle's final recommendations, for he was anxious to purchase his ticket.

* * *

The consultations lasted forever as the patients lapsed into relating their stories. Each one had a special case to bring up. Stories of a personal nature often overshadowed medical matters: one woman complained she was overworked, drained by too many children, and a lazy, demanding husband; another was unable to procure all of her prescribed medication because her medical allowance had been unfairly cut.

Chambord was called to witness, as if to push him to intervene for those who confided in him. His people had finally adopted him. He was happy to feel that they all came to him with their personal problems. He remembered something from Duhamel that he had written on one of the endpapers of the consultation register: "A doctor is a man who, either because he likes to or because he has to, meddles in what does not concern him." But wasn't he, Chambord, entitled to meddle in everything that concerned the lives of his fellow countrymen?

"Next!"

A woman of about fifty entered, a smile of confidence on her face. She and her family thought a lot of Chambord, who had always responded promptly whenever they called, even at night.

The Bastards

"It's my brother who keeps insisting that I come and see you. I wonder if it's worth bothering you for such a trifle."

After giving her a thorough examination, he said: "You have to have an operation as soon as possible."

"Why?"

"There are ganglions already . . . from that little lump there. You have to act quickly. That's the best way to avoid an unpleasant surprise."

"You think so?"

"I'll give you a note for the surgeon."

"No use. I'll go to Suriname."

"You can have a safe operation right here."

"I prefer to *cross the border,* to see a Dutch doctor."

"And why is that?"

"No real reason . . . I have family over there."

Every time he had tried to find out what caused some patients needing surgery to make such a trip, he had come up with the same result: "they preferred" . . . "no real reason" . . . "family over there" . . .

At first, he had insisted, had stood up for his local counterpart, but his zeal had quickly dissipated when faced with this wall of excuses, inferences, and bouts of silence. And, he wondered, would his counterpart have stood up for him, Chambord? Wasn't their relationship characterized for some time precisely by a lack of relationship?

"Enjoy your trip, then. If the Dutch surgeon thinks that you need postoperative care, let him drop me a note."

He stopped examining another woman patient to take a phone call.

"Hello, doctor! This is the post office. There's a telegram for you. Shall I read it?"

"Sure."

"Arriving Saint-Laurent tomorrow by scheduled flight. It's signed: Alain Cambier."

He thanked the person on the other end and hung up. "Well, Cambier's back! Returning like that, out of the blue, that's just like him!"

An Unwed Mother Called Guiana

He returned to the room where his patient, perched on the examination table with her legs spread apart and her heels resting in the stirrups, was holding a speculum in place with her fingers. He adjusted his head mirror, took a pair of forceps he used to hold swabs, and set to work once more.

"Tell me, doctor, is everything all right?"

"The cervix is not completely closed, and there's still some inflammation."

She was about to be released from the hospital where she had spent a week. As soon as she was admitted, she had had to have her womb scraped as a result of hemorrhaging and severe abdominal pain. She had insisted on returning to Chambord's care after the operation. She was a white woman in her early thirties. "*They* trust me with their lives, but question my ability to run my own."

"I'm going to prescribe something for you at home."

As she put her clothes back on, he went to his office and opened a file in which he wrote his observations, though he stopped short of making a diagnosis.

She came over and sat down.

"You think everything's fine, doctor?"

"Sure looks so. At any rate, you can't afford to take that sort of chance. It could backfire on you next time."

"I don't want any more children."

"You'll just have to avoid conceiving them, then. There are lots of ways."

"That's a lot of crap!"

"Not so fast! Don't forget that this type of affair can reach the ears of the police."

"Gélazothes doesn't scare me one bit," she said. "He'd better check out what's happening right under his nose instead of sticking his nose in other people's business."

She was obviously referring to the latest scandal involving the commissioner who had beaten his wife to a pulp after an official ball at the Town Hall. He had not forgiven her for dancing with one of Vincent's staff.

She smiled pensively as she shook Chambord's hand. He felt

The Bastards

some measure of pity for this woman grown old and ugly before her time. He wrote on the observation sheet: "Diagnosis: Miscarriage."

Someone entered. It was Rinefour. A Guianese businessman, and a great lover of tennis despite a recent fracture of the wrist caused by a crank handle, he was young for his years. Taking advantage of his handicap, he had again started fishing, and often took Chambord along with him.

"I didn't come for an examination."

"Obviously not, looking as healthy as you do."

"I could have had an accident, like the last time."

"You never know, you may have fallen on your ass during a game."

They burst out laughing. They spent some good times together. Almost every night, they would shut themselves up in the back of the store with Reyor, Rinefour's partner, and jokes would flow left and right until the wives came and called their husbands away. Chambord would skedaddle off, his old car noisily backfiring along the avenue.

"What brings you here?"

"I just heard that giltheads are plentiful. How about a spin on the lake this afternoon?"

"What's the tide going to be like?"

"Rising a bit."

"Good! We must head for the strait that connects with the river."

"I understand."

"Yes, but my siesta goes down the drain if we go."

"You're worse than those Europeans. Two years, and you're still into siestas. Don't tell me you're thinking of taking a cure in Vichy while you're on vacation?"

This line of argument always hit home. Chambord did not like it to appear that he could not withstand the climate. In fact, he withstood it very well indeed, but it did take its toll on him. He thought it necessary to take it easy whenever the opportunity arose.

"What time do we leave?"

"Two o'clock . . . half past one, if you're free. We have to get the live bait ready before we leave."

Always the same old story! In the hope of catching one gilthead, you first had to sit there like an idiot for hours catching small fishes, and sometimes, with all the piranha, this proved somewhat difficult. Then you had to keep them alive in a bucket of water and lug the whole thing to the lake. Once there, you had to attach one by its back to the fish hook, cast your line, and follow the movement of the float as it is carried by the bait; your eyes would hurt from blinking, especially when everything kept bobbing up and down. You had to keep quiet, follow the float—that's the only way to tempt the gilthead. The float would suddenly disappear under the water. The fish would be eating right there, not hurrying. You would wait until the prey was well lodged in its stomach. That's when you would strike. After a short struggle, the wild catch, generally weighing several pounds, would be landed in the grass.

Chambord suggested: "All you have to do is what the Indians did. You put bottles with cassava flour at the bottom of the water. Then, every time you want to go gilthead fishing, you simply collect your bottles full of small fishes."

"I tried that. Problem is, there are people who collect the bottles before me."

"I see. O.K., see you at two."

Rinefour thought it a good idea to offer some further enticement: "It's mango season. There's always plenty of those if we don't catch any giltheads."

Then, without any transition, he added: "Say, I hear you played a joke on one of the nuns?"

"What nun?"

"The one working in the linen room."

"Me?"

"Yes, Some story about a bra."

"Story! There's no story. I had prescribed a particular medication for an old man in the hospice who was having trouble passing water. After his treatment, his breasts began to grow.

The Bastards

Since he was pestering me, I told him to go to the linen room for a bra. The nun took his measurements, and cut her cloth. I couldn't believe she would take it seriously."

"At any rate, the whole thing made all those old people laugh!"

At that, Chambord stood up. It was time to go to the dispensary.

CHAPTER TWO

For over an hour, the small plane had skimmed the top of the forest.

After circling over the Maroni, it made a bumpy landing on the clay runway overrun with greenery. As it slowed down, police officers once more struggled to chase away the buffaloes in the direction of the tall grass.

The pilot put down his headphones, then crept out of the cabin behind the passengers.

A few scattered vehicles near a tumbledown hangar spewed forth their occupants, who came and joined those from the plane. Among those people coming toward the plane Cambier recognized only Chambord, who flung his arms around him, happy to find a link with his past.

"Not too shaken up over those clearings?"

"Not really."

A gust of wind raised the red dust. Chambord led his friend to a car.

In France, his constant wearing of a tie, as he unabashedly followed the dictates of current fashion, gave him an air of unusual elegance, so much so that Cambier thought him a bit of a show-off. Here, on the contrary, he was in shirt sleeves and sandals.

As the car made its way along a potholed road lined with coconut trees, he started to prepare Cambier for what awaited him.

"This is the first time you've come this far?"

"Yes."

"Weird place. Nothing, besides the hospital and the saw-mill. Our people are wallowing in idleness and mediocrity.

And to think that Saint-Laurent is the second largest town in the country."

He was about to describe his world. However, what was important to Cambier was to see his sister again, to learn what was wrong with her, and what her chances of recovery were.

"How's Caroline?"

"Her condition is stable. She's managing to take an interest in herself. When I went to see her a short while ago, she looked as if she was aware that you're really coming."

"Why was she put here?"

"An arrangment between the psychiatrist and myself."

"An arrangement?"

"When I told him that Caroline was the sister of an old friend of mine from university days, he preferred to move her away from the cesspool that masquerades as a psychiatric home in Cayenne. Here, she has a private room. She can walk about the hospital."

Outside a small factory belching smoke, a few buffaloes casually crossed the road and forced Chambord to slow down. They were led by a man with tattoos, wearing a pair of shorts and a vest but no shoes; he waved at them.

"An old-white!" Chambord said. "You'll see others. Most of them are quite nice. They hit the bottle quite a bit."

Old-whites was the shortened term used in the local vernacular to refer to the former inmates of the Transportation Camp, of the *Great College* as the Guianese called it. The wound had been excised, but it was slowly forming a scar, and some condemned men were still around, thrown into the street by this radical operation.

"There are still many of them?"

"Enough! Some have been able to readapt; there are even those who have become middle-class."

The car sputtered around a bend and crossed the gateway to the hospital. The concierge, sitting in front of his lodge, was engaged in a game of checkers with an old man in striped pajamas.

Chambord observed: "You see! The establishment is supplying linen for the patients. The stripes are indicative of a type of survival: red when the prison was in operation, they're now blue."

He stopped in front of a white building with grey slatted shutters, in which his office was located. Of stone construction, the hospital seemed to Cambier really excessive. Sand-covered drives surrounded a dozen buildings.

"How large is the establishment?"

"Its size surprises you as well?"

"Indeed. For such a small town."

"Saint-Laurent had some ten thousand inhabitants in former years, and among them were a large percentage of convicts, who thought nothing of checking themselves in as patients. That was understandable. The doctors themselves were very complacent—we love to play tricks on the police. We therefore needed a large hospital. Since labor was cheap, no expense was spared."

"What capacity?"

"Three hundred and fifty beds."

"All occupied?"

"In the hospice, yes. Three quarters of the staff is posted there."

Two nuns passed by in a rustle of habits. The whiteness of their dress emphasized the paleness of their faces, but they were alert and, for all appearances, in good health.

"They're going to the community. The congregation insisted that they move about in twos."

"Why?"

"Never tried to understand . . . as long as they do their work well."

A sign in the front of the building read: Outpatient Examinations. In the corridor, patients with consultation slips in their hands were jammed on benches.

Chambord preceded Cambier into the office, put on a jacket, and immediately went back out. There was a grumble of impatience from the patients.

"I'll only be a minute. Please calm down."

They took one of the paths. Some vultures, all black like morticians, were pecking at things in a stream, and when the two men drew closer they lazily flapped their wings as they moved aside.

"Your patients don't look too pleased," Cambier said, still thinking about the people sitting in the corridor.

"They can't do without me nowadays; and the feeling is mutual, the only difference being that I've never been able to see myself not going back to them. When I arrived, our relationship was tenuous. I had the impression that they did not accept me. They obviously could not understand what I was all about. I cursed their lack of discipline, their indolence. As for them, they took my criticism for God-knows-what sort of contempt. In this void that separated us, we ventured forth in search of each other. . . . We can touch each other."

He walked more slowly.

"There was a wall here; it separated the private patients from those sent by the penitentiary. I was able to break it down."

Cambier found himself once more in the presence of this willing, enthusiastic friend who had such an influence at the Club. He rediscovered him, lost in this hospital on the other side of the world, grabbing routine by the waist. To work with, he had a population riddled with problems, in a dreaded milieu where the West had spat out its dregs. Chambord tried desperately to recover everything, to help in molding the country. For him, an ex-convict, whatever his past or his race, represented a share in investment capital. He was able to break down one wall and, at the same time, was starting on the other invisible one separating two worlds.

A small, worn-out man shuffled up. His feet pointed outwards, and this deformity forced him to thrust his pelvis forward in an obscene manner.

"Good morning, doctor," he said cheerfully. "It's my day out."

"Hello, Fernandez."

"I'm a real scamp. The greatest pimp ever. I'm going for my dough."

"You're collecting your pension today?"

Fernandez was a war veteran. After his expulsion from Argentina, he had arrived in Marseilles at the beginning of the Great War and enlisted in the Legion. Wounded, evacuated, and reformed, he had fallen into his illicit activities once more, and soon found himself in prison.

Although he had been relegated to the rank of outcast, the state still continued to pay him a set allowance. Society had vomited this undesirable body, but kept it going, prolonged its existence like those anatomical parts, like those monsters that find a sort of rehabilitation in museums built and maintained with public funds.

He approached Chambord and Cambier. Up close, he resembled an owl. He had a dirty cap on his flattened skull; his small, shifty eyes shone in the crescent of shade made by the visor on his sockets; his hooked nose almost reached his undershot jaw over his toothless mouth.

"My pension? I don't need it. I've got women in town walking the streets for me. Then, you know, there's no safe I can't crack. I just take a tiepin, and poof! it's all over with the safe, and I'm rolling in dough."

He hobbled away, his back bent, ridiculously thin in his linen suit that swung from side to side as if on a hanger.

"Totally crazy!" Chambord said. "A paranoiac. Most of them are mythomaniacs. They all think themselves former public enemies number one."

Totally crazy! Chambord did not realize what a blunder he had made. Cambier felt his heart leap as he thought that his own sister was part of this pitiful world of the crazy. He once more saw himself on that road he had made his own one day in his despair, the one for exceptional beings. The daughter of a middle-class family, sister of a dentist, was rubbing shoulders with extraordinary beings: the spineless, the perverse, murderers, the banished, who were sometimes supported because they had acquired "rights over us." His sister was isolated; she *could walk about the hospital*. Fernandez, a jailbird, had *his day out*.

At the other end of the path stood a wall overlooking the river, while, on either side, coconut trees rose in bushy columns, their shadows dancing over the hibiscus beds. Gaily-

The Bastards

colored humming birds flew back and forth collecting nectar from flowers.

A flight of steps led to the floor where Caroline was. Her room, though private, was no less a fortress: an iron gate acted as a double door.

"Get me the key to the padlock," Chambord barked at the young woman in attendance, who was looking at them as she wiped her hand on her apron.

Cambier caught sight of his sister through the bars. He was seeing her for the first time after so many years apart. She was sitting in front of a table, painstakingly brushing her long hair hanging loosely on her shoulders. She was humming a tune without any rhythm, her face contorting at the reflection of herself in the mirror before her. Against the pale blue background of the wall, her profile stood out like the exact replica of her father's.

She had heard them arrive. Why didn't she come toward her brother? Why didn't she offer him her hand, or her cheek, through the iron gate?

"Caroline! . . . I've come to see you."

She listened, but did not turn around. Her hand froze in a weary gesture. On the table, she placed a barrette she was holding between her lips.

"Marcel! Marcel!" she whispered.

Cambier clutched Chambord. Where was the stabilization everyone had spoken of? He found himself faced with a sick woman held prisoner to her autism, to her room-cum-cell, to the predestined environment.

"I'll explain."

The iron door squeaked on its hinges. Cambier walked toward his sister. As he leaned over to kiss her, she suddenly grew stiff, and as she recoiled from him, she tipped over the mirror. In the faint light of the room could be seen two fugitive shadows engaged in an unreal duel.

He wanted to reach out and touch her, but she eluded him, as if sick to the stomach at the thought of being touched. He said painfully: "Caroline, you recognize me. I'm Alain, your brother."

She got up and threw herself on her bed, sobbing.

He thought that seeing him again had made her emotional and was about to run toward her to soothe her, to reassure her. A face, full of hatred, looked up from the pillow where tears had left damp circles.

"What did you bring me?" she asked angrily.

"Look. Books, fruits, sweets!"

"To do what?"

"Well . . . "

"Listen to me. You too are against me, just like Chambord and the rest of them. You want to kill Marcel in me. I'm not mad. I want Marcel . . . I hate your books, your sweets . . . Love keeps me alive."

"Come now, Caroline, you know I'm on your side."

Her reply was disconcerting, the kind a mad woman would give: "Love, you understand? Love, that virgin hanging by her feet from the mast of eternity!"

Chambord joined in the exchange. His hypnotizing eyes stared straight at her. He sat beside her and held her hands.

"Caroline, remember what we agreed. No one here wants to harm you. I'm your friend. I'm the one who asked for you to be sent here so I could help you find Marcel. We must succeed. You promised you'd cooperate."

"I promised," she murmured, as if to convince herself.

"We must succeed. Alain is here. You must tell him what you expect from him, from us. He's here to find out."

"He's a traitor. His books, his sweets . . . all traps!"

"O.K., I'll take them away."

"No. Leave them. They are from Marcel."

She threw her arms around Cambier's neck. He felt warm lips on his skin, and that hysterical embrace had the same chilling effect as an act of incest. He could not bring himself to ease out of it. As he looked over his sister's shoulder, his eyes pleaded with Chambord. His friend made a sign indicating that he was going to leave, then tiptoed out as Caroline drowned herself, and her brother, in a show of effusiveness.

* * *

The orderly took Cambier's suitcase, and accompanied him to Chambord's residence, the back door of which looked directly onto the hospital. They came to a large living room where the windows were wide open.

"The bedrooms are upstairs," the orderly said.

He refused the tip that Cambier, still accustomed to certain metropolitan practices, had spontaneously offered. He continued: "Doctor says that if you want some refreshments, there's beer in the refrigerator."

"Very well. What's your name?"

"Alexis."

"Been here long?"

"Thirty years."

Cambier went no further. He had understood that Alexis was an old-white, a man who must have come to the Great College quite young, for he seemed to be in his fifties.

In turn, Alexis asked him: "A relative of the doctor?"

"A friend. My sister's undergoing treatment here . . . Mademoiselle Cambier."

"Cambier?"

"Yes. The mad woman."

He regretted having called her mad. He had pronounced the word like an exorcism. Mad! That was how far his father's prejudices had taken him. The venom spat on Caroline had pushed her to the edge of despair, but the daughter had retained the imprint of the paternal mold. The resemblance, like an avenger, grew even stronger beyond the madness and death.

"The doctor takes good care of Mademoiselle Caroline," Alexis said, as he bowed his head and moved away, visibly upset.

Cambier poured himself a glass of beer and sat down on a red couch. The day he had landed in his country, he still had the impression that his sister was part of a long line of family illnesses. By the following day, he began to have doubts. Doubt had gripped him as soon as he was up, following a telephone call.

He was lathering himself with shaving cream before the mirror. Beneath this daily coat of ermine, his face looked like that of a demipatriarch: jet-black hair, snow-white chin. The telephone rang and surprised him with his shaving brush in his hand.

"Hello, Doctor Cambier?"

"*Mister* Cambier! I'm not a medical doctor, only a dentist."

He did not recognize that voice which, after the initial flattery, now proceeded to address him in very familiar terms: "I just heard you're here. Did you have a pleasant trip? What do you think of your country?"

He was becoming angry. A shadow was pursuing him right into his bedroom, was questioning him, and was avoiding identifying itself.

"Who is this?"

"Daubrant."

"Who?"

"Marcel Daubrant, your friend José's brother. You remember José, your childhood buddy."

"Of course!"

"I'm his big brother."

"Oh, yes! What was I thinking of? How's life with you these days?"

"Same as usual; I'm in business. Can you have lunch with me today? I'll pass by and pick you up in the car."

"O.K. What time?"

"About quarter past one, after we close."

He returned to getting ready and could not stop thinking of Marcel. A particular scenario sprang to life before his eyes; many sequences were missing, but he began to picture certain tableaus.

The Daubrants lived quite close to his house. Their café was the focal point for a clientele of initiates who saw their vocation as being to prove how great rum really was. Marcel, a robust athletic type full of rich African blood in his veins, and Caroline were in love. Cambier's father was not at all pleased with this: "Who does this Negro, this bar keeper, think he is?"

In spite of the scandals and the threats, his daughter held firm. She would spend endless hours on the balcony waiting to catch a glimpse of the young man. The two had concocted a system of communication that the father had finally discovered. "Never, you hear me, never will I accept this ragamuffin in my house!" This outburst would bring on his heart attack; he would slump down in a chair, and his wife would give him some drops. Caroline would scamper off to her room and shut herself in, heaving with sobs.

Marcel came by for Cambier at the agreed time. How little he had changed! A handsome man, very dark, meticulous in his dress, as if to reject prejudice; his American car, sparkling with chrome, took them to a hotel restaurant near the Bourda beach.

All along the way, Marcel remained silent. He had shaken his young friend's hand with such warmth that it had left Cambier embarrassed. His actions betrayed exactly how he felt; no words could have made these feelings more tangible.

He drove fast, without any hint of ostentatiousness in his movements, but the worried look on his face, and the lengthy bit of ash he forgot to flick from his cigarette, betrayed the nagging presence of memories. With the car purring peacefully along, and with its driver pensive and despondent, conversation was out of the question.

The restaurant was almost empty. Fans toiled unsuccessfully at making the air more refreshing, while the Afro-Cuban music coming from a speaker went virtually unnoticed.

"What will you have as an aperitif?"

"Whatever you have."

"I'm a rum-punch lover, you know."

"Then I'll have a rum-punch too."

Marcel clapped his hands to get the waiter's attention.

"Two punches, with lemon!"

He got straight to the point. What was on his mind spilled out like a hiccup.

"Any news about Caroline?"

"Yes. From my uncle."

"Oh, him!"

He hated Cambier's uncle. Soon, there would be two of them hating him.

"You don't seem very fond of him."

"Son of a bitch! He's another one of those people making much of their light skin, apparently forgetting that his mother is black."

Cambier felt sure that the uncle was ashamed of his own

mother. Previously, when he had wanted to find out how she was doing, he had been told that they only saw her every now and then and that they hadn't been able to tell her he was coming. He had nevertheless hurried over to see her, only to find her all alone, lacking affection, but wonderful as always.

The mere fact that he brought up the conversation he had had with his uncle and aunt concerning his grandmother meant that he was siding wholeheartedly with Marcel.

"Say, Marcel, why don't you tell me what happened with Caroline and yourself?"

"That's simple. Your father, for all his insults, was a nice fellow. The only problem was that he carried no weight as far as his brother, his wife, and his sister-in-law were concerned. So, he preferred to torture Caroline, to keep her from everyone rather than give her to me, despite the proof!"

"What proof?"

"Listen, Alain, what I'm about to tell you is very serious. Right now, it's only your uncle, your aunt, and I who know about it, since the others are either dead—your father and mother—or unable to remember—Caroline. Sorry I had to burden you with such a list!"

Cambier was deeply moved by the mention of this sorry honor roll, but he did not hold it against Marcel. A floodgate had just been opened; the sudden gush of freedom must inevitably cause splashing.

The waiter returned with his tray. As he leaned over, he grazed Cambier's face with his tinsel epaulette. He apologized profusely, despite protests designed to have him leave as soon as possible. Would Marcel continue his tale?

"We might as well place our orders now," he said.

"I'll stick with the set menu."

"Why?"

"I'm not very hungry."

"Oh!" he said, disappointed. "Have you seen what's on it?"

"No."

"Let me read it for you. Hors-d'oeuvre . . . "

"Assorted, of course."

"Exactly. Armadillo stew . . . "

"Armadillo?"

"Yes, armadillo stew. Rice creole, fruits. Good. And for wine, bordeaux?"

The waiter anticipated Cambier's reply. He asked: "Red?"

"O.K."

Marcel was sipping his punch.

"What's this secret you wanted to tell me?"

"Well, in the face of your father's objections, Caroline and I wanted to force his hand."

"And how did you plan doing that?"

"We met secretly. After a while, she told me we had succeeded. She was pregnant."

Cambier was visibly alarmed, and this forced Marcel to stop. In his naiveté and surprise he looked pitiful, and seemed consumed with menacing animosity, like his father who had suddenly found himself trapped under a landslide and was forced to wait for the enemy's shovel to rescue him.

Marcel, visibly disconcerted, waited for some encouragement to continue. He had said both too much and too little. He could not leave things where they were.

"Go on!"

He hesitated. He looked for words that would do the least damage, but all his efforts led only to cutting phrases that were all the more painful in their clumsy conciseness.

"One day, your father sent for me. I thought he was going to tell me something like: 'Caroline told me everything. It's impossible to turn back now; I'm forced to agree.' I expected him to give in meekly. But, instead, it was terrible. He was on the warpath. He closed the door to his study, shutting me in with him. . . . By the way, I remember there was a photo of you in a frame next to a bookend."

"Yes. Then?"

"Then he called me every name imaginable: ragamuffin, nigger, orangutang . . . You name it. He said he would never agree to give me his daughter, that he would do whatever was necessary to prevent it. Shortly afterwards, Caroline left for Martinique. When she returned two months later, she had not gotten any bigger. Soon after, she began having her attacks;

then . . . then they put her in the mental hospital because your mother was no longer there to take care of her."

The armadillo stew that Cambier had found so delicious, now made him feel sick. His father had refused to give Caroline to Marcel. He himself had used everything at his disposal to fight against routine, and only ended up missing Charlotte. Marcel's perseverance in adversity was similar to his. He surprised himself by feeling close to this man, even to the point of identifying with him. Race separated Marcel from Caroline to the same extent that it separated him from Charlotte. For him, the racial factor had not backfired, had not worked against him. But Marcel's case would be exactly like his, even if that gulf were suddenly bridged. Can one marry a woman who has lost her mind?

"Would you have married Caroline if she had a contagious disease?"

"Yes."

"Are you sure?"

"I'd have her cared for. I'd expose myself to any disease for her."

"You would?"

"Have you ever felt the need to have just one woman with you, one woman and no other? To take her just as she is, because . . . "

"Because?"

"Because without her . . . it's even worse."

If Marcel had had the slightest idea of the other drama, if he had, willingly, tried to make it more pressing, he could not have been more successful. From this man without culture had just come the postulate that had escaped him but a short while before: "I should have confided in Charlotte." She would have found in his *certainty* an antidote to the routine that had taken from her a man for whom everything became henceforth *even worse*.

Over dessert, Marcel made a confession that reeked of serene tenacity: "Socially, I'm a success. I have money, and my business is doing well. I have only to snap my fingers, and those little middle-class ladies would stand in line to marry me, and even the mulattoes at that! I don't want anyone else besides your sister. She wanted me when I was just a black man with nothing to offer. It has to be her or no one else!"

"Do you think she'll ever get over it?"

"I haven't the slightest idea. I want only her. It's no use the gossipmongers saying I'm a pervert, that won't change a thing."

"They're saying that?"

"You'll hear it sooner or later."

They were about to leave each other, and Caroline's shadow still clouded their every thought.

Marcel drained his cup of bitterness to the dregs. The rigidity of routine, after snatching Caroline from him, further burdened him with slander, in punishment, as it were, for having kept his certainty in the midst of such adversity. His negritude disqualified him in the eyes of those who, in reality, existed— at least in half of their being—only thanks to this African blood they hated him for. Their intellectual barrenness prevented them from experiencing that throbbing within them that came from the very Africa they denied. Thus, they believed that they could flatter their way into Europe's esteem. But Europe quite rightly despised them. Tomorrow, it will be victorious Africa's turn not to be taken in by their demagogic turnaround.

In the face of all their insults, Marcel remained untarnished, free to reclaim a continent at any moment. They, on the other hand, victims of their own carelessness, were already suffering the lot of bastards.

"I had to come all the way back here to face color prejudice again. Things are different in France."

"José understood that; he got married over there and no longer wants to return home. He'd be too ashamed."

"Obviously, when one has evolved . . . "

"It's more a case of thinking about his wife. He would be ashamed . . . for her."

Once again, Marcel, without realizing it, had set wheels in motion; a hill, steep, accusing, and strewn with stones appeared before Cambier, and like José, he was afraid to climb it. José had married and had given up his country, whereas he had given up Charlotte, and was now here. Hadn't they both yielded to routine?

* * *

Cambier looked at his watch. It was past one o'clock.

He crossed the gravelly garden where a few flower beds lay lost beneath tall, untended bushes. He went out into the street and felt as if he were stifling in his jacket. On the mud sidewalks, sawed-off tree trunks were piled helter-skelter. From their bark sprouted lush, almost explosive, grass. There was not the slightest hint of shade, except near the municipal tax office, where some surviving mango trees seemed to huddle in the sun.

He walked straight ahead, and was beginning to notice the swirl of the river as it struggled against the rising tide, when he heard someone calling.

"Hey! But that's Cambier!"

Saivol, an old friend from Cayenne, had recognized him. He was big and robust, and his legs bulged in shorts that were too tight. He was standing in front of the office of his shipping company.

As he came nearer, Cambier noticed the air of power Saivol exuded. They hugged so tightly, he felt his body would break. He was taken inside, and introduced to colleagues. He imagined these gigantic bodies reduced to the depressing demands of bureaucracy—still more of his countrymen forced to remain at a level far below their competence.

"I'm looking for the dispensary. I'd like to see Chambord."

"You're right on target this time. The dispensary's just behind here."

Saivol went toward a partition against which stood a pile of papers tied in a bundle. He knocked a few times and waited. Shortly afterward, a knock similar to his repeated the code against the wall.

"Hi, Chambord. I think I'll be forced, once again, to offer you an aperitif."

"Sorry, old buddy. I still have quite a lot to do here. Besides, someone's waiting for me."

"Is that so? Can we know if she's a brunette or a blonde?"

"Who?"

"The woman waiting for you."

"Jackass! It's a man."

"You caught me this time. I'd never have believed it. But you're excusable. After all, loneliness can make a person do anything."

Chambord paused. Saivol became serious: "I wanted to let you know that Cambier is waiting for you."

"Have him come over here."

At the entrance to the dispensary, there was an even bigger throng of patients than at the hospital. Over there, the patients paid for their services, were more sophisticated; here, they were mainly natives or locals: Indians or blacks who had gone back to the tribal way of life on the banks of the river, either upstream or downstream from Saint-Laurent, after escaping the yoke of slavery.

Potbellied infants clung to their mothers; Indian women in brightly colored material, with a shoulder or a breast exposed, took their places beside black women in their long wrap skirts. The men—fewer in number and wearing glass beads, and among whom was a sprinkling of old-whites—remained indifferent to the din.

This entire group of poor people, barefooted and oblivious of the vicissitudes of the rich, depended entirely on Chambord's wisdom to solve its problems.

"You're going to put on a jacket and give me a hand."

"O.K."

"Some want extractions. I'll leave that to you."

A female assistant took care of Cambier. He dressed and took up a tray in which there were pairs of forceps with parts of the chrome missing. He began to work on diseased mouths, while Chambord poked at bellies and listened to hearts. In that series of operations, he managed to forget all that was troubling him.

Suddenly, Chambord raised his voice. He was quarreling with an Indian woman in a language that Cambier did not understand. In a reflexive action occasioned by her modesty, she was stubbornly holding her hand over her pubic area.

When Chambord got fed up and energetically showed her the door, she finally gave in.

"It's always the same thing. They walk about almost naked, then come here and kick up a fuss when we want to give them an examination!"

On leaving the dispensary, they stopped at Saivol's office, where a bunch of happy-go-lucky fellows came to discuss things over a drink before going to eat. Their group was appropriately called the Destroyers' Club, to show in what esteem they held the punch-aperitif. If they neglected the early-morning drink, the starter, or the one at eleven o'clock, the booster, they appreciated the *destroyers* that came before lunch.

The group included Fedène, Rinefour, Reyor, and Rangul, the eternal joker who was now working in a business establishment, but who was seriously considering opening a bakery-patisserie. There was also Méverit, the schoolteacher, who was getting ready to return to his pupils.

All their lives, or almost all, depended on business in a country which produced nothing, and where the people refused to produce anything because, for a hundred years or so, physical labor had been represented as punishment inflicted on convicts. Chambord himself seemed to subscribe to this shirking of responsibility. He asked Saivol if he knew when the next cargo ship was due. This would afford him the opportunity to stuff himself with food, either at his residence or on board ship, in the company of the captain.

On every occasion, the shipment of food supplies arrived like manna from heaven in this region that allowed itself to starve to death in the midst of its untouched wealth.

At Chambord's home, an Englishwoman who came to do the cleaning and who spoke very little French served the meal.

Chambord ate heartily, washing the food down with ice cold beer. "Freedom revolves around choice, even if we choose not to be free." Was he aware that he was free? Where was the choice? Such were the questions that Cambier asked himself as he observed him.

Up to the time he sat down to eat under the sad, watchful

The Bastards

eyes of the Englishwoman, he did not know what was going to be on the menu. He would return home with a roar of his engine, leaving the car in a garage next to the room of an Arab guard—an ex-convict—and would abandon himself to the care of the servant, another one of those uprooted women who had fled her wretched island. Then he would fall off into a deep siesta from which he would awake all groggy before taking an invigorating shower. This represented an unending chain of abandon and escape. All these transplanted people abandoned themselves to him, and he in turn abandoned himself to his milieu.

Every day he found himself forced to listen to mythomaniacs and their ramblings, to see undernourished children, to fight the prudishness of the native women, to share other people's worries and misfortunes, to yield to the curiosity of a sleepy-eyed, distant servant, to be watched by a former detainee, with another ex-detainee, Alexis, being in charge of the mess.

Was he aware of his influence on all these beings? His life was an open book: in a hospital where some one thousand eyes were trained on him; in a dispensary where other eyes kept watch as well; in the streets where everyone tracked him down by the very sound of his old jalopy; in that apartment with its wide open windows and doors. He was a public character, public property. He belonged to everyone, and nothing belonged to him.

Cambier thought it all strangely pathetic.

"At last, another day's over!" he said.

"It's never over."

The words fell mercilessly on his ears, as if a sentence was passed on Cambier, who was left at a loss. Not content with giving himself to his milieu, Chambord now gave him the right to dispose of his person at any time. He made his admission without bitterness. What potion had he drunk to lose all awareness of his sacrifice in this manner? He had given up an opportunity for success in France itself. Was he still thinking of his former boss, of Farnabe, of his little provincial circle? How distant, how insipid that must all seem henceforth! Only the reality of a people was important. He had thrown himself headlong into it, spurred on by visions of hope. Had these not given way to resignation in this prison without bars, where any slight impulse to escape was thwarted by a void: the vast, peaceful river, despairingly innocent, and the forest, even more extensive, more innocently foreboding?

"You do have set hours, and time to relax?"

The question appeared to catch him by surprise. He put his glass down, and used his napkin to wipe away the foam from the beer, which was leaving a white line around his lips.

"Want to hear how I live?"

"Sure."

"Mornings, at eight o'clock, I arrive at the hospital and make my rounds in the wards. Starting at ten, I see outpatients till about twelve. Then I go to the dispensary and sometimes leave around two. I have lunch, and take a little siesta till four. Then it's back to the hospital for follow-up visits, x-rays, laboratory work, files to be written up, and classes for the nurses. Somewhere around seven, I begin house calls. At times, there are emergency calls at night."

"Where do you get time to relax in all that?"

"I do. I go to the cinema. If I'm needed, someone comes to get me. I go fishing or hunting with friends. By the way, yesterday, for example, I went gilthead fishing with Rinefour instead of taking my siesta; as a matter of fact, we came back empty-handed."

"You like that sort of life?"

"Would you believe I've put on weight! What more can I tell you?"

"Still, loneliness . . . "

"I'm not lonely. I've got my friends, my patients. In fact, they're becoming one and the same; with a bit of good luck, I can make a patient my friend; and with a bit of bad luck, a friend can end up becoming my patient."

"In the final analysis, you think you achieved all the goals we set ourselves long ago."

"You've touched the one point that bothers me. I haven't succeeded on that score. The terrain is full of pitfalls. There-

The Bastards

fore, I wanted to start a movement to jolt our countrymen out of their apathy. Some Frenchmen living here even agreed to help me, but in spite of that, we were accused of separatism. We were honored, among other things, with reports from the office of general information. We're being sabotaged from on high."

"And what about the 'colonial relationship'?"

"Over here, you see, colonialism is not so much a way of doing things as it is a state of mind."

"Our people . . . "

"They're suffering from the ambiguity of our situation. In their eyes, we're almost Europeans—I say *almost*—and they're happy with that. When we criticize a certain Europe, they don't understand what we're talking about. They question our good faith when we say that the metropolitan white has nothing in common with the puppets sent down here to us. We are not understood. The administration is not unaware of this malaise; in fact, it encourages it."

"In what way?"

"It isolates us by handing out, and often to our own countrymen, undeserved honors. In this town, for instance, several key positions are held by people without any academic qualifications or any competence. What can people like that learn from any reform, from any evolution in our status? Our intentions, however honorable they might be, will always come to nought, because they are consumed by this cancer."

The ambiguity of our situation! He had hit upon the correct way of describing their plight, and had said it without any attempt to explain it any more profoundly. Cambier would have loved to analyze it.

The river and the forest confined the world of all the inhabitants, whatever their race. In that sea of humanity, there were men burning with ideals in their hearts, men like Chambord, opposed to other men whose main concern was to safeguard a system that protected them.

As a result, there evolved an incongruous collusion, held together by demagogy. People were simply bought, were laden with honors to arouse that combative spirit that some wanted elevated to an ideology. It was necessary to enclose all the Chambords in an imponderable network, but the inept collusion was doomed to failure. At best, all it could do was set back the fateful date of a bitter and irreversible collapse.

Chambord drank in silence, lost in a distant reverie. His eyes never left Cambier, but he really did not see him. The periscope he wanted to use to look at his friend was working in the opposite direction. It was within himself that an eye was peering, revealing, in half tones, spaces of speckled shadow, dotted with diffused, moonlit clearings.

Cambier delved deep into his host, earnestly striving to discover him. What did he find? It was not Night, that impenetrable privilege avoiding capture like water in a hand trying to close around it. Nor was it dazzling brightness either, those innumerable facets with their constant sparkling that forces you to blink, to close your eyes in order to grope blindly along.

What he thought he saw, what Chambord really wanted him to see, constituted a compromise between pride and abandon.

Chambord controlled himself, clearly delimited his eagle's nest, and, at the same time, kept his eyes fixed on the paths leading to it—those paths stewn with flint, paths of servitude, that all his countrymen were condemned to travel in both directions.

Cambier had in times past taken off in a flash, but, once at the summit, he found himself trapped, and his family problems had come along to undermine his serenity.

Turenne's ambition was to climb this calvary on foot, without any thought of mortification, although this pilgrimage was to be made together with Brigitte and their child.

Ségaye, to the great distress of his pharmacist father in Saint-Laurent, had opted to flee, and had gone to live in the south of France. As for Décamport and Sugert, no one knew what had become of them.

For his part, Chambord had reached the summit. He realized that he was not achieving his goal, that he had to retrace his steps, going back to meet those who had not been able to follow him, and who were the only ones capable of under-

The Bastards

standing what he had to say. They would meet him halfway, drenched in shadow and light, newly escaped from a tower of Babel where he was surrounded by hostile companions who were different from him.

Almost reluctantly, he admitted: "Empires are won in dispensaries, and lost in offices."

"Could it be you're discouraged?"

"No, worried. I fear that one day violence and hatred will suddenly flare up. For come it will, that day when our people feels itself wronged. In its anger, it will overrun men like us."

Cambier thought he understood that Chambord was not giving up, that on the contrary he was outlining a problem, collecting data in search of a better solution. By his presence alone, he was happy just to control the drifting of his people, while waiting for those who would come along to help him up against the current. Around him, too many men had foundered in a sea of discouragement after trying to do something and had found themselves unable to survive. These were not cowards; these were not people unaware of what was happening. They thought long and hard about their deception. Everywhere, one met only indifferent men, marked by burning memories, preferring to cling to a precarious balance rather than try to shake off their languor. New blood was needed to motivate those who operated only by fits and starts, to carry along those who voluntarily withdrew from the struggle.

"If all the guys agreed to come back at the end of their studies, things would definitely be different."

There was a look of doubt on Chambord's face, as if a fleeting argument prevented him from agreeing with this point of view.

"Possible. But I'm convinced that, the way things are going now, the people will overrun us, either through a sudden rush of excitement that will come like a tidal wave, or because they have found demagogues treacherous enough to arouse them and take advantage of them. Whatever happens, we'll be powerless to control them, for they will have grown accustomed to seeing our authority challenged."

This prediction bothered Cambier. "We are people without

a past, without a future. The illiterate are happier than us; they have no memory, no projects. Our learning makes us discover the void around us, as well as our inability to fill it."

They had pursued difficult studies, spurred on by the idea that one day they would earn the trust of their people and of the administration that had encouraged them to attend the university. They had played the game. They returned home, convinced that their culture, their experience, their pivotal position would make them indispensable intermediaries while waiting to become genuine trustees. However, that only served to arouse suspicion around them. Without culture, they would have justified that conditional paternalism, complacently advanced as an argument in favor of colonialism. Armed with their references, they became questionable. And who was doing the questioning? Men who, far too often, had been anxious, owing to their mediocrity, to come and fade into oblivion in this country.

In France, Chambord had never come face to face with such questioning. Conscious of the traps that were in store for him here, he had rid himself of any vindictiveness before considering returning among his countrymen. Once back home, he realized that his search for purity had been only a futile precaution: those who, while in France, had initiated him to all those lofty principles turned out to be false prophets, in the sense that they had sent as servants certain messengers inspired by a touch of treason.

"Those who oppose us, are they doing anything for this country? Do they have a vocation?" Cambier enquired.

"You have only to look around you and you'll see: a country three times the size of Belgium, colonized for three centuries now. What is there? Thirty thousand inhabitants, and not even sixty miles of paved roads; the only decent way from here to Cayenne is by plane. By land, the trip is a veritable adventure, and it's not at all unwise to make one's will before setting out. There's no industry, no infrastructure. . . . "

"But our country was a major gold producer long ago."

"That's right. From three tons before the war, our gold production has fallen to three hundred kilograms, according to official figures. Do they really expect us to believe that the subsoil had suddenly dried up?"

"Aren't they thinking of starting up operations again?"

"They started by outlawing gold prospecting, thus reducing all the poor miners who made their living this way to begging alms. Today they're all in the hospice in Saint-Laurent. Our deposits have been given over to companies who maintain that our subsoil is empty, but who, in spite of everything, have not seen fit to take their experts elsewhere."

"What about the administration?"

"What can you expect from people who have no shame, no imagination?"

"After all, we don't have only mediocre people here, do we?"

"No, of course not. But the good men are quickly disheartened or broken. They are seen as troublemakers. Here in Saint-Laurent, we have Vincent, who's all right, the only one who really knows what he wants. We younger ones like him a lot, even if we don't always agree with him. Unfortunately, there is a rumor that he'll be leaving any day now."

"Disciplinary action?"

"You can never know. Everything is hushed up. You know how it's done? They give the most important job, or even an official honor, to the civil servant causing the problem."

A faint gesture of his hand accompanied the look of disgust on his face. He added: "There's always the dandy."

"The dandy?"

"Bertrand, the man who has Cayenne firmly under his control, a barrage of words and a dearth of ideas."

Bertrand had not abandoned his great fight against wastage. Everything was grist to his mill, but it was clear to all concerned that his administration would be catastrophic. In two years nothing had been done, yet expenses had not gone down. Under those conditions, how could he make viable a country where so much was still to be accomplished?

One day, Bertrand had sent for Chambord to seek his help in organizing World Leprosy Day in Saint-Laurent. Their meeting had lasted two hours, during which time the dandy had rambled endlessly from digression to digression. "Doctor, this country is all screwed up. What a big waste! Too many gendarmes, too many customs officers, too many petty civil service clerks, too many police officers! Look, just yesterday, I received a police report on your political activities. Obviously, I'm obliged to forward it to my superiors. The police service here is like an upturned pyramid. It is supported by one man alone: the investigator. Reports go all the way up to the minister without any control. I can only repeat what I say all the time: two years in this country is too much; four years, and you're rotten; after six years, you're fit for prison." His predecessor had stayed in Guiana over six years. Vincent had been there for five. He, Bertrand, intended to retire quietly after his two-year stint. Good old Bertrand, he was talking about gold!

"If stupidity could be given away, the dandy would be its main supplier!" Chambord added.

The hostility against certain men like Chambord was only a futile preservation reflex. It was the result of great fear, the fear of that collective and sudden awareness that would one day carry the country along in the wake of organized, down-to-earth men. This awareness would overthrow the decrepit system maintained by a bunch of mystifiers, who showed rare acrobatic skill. They proceeded, without faltering, on their tightrope, controlled from above, flattered from below. They managed to paralyze those above them with false reports, and to stifle those below them through deliberate generosity or intimidation.

But a circus act is always a precarious performance. Hidden in the dark, the Devil watches, laughing at the applause going to the head of the tightrope walker and convincing him of his infallibility. One day, he goes out on the stage and strikes like a thunderbolt.

During the night, a storm pounded the roofs with the noise of galloping hooves. Whenever there was a letup in the pounding, the swishing of the palm leaves buffeted by the wind created an atmosphere of terror.

Despite the coolness brought by the breeze as it rippled through his mosquito net, Cambier had trouble sleeping. He had seen Caroline again, and Chambord had finally told him what he was expecting to hear.

"This morning you promised to explain . . . about my sister."

"I was just thinking about that. Do you have any idea what could be wrong?"

"Must be some sort of shock. I saw Marcel in Cayenne."

"Emotional, to be more precise. Marcel is only part of the whole picture; what set it off goes beyond him."

Cambier had failed to perceive this nuance. Heading straight for his goal, and ignoring all the intervening stages, he looked first of all at a specific area. It mattered little to him whether the shock was emotional or otherwise; Caroline had become insane after a peculiar fight that pitted her against her father. She had lost the battle. A feeling of defeat had been shattered into myriad idle impulses, and their chain reactions were still rumbling deep within her in multiple explosions. Only Marcel could break the chain, could snatch Caroline from the jolts that had thrown her off balance.

"My parents objected to the marriage. She must have been shattered over this refusal."

Chambord took the time to light a cigarette, and his face disappeared behind a small blue cloud. He threw the match over his shoulder through a window above the couch. As his features became clearly defined once more, Cambier thought he detected a look of embarrassment—an admission was forthcoming, softened by soothing words.

"There's more than that. Here's what the psychiatrist reported to me: Caroline's state is now irreversible, but only became so after your father died. Up to that time, the conflict existed in veiled form. Then things suddenly came to a head."

"For what reason?"

Chambord paused once more. His friendship with Cambier, their former intimacy, stood in his way, making it difficult for Chambord to confide in him. It would have been simpler if there had not been between them that slice of life with its sentimentality, throbbing with shared adventures, with complicity. Could Cambier suddenly become merely the brother of a patient, a relative anxiously seeking information?

"Do you recall the circumstances under which your father died?"

"Vaguely. It happened the night after I took my *baccalauréat*. I was at the cinema. Hortense came to get me; she was in tears. She told me that my father was seriously ill; in fact, he was already dead."

He could not see what circumstances could have surrounded that event, to the point of influencing a doctor. Ordinarily, the father showed only his anger: sometimes it was to upbraid Hortense and punish her severely for her poor grades at school; at other times, it was to threaten Caroline on account of Marcel.

"Two members of your family reacted badly to emotions: your father and Caroline, the very ones who were enemies. The day you took your *baccalauréat,* emotions were running high. Your sister had barely returned from a trip to Martinique destined, apparently, to make her forget certain projects. That day, she had a heated altercation with your father, accusing him of cruelty on which, by the way, the psychiatrist was unable to have her elaborate. Be that as it may, she threatened to call in the law for your father."

"She was pregnant with Marcel's child. That's why she was sent away."

"I didn't know that."

The Bastards

"When she came back, she was no longer pregnant. You understand?"

"She'd had an abortion."

"She'd been helped . . . or forced."

"She never said a word about that. Obviously, that . . . accident must have intensified her feeling of frustration. In short, she threatened your father, who had a heart attack, as usually occurred every time he experienced violent emotion. A few hours later, he was dead. He had taken his whole bottle of drops."

"Suicide?"

"Listen, Cambier, I think you're a levelheaded man."

Levelheaded! That exaggerated reputation had preceded him. His uncle, always one for words of consolation, had said to his aunt the day before: "Alain is the most levelheaded in the family. Let him manage his affairs as he pleases!" His degree had been made into a shield that hid an internal storm. He had managed to obtain it, therefore he was levelheaded! Since his return, every attempt he made to find out what had happened had ended up with unexpected revelations. Those who observed his life-style conceded his right to resort to reason, in order to soothe the shocks they were inflicting upon him.

"There's no point in being levelheaded. . . . "

"It wasn't proven that it was suicide. But that's not really important. Caroline saw your father drink and saw him die. She felt responsible, so much so that she shouted: 'It's my fault!' and called down on herself God-knows-what curse. That's how it all started."

After his father died, Cambier had remained close to Caroline, never suspecting the turn things had taken. Even if he had not fled their house, would his sister have sought refuge in him? Their lives unfolded in a common setting, but all community ended right there.

"So, no hope then?"

"The psychiatrist doesn't expect any worsening or any improvement. She's remaining stable."

"And how's her blood?"

"Blood? What blood?"

"The tests?"

"Everything's normal as far as that is concerned."

He had thus learned everything about his sister's illness. Before leaving Saint-Laurent, he would return to see her, would take advantage of a moment of lucidity to have himself recognized by her. Could he leave without that at least? He would speak of Marcel to Caroline; he would tell her that everything was ready for her; that Marcel and he were waiting for her. He maintained a ray of hope. She must beat this evil disease. He would give her to Marcel.

He now had Hortense left to see. Unlike the case of the elder sister, for whom everything took place on the inside, he fully expected to read the younger's catastrophe on her skin. He would see a hideous octopus stick to a body, crawl, and reach out its tentacles. He would find Hortense rendered incapable, like Caroline, of hurting, and abandoned to her distress.

Chambord would drive him as far as the leper sanitorium, lost in the bush some twenty-odd miles from Saint-Laurent.

* * *

They set out early. As soon as they were in the outskirts of the town, immediately after the cemetery surrounded by bamboo, the car began to create splashes of muddy water. The road, with large potholes made by other vehicles, wound its way in the heart of the forest. Wooden bridges without guardrails spanned swollen rivers carrying trunks of trees uprooted by the storm. Every now and then, a turn in the road brought them past a dilapidated farm.

"There are countrymen who do not desert the land after all!" Cambier said.

"Don't fool yourself. All those tumbledown hovels are inhabited by old-whites. Furthermore, they rarely work the land. They're more interested in hunting: big game, butterflies . . . where the money is."

"Why?"

"Our blue butterflies are in great demand overseas . . . look, there's one."

The Bastards

In some undergrowth, a blue gauze flitted about in a movement that was at once haphazard and delicate. It sparkled briefly as a ray of sunlight hit it.

"I know this forest like the back of my hand. I come here often to frighten the parrots and the toucans."

"Clumsy!"

"Not exactly. I always bring back something. Our birds are so tame! But, once I'm in the woods, I walk about, I make noise, I go everywhere, the game as such . . . "

"And the snakes?"

"You too, you believe all those tall tales! In two years, I've never had anyone come to me with a bite. Of course, that doesn't prove anything, for there are local remedies that most of the people living in these parts use. But personally, I've come across a snake only once; it had beautiful red, yellow, and black rings. I almost felt like touching it. It escaped. All wild animals are afraid of man. For instance, crocodiles are the most cowardly animals I know. It's impossible to get close to them, except at night."

"At night?"

"You can catch them only at night, when they surface. You see their small, bright eyes level with the water; you shoot straight between the eyes. When they're hit, they dive to the bottom, and you have to go looking for them down there."

"And suppose they're only injured?"

"You hold their jaws with one hand, and their tails with the other, and you can bring them out like that. It's fascinating."

Chambord was in love with this country, its fauna, its flora, its dangers. Not for an empire would he have abandoned this muddy road, those coral snakes, those crocodiles. He had attained a supreme degree of contentment in this nature that had given birth to him, and this made him forget the ideological obstacles he found so discouraging. Was he a prisoner, a hostage, as Cambier had thought?

"We have to bear right," he said, as they came to a fork in the road.

"Where does that other road lead to?"

"Mana, about twelve miles from here. Long ago, there was a convict camp at the top of that hill. There are still ruins: dormitories, workshops, guards' quarters. The entire facility has been taken over by a fellow who's into lumbering. In our country, it's only wood that does any work."

The road became more uneven, with more holes but less mud, since the nature of the terrain had changed. They were now driving along a strip of sand.

"As soon as you see the primitives' settlement, you'll know that we don't have far to go."

In one of the clearings, tractors, lying idle since it was Sunday, stood alongside the trunks they had pulled previously; their tracks had left deep ruts in the soil.

They reached the small agglomeration of primitives. The threadbare shacks seemed to spring from the jungle. Naked children with beads around their waists were running at the side of the road. The men had surprising figures: very muscular chests, and thin legs.

"They spend their lives on the river," Chambord said.

"So?"

"They use mainly their arms . . . to paddle."

Every word Chambord uttered led Cambier to discover a little more about that country where he, too, was born, where he had grown up, but of which he knew nothing. He had had to come all the way to Saint-Laurent to see up close one of the primitives: a black-skinned one here, a red-skinned one there. All those men belonged to the same people: his own. He discovered them as he acknowledged he had always stayed aloof from them, from their languages, from their customs. What sort of humanism was it that made men like him ignorant of their own country, that made them go away from it, that made them so happy for so long that they had fled, as if they had received a promotion? What name could he give to that mystification that concealed all that belonged to them, that persuaded them they had no achievements, no possessions? Was it done deliberately, or had the mystifiers mystified themselves?

They came upon a cluster of little houses with red roofs. A

steeple rose above them. There were flowers everywhere. In the middle of the imposing forest, this note of gaiety, coming from an organized world, had a brutally calming effect.

"Here we are."

"*This* is the sanitorium? I was expecting to see a hospital."

"Each patient lives in one of these buildings. There are even couples; only, if babies are born, they are sent to the day nursery in Saint-Laurent. Sooner or later, they are put in foster homes."

The car came to a halt in front of the building where the nuns lived. Down from this building, a meandering river contrasted harmoniously with the greenery. A canoe tied up to a tiny pier was riding the currents.

The first word from the mother superior was about Hortense.

"Your sister has been impatient. Ever since I told her about the call from Doctor Chambord, she can't keep still."

Cambier threw himself at his sister, who had come running, alerted by the noise of the engine. She was aglow with freshness, with apparent health. He had expected to see her disfigured, her body all swollen and puffy. Instead, he found himself in the presence of an elegant, well made-up young woman. He felt weak with joy, and all his apprehension disappeared, to be replaced by unspeakable happiness. His sister, his little sister, would be able to make a new start in life, to return to their house.

"Come, Alain. Come over to my place," she said, still holding on to him.

Once there, they found the moving disorder so characteristic of young girls' rooms; picture magazines were scattered on the furniture; there were a record player and some records on a round-topped chest. A crucifix was hanging over the doorway connecting the room where they were to the bedroom.

Hortense was so anxious to talk about herself and her brother that she forgot to enquire about Caroline. As for him, everything he had prepared dissipated before so much joy. His sister did not need any consolation.

"You like it here?"

An Unwed Mother Called Guiana

"Oh, yes. I've been here four months now. Everyone is so nice: the doctor, the nuns, my friends. . . . "

"You're practically cured, as far as I can see."

"Yes, but I want to remain with the nuns, with the others, with Caroline. I feel close to her here. How is she? You saw her?"

"She's more or less the same. Chambord's trying his best to get her to improve."

"You think you can cure her?" she asked Chambord.

"We're trying."

She offered them coffee, and they spoke about Caroline, about the family.

Hortense had definite ideas about the whole affair. The uncle and aunt, mesmerized by their phobia, deserved only indifference or contempt. Caroline was a lost cause, for her being sent away constituted an admission of powerlessness on the part of the specialists. Despite Chambord's denial, she persisted in seeing things this way. Henceforth, resignation was to replace all medication. Complaining would not change a thing.

"Why don't you want to leave this place?"

"I've done some thinking. I've come to understand many things."

"For example?"

"In town, they're afraid of people like me. I prefer not to go back."

"What can that do, the fear of others? You'll be living with me."

"Isolated, with no one to talk to?"

"I'm thinking of opening my office as early as next week. We need a woman in the house."

"Then it's better to get married."

She spoke these words as she stood up and went into the bedroom, returning with an album. He thought she was about to show him family souvenirs. Instead, she showed photos of herself at various stages of her illness.

"Here's one of me, at the very beginning."

She showed the photograph. She was hideous, her cheeks jutting out, her lips swollen, her eyes all puffed up. There was no reaction from Chambord to this caricature; he had seen others. But how could Hortense remain so calm? What was it that was driving her to this mortification?

"What ever made you take these photos? Why are you keeping them?"

"The first time, it happened rather casually. I was still at the hospital. One day, the doctor began to take photographs of the patients. I, after all, was Mademoiselle Cambier, the daughter of someone important; they couldn't very well force me! I demanded to be treated like the others. Later on, I happened to look at myself in a mirror and to compare myself to my first photo. So, I continued to have my photograph taken. For us, photos are more important than all those good words."

The back of every shot bore a date. In each case, the improvement was immediately obvious. Hortense was indeed the most levelheaded in the family, she whom her mother reproached for being too much like her grandmother, the black woman.

She showed them around the sanitorium. There was, not far from a chapel, a statue of the nun who had founded the establishment. Hands crossed over her heart in an attitude of devout humility, she was facing the river.

They went into a linen and laundry room, where a washing machine had just been installed. They found a young woman hard at work doing embroidery. Her bent, worn out fingers held the needle clumsily. She smiled as Cambier got closer; he was not unfamiliar with this face, but could not place it. Hortense had guessed his predicament, but avoided doing anything to help him.

"Hello, Alain!" the young woman said, extending her hand to him.

His own hand, somewhat hesitantly, took the one offered. All of a sudden, it clicked. He shouted: "Ginette!"

Chance brought him a revelation that he had not even thought of seeking: Wasn't Ginette responsible for Hortense's illness? They had grown up together. "Between her house and ours was only a low, broken-down wall." Ginette's father was considered a disabled ex-serviceman. He was alleged to have

frozen his hands while in the trenches, and several fingers had
been amputated; the stumps were still extremely painful.
When he heard him complaining and lecturing his wife, Cambier's father would grumble between his teeth: "This whole
thing will come to a bad end! He's a leper. He'd be better off
looking after himself, rather than running after a pension. . . .
It's his daughter who'll suffer for it." Without suspecting it, he
had predicted that destiny, proving him right, would strike his
own daughter. Hadn't Ginette, as they tried to show each
other how much pain they could endure, innocently infected
Hortense with her disease? When they amused themselves by
sticking aloe prickles in their arms, Ginette would feel nothing.
"Didn't she *already* have leprosy?" And there was Hortense
sticking herself with the prickle her friend had already used!

"You came to see Hortense. She's leaving soon."

"I think so."

"She's lucky. I . . . "

"Your turn will come as well."

"Now you're a . . . "

She broke down, sobbing. The others tried to console her.

"Come now, you mustn't cry."

"I'll remain here. I don't want to leave."

"You'll see. Everything will work out."

"Don't pay me any mind. I just got a little upset," she said.

* * *

They returned to Saint-Laurent late in the morning. Cambier
accompanied Chambord to the hospital, and while his friend
made his rounds, he went to see Caroline, but was no happier
than the day before. She was delirious.

Once again, he came face to face with that same look of hatred, those same menacingly angry eyes that had already made
such an impression on him. To all appearances, Caroline had
not washed and dressed, but she had plastered powder and
makeup over herself. She had put on back to front a ragged
dressing gown, and her nightdress hung hideously to one side,
making her look like a twisted, hunchbacked woman. She was
wearing odd sizes of slippers, and to add to the weird nature

The Bastards

of her garb she was making large gestures with her arms and was impressively muttering grandiloquent words interspersed with snatches of the liturgy in Latin. She was doing a parody of the mass.

He looked at her for an instant through the bars, but could not stand this spectacle. He fled in disgust.

Chambord rejoined him in the office. The faithful Alexis was standing in the gallery smoking nonstop.

"Well, how did you find her today?"

"We didn't say a word to each other."

"She refused to speak to you?"

"I'm the one who didn't dare."

"Why?"

"It was impossible to approach her. She . . . "

"Oh yes, I see. Every Sunday it's like that. Tomorrow everything will be all right."

"I'd like her to recognize me before I leave, and my flight's tomorrow morning."

"I can't promise you anything."

"You just said that tomorrow . . . "

"Yes. But it could happen later on in the week."

"I want to talk to her about Marcel, to promise her . . . "

"I speak to her about him every day."

"And what's her reaction?"

"Listen, all we say to Caroline and nothing amount to the same thing. Her world is within her and monopolizes her behavior. We can't get through to her."

"By insisting . . . "

"Where would that get us? There's a dam between that world of hers and ours. Communication is only one-way, through the overflow, through what spills over."

From then on, Cambier understood that Caroline was lost. Hortense, despite her apparent childishness, had made a quicker, better prediction than he had. Chambord, deliberately and rightfully cautious, had displayed an ambiguity that could not sustain illusion for any length of time. He had contradicted himself on several occasions. Cornered into giving an answer, he had come out with words that were cruelly pessimistic.

An Unwed Mother Called Guiana

"Actually, I've lost both my sisters: one stays closed up in her frenzied world, the other's in an establishment that she persists in thinking of as a refuge from society."

He remained alone, condemned to go mournfully through a crowd whose questionable neutrality bordered on persecution. His uncle and his aunt, all too happy to be rid of a burden as far as he was concerned, were beginning to breathe easy. He had only Marcel left, yet another sacrificial victim, who would join him as a partner in his grief; and their sinister capital would grow with undesirable interest.

Carnival Sunday in Saint-Laurent.

Africa was on display in the streets, thrown by the armful in showers of bright colors, of rhythms, of trances. The crowd of bystanders got in the way of the disguised automatons. Red devils were parading, with their long, stiff tails banging against their calves, or at times thrust forward in an indecent manner.

Africa was being jostled at ground level, was shouting, was jumping in the air. A white trail undulated—a secular procession of persons in penitent's hoods. A rope stretched from shoulder to shoulder, clutched, like a cashbook, ran between the bodies—an umbilical cord serving as a link to the black mother. "*Ohé, Zombis baré yo!*"

Africa was on view in the streets, innocent, violent, unsuspected.

An invisible drum emitted a captivating call, repeated in identical fashion to the point of obsession. On a truck, an orchestra was striving to make itself heard, but only the drum, only Africa, could be heard.

Bodies decorated with cane leaves were portraying a rustic scene. Cutlass blades glinted in the sun, threatening the greenery—a time-honored gesture of the sons of Africa working, sweating under the master's whip.

The car was besieged, almost raised off the ground by this crowd. Chambord was forced to stop. A red devil, its breasts erect and pointed, its rear plump—a woman, no doubt—imitated a deep voice as it assailed him with an ambiguous stream of words in the Guianese patois.

Bobbies in jute sacks were having a good frolic. The unending parade kept going, delirious with festivity, abandon, rhythm, and negritude. "*Ohé, Zombis baré yo!*"

Cambier, suddenly liberated, looked on at this madness. "This Night that is inside me, and that I cannot define, isn't it *quite simply* Africa?"

The car was able to find a clearing and leave.

They came to an Indian village situated on the outskirts of Saint-Laurent. The shacks, exposed to the elements, were spread out at the junction of the river and a winding tributary that lay in the shadow cast by large trees with mud-stained roots. Some men, stretched out in hammocks, awoke at the sound of the engine. A few couples approached Chambord to show him infants he had looked after. In the distance, on the grass, some youngsters were playing with a ball, while behind one of the shacks little girls were spinning madly around in a Provençal dance.

"Hear that?" Chambord said. "You can find traces of our Gallic ancestors even here in the depths of the jungle."

"That's Assimilation."

"What Assimilation? The Indians have no civil status; they do not vote. Then what's the point of drumming things into their heads? Later on, these children will return to their own tribe, never to leave again."

"Would you be against their . . . "

"It's not a question of being for or against. It's more than that; it's a question of human dignity, of social balance. We're in the process of bastardizing them, the way it was done to us. But I'm reassured by at least one thing: at boarding school where an attempt is being made to westernize them, the little Indian girls continue to sleep in their hammocks. Even at the hospital, some of the Indians refuse to sleep in beds. All that is significant."

"What do you mean?"

"I see that as a form of resistance, a form of refusal to surrender, and it's very reassuring. As long as the authorities persist in taking them out of their tribes at all costs, there'll be nothing but failures: a waste of time and money, and, to crown it all, a risk of social upheaval weakening the tribes. Assimilation will replace malaria!"

The young Indian was taken away from his milieu; he was baptized, raised, and sent to school up to adolescence. The educator was proud of the job he had done. Chambord however saw no reason for rejoicing. Once back in his tribe, the Indian lost all constructive contact with the world that had tried to mold him: no more going to church, no more reading books, no more speaking French. All he had learned gradually dwindled away, and his memory became as empty as an hourglass. He was forced to readapt. Far from being a motivating force, he became a dead weight for his people.

"Is the situation the same with the black primitives?"

"Young blacks are not taken care of like that. At least, for them, it means less of a risk of bastardization, and in a way, that's much better. But this segregation of blacks and Indians is no less disturbing; it only goes to show that in the hearts of the educators there's some hatred of blacks."

"Isn't that going a bit far?"

"Long ago, the Indian was not enslaved the way the blacks were. The segregation currently practiced against blacks is simply a case of history repeating itself."

"What can we do then? You think it a mistake every time someone is cared for; you smell racism every time someone is abandoned. You have to choose."

"Yes, but choosing doesn't mean improvising. One must first of all get to the very depths of what reality itself means for these primitive people, of what their aspirations are; otherwise, their friends will be the death of them."

He expounded his views. It was not that the primitives were deprived, they were just decadent. In the past, they had something: a civilization, a god or gods, a sense of belonging to tribe or nation. These values, however modest, helped create a balance, a joie de vivre. Adventurers, honored in Western history textbooks, had destroyed everything and annihilated these so-called savages with their own brand of savagery. Indian cities had been lost to fire and bloodshed; black societies, originally from the valley of the Nile and regrouped in West

The Bastards

Africa, had suffered the same fate. Guiana had become the refuge of all those uprooted men that Europe had spat out: criminals, commoners. Those very people whose ancestors had plundered, desecrated, and burnt now wanted their victims to believe that they were nothing, and that they had never left the realm of stupidity and nothingness. Everything transpired as if the primitive's origin on the planet was being contested, as if his appearance was a present-day affair—a sort of sudden, unexpected birth.

Chambord felt that in this chaos of mystification and contestation, people like him had something to say. They had to struggle on all fronts: to look after their own defense and to defend the primitives as well. At least, one had to make sure that no further harm was done to them, if one could not actually do any good for them.

As far as he was concerned, there was only one fight. The black primitives were the link between himself and Africa, that ancestral, historic Africa cemented in his mind. Their common ancestors, sold to slave traders, had one day ended up on the shores of the Caribbean, where their existence was guided by one principle alone: slavery, punctuated by the stultifying rhythm of the whip, symbol of their wretchedness, of their horror of living. Some had had the incredible courage to escape from their executioners, in spite of the lessons to be learned in the punishment meted out to any runaway black that was caught. They had ventured into the jungles of the Amazon, had confronted dangers that, in fact, were no worse than the treatment inflicted on men by other men whose pigmentation was different. They had adapted to that forest and had restored their tribes in it, safe from the intentions, good or bad, of the conquerors. Others, resigned to their lot, or already bastardized, had endured the atrocities up to the bitter end, up to the day their own masters discovered the flame of liberation in their own souls. But what insults, what threats Schoelcher and his friends must have had to endure!

Chambord descended from that half-freed fraction. It was his duty to complete the operation without losing sight of the other fraction that had accepted obscurantism in exchange for

its negritude, for its freedom. To ignore these primitives would
have been, on his part, tantamount to practicing neocolonialism, to admitting implicitly that he was standing on a ladder,
with men above and below him, and to agreeing to a deplorable gelling of humanity. He could not deny these disinherited
people the possibility of improvement from within, since his
own case stood out as proof. His position could therefore
brook no compromise. The black primitives, as former slaves,
came from the same source as he, and, as primitives, remained
solidly united with the Indians. Struggling for true freedom
meant uplifting them both.

"What do you mean by negritude?" Cambier asked.

"For me, fidelity to Africa."

They set off once more, driving away from Saint-Laurent.
After passing the only metal bridge in the area, Chambord
slowed the car down.

"This savannah with the mango trees is a lovely spot. It
stretches all the way to the lake where I was day before yesterday, all the way to the river: picnics, fishing . . . "

"And what's on the other side of the road? Those bamboo
trees?"

"It's worth a look. Come with me!"

They left the car at the side of the road. Chambord's bag, his
instruments, and his first-aid medication were on the back seat.

"You're not locking the door?"

"We're no longer in Europe. Our countrymen do not steal.
The old-whites who came here because they had committed
murder do not stoop to pilfering. It's a question of prestige."

"On the contrary, I thought . . . "

"The proof: there's no prison in Saint-Laurent. Whenever,
by chance, there's someone to lock up, the policemen are not
amused. They have to accompany this person to Cayenne,
sometimes by plane."

They jumped down from the roadway onto the grass with
its sparse undergrowth. A few buffaloes were grazing, totally
oblivious to the black birds perched on their backs in search

of some morsel. The clusters of bamboo were swaying in the breeze, and obsessing cracking sounds accompanied the movement of the long stalks as they hit against one another. Chambord slid through them sideways; his friend followed him tenuously, for he could not help thinking of rattlesnakes. Upon crossing the edge, he could not contain his astonishment: "What's that over there?"

"As you can see, it's a tomb."

"Whose?"

"Some officer, they say. Probably died quite some time ago; yet another one who refused to be buried in the same cemetery as the old-whites!"

"But his body must have been sent back to France."

"Makes no difference. It's the symbol that counts. The tomb remains."

"A symbol?"

"Yes, you can do what you want, you cannot make yourself different from your fellowmen. Take for instance this man. What difference is there between his body and that of an old-white? All he got for his pride is solitude, oblivion. For visitors, he has only the birds that live in the bamboo, and mess on his tomb all day long."

"And you, sometimes!"

"I'll even go so far as to say I enjoy coming here."

"In doing so, isn't that a way of proving you're not like the others . . . those who never come?"

"Possibly, but I'm in no way proud of what I do. As far as I'm concerned, that man was an idiot. A man who tries to set himself apart is always an outcast and a fool."

These last words vibrated inside Cambier and kept echoing and echoing.

The man had turned to dust under that tombstone, had pursued exception till the day he died. For years, he, Cambier, had slaked his thirst for exception. He had felt an unexplorable world brewing inside him—his Night—and he had realized, faced with the plethora of his countrymen, that this Night was within each one of them, that it was common to them all, both in origin and in expression. A people inattentive to its own needs, that refused to study anything seriously, to prove anything, had shown him what path he had to take.

He had wanted to love a woman "by way of exception," but he had never been able to get a grasp on this love nor to dominate it. "That virgin hanging by her feet from the mast of eternity!" Who had said that? His sister? Yes, a madwoman! And what did she mean, despite her madness, despite that fog that acted as a screen between herself and others? That love is quite a feeling, always new, always thwarted, always eternal!

He had, for years, slaked his thirst for exception. It had led him to loneliness, just like that officer lost in the open savannah, close to a patch of bamboo.

On the moss-covered tombstone, no name was engraved.

CHAPTER FOUR

"Heads will roll!" Gélazothes had predicted, using words that
were all too true in Saint-Laurent when an unpardoning guillotine spelled the end of the convicted habitual criminals.

Today, he was repeating to his men: "I told you so!"

Vincent was leaving the country for good, and all his friends
had accompanied him to the airport. Gélazothes insinuated
that he had been dismissed.

From his vantage point off in one corner, he stared at each
of those who were defying him by coming in a show of public
support for his enemy. His eyes hidden behind dark shades, he
shot fierce looks at them and cursed them under his breath.

Among them were the mayor ("That little two-bit mayor,
who has the nerve to speak to me as if he had real power"),
the vice-chairman of the hospital board ("I can just picture
that squirt ending his days at some unheard of faculty of medicine"), the parish priest ("He'd be better off praying for the
soul of one of his colleagues who gets his parishioners pregnant"), the surgeon ("Unqualified butcher"), a few policemen,
including Fontès ("Pitiful! Just look at their salary scale"),
and, finally, Chambord ("As for that one, he'd better take
stock of himself. His goose is cooked!").

Gélazothes was fond of the expression "take stock of oneself," which he had no doubt picked up from his close contact
with crooks. It was with these words that he had warned his
wife when, upon emerging from the stupor of alcohol, he had
seen her dancing with one of Vincent's staff. The wretched
woman, brutally dragged from the dance floor, had been
hustled to the couple's home, where a cruel beating had made
her forget her taste for dancing forever. With his right hand

poised to strike, he kept his left index finger on his lips: "Hush!" but the victim kept bawling and asking for forgiveness. So, he proposed a sort of deal: "I know you've got another man. Tell me who it is!" The neighbors, roused from their beds by this nocturnal disturbing of the peace, could not believe their ears.

He noticed the thin face of the lanky Verdanson, who was emerging from the group of Vincent's friends. "I hadn't seen him. Was he trying to hide? Coward!"

Verdanson worked at the subprefecture. He was the last European to continue seeing the commissioner. He would really have liked to rid himself of this thankless task, but his wife's inconsiderate gossiping had disclosed too much to the police officer. If they had many things on each other, only Gélazothes could be dangerous. As it turned out, the day after the never-to-be-forgotten beating, Gélazothes was to have lunch at Verdanson's home. At exactly twelve noon, he had turned up to say he could not make it: "We can't come over. My wife's indisposed; her head is swollen!" What would Verdanson have gained from a scandal that did not frighten even the person responsible for it?

That was the type of man Gélazothes was: alone, but feared. He enjoyed being one of Bertrand's closest friends, and pledged that he would clean up the entire Maroni region. Even the Guianese would be included.

Vincent was leaving without great ceremony. He was in shirt-sleeves, with a hint of a smile on his face as he went from one person to the other, exchanging a few pleasantries with them.

"I'm leaving a very bitter man."

"We'll miss you."

"I couldn't refuse my new job. I was chosen from among many 'possible' candidates."

"That shows they respect your competence."

"Perhaps you'll come back one day as prefect."

"I'd love that."

Chambord, who remained silent, nevertheless suspected that such an eventuality was highly improbable.

The next day, the four-engined plane that Vincent had boarded in Cayenne departed from its regular course, and made a low circular pass over Saint-Laurent. People ran out into the streets, and their hearts missed a beat.

Henceforth, the way was clear. Gélazothes was ecstatic.

A few days later, a surprising piece of news spread through the small town: Gélazothes was being transferred, and had to leave immediately.

The prophesy was being fulfilled. One more head was rolling: that of the prophet himself.

Gélazothes, upset by the shock of this turnaround in events, was a sorry sight. This great warrior, afraid of flying, chose to take a coasting vessel that was in Saint-Laurent at the time. The ship's captain, a Martinican, was a very good friend of Chambord, Saivol, Fedène, and a few others. As luck would have it, there were no cabins free, and Gélazothes spent the entire voyage on deck, with his wife and his dog, eating food bought in the various ports of call. Several Europeans even came to ridicule him as he left. They called to one another as they stood on the quay: "You can take stock of yourself!" Champing at the bit, he looked at them with contempt, and muttered under his breath: "Only dirt can soil you!"

* * *

Chambord had not felt it coming. In spite of his two years here, he persisted in prejudging others' reflexes by criteria he had learned in France.

Over there, a man was free to act as he pleased. No extra-professional considerations came into play in the appreciation of his work or in an eventual promotion decision. In every man lurked two individuals: the wage earner and the citizen.

Here, on the contrary, the panels of the diptych remained closely linked, dependent, intermingled. No man, even less a Guianese, could expect to be on the administration's payroll wihout becoming its pawn.

Chambord had thought he could give a good account of himself by doing his best at what was expected of him professionally. But those in high places wanted to see in him only a robot, a privileged robot, and, as such, an accomplice. Any difference in concept was already an act of deviationism, an act of treason.

Wasn't he told: "Frankly speaking, isn't it the white man who *allowed* the formation of the black elite?" He, to be honest, had always thought that he had received no gifts, that he had had to face the same requirements as anybody else in order to get where he was. Today, he was being made to understand that, in a word, his life depended on administration largesse, and that by deviating from its methods he was showing his ingratitude.

He read again the official letter he had just received. Of course, he was not being denied the benefit of a new contract—this type of formal reply not tallying with the principles of local diplomacy—but the conditions imposed were such that he would no doubt find himself forced to leave.

He asked himself: "Who could have done that to me?" Three names came to mind: Gélazothes, Arnaud, and Mirabel, the doctor that Poncet had called a traitor and who had replaced him since Bertrand had had the director of health recalled to France. The commissioner had written so many reports that their number and variety removed any shred of truthfulness from them. But had Arnaud forgotten the insult caused by his earlier refusal of an invitation to lunch? Had Mirabel forgotten that he, Chambord, had called him a colonialist, officially, in writing?

"They want to humiliate me, to force me to disappear." He did not want to disappear. His country needed him. He would play a good trick on them by deciding to remain, by accepting their conditions. He would accept.

The dandy had once told him: "When they remain too long in the same sector, doctors become like little black kings. I don't ever want that again! I'm going to issue a decree making it compulsory to change jobs every two years." But Chambord could not be transferred, since he had obtained his position through competitive examination. So, they decided to harass him. "Those sons o' bitches!" They were beginning to be afraid of him, to worry that he would turn into a little black king. Since this was the case, he would remain with his people to help them defend themselves. He would even take a cut in salary.

But, if he did this, wouldn't he be capitulating in a way? There was still this dilemma; he wanted to encourage his people to raise their heads, and there he would be, showing them an example of submission. No, he could not accept. Accepting would mean self-condemnation. But to refuse, to leave, wasn't that condemning his people?

He brought his car to a screeching stop in front of Rinefour's store. He slammed the door and burst into his friend's office.

"I'd like to talk to you."

"You're in luck. I've just finished my mail."

"First, read this!"

"Those swine!" Rinefour said as he returned the letter. "We're in a hell of a mess with people like that."

"What do you advise me to do?"

"Tell them to go to hell. Don't let them deter you."

"I want to stay."

"So you can starve, and vegetate, and grow rusty without the slightest benefit to yourself?"

"I don't give a shit about money. I'm thinking of you people. My presence . . . "

"Of us? What will it take for you to understand that our countrymen are not 'with it'? They're all a bunch of cowards! There's probably one thing to do for you to remain here, with dignity: a petition. They love you, they want to keep you, but they will not be bold enough to sign. They're afraid. Remember the club. Remember how they all made themselves scarce after Gélazothes issued his first threats."

"They did sign a petition to keep a white doctor who had slapped our director. If they love me like you say, they'll sign."

"Don't believe that. I repeat, they'll be afraid to support you; it could be taken the wrong way. Although I'll regret it, my advice to you is to make a life for yourself somewhere else. You're too straightforward for them. You'll always be the only one to suffer, in whatever form that might be."

"And what if I started my own practice?"

"The administration will immediately come up with some

other damned doctor who's drawing a salary and who will steal all the patients with official allowances. Now, over here, that's all there is. How will you live? Is it this mediocrity that's tempting you?"

"I still have a month ahead of me to make a decision," Chambord said as he left.

The consultations brought their daily litany of complaints: each patient described his ailment or spoke to Chambord about a problem. He had to reassure some after lending a sympathetic ear to their accounts of what was wrong with them; others he had to promise that everything would be all right very soon. He was a source of consolation for all, and people came to him for both the words and the medication to overcome their grief. They left full of reassurance and optimism. He would remain in his office, crestfallen, alone, unable to foresee any solution to the battle he was waging against himself, one that his pride was in the process of abandoning.

"I'm too much alone." He had not thought he had said the right thing when he told Cambier that there was an attempt to isolate men like them. Whom could he trust? From whom could he expect anything whatsoever? Those around him, too much in the habit of being on the receiving end, could give him nothing. When he left—for he was sure he would be driven to leave—who would come and exhort his people to react? It would all be over! No more contact with a mass of subjugated people unaware of their destiny, that mass that did not even see that it needed him. Over, too, those lengthy consultations during which all the wretchedness he found so fascinating would be exposed: a Boni had *aches all over his skin,* which, translated, meant he was suffering from rheumatism; a Roucouyenne Indian said that his child was ten years old, and that he, the father, was *many years old,* all of which meant simply that the child was a child and the father an adult, any number above ten being considered under the heading "many." And if ever a Guianese complained of a *heartache,* it was obviously a case of his stomach burning him because of intestinal worms.

The Bastards

He would therefore have to leave all that: those languages with their limited vocabulary, forcing them to develop special codes; those charming, trusting people. Didn't they understand he was indispensable? "No one is irreplaceable!" What was going to become of these men, these women, these children?

The telephone rang.

"Doctor, we're waiting for you to examine the infants."

"I'm coming."

He hadn't thought about them, those little bits of men now starting life without a clue as to what it holds in store for them. What rotten luck to be born in this part of the world where future and past were meaningless words!

He had to go to them, to check their weight charts, to examine their throats, to collect specimens in the flat of his big left hand, while his right slid the stethoscope along their chests, to look at the color of their stools, to advise the mothers on the choice of milk, to step aside suddenly to avoid being doused with urine from little penises or little vulvae full of talcum powder. "After killing my past, circumscribing my future, they're even stealing my present from me!"

He would leave. He was entitled to vacation in France; to give it up would be to help the dandy in his campaign against government waste. Once there, he would find himself banished, dismissed, ostracized. How could he bring himself, at present, to live in France with that open wound he could already feel bleeding in his side? He was being sent back to that land of freedom that he had loved so much. But this liberty he was going to enjoy all by himself, would it really be *the* liberty? "One does not escape from one's condition, from one's milieu!"

He was now an out-and-out bastard, since his own mother, Guiana, was disowning him.

He stood up and went outside.

* * *

The sharp grass of the savannah at the edge of the forest was now parched a reddish brown by the "Indian summer." The muddy waters of Balaté Creek and the river flowed lazily between little islands of greenery. It had rained in the interior.

An Unwed Mother Called Guiana

Chambord was driving toward Saint-Jean.

He had not been able to take his siesta. He felt uncomfortable, fidgeting constantly, and unable to keep still. He had left immediately after lunch.

In his rearview mirror, he saw a cloud of red dust created by the car. By straightening himself in his seat, he could see a corner of his face: "I've aged ten years since this morning."

Why was he going to Saint-Jean? He honestly did not have any idea. He had already seen what was worth seeing: the sawmill, the workshop, the residences occupied by those central European immigrants the administration had wanted to relocate. Before them, convicts—among whom there had even been women—had been sent here to the various camps. How many old-whites in detention in Saint-Laurent must have run away to pay a nocturnal visit to one of their colleagues of the opposite sex, covering on foot the ten-odd miles separating both their settlements! In no time, the relegation of women convicts was discontinued. "There must have been too many births."

Now, *displaced persons* were being relocated in Saint-Jean. They had been offered the former quarters reserved for the guards and their families. A few technicians, French for the most part, remained behind to keep an eye on these people. This entire little world enjoyed comfortable accommodations, decent salaries, social security, and family allowances. "Meanwhile, my people are rotting in hovels!"

This land that had given birth to Chambord seemed to him more hospitable to outsiders than to its own sons: *that* was its vocation: a model stepmother, unworthy mother!

He remembered what Rinefour had said: "They love you, they want to keep you, but they will not be bold enough to sign." They loved him, but they were afraid. The dandy and his cronies had struck because they too were afraid: a kick by a horse scared of its own shadow.

He gravitated in a world in which fear conditioned every gesture, every word. No, he was not afraid. This meant that he had no right being here: he had to go. A danger, he was condemned to be ostracized.

Already, he felt himself no more than an anachronism, than

someone living in suspense, powerless to stop the insipid pantomime of those around him. He would have liked to intervene, but they were not speaking the same language; his world
had absolutely no connection with the world of fear. He saw
them doing a wild dance of ghosts, oblivious of his presence,
of his input that shocked, penetrated, and came back out of
them without, to all appearances, moving them in the least.
For them, he did not exist. Only fear existed: the paradoxical
fear of ghosts afraid of those they frighten, a fear that was
both active and provoked, a fear of fear, anarchy on the edge
of an abyss ready to engulf them all.

Couldn't he do something for them? He knew that a fatal
catastrophe awaited them. Was it possible to bring together
people so much like him in social status, so unlike him in their
preoccupations? He had been with them every day for two
years; he had split their ranks, and they had not noticed
a thing.

They were part of the same troops and were not aware of
their loneliness. They let themselves be swept away in a whirlwind whose link with History was contested. Sooner or later,
they would be pulverized. They would come to the end of an
unknown course and return to the original nothingness without obtaining their promotion.

He, Chambord, was standing at the side of the road, one
foot in History. He was looking at the parade go by, impatient
to join it, for he had fleetingly glimpsed the victory for those
sacrificial victims sleepwalking their way to battle, unaware
that the struggle was at their own doorstep, at the doorstep
of History, and that it had been going on for centuries. He
wanted to say to them: "Where are you going? What are you
searching for elsewhere? The battle is within you. You must
conquer your illusions, your silence, your fear." The cohort
continued its way, deaf to his curses. It did not hear, nor did it
see this lucid man making it a gift of himself.

The adventure was at a turning point; it would explode in a
din of shouts and lamentations. It was then that the cohort
would awake, disband, and self-destruct.

Chambord saw only deception, betrayal of confidence, tears

of blood. But he still held out hope; that was all he had done over the past two years. "You'll always be the only one to receive the blows, wherever they come from." What was he waiting for to understand that nobody wanted to decipher his messages? Soon men from his own country would rise up and spit in his face, would chase him as if he had the plague. And he would shout to them: "I'm one of you! I want to save you!" But no one would want to be saved in this manner, and the very ones he would have wanted to elevate to the rank of free men would stone and chase him away. . . .

He came to a halt, made a quick maneuver, and drove back.

As he approached Saint-Laurent, he already regretted returning. Should he take his clothes off, stretch out on his bed, turn over questions in his mind, then take a shower before going back to the hospital? He passed his house without stopping. He was on his way to see Fedène.

"I've come to show you a letter."

He handed the sheet of paper to Fedène who, having had to interrupt his siesta, came downstairs in only his undershorts.

"Doesn't surprise me from them!" he answered, returning the sheet of paper, which, by dint of being unfolded, refolded, manipulated, was beginning to show signs of wear.

"Rinefour is speaking of a petition, but claims that many of our countrymen will balk at signing."

"They're afraid. For centuries, they have been vegetating in their fear, and have been living from fine words and mystification."

"I'll go away," Chambord said despondently.

"You have to stay."

"If I stay, that would mean that I'm giving in to their arbitrariness, that I'm surrendering. My dignity . . . "

"Your dignity commands you, precisely, to forget about the victimization, to remain with your people."

"My people will not support me. . . . "

"If they don't know how to be bold, it's because up to now too many men like you became fugitives. There's a band of faithful followers who continue, through thick and thin, to come to our club. They believe in you, and it's for that reason that they persist in their action. We have to encourage them to continue."

"Others can continue in my place."

"Yes, others will come. There'll always be more, for it is inevitable that we will wake up to what is happening to us. But, for the time being, it's because of you that the guys are holding on. If you go away, it'll all be over for them. They'll feel abandoned by the one for whom they took risks. That'll be a heavy burden for the future."

He drank slowly a glass of beer Fedène had offered him. What an imbroglio! One minute he was being advised to leave; the next he was being encouraged to remain. He was born in this country; he had grown up in this milieu, and he had to examine himself to ascertain whether or not he would become a fugitive.

Foreigners all found this country pleasant, even the convicts who were sent there to do hard labor. Whenever they were asked about their past suffering, they would shrug their shoulders: "Oh, yes, sure, on the Salut Islands it was tough, but in Saint-Laurent, we lived like kings, doctor."

Nobody had ever seen, except in the scandal-oriented tabloids, a convict dragging an iron ball on his foot. Most of them were able to make use of whatever expertise they possessed (wasn't there even a doctor among them?), working as servants for the guards or other private citizens. For instance, wasn't the hairdresser imprisoned for murdering his mistress ("To teach her how to live!"), who invented a new hairstyle every two weeks, in the habit of saying: "Had I known that prison life was so nice, I'd have killed my wife long ago!"

Why, then, couldn't he fit in as well, Chambord wondered. Didn't he lead the same type of life as those outcasts?

In times past, this country was the only colony where the black man experienced absolutely no prejudice from the white man. Prison, with its huge contingent of the dregs of European society, nipped any arrogance in the bud. Nowadays, there was no more prison. All that remained were scattered pockets of men compelled to accept a duality as either men banned from setting foot in France or those who had opted to remain rather than return to their country and place themselves at the mercy of their countrymen's prejudice. Some newcomers, more often than not on the run from upheavals in the colonies where they ran riot, brought with them deplorable habits. "Am I not a victim of racism?"

"They want to behead the country. Every Guianese of worth is a bad example to his people."

"We must play the game *our* way."

"What's the use? They've all ganged up against us, betrayed us. Our going to university spoils things for them. Colonization as currently practiced can succeed only to the extent that we wallow in our mediocrity."

"You see why you must stay and fight everything."

"I feel so alone. . . . "

"Others will come. . . . If those who abandon ship inspire others to do the same, if they make a few converts, the 'nonquitters' on the other hand inspire others to return and stay. It's a vicious circle. It's up to us to be smart enough to make it work to our benefit."

* * *

Cambier had now completed setting up shop. He had hung in front of the family house a sign with his name, degrees, and office hours. His first patient was soon walking through the door.

He had received tremendous support from his uncle, who had done his utmost to introduce him to friends, to get him into certain milieus that, by virtue of his youth, he had never frequented before. He had left while still almost a teenager, had stayed away for years, returning now as a dentist. That sort of experience created a hole in one's existence. Could those who had known him before he left, and who still thought of him as a troublesome youngster, now conceive of calmly opening their mouths for him?

His uncle had shown heartwarming concern for him and had been diplomatic in his dealing with everyone. As a result, he had redeemed himself in the eyes of his nephew, who, to his surprise, actually began to like him, just like in the past.

The Bastards

Wasn't he merely a complex, irresponsible man? "I was unfair to him!"

Now there was life, that mountain of false principles he had despised so much only a short time before. He had tried to exist, because he had imagined that existing was *something else besides,* and *more than* living. He had come up with a code of ethics—the Real—thinking that he could thus escape the rest—Reality—but he had only managed to create new constraints for himself. He had lived, despite the horror of Living, for living is not a reflexive act. "Wanting to escape life is a childish illusion." He realized that today, in this office where he was preparing an amalgam to fill a patient's tooth.

That's the way things were, and it was sheer vanity wanting to change them. Even in that room, everything followed a certain order. The black cat, Négro, had installed himself on a window sill and was purring quietly. The noises from the street were muffled by the frosted panes; a fan toiled away in a corner, dispensing a light breeze. The patient sat huddled up, one hand on his jaw.

It was all part of the normal run of life, even the faithfulness of that cat, which had not left the house, despite the fact that its owners had disappeared. Even the Archangel himself, were he to appear suddenly with his sword, could not change anything. The devil of life could not be harmed by his attack. Everything would continue as usual.

"Come and see me in four days."

"And suppose the dressing comes off in the meanwhile?"

"Don't worry. Even if it shifts a bit, there'll always be enough to hold it till the next appointment."

As he had a half hour free, Cambier went and sat at his desk. He was going to write to Turenne, but did not know where to begin. For two years, there had been nothing between them but silence, perhaps even oblivion. Through Chambord, he had learned of the birth of the son Brigitte had given Turenne.

Charlotte! All of a sudden, he began to think about her. Thoughts flashed quickly through his mind. What had become of her? Shouldn't he also drop her a line to say he was still holding on? Too late! Between them, life had done what it had to do. He no longer had the right to emerge from the shadows after such a long silence; nor did he have the right to think only about himself. Caroline and Hortense needed him too much. Was this the time to fall back on past sentimental considerations?

"A river does not flow past the same place twice." A couple cannot grow strong on a foundation of impulses. A patient snatched from the jaws of death is very often a dead man on reprieve. No, the misunderstanding had lasted too long.

"It's better you get married," Hortense had said to him. Perhaps, but not to Charlotte. Could he make another woman happy, with all that *certainty* creeping around inside him?

"It has to be her or no one else," Marcel had insisted concerning Caroline.

"Charlotte or no one else!" Between him and her there would always be that *virgin hanging by her feet from the mast of eternity.*

He thus found himself depositary and keeper of the family vicissitudes. Earlier on, he had believed in the existence of a germ; it did exist, but was something more cunning, more toxic than a microbe: namely, prejudice.

"In town they're afraid of people like me." Hortense knew what she was talking about.

"Who does this Negro, this barkeeper, think he is?" Caroline and Marcel would forever bear the stigma of that Refusal.

The mountain of false principles was nothing more than that cumberson heritage Cambier could not escape, and for which he was called upon to pay heavy estate duties. He must take total possession of it, in order to destroy it, to deny it by paying with that bloodred currency he could feel coagulating in his veins.

"Just like your grandmother, the Negro. I'm sorry you're so much like her." His own mother used to say that. Had Africa committed such heinous crimes for her children to reject her like that? Was it a crime to have undergone centuries of servitude, of whippings, of contempt?

In a flash, he made a decision. He would immediately go

and find his grandmother, would kiss her and take her with him. He would give no explanation. He would insist. He would bring her to live with him, in this house. He would put her in charge. It would be the black woman's turn to become one of those giving the orders.

He had found the path he was to take; it was beautiful and led in one direction. And this time, he would not let his chance slip by. By rehabilitating his grandmother, he was rehabilitating himself, and Africa, and Guiana, and all their children.

He jumped up and crossed the waiting room.

"Fix up the master bedroom right away," he shouted at his maid.

The master bedroom! The bedroom in which his parents had slept! Henceforth, it would be occupied by that woman they had been ashamed of, that woman who had given them all life and who, despite all her trials and tribulations, had buried almost all of them.

He jumped into his car, and drove off in the direction of the suburbs.

* * *

Dawn made its triumphant appearance over sleepy Saint-Laurent. In the distance, a cock crowed to greet the first rays of light.

Chambord had not slept a wink all night. Imprisoned under his mosquito net that billowed in the light breeze like a sail, he had heard every possible noise.

The day before, a banquet given in his honor by his friends from the club had brought together around him both Guianese and Europeans. Their words still echoed in his ears: "We refuse to believe that you're leaving for good. The task is hard, the road is long, but we'll make it if we know how to be bold. While you're away, you'll always be for us the one who'll be returning shortly."

The drums of the Boni had fallen silent only very late in the night. What a spell this rhythm must cast on those men and women dancing half-naked, who, from this plot of land won back from adversity, shouted incantations in the direction of distant Africa, and who were befuddled by an ancestral language on the shores of a liquid monster glimmering in the moonlight, deified, overwhelming man with wonder.

Chambord had felt an irresistible resonance within him. Africa—carnal, maternal, powerful, his own—penetrated his being, subdued him, reminded him that he could not get away from her. Nowhere else had he experenced such fullness except in the face of this Maroni, of these primitives, of this Nature. And here he was, forced to flee!

Was this the lot of his race? To flee, always to flee? His ancestors had had to flee the banks of the Nile, chased by conquerors from the East. They had found refuge in the forest, where they had gone back to their primitive way of life. They had walked, run, westward until the day an ocean put an end to their exodus. Now, the forest was behind them, forming an impregnable rampart. They could once more begin to hope. But other conquerors had come, by sea this time, and had overpowered them, raided them, carried them off and dumped them in the New World.

Now that he thought he was finally at home, he had to pack up once more and leave, to fall back on a historic vocation. Wouldn't it have been better to remain at the stage those dancers were at today, those drum beaters ignorant of their past, but peaceful and content with their present-day lot?

He was about to doze off when the air was rent with the screeching of the night-soil workers' cart ("All your countrymen are in the same boat!"). In a flash, foul smells poisoned the air. He did not find them in any way repugnant. "My last night here!"

At eight o'clock, he would be taking the plane to Cayenne, then on to France. "France, that wonderful country perpetually betrayed, which no longer understands when we revolt." How could France foresee, since it never managed to know? Whenever members of parliament or technicians came on mission to Guiana, they were systematically deceived, intoxicated by reassuring, untrue accounts. They passed in the midst of a people bound hand and foot without seeing them, without making themselves seen. From what they heard, the people were happy, and they thought, naively, that happiness could come from a lack of responsibility.

The Bastards

A senior civil servant arrived one day. He needed a whole year to adapt, to understand. He tried to start working, but he hardly had the time to go very far, because the fateful end of the two-year term soon came crashing down on him like a gong.

A few men with ability, and filled with a praiseworthy vocation, came ashore. They did not remain very long. Sometimes, they were appalled by the overall mediocrity, sometimes they were recalled to other, more important positions where they could use their full potential.

Who else but the Guianese themselves would be able to break new ground by creating a situation of permanence? Was this not what he, Chambord, would have wanted to try? And attempts were being made to eliminate him through humiliation. . . .

He still had the last of his packing to do; he had to dash over to the hospital and pass by his office to say good-bye to his patients. Those in the medical ward were mere birds of passage; they would soon be able to return to their families, to forget a painful albeit recuperative stay. But those in the hospice who had nobody else in the world besides him? Those in the tuberculosis ward that he had initiated? Those in the psychiatric wing that he visited on an almost daily basis? What was going to become of them?

They were all misfits, permanently lost to their milieu. They had all been formerly chased from their homes by wretchedness or despair and had come here young, ambitious, and with the secure feeling that they would be restored to good health. They felt, too, that they would one day find in their wash-trough or under their spades one of those legendary huge nuggets that bestrewed the gold-filled sands of Guiana.

Today, they were poor, even more destitute than before, for they were unable to continue believing in a happiness that their old age rendered impossible.

One of them would wake with a start, dress hurriedly, and make preparations to leave the establishment in the middle of the night, shouting his joy at having had a revelation in a dream, a hope for wealth. "I know where to find nuggets. Release me. Let me go!"

Another would become aggressive, threatening: "I'll kill you! It's you who stole my gold!" Attempts would be made to reason with him; he would be given an injection to sedate him. Then, one day, there was a rush in extremis to prevent him from hanging himself from a tree.

Some did not wallow in their madness. He, Chambord, would say to them at times: "Why don't you let them send you back home? Back home, in the Antilles, you'll be with family and friends." "Never!" they would reply, and that one word said more than a lengthy speech.

Yes, what would become of those fallen men, those princes of wretchedness who had trusted him so implicitly and who would do no more than just wither away and die?

He began to sob in his pillow. . . .

The cold shower stung his body. He did not want to think that this was the last time he was shuddering under that water, but this sad thought fixed itself in his mind, fascinating him.

As he packed, he took note of what he was carrying with him. None of the trinkets that he took up almost mechanically was meant for him. Did he need anything with all these memories already cluttering his mind?

Sharp-pointed miniature feathered arrows, strapped together with multicolored wires, were in a bamboo sheath decorated with geometric figures. He would give his boss this souvenir from the Galibis Indians.

A light woven disc, the size of a pie dish, had between its mesh dried wasps, ants, and hornets attached with bits of wire: it was a *maraké*, a sort of instrument of torture that the Roucouyenne Indians applied to the bodies of adolescents during their initiation ceremonies. The candidate was supposed to suffer innumerable stings without wincing. It was only after that experience that he became worthy of joining the men of the clan, of hunting, of going to war, of taking a wife. Each young Roucouyenne was obliged to undergo three *maraké* tests. "Farnabe would love to have this trophy."

A large Boni paddle, so large it came up to your shoulder, was all sculpted, carved with circles and diamond shapes. "I'll insist on having this placed in the Foyer, mounted slantwise on the wall in the drawing room."

The Bastards

Four months! Four months away from a world where nothing was the same as it was in France, but where everything grabbed you deep in your soul, where everything bewitched you, where everything captured you forever. He would once more see Farnabe and his family. A warm show of affection would surround him; white people would treat him as one of their own. And here? Whites opposed him, and his countrymen did not dare show publicly how much they loved him.

He continued to be a part of that race of men with white minds in black bodies. He no longer had any choice, too marked in his very constitution by three hundred years of exile and domination. That was his destiny: to be condemned forever to wander in search of a promised land beyond a backward-looking Guiana, on this side of a forward-looking Europe; to vegetate, without any real options, between those who forget themselves for having suffered too much, and others who forget you because they are too preoccupied making others suffer.

He had wanted to affirm what made him different from the white man, but his case was insignificant to a white administration that did not condescend to look down on him except to crush him. He had also wanted to go back to his milieu, to rediscover together with his people those pure paths of yore, lost today under brambles. His countrymen, on the other hand, blinded or dispossessed of themselves, placed him outside their world and made him feel how different from them he had become.

He was now at the hospice.

Old women surrounded him, held him back by his jacket, wiped away a tear. He felt arising in him an emotion that would once more manifest itself in his eyes, but he controlled himself. An old woman kissed his hands. He could not hold it any longer. He ran off hurriedly so as not to display any weakness.

Among the men, there was less of a show of emotion. Each outburst drove back his grief, brought forth simple words that were moving by their very simplicity.

He completed his rounds among the tuberculosis patients,

where he had relived the exciting atmosphere of his internship years. A blind old-white with one leg, who was suffering from tuberculosis complicated by bouts of asthma, called him: "I can't see you. Let me touch your face." Every stroke of those fingers (those same fingers that had killed in the past, and that today were eloquent interpreters of gratitude) felt like a firebrand on Chambord's face.

A hum was heard over the commune—the plane was arriving and would be leaving almost immediately. He had to jump into a car and rush to the airfield.

The nun who accompanied him on his visit, and who had previously been so caustic in her comments, took leave of him in the following terms: "We hope you'll return, doctor."

He stayed two days in Cayenne at Cambier's place. He continued to go from office to office. In the plane, he had made his decision: he would return, *would accept* anything to remain with his people.

Cambier showed him a letter from Turenne, who was getting ready to defend his thesis and was wondering what he would do with his life. Should he return to Guiana? Did he have the right to impose this new life on Brigitte, who, never mind what she said, was not prepared for such a break with the easy life of France?

And Chambord thought: "Of us three, only Turenne went with Europe to the very end. His presence here is indispensable, if only to show us that our desire to reconquer what is ours does not necessarily imply hatred of the white man."

He climbed the steps, a raincoat on his arm and a briefcase in his hand. All around the runway the damp savannah was misty under the sun's first rays. "Tomorrow night, in Orly, I'll be shivering with cold. Day after tomorrow, I'll see Montpellier once more." His free hand waved good-bye to Cambier: "See you soon!" he said. "I'll be returning with Turenne and Brigitte."

Caraf Books
Caribbean and African Literature
Translated from French

Serious writing in French in the Caribbean and Africa has developed unique characteristics in this century. Colonialism was its crucible; African independence in the 1960s its liberating force. The struggles of nation-building and even the constraints of neocolonialism have marked the coming of age of literatures that now gradually distance themselves from the common matrix.

CARAF BOOKS is a collection of novels, plays, poetry, and essays from the regions of the Caribbean and the African continent that have shared this linguistic, cultural, and political heritage while working out their new identity against a background of conflict.

An original feature of the CARAF BOOKS collection is the substantial critical introduction in which a scholar who knows the literature well sets each book in its cultural context and makes it accessible to the student and the general reader.

Most of the books selected for the CARAF collection are being published in English for the first time; some are important books that have been out of print in English or were first issued in editions with a limited distribution. In all cases CARAF BOOKS offers the discerning reader new wine in new bottles.

The Editorial Board of CARAF BOOKS consists of A. James Arnold, University of Virginia, General Editor; Kandioura Dramé, University of Virginia, Associate Editor; and two Consulting Editors, Abiola Irele of the University of Ibadan, Nigeria, and J. Michael Dash of the University of the West Indies in Mona, Jamaica.